# THE IVORY TRAIL

# THE IVORY TRAIL

## BY TALBOT MUNDY

Frontispiece by

JOSEPH CLEMENT COLL

**WILDSIDE PRESS**

# THE IVORY TRAIL

This edition published in 2007 by Wildside Press, LLC.
www.wildsidepress.com

# MORE WILDSIDE CLASSICS

# THE NJO HAPA* SONG

*Green, oh greener than emeralds are, tree-tops beckon the
   dhows to land,*
*White, oh whiter than diamonds are, blue waves burst on the
   amber sand,*
*And nothing is fairer than Zanzibar from the Isles o' the West
   to the Marquesand.*

> *I was old when the world was wild with youth*
> *(All love was lawless then!)*
> *Since 'Venture's birth from ends of earth*
> *I ha' called the sons of men,*
> *And their women have wept the ages out*
> *In travail sore to know*
> *What lure of opiate art can leach*
> *Along bare seas from reef to beach*
> *Until from port and river reach*
> *The fever'd captains go.*

*Red, oh redder than red lips are, my flowers nod in the blazing
   noon,*
*Blue, oh bluer than maidens' eyes, are the breasts o' my waves
   in the young monsoon,*
*And there are cloves to smell, and musk, and lemon trees, and
   cinnamon.*

---

*The words "Njo hapa" in the Kiswahili tongue are the equiv-
alent of "come hither!"

# THE IVORY TRAIL

## CHAPTER ONE

ESTIMATES of ease and affluence vary with the point of view. While his older brother lived, Monty had continued in his element, a cavalry officer, his combined income and pay ample for all that the Bombay side of India might require of an English gentleman. They say that a finer polo player, a steadier shot on foot at a tiger, or a bolder squadron leader never lived.

But to Monty's infinite disgust his brother died childless. It is divulging no secret that the income that passed with the title varied between five and seven thousand pounds a year, according as coal was high, and tenants prosperous or not— a mere miserable pittance, of course, for the Earl of Montdidier and Kirkudbrightshire; so that all his ventures, and therefore ours, had one avowed end—shekels enough to lift the mortgages from his estates.

Five generations of soldiers had blazed the Montdidier fame on battle-grounds, to a nation's (and why not the whole earth's) benefit, without replenishing the family funds, and Monty (himself a confirmed and convinced bachelor) was minded when his own time should come to pass the title along to the next in line together with sufficient funds to support its dignity.

To us—even to Yerkes, familiar with United States merchant kings—he seemed with his thirty thousand dollars a year already a gilded Crœsus. He had ample to travel on, and finance prospecting trips. We never lacked for working capital, but the quest (and, including Yerkes, we were as keen as he) led us into strange places.

So behold him—a privy councilor of England if you please

1

—lounging in the lazaretto of Zanzibar, clothed only in slippers, underwear and a long blue dressing-gown. We three others were dressed the same, and because it smacked of official restraint we objected noisily; but Monty did not seem to mind much. He was rather bored, but unresentful.

A French steamer had put us ashore in quarantine, with the grim word cholera against us, and although our tale of suffering and Monty's rank, insured us a friendly reception, the port health authorities elected to be strict and we were given a nice long lazy time in which to cool our heels and order new clothes. (Guns, kit, tents, and all but what we stood in had gone to the bottom with the German cholera ship from whose life-boat the French had rescued us.)

"Keeping us all this time in this place, is sheer tyranny!" grumbled Yerkes. "If any one wants my opinion, they're afraid we'd talk if they let us out—more afraid of offending Germans than they are of cholera! Besides—any fool could know by now we're not sick!"

"There might be something in that," admitted Monty.

"I'd send for the U. S. Consul and sing the song out loud, but for you!" Yerkes added.

Monty nodded sympathetically.

"Dashed good of you, Will, and all that sort of thing."

"You English are so everlastingly afraid of seeming to start trouble, you'll swallow anything rather than talk!"

"As a government, perhaps yes," admitted Monty. "As a people, I fancy not. As a people we vary."

"You vary in that respect as much as sardines in a can! I traveled once all the way from London to Glasgow alone in one compartment with an Englishman. Talk? My, we were garrulous! I offered him a newspaper, cigarettes, matches, remarks on the weather suited to his brand of intelligence— (that's your sole national topic of talk between strangers!)— and all he ever said to me was 'Haw-ah!' I'll bet he was afraid of seeming to start trouble!"

"He didn't start any, did he?" asked Monty.

"Pretty nearly he did! I all *but* bashed him over the bean with the newspaper the third time he said 'haw-ah!'"

Monty laughed. Fred Oakes was busy across the room with his most amazing gift of tongues, splicing together half-a-dozen of them in order to talk with the old lazaretto attendant, so he heard nothing; otherwise there would have been argument.

"Then it would have been you, not he who started trouble," said I, and Yerkes threw both hands up in a gesture of despair.

"Even you're afraid of starting something!" He stared at both of us with an almost startled expression, as if he could not believe his own verdict, yet could not get away from it. "Else you'd give the *Bundesrath* story to the papers! That German skipper's conduct ought to be bruited round the world! You said you'd do it. You promised us! You told the man to his face you would!"

"Now," said Monty, "you've touched on another national habit."

"Which one?" Yerkes demanded.

"Dislike of telling tales out of school. The man's dead. His ship's at the bottom. The tale's ended. What's the use? Besides—"

"Ah! You've another reason! Spill it!"

"As a privy councilor, y'know, and all that sort of thing—"

"Same story! Afraid of starting something!"

"The Germans—'specially their navy men—drink to what they call *Der Tag* y'know—the day when they shall dare try to tackle England. We all know that. They're planning war, twenty years from now perhaps, that shall give them all our colonies as well as India and Egypt. They're so keen on it they can't keep from bragging. Great Britain, on the other hand, hasn't the slightest intention of fighting if war can be avoided; so why do anything meanwhile to increase the tension? Why send broadcast a story that would only arouse international hatred? That's their method. Ours—I mean our government's—is to give hatred a chance to die down. If our papers got hold of the *Bundesrath* story they'd make a deuce of a noise, of course."

"If your government's so sure Germany is planning war,"

objected Yerkes, "why on earth not force war, and feed them full of it before they're ready?"

"Counsel of perfection," laughed Monty. "Government's responsible to the Commons—Commons to the people—people want peace and plenty. No. Your guess was good. We are in here while the government at home squares the newspaper men."

"You don't mean to tell me your British government controls the press?"

"Hardly. Seeing 'em—putting it up to 'em straight—asking 'em politely. They're public-spirited, y'know. Hitting 'em with a club would be another thing. It's an easy-going nation, but kings have been sorry they tried force. Did you never hear of a king who used force against American colonies?"

"Good God! So they keep you—an earl—a privy councilor—a retired colonel of regulars in good standing—under lock and key in this pest-house while they bribe the press not to tell the truth about some Germans and start trouble?"

"Not exactly," said Monty.

"But here you are!"

"I preferred to remain with my party."

"You mean they'd have let you out and kept us in?"

"They'd have phrased it differently, but that's about what it would have amounted to. I have privileges."

"Well, I'm jiggered!"

"I rather suspect it's not so bad as that," said Monty. "You're with friends in quarantine, Will!"

For a quarantine station in the tropics it was after all not such a bad place. We could hear the crooning of lazy rollers on the beach, and what little sea-breeze moved at all came in to us through iron-barred windows. The walls were of coral, three feet thick. So was the roof. The wet red-tiled floor made at least an impression of coolness, and the fresh green foliage of an enormous mango tree, while it obstructed most of the view, suggested anything but durance vile. From not very far away the aromatic smell of a clove warehouse located us, not disagreeably, at the farther end of one of Sindbad's journeys, and the birds in the mango branches cried and were colorful with hues and notes of merry extravagance. Zanzibar is no parson's paradise—nor the center of much high society. It reeks of unsavory history as well as of spices. But it has its charms, and the Arabs love it.

It had Fred Oakes so interested that he had forgotten his concertina—his one possession saved from shipwreck, for which he had offered to fight the whole of Zanzibar one-handed rather than have it burned.

("Damnation! it has silver reeds—it's an English top-hole one—a wonder!")

So the doctors who are kind men in the main disinfected it twice, once on the French liner that picked us out of the *Bundesrath's* boat, and again in Zanzibar; and with the stench of lord-knew-what zealous chemical upon it he had let it lie unused while he picked up Kiswahili and talked by the hour to a toothless, wrinkled very black man with a touch of Arab in his breeding, and a deal of it in his brimstone vocabulary.

Presently Fred came over and joined us, dancing across the wide red floor with the skirts of his gown outspread like a ballet dancer's—ridiculous, and perfectly aware of it.

"Monty, you're rich! We're all made men! We're all rich! Let's spend money! Let's send for catalogues and order things!"

Monty declined to take fire. It was I, latest to join the partnership and much the least affluent, who bit.

"If you love the Lord, explain!" said I.

"This old one-eyed lazaretto attendant is an ex-slave, ex-accomplice of Tippoo Tib!"

"And Tippoo Tib?" I asked.

"Ignorant fo'castle outcast!" (All that because I had made one voyage as foremast hand, and deserted rather than submit to more of it.) "Tippoo Tib is the Arab—is, mind you, my son, not was—the Arab who was made governor of half the Congo by H. M. Stanley and the rest of 'em. Tippoo Tib is the expert who used to bring the slave caravans to Zanzibar—bring 'em, send 'em, send for 'em—he owned 'em anyway. Tippoo Tib was the biggest ivory hunter and trader who ever lived since old King Solomon! Tippoo Tib is here—in Zanzibar—to all intents and purposes a prisoner on parole—old as the hills—getting ready to die—and proud as the very ace of hell. So says One-eye!"

"So we're all rich?" suggested Monty.

"Of course we are! Listen! The British government took Tippoo's slaves away and busted his business. Made him come and live in this place, go to church on Sundays, and be good. Then they asked him what he'd done with his ivory. Asked him politely after putting him through that mill! One-eye here says Tippoo had a million tusks—a million!—safely buried! Government offered him ten per cent. of their cash value if he'd tell 'em where, and the old sport spat in their faces! Swears he'll die with the secret! One-eye vows Tippoo is the only one who knows. There were others, but Tippoo shot or poisoned 'em."

"So we're rich," smiled Yerkes.

"Of course we are! Consider this, America, and tell me if Standard Oil can beat it! One million tusks! I'm told—"

"By whom?"

"One-eye says—"

"Oh!"

"You'll say 'Oh!' at me to a different tune, before I've done! One-eye says it never paid to carry a tusk weighing less than sixty pounds. Some tusks weigh two hundred—some even more—took four men to carry some of 'em! Call it an average weight of one hundred pounds and be on the safe side."

"Yes, let's play safe," agreed Monty seriously.

"One hundred million pounds of ivory!" said Fred, with a smack of his lips and the air of a man who could see the whole of it. "The present market price of new ivory is over ten shillings a pound on the spot. That'll all be very old stuff, worth at least double. But let's say ten shillings a pound and be on the safe side."

"Yes, let's!" laughed Yerkes.

"One thousand million—a billion shillings!" Fred announced. "Fifty million pounds!"

"Two hundred and fifty million dollars!" Yerkes calculated, beginning to take serious notice.

"But how are we to find it?" I objected.

"That's the point. Government 'ud hog the lot, but has hunted high and low and can't find it. So the offer stands ten per cent. to any one who does—ten per cent. of fifty million—lowest reckoning, mind you!—five million pounds! Half for Monty—two and a half million. A million for Yerkes, a million for me, and a half a million for you all according to contract! How d'you like it?"

"Well enough," I answered. "If it's only the hundredth part true, I'm enthusiastic!"

"So now suit yourselves!" said Fred, collapsing with a sweep of his skirts into the nearest chair. "I've told you what One-eye says. These dusky gents sometimes exaggerate of course—"

"Now and then," admitted Monty.

"But where there's smoke you mean there's prob'ly some one smoking hams?" suggested Yerkes.

"I mean, let's find that ivory!" said Fred.

"We might do worse than make an inquiry or two," Monty assented cautiously.

"Didums, you damned fool, you're growing old! You're wasting time! You're trying to damp enthusiasm! You're —you're—"

"Interested, Fred. I'm interested. Let's—"

"Let's find that ivory and to hell with caution! Why, man alive, it's the chance of a million lifetimes!"

"Well, then," said Monty, "admitting the story's true for the sake of argument, how do you propose to get on the track of the secret?"

"Get on it? I *am* on it! Didn't One-eye say Tippoo Tib is alive and in Zanzibar? The old rascal! Many a slave he's done to death! Many a man he's tortured! I propose we catch Tippoo Tib, hide him, and pull out his toe-nails one by one until he blows the gaff!"

(To hear Fred talk when there is nothing to do *but* talk a stranger might arrive at many false conclusions.)

"If there's any truth in the story at all," said Monty, "government will have done everything within the bounds of decency to coax the facts from Tippoo Tib. I suspect we'd have to take our chance and simply hunt. But let's hear Juma's story."

So the old attendant left off sprinkling water from a yellow jar, and came and stood before us. Fred's proposal of tweaking toe-nails would not have been practical in his case, for he had none left. His black legs, visible because he had tucked his one long garment up about his waist, were a mass of scars. He was lean, angular, yet peculiarly straight considering his years. As he stood before us he let his shirt-like garment drop, and the change from scarecrow to deferential servant was instantaneous. He was so wrinkled, and the wrinkles were so deep, that one scarcely noticed his sightless eye, almost hidden among a nest of creases; and in spite of the wrinkles, his polished, shaven head made him look ridiculously youthful because one expected gray hair and there was none.

"Ask him how he lost his toe-nails, Fred," said I.

But the old man knew enough English to answer for himself. He made a wry grimace and showed his hands. The finger-nails were gone too.

"Tell us your story, Juma," said Monty.

"Tell 'em about the *pembe*—the ivory—the much ivory— the *meengi pembe*," echoed Fred.

"Let's hear about those nails of his first," said I.

"One thing'll prob'ly lead to another," Yerkes agreed. "Start him on the toe-nail story."

But it did not lead very far. Fred, who had picked up Kiswahili enough to piece out the old man's broken English, drew him out and clarified the tale. But it only went to prove that others besides ourselves had heard of Tippoo Tib's hoard. Some white man—we could not make head or tail of the name, but it sounded rather like *Somebody belonging to a man named Carpets*—had trapped him a few years before and put him to torture in the belief that he knew the secret.

"But me not knowing nothing!" he assured us solemnly, shaking his head again and again.

But he was not in the least squeamish about telling us that Tippoo Tib had surely buried huge quantities of ivory, and had caused to be slain afterward every one who shared the secret.

"How long ago?" asked Monty. But natives of that part of the earth are poor hands at reckoning time.

"Long time," he assured us. He might have meant six years, or sixty. It would have been all the same to him.

"No. Me not liking Tippoo Tib. One time his slave. That bad. Byumby set free. That good. Now working here. This very good."

"Where do you *think* the ivory is?" (This from Yerkes.) But the old man shook his head.

"As I understand it," said Monty, "slaves came mostly from the Congo side of Lake Victoria Nyanza. Slave and elephant country were approximately the same as regards general direction, and there were two routes from the Congo—the southern by way of Ujiji on Tanganyika to Bagamoyo on what is now the German coast, and the other to the north of Victoria Nyanza ending at Mombasa. Ask him, Fred, which way the ivory used to come."

"Both ways," announced Juma without waiting for Fred to interpret. He had an uncanny trick of following conversation, his intelligence seeming to work by fits and starts.

"That gives us about half Africa for hunting-ground, and a job for life!" laughed Yerkes.

"Might have a worse!" Fred answered, resentful of cold water thrown on his discovery.

"Were you Tippoo Tib's slave when he buried the ivory?" demanded Monty, and the old man nodded.

"Where were you at the time?"

Juma made a gesture intended to suggest immeasurable distances toward the West, and the name of the place he mentioned was one we had never heard of.

"Can you take us to Tippoo Tib when we leave this place?" I asked, and he nodded again.

"How much ivory do you suppose there was?" asked Yerkes.

"*Teli, teli!*" he answered, shaking his head.

"Too much!" Fred translated.

"Pretty fair to middling vague," said Yerkes, "but"—judicially—"almost worth investigating!"

"Investigating?" Fred sprang from his chair. "It's better than all King Solomon's mines, El Dorado, Golconda, and Sindbad the Sailor's treasure lands rolled in one! It's an obviously good thing! All we need is a bit of luck and the ivory's ours!"

"I'll sell you my share now for a thousand dollars—come—come across!" grinned Yerkes.

There was a rough-house after that. He and Fred nearly pulled the old attendant in two, each claiming the right to torture him first and learn the secret. They ended up without a whole rag between them, and had to send Juma to headquarters for new blue dressing-gowns. The doctor came himself—a fat good-natured party with an eye-glass and a cocktail appetite, acting *locum-tenens* for the real official who was home on leave. He brought the ingredients for cocktails with him.

"Yes," he said, shaking the mixer with a sort of deft solicitude. "There's more than something in the tale. I've had a try myself to get details. Tippoo Tib believes in up-to-date physic, and when the old rascal's sick he sends for me. I offered to mix him an elixir of life that would make him outlive Methuselah if he'd give me as much as a hint of the general direction of his cache."

"He ought to have fallen for that," said Yerkes, but the doctor shook his head.

"He's an Arab. They're Shiah Muhammedans. Their Paradise is a pleasant place from all accounts. He advised me to drink my own elixir, and have lots and lots of years in which to find the ivory, without being beholden to him for help. Wily old scaramouch! But I had a better card up my sleeve. He has taken to discarding ancient prejudices—doesn't drink or anything like that, but treats his harem almost humanly. Lets 'em have anything that costs him nothing. Even sends for a medico when they're sick! Getting lax in his old age! Sent for me a while ago to attend his favorite wife—sixty

years old if she's a day, and as proud of him as if he were the
king of Jerusalem. Well—I looked her over, judged she was
likely to keep her bed, and did some thinking.

"You know their religious law? A woman can't go to Paradise without special intercession, mainly vicarious. I found
a mullah—that's a Muhammedan priest—who'd do anything
for half of nothing. They most of them will. I gave him
fifty dibs, and promised him more if the trick worked. Then
I told the old woman she was going to die, but that if she'd
tell me the secret of Tippoo Tib's ivory I had a mullah handy
who would pass her into Paradise ahead of her old man. What
did she do? She called Tippoo Tib, and he turned me out of
the house. So I'm fifty out of pocket, and what's worse, the
old girl didn't die—got right up out of bed and stayed up!
My rep's all smashed to pieces among the Arabs!"

"D'you suppose the old woman knew the secret?" I asked.

"Not she! If she'd known it she'd have split! The one
ambition she has left is to be with Tippoo Tib in Paradise.
But he can intercede for her and get her in—provided he feels
that way; so she rounded on me in the hope of winning his
special favor! But the old ruffian knows better! He'll no
more pray for her than tell me where the ivory is! The Koran
tells him there are much better houris in Paradise, so why
trouble to take along a toothless favorite from this world?"

"Has the government any official information?" asked
Monty.

"Quite a bit, I'm told. Official records of vain searches.
Between you and me and these four walls, about the only
reason why they didn't hang the old slave-driving murderer
was that they've always hoped he'd divulge the secret some
day. But he hates the men who broke him far too bitterly
to enrich them on any terms! If any man wins the secret
from him it'll be a foreigner. They tell me a German had
a hard try once. One of Karl Peters' men."

"That'll be Carpets!" said Monty. "Somebody belonging
to Carpets—Karl Peters."

"The man's serving a life sentence in the jail for torturing
our friend Juma here."

"Then Juma knows the secret?"

"So they say. But Juma, too, hopes to go to Paradise and wait on Tippoo Tib."

"He told us just now that he dislikes Tippoo Tib," I objected.

"So he does, but that makes no difference. Tippoo Tib is a big chief—*sultani kubwa*—take any one he fancies to Heaven with him!"

We all looked at Juma with a new respect.

"I got Juma this job in here," said the doctor. "I've rather the notion of getting my ten per cent. on the value of that ivory some day!"

"Are there any people after it just now?" asked Monty.

"I don't know, I'm sure. There was a German named Schillingschen, who spent a month in Zanzibar and talked a lot with Tippoo Tib. The old rascal might tell his secret to any one he thought was England's really dangerous enemy. Schillingschen crossed over to British East if I remember rightly. He might be on the track of it."

"Tell us more about Schillingschen," said Monty.

"He's one of those orientalists, who profess to know more about Islam than Christianity—more about Africa and Arabia than Europe—more about the occult than what's in the open. A man with a shovel beard—stout—thick-set—talks Kiswahili and Arabic and half a dozen other languages better than the natives do themselves. Has money—outfit like a prince's —everything imaginable—rifles—microscopes—cigars—wine. He didn't make himself agreeable here—except to the Arabs. Didn't call at the Residency. Some of us asked him to dinner one evening, but he pleaded a headache. We were glad, because afterward we saw him eat at the hotel—has ways of using his fingers at table, picked up I suppose from the people he has lived among."

"Are you nearly ready to let us out of here?" asked Monty.

"Your quarantine's up," said the doctor. "I'm only waiting for word from the office."

We drank three rounds of cocktails with him, after which

he grew darkly friendly and proposed we should all set out together in search of the hoard.

"I've no money," he assured us. "Nothing but a knowledge of the natives and a priceless thirst. I'd have to throw up my practise here. Of course I'd need some sort of guarantee from you chaps."

The proposal falling flat, he gathered the nearly empty bottles into one place and shouted for his boy to come and carry them away.

"Think it over!" he urged as he got up to leave us. "You might take a bigger fool than me with you. You'd need a doctor on a trip like that. I'm an expert on some of these tropical diseases. Think it over!"

"Fred!" said Monty, as soon as the doctor had left the room, "I'm tempted by this ivory of yours."

But Fred, in the new blue dressing-gown the doctor had brought, was in another world—a land of trope and key and metaphor. For the last ten minutes he had kept a stub of pencil and a scrap of paper working, and now the strident tones of his too long neglected concertina stirred the heavy air and shocked the birds outside to silence. The instrument was wheezy, for in addition to the sacrilege the port authorities had done by way of disinfection, the bellows had been wetted when Fred plunged from the sinking *Bundesrath* and swam. But he is not what you could call particular, as long as a good loud noise comes forth that can be jerked and broken into anything resembling tune.

"Tempted, are you?" he laughed. He looked like a drunken troubadour en deshabille, with those up-brushed mustaches and his usually neat brown beard all spread awry. "Temptation's more fun than plunder!"

Yerkes threw an orange at him, more by way of recognition than remonstrance. We had not heard Fred sing since he tried to charm cholera victims in the *Bundesrath's* fo'castle, and, like the rest of us, he had his rights. He sang with legs spread wide in front of him, and head thrown back, and, each time he came to the chorus, kept on repeating it until we joined in.

There's a prize that's full familiar from Zanzibar to France;
From Tokio to Boston; we are paid it in advance.
It's the wages of adventure, and the wide world knows the feel
Of the stuff that stirs good huntsmen all and brings the hounds
　　to heel!
It's the one reward that's gratis and precedes the toilsome
　　task—
It's the one thing always better than an optimist can ask!
It's amusing, it's amazing, and it's never twice the same;
It's the salt of true adventure and the glamour of the game!

## CHORUS

It is tem-tem-pitation!
The one sublime sensation!
You may doubt it, but without it
There would be no derring-do!
The reward the temptee cashes
Is too often dust and ashes,
But you'll need no spurs or lashes
When temptation beckons you!

Oh, it drew the Roman legions to old Britain's distant isle,
And it beckoned H. M. Stanley to the sources of the Nile;
It's the one and only reason for the bristling guns at Gib,
For the skeletons at Khartoum, and the crimes of Tippoo Tib.
The gentlemen adventurers braved torture for its sake,
It beckoned out the galleons, and filled the hulls of Drake!
Oh, it sets the sails of commerce, and it whets the edge of
　　war,
It's the sole excuse for churches, and the only cause of law!

## CHORUS

It is tem-tem-pitation! etc., etc.

No note is there of failure (that's a tune the croakers sing!)
This song's of youth, and strength, and health, and time that's
　　on the wing!
Of wealth beyond the hazy blue of far horizons flung—
But never of the folk returning, disillusioned, stung!
It's a tale of gold and ivory, of plunder out of reach,
Of luck that fell to other men, of treasure on the beach—

A compound, cross-reciprocating two-way double spell,
The low, sweet lure to Heaven, and the tallyho to hell!

## CHORUS

> It is tem-tem-pitation!
> The one sublime sensation!
> You may doubt it, but without it
> There would be no derring-do!
> It's the siren of to-morrow
> That knows naught of lack or sorrow,
> So you'll sell your bonds and borrow,
> When temptation beckons you!

Once Fred starts there is no stopping him, short of personal violence, and he ran through his ever lengthening list of songs, not all quite printable, until the very coral walls ached with the concertina's wailing, and our throats were hoarse from ridiculous choruses. As Yerkes put it:

"When pa says sing, the rest of us sing too or go crazy!"

I went to the window and tried to get a view of shipping through the mango branches. Masts and sails—lateen spars particularly—always get me by the throat and make me happy for a while. But all I could see was a low wall beyond the little compound, and over the top of it headgear of nearly all the kinds there are. (Zanzibar is a wonderful market for second-hand clothes. There was even a tall silk hat of not very ancient pattern.)

"Come and look, Monty!" said I, and he and Yerkes came and stood beside me. Seeing his troubadour charm was broken, Fred snapped the catch on the concertina and came too.

"*Arabian Nights!*" he exclaimed, thumping Monty on the back. "Didums, you drunkard, we're dead and in another world! Juma is the one-eyed Calender! Look—fishermen—houris—how many houris?—seen 'em grin!—soldiers of fortune—merchants—sailors—by gad, there's Sindbad himself! —and say! If that isn't the Sultan Haroun-al-Raschid in disguise I'm willing to eat beans and pie for breakfast to oblige Yerkes! Look—look at the fat ruffian's stomach and swagger, will you?"

Yerkes sized up the situation quickest.

"Sing him another song, Fred. If we want to strike up acquaintance with half Zanzibar, here's our chance!"

"Oh, Richard, oh, my king!" hummed Monty. "It's Cœur de Lion and Blondell over again with the harp reversed."

If Zanzibar may be said to possess main thoroughfares, that window of ours commanded as much of one as the tree and wall permitted; and music—even of a concertina—is the key to the heart of all people whose hair is crisp and kinky. Perhaps rather owing to the generosity of their slave law, and Koran teachings, more than to racial depravity, there are not very many Arabs left in that part of the world with true semitic features and straight hair, nor many woolly-headed folk who are quite all-Bantu. There is enough Arab blood in all of them to make them bold; Bantu enough for syncopated, rag-time music to take them by the toes and stir them. The crowd in the street grew, and gathered until a policeman in red fez and khaki knickerbockers came and started trouble. He had a three-cornered fight on his hands, and no sympathy from any one, within two minutes. Then the man with the stomach and swagger — he whom Fred called Haroun-al-Raschid—took a hand in masterly style. He seized the policeman from behind, flung him out of the crowd, and nobody was troubled any more by that official.

"That him Tippoo Tib's nephew!" said a voice, and we all jumped. We had not noticed Juma come and stand beside us.

"I suspect nephew is a vague relationship in these parts," said Monty. "Do you mean Tippoo's brother was that man's father, Juma?"

"No, bwana.* Tippoo Tib bringing slave long ago f'm Bagamoyo. Him she-slave having chile. She becoming concubine Tippoo Tib his wife's brother. That chile Tippoo Tib's nephew. Tea ready, bwana."

"What does that man do for a living?"

---

*Bwana, Swahili word meaning master.*

"Do for a living?" Juma was bewildered.

"What does he work at?"

"Not working."

"Never?"

"No."

"Has he private means, then?"

"I not understand. Tea ready, *bwana.*"

"Has he got *mali**?" Fred demanded.

"*Mali?* No. Him poor man."

"Then how does he exist, if he has no *mali* and doesn't work?"

"Oh, one wife here, one there, one other place, an' Tippoo Tib byumby him giving food."

"How many wives has he?"

"Tea ready, *bwana!*"

"How do they come to be spread all over the place?" (We were shooting questions at him one after the other, and Juma began to look as if he would have preferred a repetition of the toe-nail incident.)

"Oh, he travel much, an' byumby lose all money, then stay here. Tea, him growing cold."

There is no persuading the native servant who has lived under the Union Jack that an Englishman does not need hot tea at frequent intervals, even after three cocktails in an afternoon. So we trooped to the table to oblige him, and went through the form of being much refreshed.

"What is that man's name?" demanded Monty.

"Hassan."

"Do you know him?"

"Everybody know him!"

"Can you get a message to him?"

"Yes, *bwana.*"

"Tell him to come and talk with us at the hotel as soon as he hears we are out of this."

We did not know it at the time (for I don't think that Monty guessed it either) that we had taken the surest way

---

*Mali,* Swahili word meaning *possessions, property.*

of setting all Zanzibar by the ears. In that last lingering stronghold of legal slavery,* where the only stories judged worth listening to are the very sources of the Thousand Nights and a Night, intrigue is not perhaps the breath of life, but it is the salt and savory. There is a woolly-headed sultan who draws a guaranteed, fixed income and has nothing better to do than regale himself and a harem with western alleged amusement. There are police, and lights, and municipal regulations. In fact, Zanzibar has come on miserable times from certain points of view. But there remains the fun of listening to all the rumors borne by sea. "Play on the flute in Zanzibar and Africa as far as the lakes will dance!" the Arabs say, and the gentry who once drove slaves or traded ivory refuse to believe that the day of lawlessness is gone forever. One rumor then is worth ten facts. Four white men singing behind the bars of the lazaretto, desiring to speak with Hassan, "nephew" of Tippoo Tib, and offering money for the introduction, were enough to send whispers sizzling up and down all the mazy streets.

Our release from quarantine took place next day, and we went to the hotel, where we were besieged at once by tradesmen, each proclaiming himself the only honest outfitter and "agent for all good export firms." Monty departed to call on British officialdom (one advantage of traveling with a nobleman being that he has to do the stilted social stuff). Yerkes went to call on the United States Consul, the same being presumably a part of his religion, for he always does it, and almost always abuses his government afterward. So Fred and I were left to repel boarders, and it came about that we two received Hassan.

He entered our room with a great shout of *"Hodi!"* (and Fred knew enough to say *"Karibu!"*)—a smart red fez set at an angle on his shaven head, his henna-stained beard all newly-combed—a garment like a night-shirt reaching nearly to his heels, a sort of vest of silk embroidery restraining his

---

*Slavery was not absolutely and finally abolished in Zanzibar until 1906, during which year even the old slaves, hitherto unwilling to be set free, had to be pensioned off.

stomach's tendency to wobble at will, and a fat smile decorating the least ashamed, most obviously opportunist face I ever saw, even on a black man.

"*Jambo, jambo;*"* he announced, striding in and observing our lack of worldly goods with one sweep of the eye. (We had not stocked up yet with new things, and probably he did not know our old ones were at the bottom of the sea.) He was a lion-hearted rascal though, at all events at the first rush, for poverty on the surface did not trouble him.

"You send for me? You want a good guide?"

The Haroun-al-Raschid look had disappeared. Now he was the jack-of-all-trades, wondering which end of the jack to push in first.

"When I need a guide I'll get a licensed one," said Fred, sitting down and turning partly away from him. (It never pays to let those gentry think they have impressed you.) "What is your business, Johnson?"

"My name Hassan, sah. You send for me? You want a headman. I'm formerly headman for Tippoo Tib, knowing all roads, and how to manage *wapagazi,*† *safari,*‡ all things!"

"Any papers to prove it?" asked Fred.

"No, sir. Reference to Tippoo Tib himself sufficient! He my part-uncle."

"Ready to tell any kind of a lie for you, eh?"

"No, sir, always telling truth! You got a cook yet?"

"Can you cook?" Fred answered guardedly.

"Yes, sah. Was cook formerly for Master Stanley, go with him on expedition. Later his boy. Later his headman. You want to go on expedition, I getting you good cook. Where you want to go?"

"Are you looking for a job?" asked Fred.

"What you after? Ivory?"

"Maybe."

"I know all about ivory—I shoot, trade ivory along o' Tippoo Tib an' Stanley. You engage my services, all very well."

*Jambo*, good day.
†*Wapagazi*, plural of *pagazi*, porter.
‡*Safari*, journey, and, by inference, outfit for a journey.

"Go and tell Tippoo Tib we want to see him. If he confirms what you say, perhaps we'll take you on," said Fred.

"Tell Tippoo Tib? Ha-ha! You want to find his buried ivory—that it? All white men wanting that! All right, I go tell him! I come again!"

"Come back here, you fat rascal!" ordered Fred. "What do you mean about buried ivory? What buried ivory?"

Hassan's face lost some of its transcendent cheek. Even the dyed beard seemed to wilt.

"What you wanting?" he asked. "Hunt, trade, travel—what your business?"

"Fish!" Fred answered genially.

"*Samaki?*"

"Yes—*samaki*—fish!"

Having no experience of Arabs, and part-Arabs, I wondered what on earth Fred could be driving at. But Hassan wondered still more, and that was the whole point. He stood agape, looking from one to the other of us, his fat good-natured face an interrogation mark.

"I go an' tell *bwana* Tippoo Tib!" he announced, and departed swiftly.

"What's the idea of fish, Fred?" I asked.

"Oh, just curiosity. The way of getting information out of colored folk is to get them so frantically curious they've no time to think up lies. Tobacco would have done as well—anything unexpected. A bird flying, and a black man lying, are both of 'em easy to catch or confuse unless they know which way they're heading. Let's go and look at the bazaar."

But in order to look one had to reach. We left the great heavy-beamed hotel that had once been Tippoo Tib's residence, but were stopped in the outer doorway by a crowd of native boys, each with a brass plate on his arm.

"Guide, sah!—Guide, sah!—My name McPhairson, sah!—My name Jones, sah!—My name Johnson, sah! Guide to all the sights, sah!"

They were as persistent and evilly intentioned as a swarm of flies, and bold enough to strike back when anybody kicked them. While we wrestled and swore, but made no headway,

we were accosted by a Greek, who seemed from long experience
able to pass through them without striking or being struck.
We were not left in doubt another second as to whether our
friend Hassan had dallied on the way, and held his tongue
or not.

"Good day, gentlemen! I hear you are after fish! Hah!
That is a good story to tell to Arabs! You mean fishing for
information, eh? Ha-hah!"

He turned on the swarm of boys, who still yelled and struggled about our legs.

"*Imshi!** *Voetsak!*† *Enenda zako!*‡ *Kuma nina,
wewe!*"¶ In a minute he had them all scattering, for only
innocence and inexperience attract the preying youth of Zanzibar. "Now, gentlemen, my name is Coutlass—Georges Coutlass. Have a drink with me, and let me tell you something."

He was tall, dark skinned, athletic, and roguish-looking
even for the brand of Greek one meets with south of the
Levant—dressed in khaki, with an American cowboy hat—
his fingers nearly black with cigarette juice—his hands unusually horny for that climate — and his hair clipped so
short that it showed the bumps of avarice and other things,
said to reside below the hat-band to the rear. Yet a plausible,
companionable-seeming man. And Zanzibar confers democratic privilege, as well as fevers; impartiality hovers in the
atmosphere as well as smells, and we neither of us dreamed of
hesitating, but followed him back into the bar—a wide, low-
ceilinged room whose beams were two feet thick of blackened,
polished hard wood. There we sat one each side of him in
cane armchairs. He ordered the drinks, and paid for them.

"First I will tell you who I am," he said, when he had
swallowed a foot-long whisky peg and wiped his lips with his
coat sleeve. "I never boast. I don't need to! I am Georges

---

*Imshi* (Arabic), get to hell out of here!
†*Voetsak* (Cape Dutch), ditto.
‡*Enenda zako* (Kiswahili), ditto.
¶*Kuma nina* (Kiswahili). An opprobrious, and perhaps the
commonest expletive in the language, amounting to a request for
details of the objurgee's female ancestry. By no means for use
in drawing-rooms.

Coutlass! I learned that you have an English lord among your party, and said I to myself 'Aha! There is a man who will appreciate me, who am a citizen of three lands!' Which of you gentlemen is the lord?"

"How can you be a citizen of three countries?" Fred countered.

"Of Greece, for I was born in Greece. I have fought Turks. Ah! I have bled for Greece. I have spilt my blood in many lands, but the best was for my motherland!—Of England, for I became naturalized. By bloody-hell-and-Waterloo, but I admire the English! They have guts, those English, and I am one of them! By the great horn spoon, yes, I became an Englishman at Bow Street one Monday morning, price Five Pounds. I was lined up with the drunks and pick-pockets, and by Jumbo the magistrate mistook me for a thief! He would have given me six months without the option in another minute, but I had the good luck to remember how much money I had paid my witnesses. The thought of paying that for nothing—worse than nothing, for six months in jail!—in an English jail!—pick oakum!—eat skilly!—that thought brought me to my senses. 'By Gassharamminy,' I said, 'I may be mad, but I'm sober! If it's a crime to desire to be English, then punish me, but let me first commit the offense!' So he laughed, and didn't question my witnesses very carefully—one was a Jew, the other an ex-German, and either of them would swear to anything at half price for a quantity—and they kissed the Book and committed perjury—and lo and behold, I was English as you are—English without troubling a midwife or the parson! Five pounds for the 'beak' at Bow Street—fifty for the witnesses—fifty-five all told—and cheap at the price! I had money in those days. It was after our short war with Turkey. We Greeks got beaten, but the Turks did not get all the loot! By prison and gallows, no! When our men ran before a battle, I did not run—not I! I remained, and by Crœsus I grew richer in an hour than I have ever been since!"

"That's two countries," said I. "Which is the third that has the honor to claim your allegiance?"

"Honor is right!" he answered with a proud smile. "I, Georges Coutlass, have honored three flags! I am a credit to all three countries! The third is America—the U. S. A. You might say that is the corollary of being English—the natural, logical, correct sequence! The U. S. laws are strict, but their politics were devised for—what is it the preachers call it— ah, yes, for straining out gnats and swallowing camels. By George Washington they would swallow a house on fire! There was a federal election shortly due. One of the parties —Democratic—Republican—I forget which—maybe both!— needed new voters. The law says it takes five years to become a citizen. Politics said fifteen minutes! The politicians paid the fees too! I was a citizen—a voter—an elector of presidents before I had been ashore three months, and I had sold my vote three times over within a month of that! They had me registered under three names in three separate wards! I didn't need the money—I had plenty in those days—I gave the six dollars I received for my votes to the Holy Church, and voted the other way to save my conscience; but the fun of the thing appealed! By Gassharamminy! I can't take life the way the copy-books lay down! I have to break laws or else break heads! But I love America! I fought and bled for America! By Abraham Lincoln, I fought those Spaniards until I don't doubt they wished I had stayed in Greece! Yes, I left that middle finger in Cuba—shot through the left hand by a Don, think of it, a Don! When I came out of hospital — and I never saw anything worse than that hot hell!—I got myself attached to the commissariat, and the pickings were none so bad. Had to hand over too much, though. That is the worst of America, there is no genuine liberty. You have to steal for the man higher up. If you keep more than ten per cent., he squeals. He has to pass most of it on again to some one else, and so on, and they all land in jail in course of time! Give me a country where a man can keep what he finds! There was talk about congressional inquiries. Then a friend of mine—a Greek—who had been out here told me of Tippoo Tib's ivory, and it looked all right to me to change scenes for a while. I had citizenship papers—U. S., and English, and a Greek passport in case of accident. Traveling looked good to me."

"If you traveled on a Greek passport you couldn't use citizenship papers of any other country," Fred objected.

"Who said I traveled on a Greek passport? Do you take me for such a fool? Who listens to a Greek consul? He may protest, and accept fees, but Greece is a little country and no one listens to her consuls. I carry a Greek passport in case I should find somewhere someday a Greek consul with influence—or a Greek whom I wish to convince. I traveled to South Africa as an American. I went to Cape Town with the idea of going to Salisbury, and working my way up from there as a trader into the Congo. I reached Johannesburg, and there I did a little I. D. B. and one thing and another until the Boer War came. Then I fought for the Boers. Yes, I have bled for the Boer cause. It was a damned bad cause! They robbed me of nearly all my money! They left me to die when I was wounded! It was only by the grace of God, and the intrigues of a woman that I made my way to Lourenco Marquez. No, the war was not over, but what did I care? I, Georges Coutlass, had had enough of it! I recompensed myself en route. I do not fight for a bunch of thieves for nothing! I sailed from Lourenco Marquez to Mombasa. I hunted elephant in British East Africa until they posted a reward for me on the telegraph poles. The law says not more than two elephants in one year. I shot two hundred! I sold the ivory to an Indian, bought cattle, and went down into German East Africa. The Masai attacked me, stole some of the cattle, and killed others. The Germans, damn and blast them, took the rest! They accused me of crimes—me, Georges Coutlass!—and imposed fines calculated carefully to skin me of all I had! Roup and rotten livers! but I will knock them head-over-halleluja one fine day! Not for nothing shall they flim-flam Georges Coutlass! Which of you gentlemen is the lord?"

We bought him another drink, and watched it disappear with one uninterrupted gurgle down its appointed course.

"What did you do next?" Fred asked him before he had

recovered breath enough to question us. "I suppose the Germans had you at a loose end?"

"Do you think that? Sacred history of hell! It takes more than a lousy military German to get Georges Coutlass at a loose end! They must get me dead before that can happen! And then, by Blitzen, as those devils say, a dead Georges Coutlass will be better than a thousand dead Germans! In hell I will use them to clean my boots on! At a loose end, was I? I met this bloody rogue Hassan—the fat blackguard who told me you have come to Zanzibar for fish—and made an agreement with him to look for Tippoo Tib's buried ivory. Yes, sir! I showed him papers. He thought they were money drafts. He thought me a man of means whom he could bleed. I had guns and ammunition, he none. He pretended to know where some of Tippoo Tib's ivory is buried."

"Some of it, eh?" said Fred.

"Some of it, d'you say?" said I.

"Some of it, yes. A million tusks. Some say two million! Some say three! Thunder!—you take a hundred good tusks and bury them; you'll see the hill you've made from five miles off! A hundred thousand tusks would make a mountain! If any one buried a million tusks in one spot they'd mark the place on maps as a watershed! They must be buried here, there, everywhere along the trail of Tippoo Tib—perhaps a thousand in one place at the most. Which of you two gentlemen is the lord?"

"Did Hassan lead you to any of it?" Fred inquired.

"Not he! The jelly-belly! The Arab pig! He led me to Ujiji—that's on Lake Tanganika—the old slave market where he himself was once sold for ten cents. I don't doubt a piece of betel nut and a pair of worn-out shoes had to be thrown in with him at the price! There he tried to make me pay the expenses in advance of a trip to Usumbora at the head of the lake. God knows what it would have cost, the way he wanted me to do it! Are you the lord, sir?"

"What did you do?" asked Fred.

"Do? I parted company! I had made him drunk once. (The Arabs aren't supposed to drink, so when they do they

get talkative and lively!) And I knew Arabic before ever I
crossed the Atlantic—learned it in Egypt—ran away from a
sponge-fishing boat when I was a boy. No, they don't fish
sponges off the Nile Delta, but you can smuggle in a sponge
boat better than in most ships. Anyhow, I learned Arabic.
So I understood what that pig Hassan said when he talked
in the dark with his brother swine. He knew no more than
I where the ivory was! He *suspected* most of it was in a
country called Ruanda that runs pretty much parallel with
the Congo border to the west of Victoria Nyanza in German
East Africa, and he was counting on finding natives who could
tell him this and that that might put him on the trail of it!
I could beat that game! I could cross-examine fool natives
twice as well as any fat rascal of an ex-slave! Seeing he had
paid all expenses so far, however, I was not much to the bad,
so I picked a quarrel with him and we parted company.
Wouldn't you have done the same, my lord?"

But Fred did not walk into the trap. "What did you do
next?" he asked.

"Next? I got a job with the agent of an Italian firm to go
north and buy skins. He made me a good advance of trade
goods—*melikani*,* beads, iron and brass wire, *kangas,*† and
all that sort of thing, and I did well. Made money on that
trip. Traveled north until I reached Ruanda—went on until
I could see the Fire Mountains in the distance, and the country all smothered in lava. Reached a cannibal country, where
the devils had eaten all the surrounding tribes until they had
to take to vegetarianism at last."

"But did you find the ivory?" Fred insisted.

"No, or by Jiminy, I wouldn't be here! If I'd found it I'd
have settled down with a wife in Greece long ago. I'd be
keeping an inn, and growing wine, and living like a gentleman! But I found out enough to know there's a system that
goes with the ivory Tippoo Tib buried. If you found one

---

*Melikani*, the unbleached calico made in America that is the
most useful trade goods from sea to sea of Central Africa.
†*Kanga*, cotton piece goods.

lot, that would lead you to the next, and so on. I got a suspicion where one lot is, although I couldn't prove it. And I
made up my mind that the German government knows darned
well where a lot of it is!"

"Then why don't the Germans dig it up?" demanded Fred.

"Aha!" laughed Coutlass. "If I know, why should I tell!
If they know, why should they tell? Suppose that some of
it were in Congo territory, and some in British East Africa?
Suppose they should want to get the lot? What then? If
they uncovered their bit in German East Africa mightn't that
put the Congo and the British on the trail?"

"If they know where it is," said I, "they'll certainly
guard it."

"Which of you is the lord?" demanded Coutlass earnestly.

"What do you suppose Hassan is doing, then, here in Zanzibar?" asked Fred.

"Rum and eggs! I know what he is doing! When I
snapped my thumb under his fat nose and told him about the
habits of his female ancestors he went to the Germans and informed against me! The sneak-thief! The turn-coat! The
maggot! I shall not forget! I, Georges Coutlass, forget
nothing! He informed against me, and they set *askaris**
on my trail who prevented me from making further search.
I had to sit idle in Usumbura or Ujiji, or else come away;
and idleness ill suits my blood! I came here, and Hassan
followed me. The Germans made a regular, salaried spy of
him—the semi-Arab rat! The one-tenth Arab, nine-tenths
mud-rat! Here he stays in Zanzibar and spies on Tippoo Tib,
on me, on the British government, and on every stranger who
comes here. His information goes to the Germans. I know,
for I intercepted some of it! He writes it out in Arabic, and
provided no woman goes through the folds of his clothes
or feels under that silken belly-piece he wears, the Germans
get it. But if a woman does, and she's a friend of mine, that's
different! Are you the lord, sir?"

"What do you propose?" asked Fred.

---

*Askari*, native soldier.

"Help me find that ivory!" said Coutlass. "I have very little money left, but I have guns, and courage! I know where to look, and I am not afraid! No German can scare me! I am English—American—Greek!—better than any hundred Germans! Let us find the ivory, and share it! Let us get it out through British territory, or the Congo, so that no German sausage can interfere with us or take away one tusk! Gee-rusalem, how I hate the swine! Let us put one over on them! Let us get the ivory to Europe, and then flaunt the deed under their noses! Let us send one little tip of a female tusk to the Kaiser for a souvenir—female in proof it is all illegitimate, illegal, outlawed! Let us send him a piece of ivory and a letter telling him all about it, and what we think of him and his swine-officials! His lieutenants and his captains! Let us smuggle the ivory out through the Congo —it can be done! It can be done! I, Georges Coutlass, will find the ivory, and find the way!"

"No need to smuggle it out," said Fred. "The British government will give us ten per cent., or so I understand, of the value of any of it we find in British East."

Georges Coutlass threw back his head and roared with laughter, slapped his thighs, held his sides—then coughed for two or three minutes, and spat blood.

"You are the lord, all right!" he gasped as soon as he could get breath. "No need to smuggle it! Ha-ha! May I be damned! Ten per cent. they'll give us! Ha-ha! Generous! By whip and wheel! they're lucky if we give them five per cent.! I'd like to see any government take away from Georges Coutlass ninety per cent. of anything without a fight! No, gentlemen! No, my Lord! The Belgian Congo government is corrupt. Let us spend twenty-five per cent.—even thirty—forty—fifty per cent. of the value of it to bribe the Congo officials. Hand over ninety per cent. to the Germans or the British without a fight?—Never! Never while my name is Georges Coutlass! I have fought too often! I have been robbed by governments too often! This last time I will put it over all the governments, and be rich at last, and go home to Greece to live like a gentleman! Believe me!"

He patted himself on the breast, and if flashing eye and frothing lip went for anything, then all the governments were as good as defeated already.

"You are the lord, are you not?" he demanded, looking straight at Fred.

"My name is Oakes," Fred anwered.

"Oh, then you? I beg pardon!" He looked at me with surprise that he made no attempt to conceal. Fred could pass for a king with that pointed beard of his (provided he were behaving himself seemly at the time) but for all my staid demeanor I have never been mistaken for any kind of personage. I disillusioned Coutlass promptly.

"Then you are neither of you lords?"

"Pish! We're obviously ladies!" answered Fred.

"Then you have fooled me?" The Greek rose to his feet. "You have deceived me? You have accepted my hospitality and confidence under false pretense?"

I think there would have been a fight, for Fred was never the man to accept brow-beating from chance-met strangers, and the Greek's fiery eye was rolling in fine frenzy; but just at that moment Yerkes strolled in, cheerful and brisk.

"Hullo, fellers! This is some thirsty burg. Do they sell soft drinks in this joint?" he inquired.

"By Brooklyn Bridge!" exclaimed Coutlass. "An American! I, too, am an American! Fellow-citizen, these men have treated me badly! They have tricked me!"

"You must be dead easy!" said Yerkes genially. "If those two wanted to live at the con game, they'd have to practise on the junior kindergarten grades. They're the mildest men I know. I let that one with the beard hold my shirt and pants when I go swimming! Tricked you, have they? Say— have you got any money left?"

"Oh, have a drink!" laughed the Greek. "Have one on me! It's good to hear you talk!"

"What have my friends done to you?" asked Yerkes.

"I was looking for a lord. They pretended to be lords."

"What? Both of 'em?"

"No, it is one lord I am looking for."

"One lord, one faith, one baptism!" said Yerkes profanely. "And you found two? What's your worry? I'll pretend to be a third if that'll help you any!"

"Gentlemen," said the Greek, rising to his full height and letting his rage begin to gather again, "you play with me. That is not well! You waste my time. That is not wise! I come in all innocence, looking for a certain lord—a real genuine lord—the Earl of Montdidier and Kirscrubbrightshaw —my God, what a name!"

"I'm Mundidier," said a level voice, and the Greek faced about like a man attacked. Monty had entered the barroom and stood listening with calm amusement, that for some strange reason exasperated the Greek less than our attitude had done, at least for the moment. When the first flush of surprise had died he grinned and grew gallant.

"My own name is Georges Coutlass, my Lord!" He made a sweeping bow, almost touching the floor with the brim of his cowboy hat, and then crossing his breast with it.

"What can I do for you?" asked Monty.

"Listen to me!"

"Very well. I can spare fifteen minutes."

We all took seats together in a far corner of the dingy room, where the Syrian barkeeper could not overhear us.

"My Lord, I am an Englishman!" Coutlass began. "I am a God-fearing, law-abiding gentleman! I know where to look for the ivory that the Arab villain Tippoo Tib has buried! I know how to smuggle it out of Africa without paying a penny of duty—"

"Did you say law-abiding?" Monty asked.

"Surely! Always! I never break the law! As for instance —in Greece, where I had the honor to be born, the law says no man shall carry a knife or wear one in his belt. So, since I was a little boy I carry none! I have none in my hand— none at my belt. I keep it here!"

He stooped, raised his right trousers leg, and drew from his Wellington boot a two-edged, pointed thing almost long enough to merit the name of rapier. He tossed it in the air,

let it spin six or seven times end over end, caught it deftly
by the point, and returned it to its hiding-place.

"I am a law-abiding man," he said, "but where the law
leaves off, I know where to begin! I am no fool!"

Monty made up his mind there and then that this man's
game would not be worth the candle.

"No, Mr. Coutlass, I can't oblige you," he said.

The Greek half-arose and then sat down again.

"You can not find it without my assistance!" he said, wrinkling his face for emphasis.

"I'm not looking for assistance," said Monty.

"Aha! You play with words! You are not—but you will!
I am no fool, my Lord! I understand! Not for nothing did
I make a friend again of that pig Hassan! Not for nothing
have I waited all these months in this stinking Zanzibar until
a man should come in search of that ivory whom I could trust!
Not for nothing did Juma, the lazaretto attendant tell Hassan you desired to see him! You seek the ivory, but you wish
to keep it all! To share none of it with me!" He stood up,
and made another bow, much curter than his former one. "I
am Georges Coutlass! My courage is known! No man can
rob me and get away with it!"

"My good man," drawled Monty, raising his eyebrows in
the comfortless way he has when there seems need of facing
an inferior antagonist. (He hates to "lord it" as thoroughly
as he loves to risk his neck.) "I would not rob you if you
owned the earth! If you have valuable information I'll pay
for it cheerfully after it's tested."

"Ah! Now you talk!"

"Observe—I said after it's tested!"

"I don't think he knows anything," said Fred. "I think
he guessed a lot, and wants to look, and can't afford to pay
his own expenses. Isn't that it?"

"What do you mean?" demanded Coutlass.

"I can't talk Greek," said Fred. "Shall I say it again in
English?"

"You may name any reasonable price," said Monty, "for
real information. Put it in writing. When we're agreed on

the price, put that in writing too. Then, if we find the information is even approximately right, why, we'll pay for it."

"Ah-h-h! You intend to play a trick on me! You use my information! You find the ivory! You go out by the Congo River and the other coast, and I kiss myself good-by to you and ivory and money! I am to be what d'you call it?—a milk-pigeon!"

"Being that must be *some* sensation!" nodded Yerkes.

"I warn you I can not be tampered with!" snarled the Greek, putting on his hat with a flourish. "I leave you, for you to think it over! But I tell you this—I promise you—I swear! Any expedition in search of that ivory that does not include Georges Coutlass on his own terms is a delusion—a busted flush—smashed—exploded—pfff!—so—evanesced before the start! My address is Zanzibar! Every street child knows me! When you wish to know my terms, tell the first man or child you meet to lead you to the house where Georges Coutlass lives! Good morning, Lord Skirtsshubrish! We will no doubt meet again!"

He turned his back on us and strode from the room—a man out of the middle ages, soldierly of bearing, unquestionably bold, and not one bit more venial or lawless than ninety per cent. of history's gallants, if the truth were told.

"Let's hope that's the last of him!" said Monty. "Can't say I like him, but I'd hate to have to spoil his chances."

"Last of him be sugared!" said Yerkes. "That's only the first of him! He'll find seven devils worse than himself and camp on our trail, if I know anything of Greeks—that's to say, if our trail leads after that ivory. Does it?"

"Depends," said Monty. "Let's talk up-stairs. That Syrian has long ears."

So we trooped to Monty's room, where the very cobwebs reeked of Arab history and lawless plans. He sat on the black iron bed, and we grouped ourselves about on chairs that had very likely covered the known world between them. One was obviously jetsam from a steamship; one was a Chinese thing, carved with staggering dragons; the other was made of iron-hard wood that Yerkes swore came from South America.

"Shoot when you're ready!" grinned Yerkes.

I was too excited to sit still. So was Fred.

"Get a move on, Didums, for God's sake!" he growled.

"Well," said Monty, "there seems something in this ivory business. Our chance ought to be as good as anybody's. But there are one or two stiff hurdles. In the first place, the story is common property. Every one knows it—Arabs—Swahili—Greeks—Germans—English. To be suspected of looking for it would spell failure, for the simple reason that every adventurer on the coast would trail us, and if we did find it we shouldn't be able to keep the secret for five minutes. If we found it anywhere except on British territory it 'ud be taken away from us before we'd time to turn round. And *it isn't buried on British territory!* I've found out that much."

"Good God, Didums! D'you mean you know where the stuff is?"

Fred sat forward like a man at a play.

"I know where it isn't," said Monty. "They told me at the Residency that in all human probability it's buried part in German East, and by far the greater part in the Congo."

"Then that ten per cent. offer by the British is a bluff?" asked Yerkes.

"Out of date," said Monty. "The other governments offer nothing. The German government might make terms with a German or a Greek—not with an Englishman. The Congo government is an unknown quantity, but would probably see reason if approached the proper way."

"The U. S. Consul tells me," said Yerkes, "that the Congo government is the rottenest aggregate of cutthroats, horsethieves, thugs, yeggs, common-or-ordinary hold-ups, and sleight-of-hand professors that the world ever saw in one Godforsaken country. He says they're of every nationality, but without squeam of any kind—hang or shoot you as soon as look at you! He says if there's any ivory buried in those parts they've either got it and sold it, or else they buried it themselves and spread the story for a trap to fetch greenhorns over the border!"

"That man's after the stuff himself!" said Fred. "All he wanted to do was stall you off!"

"That man Schillingschen the doctor told us about," said Monty, "is suspected of knowing where to look for some of the Congo hoard. He'll bear watching. He's in British East Africa at present—said to be combing Nairobi and other places for a certain native. He is known to stand high in the favor of the German government, but poses as a professor of ethnology."

"He shall study *deathnology*," said Fred, "if he gets in my way!"

"The Congo people," said Monty, "would have dug up the stuff, of course, if they'd known where to look for it. Our people believe that the Germans do know whereabouts to look for it, but dread putting the Congo crowd on the scent. If we're after it we've got to do two things besides agreeing between ourselves."

"Deal me in, Monty!" said Yerkes.

"Nil desperandum, Didums duce, then!" said Fred. "I propose Monty for leader. Those against the motion take their shirts off, and see if they can lick me! Nobody pugnacious? The ayes have it! Talk along, Didums!"

For all Fred's playfulness, Yerkes and I came in of our free and considered will, and Monty understood that.

"We've got to separate," he said, "and I've got to interview the King of Belgium."

"If that were my job," grinned Yerkes, "I'd prob'ly tell him things!"

"I don't pretend to like him," said Monty. "But it seems to me I can serve our best interests by going to Brussels. He can't very well refuse me a private audience. I should get a contract with the Congo government satisfactory to all concerned. He's rapacious—but I think not ninety per cent. rapacious."

"Good," said I, "but why separate?"

"If we traveled toward the Congo from this place in a bunch," said Monty, "we should give the game away completely and have all the rag-tag and bob-tail on our heels. As it is, our only chance of shaking all of them would be to go round by sea and enter the Congo from the other side; but that would destroy our chance of picking up the trail in German East Africa. So I'll go to Brussels, and get back to British East as fast as possible. Fred must go to British East and watch Schillingschen. You two fellows may as well go by way of British East Africa to Muanza on Victoria Nyanza, and on from there to the Congo border by way of Ujiji. Yerkes is an American, and they'll suspect him less than any of us (they'd nail me, of course, in a minute!) So let Yerkes make a great show of looking for land to settle on. We'll all four meet on the Congo border, at some other place to be decided later. We'll have to agree on a code, and keep in touch by telegraph as often as possible. Now, is all that clear?"

"We two'll have all the Greeks of Zanzibar trailing us all the way!" objected Yerkes.

"That'll be better than having them trail the lot of us," said Monty. "You'll be able to shake them somewhere on the way. We'll count on your ingenuity, Will."

"But what am I to do to Schillingschen?" asked Fred.

"Keep an eye on him."

"Do you see me Sherlock-Holmesing him across the high veld? Piffle! Give America that job! I'll go through German East and keep ahead of the Greeks!"

But Monty was firm. "Yerkes has a plausible excuse, Fred. They may wonder why an American should look for land in German East Africa, but they'll let him do it, and perhaps not spy on him to any extent. It's me they've their eye on. I'll try to keep 'em dazzled. You go to British East and dazzle Schillingschen! Now, are we agreed?"

We were. But we talked, nevertheless, long into the afternoon, and in the end there was not one of us really satisfied. Over and over we tried to persuade Monty to omit the Brussels part of the plan. We wanted him with us. But he stuck to his point, and had his way, as he always did when we were quite sure he really wanted it.

# THE NJO HAPA SONG

*Gleam, oh brighter than jewels! gleam my swinging stars in*
*the opal dark,*
*Mirrored along wi' the fire-fly dance of 'longshore light and*
*off-shore mark,*
*The roof-lamps and the riding lights, and phosphor wake of*
*ship and shark.*

> *I was old when the fires of Arab ships*
> *(All seas were lawless then!)*
> *Abode the tide where liners ride*
> *To-day, and Malays then;—*
> *Old when the bold da Gama came*
> *With culverin and creed*
> *To trade where Solomon's men fought,*
> *And plunder where the banyans bought.*
> *I sighed when the first o' the slaves were brought,*
> *And laughed when the last were freed.*

*Deep, oh deeper than anchors drop, the bones o' the outbound*
*sailors lie,*
*Far, oh farther than breath o' wind the rumors o' fabled for-*
*tune fly,*
*And the 'venturers yearn from the ends of earth, for none o'*
*the isles is as fair as I!*

## CHAPTER TWO

THE enormous map of Africa loses no lure or mystery from the fact of nearness to the continent itself. Rather it increases. In the hot upper room that night, between the wreathing smoke of oil lamps, we pored over the large scale map Monty had saved from the wreck along with our money drafts and papers.

The atmosphere was one of bygone piracy. The great black ceiling beams, heavy-legged table of two-inch planks, floor laid like a dhow's deck—making utmost use of odd lengths of timber, but strong enough to stand up under hurricanes and overloads of plunder, or to batten down rebellious slaves —murmurings from rooms below, where men of every race that haunts those shark-infested seas were drinking and telling tales that would make Munchhausen's reputation—steaminess, outer darkness, spicy equatorial smells and, above all, knowledge of the nature of the coming quest united to veil the map in fascination.

No man gifted with imagination better than a hot-cross bun's could be in Zanzibar and not be conscious of the lure that made adventurers of men before the first tales were written. Old King Solomon's traders must have made it their headquarters, just as it was Sindbad the Sailor's rendezvous and that of pirates before he or Solomon were born or thought of. Vasco da Gama, stout Portuguese gentleman adventurer, conquered it, and no doubt looted the godowns to a lively tune. Wave after wave of Arabs sailed to it (as they do to-day) from that other land of mystery, Arabia; and there isn't a yard of coral beach, cocoanut-fringed shore, clove orchard, or vanilla patch—not a lemon tree nor a thousand-year-old baobab but could tell of battle and intrigue; not a creek where the dhows lie peacefully to-day but could whisper of cargoes run by night

37

—black cargoes, groaning fretfully and smelling of the 'tween-deck lawlessness.

"There are two things that have stuck in my memory that Lord Salisbury used to say when I was an Eton boy, spending a holiday at Hatfield House," said Monty. "One was, Never talk fight unless you mean fight; then fight, don't talk. The other was, Always study the largest maps."

"Who's talking fight?" demanded Fred.

Monty ignored him. "Even this map isn't big enough to give a real idea of distances, but it helps. You see, there's no railway beyond Victoria Nyanza. Anything at all might happen in those great spaces beyond Uganda. Borderlands are quarrel-grounds. I should say the junction of British, Belgian, and German territory where Arab loot lies buried is the last place to dally in unarmed. You fellows 'ud better scour Zanzibar in the morning for the best guns to be had here."

So I went to bed at midnight with that added stuff for building dreams. He who has bought guns remembers with a thrill; he who has not, has in store for him the most delightful hours of life. May he fall, as our lot was, on a gunsmith who has mended hammerlocks for Arabs, and who loves rifles as some greater rascals love a woman or a horse.

We all four strolled next morning, clad in the khaki reach-medowns that a Goanese "universal provider" told us were the "latest thing," into a den between a camel stable and an even mustier-smelling home of gloom, where oxen tied nose-to-tail went round and round, grinding out semsem everlastingly while a lean Swahili sang to them. When he ceased, they stopped. When he sang, they all began again.

In a bottle-shaped room at the end of a passage squeezed between those two centers of commerce sat the owner of the gun-store, part Arab, part Italian, part Englishman, apparently older than sin itself, toothless, except for one yellow fang that lay like an ornament over his lower lip, and able to smile more winningly than any siren of the sidewalk. Evidently he shaved at intervals, for white stubble stood out a third of an inch all over his wrinkled face. The upper part of his head was utterly bald, slippery, shiny, smooth, and adorned by an absurd, round Indian cap, too small, that would not stay in place and had to be hitched at intervals.

He said his name was Captain Thomas Cook, and the license to sell firearms framed on the mud-brick wall bore him witness. (May he live forever under any name he chooses!) "Goons?" he said. "Goons? You gentlemen want goons? I have the goon what settled the hash of Sayed bin Mohammed —here it be. This other one's the rifle—see the nicks on her butt!—that Kamarajes the Greek used. See 'em—Arab goons —slaver goons—smooth-bore elephant goons—fours, eights, twelves—Martinis—them's the lot that was reekin' red-hot, days on end, in the last Arab war on the Congo, considerable used up but goin' cheap;—then here's Mausers (he pronounced it "Morsers")—old-style, same as used in 1870—good goons they be, long o' barrel and strong, but too high trajectory for some folks;—some's new style, magazines an' all—fine till a grain o' sand jams 'em oop;—an' Lee-Enfields, souvenirs o' the Boer War, some o' them bought from folks what plundered a battle-field or two — mostly all in good condition. Look at this one—see it—hold it—take a squint along it! Nineteen elephants shot wi' that Lee-Enfield, an' the man's in jail for shootin' of 'em! Sold at auction by the gov'ment, that one was. See, here's an Express—a beauty—owned by an officer fr'm Indy—took by a shark 'e was, in swimmin' against all advice, him what had hunted tigers! There's no goon store a quarter as good as mine 'tween Cairo an' the Cape or Bombay an' Boma! Captain Cook's the boy to sell ye goons all right! Sit down. Look 'em over. Ask anything ye want to know. I'll tell ye. No obligation to buy."

There is no need to fit out with guns and tents in London. Until both good and bad, both cowardly and brave give up the habit of dying in bed, or getting killed, or going broke, or ending up in jail for one cause and the other, there will surely always be fine pickings for men on the spot with a little money and a lot of patience—guns, tents, cooking pots, and all the other things.

We spent a morning with Captain Thomas Cook, and left

the store—Fred, Yerkes and I—with a battery of weapons, including a pistol apiece—that any expedition might be proud of. (Monty, since he had to go home in any case, preferred to look over the family gun-room before committing himself.)

Then, since the first leg of the journey would be the same for all of us, we bought other kit, packed it, and booked passages for British East Africa. Between then and the next afternoon when the British India steamboat sailed we were fairly bombarded by inquisitiveness, but contrived not to tell much. And with patience beyond belief Monty restrained us from paying court to Tippoo Tib.

"The U. S. Consul says he's better worth a visit than most of the world's museums," Yerkes assured us two or three times. "He says Tippoo Tib's a fine old sport—damned rogue—slave-hunter, but white somewhere near the middle. What's the harm in our having a chin with him?"

But Monty was adamant.

"A call on him would prove nothing, but he and his friends would suspect. Spies would inform the German government. No. Let's act as if Tippoo Tib were out of mind."

We grumbled, but we yielded. Hassan came again, shiny with sweat and voluble with offers of information and assistance.

"Where you gentlemen going?" he kept asking.

"England," said Monty, and showed his own steamer ticket in proof of it.

That settled Hassan for the time but Georges Coutlass was not so easy. He came swaggering up-stairs and thumped on Monty's door with the air of a bearer of king's messages.

"What do you intend to do?" he asked. (We were all sitting on Monty's bed, and it was Yerkes who opened the door.)

"Do you an injury," said Yerkes, "unless you take your foot away!" The Greek had placed it deftly to keep the door open pending his convenience.

"Let him have his say," advised Monty from the bed.

"Where are you going? Hassan told me England. Are you all going to England? If so, why have you bought guns? What will you do with six rifles, three shot-guns, and three

pistols on the London streets? What will you do with tents
in London? Will you make campfires in Regent Circus, that
you take with you all those cooking pots? And all that rice,
is that for the English to eat? Bah! No tenderfoot can fool
me! You go to find *my* ivory, d'you hear! You think to get
away with it unknown to me! I tell you I have sharp ears!
By Jingo, there is nothing I can not find out that goes on in
Africa! You think to cheat me? Then you are as good as
dead men! You shall die like dogs! I will smithereen the
whole damned lot of you before you touch a tusk!"

"Get out of here!" growled Yerkes.

"Give him a chance to go quietly, Will," urged Monty, and
Coutlass heard him. Peaceful advice seemed the last spark
needed to explode his crowded magazines of fury. He clenched
his fists—spat because the words would not flow fast enough—
and screamed.

"Give me a chance, eh? A chance, eh?" Other doors
began opening, and the appearance of an audience stimulated
him to further peaks of rage. "The only chance I need is a
sight of your carcasses within range, and a long range will
do for Georges Coutlass!" He glared past Yerkes at Monty,
who had risen leisurely. "You call yourself a lord? I call
you a thief! A jackal!"

"Here, get out!" growled Yerkes, self-constituted Cerberus.

"I will go when I damned please, you Yankee jackanapes!"
the Greek retorted through set teeth. Yerkes is a free man,
able and willing to shoulder his own end of any argument.
He closed, and the Greek's ribs cracked under a vastly stronger
hug than he had dreamed of expecting. But Coutlass was no
weakling either, and though he gasped he gathered himself
for a terrific effort.

"Come on!" said Monty, and went past me through the
door like a bolt from a catapult. Fred followed me, and when
he saw us both out on the landing Monty started down the
stairs.

"Come on!" he called again.

We followed, for there is no use in choosing a leader if
you don't intend to obey him, even on occasions when you

fail at once to understand. There was one turn on the wide stairs, and Monty stood there, back to the wall.

"Go below, you fellows, and catch!" he laughed. "We don't want Will jailed for homicide!"

The struggle was fierce and swift. Coutlass searched with a thumb for Will's eye, and stamped on his instep with an iron-shod heel. But he was a dissolute brute, and for all his strength Yerkes' cleaner living very soon told. Presently Will spared a hand to wrench at the ambitious thumb, and Coutlass screamed with agony. Then he began to sway this way and that without volition of his own, yielding his balance, and losing it again and again. In another minute Yerkes had him off his feet, cursing and kicking.

"Steady, Will!" called Monty from below; but it was altogether too late for advice. Will gathered himself like a spring, and hurled the Greek down-stairs backward.

Then the point of Monty's strategy appeared. He caught him, saved him from being stunned against the wall, and, before the Greek could recover sufficiently to use heels and teeth or whisk out the knife he kept groping for, hurled him a stage farther on his journey—face forward this time down to where Fred and I were waiting. We kicked him out into the street too dazed to do anything but wander home.

"Are you hurt, Will?" laughed Monty. "This isn't the States, you know; by gad, they'll jail you here if you do your own police work! Instead of Brussels I'd have had to stay and hire lawyers to defend you!"

"Aw—quit preaching!" Yerkes answered. "If I hadn't seen you there on the stairs with your mouth open I'd have been satisfied to put him down and spank him!"

It was then that the much more unexpected struck us speechless—even Monty for the moment, who is not much given to social indecision. We had not known there was a woman guest in that hotel. One does not look in Zanzibar for ladies with a Mayfair accent unaccompanied by menfolk able to protect them. Yet an indubitable Englishwoman, expensively if carelessly dressed, came to the head of the stairs and stood beside Yerkes looking down at the rest of us with a sort of well bred, rather tolerant scorn.

"Am I right in believing this is Lord Montdidier?" she asked, pronouncing the word as it should be—Mundidger.

She had been very beautiful. She still was handsome in a hard-lipped, bold way, with abundant raven hair and a complexion that would have been no worse for a touch of rouge. She seemed to scorn all the conventional refinements, though. Her lacy white dress, open at the neck, was creased and not too clean, but she wore in her bosom one great jewel like a ruby, set in brilliants, that gave the lie to poverty provided the gems were real. And the amber tube through which she smoked a cigarette was seven or eight inches long and had diamonds set in a gold band round its middle. She wore no wedding ring that I could see; and she took no more notice of Will Yerkes beside her than if he had been a part of the furniture.

"Why do you ask?" asked Monty, starting up-stairs. She had to make way for him, for Will Yerkes stood his ground.

"A fair question!" she laughed. Her voice had a hard ring, but was very well trained and under absolute control. I received the impression that she had been a singer at some time. "I am Lady Saffren Waldon—Isobel Saffren Waldon."

Fred and I had followed Monty up and were close behind him. I heard him mutter, "Oh, lord!" under his breath.

"I knew your brother," she added.

"I know you did."

"You think that gives me no claim on your acquaintance? Perhaps it doesn't. But as an unprotected woman—"

"There is the Residency," objected Monty, "and the law."

She laughed bitterly. "Thank you, I am in need of no passage home! I overheard that ruffian say, and I think I heard you say too that you are going to England. I want you to take a message for me."

"There is a post-office here," said Monty without turning a hair. He looked straight into her iron eyes. "There is a cable station. I will lend you money to cable with."

"Thank you, my Lord!" she sneered. "I have money. I am so used to being snubbed that my skin would not feel a whip! I want you to take a verbal message!"

It was perfectly evident that Monty would rather have met the devil in person than this untidy dame; yet he was only afraid apparently of conceding her too much claim on his attention. (If she had asked favors of me I don't doubt I would have scrambled to be useful. I began mentally taking her part, wondering why Monty should treat her so cavalierly; and I fancy Yerkes did the same.)

"Tell me the message, and I'll tell you whether I'll take it," said Monty.

She laughed again, even more bitterly.

"If I could tell it on these stairs," she answered, "I could cable it. They censor cablegrams, and open letters in this place."

"I suspect that isn't true," said Monty. "But if you object to witnesses, how do you propose to deliver your message to me?" he asked pointedly.

"You mean you refuse to speak with me alone?"

"My friends would draw out of earshot," he answered.

"Your friends? Your gang, you mean!" She drew herself up very finely—very stately. Very lovely she was to look at in that half-light, with the shadows of Tippoo Tib's* old stairway hiding her tale of years. But I felt my regard for her slipping downhill (and so, I rather think did Yerkes). "You look well, Lord Montdidier, trapesing about the earth with a leash of mongrels at your heel! Falstaff never picked up a more sordid-looking pack! What do you feed them— bones? Are there no young bloods left of your own class, that you need travel with tradesmen?"

Monty stood with both hands behind him and never turned a hair. Fred Oakes brushed up the ends of that troubadour mustache of his and struck more or less of an attitude. Will reddened to the ears, and I never felt more uncomfortable in all my life.

---

*The principal hotel in Zanzibar was formerly Tippoo Tib's residence, quite a magnificent mansion for that period and place.

"So this is *your* gang, is it?" she went on. "It looks sober at present! I suppose I must trust you to control them! I dare say even tavern brawlers respect you sufficiently to keep a lady's secret if you order them. I will hope they have manhood enough to hold their tongues!"

Of course, dressed in the best that Zanzibar stores had to offer we scarcely looked like fashion plates. My shirt was torn where Coutlass had seized it to resist being thrown out, but I failed to see what she hoped to gain by that tongue lashing, even supposing we had been the lackeys she pretended to believe we were.

"The message is to my brother," she went on.

"I don't know him!" put in Monty promptly.

"You mean you don't like him! Your brother had him expelled from two or three clubs, and you prefer not to meet him! Nevertheless, I give you this message to take to him! Please tell him—you will find him at his old address—that I, his sister, Lady Saffren Waldon, know now the secret of Tippoo Tib's ivory. He is to join me here at once, and we will get it, and sell it, and have money, and revenge! Will you tell him that?"

"No!" answered Monty.

I looked at Yerkes, Yerkes looked at Fred, and Fred at me. There was nothing to do but feel astonished.

"Why not, if you please?"

"I prefer not to meet Captain McCauley," said Monty.

"Then you will give the message to somebody else?" she insisted.

"No," said Monty. "I will carry no message for you."

"Why do you say that? How dare you say that? In front of your following—your gang!"

I should have been inclined to continue the argument myself—to try to find out what she did know, and to uncover her game. It was obvious she must have some reason for her extraordinary request, and her more extraordinary way of making it. But Monty saw fit to stride past her through his open bedroom door, and shut it behind him firmly. We stood looking at her and at one another stupidly until she turned her back and went to her own room on the floor above. Then we followed Monty.

"Did she say anything else?" he asked as soon as we were inside. I noticed he was sweating pretty freely now.

"Didums, you're too polite!" Fred answered. "You ought to have told her to keep her tongue housed or be civil!"

"I don't hold with hitting back at a lone woman," said Yerkes, "but what was she driving at? What did she mean by calling us a pack of mongrels?"

"Merely her way," said Monty offhandedly. "Those particular McCauleys never amounted to much. She married a baronet, and he divorced her. Bad scandal. Saffren Waldon was at the War Office. She stole papers, or something of that sort—delivered them to a German paramour—von Duvitz was his name, I think. She and her brother were lucky to keep out of jail. Ever since then she has been—some say a spy, some say one thing, some another. My brother fell foul of her, and lived to regret it. She's on her last legs I don't doubt, or she wouldn't be in Zanzibar."

"Then why the obvious nervous sweat you're in?" demanded Fred.

"And that doesn't account for the abuse she handed out to us," said Yerkes.

"Why not tip off the authorities that she's a notorious spy?" I asked.

"I suspect they know all about her," he answered.

"But why your alarm?" insisted Fred.

"I'm scarcely alarmed, old thing. But it's pretty obvious, isn't it, that she wants us to believe she knows what we're after. She's vindictive. She imagines she owes me a grudge on my brother's account. It might soothe her to think she had made me nervous. And by gad—it sounds like lunacy, and mind you I'm not propounding it for fact!—there's just one chance that she really does know where the ivory is!"

"But where's the sense of abusing us?" repeated Yerkes.

"That's the poor thing's way of claiming class superiority," said Monty. "She was born into one class, married into another, and divorced into a third. She's likely to forget she

said an unkind word the next time she meets you. Give her
one chance and she'll pretend she believes you were born to
the purple — flatter you until you half believe it yourself.
Later on, when it suits her at the moment, she'll denounce
you as a social impostor! It's just habit—bad habit, I admit
—comes of the life she leads. Lots of 'em like her. Few of
'em quite so well informed, though, and dangerous if you
give 'em a chance."

"I still don't see why you're sweating," said Fred.

"It's hot. There's a chance she knows where the ivory is!
She has money, but how? She'd have begged if she were
short of cash! It's my impression she has been in German
government employ for a number of years. Possibly they have
paid her to do some spy-work—in the Zanzibar court, perhaps
—the Sultan's a mere boy—"

"Isn't he woolly-headed?" objected Yerkes.

"Mainly Arab. It's a French game to send a white woman
to intrigue at colored courts, but the Germans are good imi-
tators."

"Isn't she English?" asked Yerkes.

"Her trade's international," said Monty dryly. "My guess
is that Coutlass or Hassan told her what we're supposed to be
doing here, and she pretends to know where the ivory is in
order to trap us all in some way. The net's spread for me,
but there's no objection to catching you fellows as well."

"She'll need to use sweeter bait than I've seen yet!" laughed
Yerkes.

"She'll probably be sweetness itself next time she sees you.
She'll argue she's created an impression and can afford to be
gracious."

"Impression is good!" said Yerkes. "I mean it's bad! She
has created one, all right! What's the likelihood of her having double-crossed the Germans? Mightn't she have got a
clue to where the stuff is, and be holding for a better market
than they offer?"

"I was coming to that," said Monty. "Yes, it's possible.
But whatever her game is, don't let us play it for her. Let
her do the leading. If she gets hold of you fellows, one at a

time or all together, for the love of heaven tell her nothing!
Let her tell all she likes, but admit nothing—tell nothing—
ask no questions! That's an old rule in diplomacy (and remember, she's a diplomat, whatever else she may be!) Old-
stagers can divine the young ones' secrets from the nature
of the questions they ask! So if you get the chance, ask her
nothing! Don't lie, either! It would take a very old hand to
lie to her in such way that she couldn't see through it!"

"Why not be simply rude and turn our backs?" said I.

"Best of all—provided you can do it! Remember, she's an
old hand!"

"D'you mean," said Yerkes, "that if she were to offer proof
that she knows where that ivory is, and proposed terms, you
wouldn't talk it over?"

"I mean let her alone!" said Monty.

But it turned out she would not be let alone. We dined
in the public room, but she had her meals sent up to her and
we flattered ourselves (or I did) that her net had been laid
in vain. Folk dine late in the tropics, and we dallied over
coffee and cigars, so that it was going on for ten o'clock when
Yerkes and I started up-stairs again. Monty and Fred went
out to see the water-front by moonlight.

We had reached our door (he and I shared one great room)
when we heard terrific screams from the floor above — a
woman's—one after another, piercing, fearful, hair-raising,
and so suggestive in that gloomy, grim building that a man's
very blood stood still.

Yerkes was the first up-stairs. He went like an arrow from
a bow, and I after him. The screams had stopped before we
reached the stairhead, but there was no doubting which her
room was; the door was partly open, permitting a view of
armchairs and feminine garments in some disorder. We
heard a man talking loud quick Arabic, and a woman—pleading, I thought. Yerkes rapped on the door.

"Come in!" said a voice, and I followed Yerkes in.

We were met by her Syrian maid, a creature with gazelle
eyes and timid manner, who came through the doorway leading to an inner room.

"What's the trouble?" demanded Yerkes, and the woman
signed to us to go on in. Yerkes led the way again impul-
sively as any knight-errant rescuing beleaguered dames, but
I looked back and saw that the Syrian woman had locked
the outer door. Before I could tell Will that, he was in
the next room, so I followed, and, like him, stood rather
bewildered.

Lady Saffren Waldon sat facing us, rather triumphant, in
no apparent trouble, not alone. There were four very well-
dressed Arabs standing to one side. She sat in a basket chair
by a door that pretty obviously led into her bedroom; and
kept one foot on a pillow, although I suspected there was not
much the matter with it.

"We heard screams. Thought you were being murdered!"
said Yerkes, out of breath.

"Oh, indeed, no! Nothing of the kind! I fell and twisted
my ankle—very painful, but not serious. Since you are here,
sit down, won't you?"

"No, thanks," said he, turning to go.

"The maid locked the door on us!" said I, and before the
words were out of my mouth three of the Arabs slipped into
the outer room. There was no hint or display of weapons of
any kind, but they were big men, and the folds of their garments were sufficiently voluminous to have hidden a dozen
guns apiece.

"She'll open it!" said Will, with inflection that a fool could
understand.

"One minute, please!" said Lady Saffren Waldon. (It was
no poor imitation of Queen Elizabeth ordering courtiers
about.)

"We didn't come to talk," said Will. "Heard screams.
Made a mistake. Sorry. We're off!"

"No mistake!" she said; and the sweetness Monty prophesied began to show itself. The change in her voice was too
swift and pronounced to be convincing. "I did scream. I was
in pain. It was kind of you to come. Since you are here I
would like you to talk to this gentleman."

She glanced at the Arab, an able-looking man, with nose

and eyes expressive of keen thought, and the groomed gray beard that makes an Arab always dignified.

"Some other time," said Will. "I've an engagement." And he turned to go again.

"No—now!" she said. "It's no use—you can't get out! You may as well be sensible and listen!"

We glanced at each other and both remembered Monty's warning. Will laughed.

"Take seats," she said, with a very regal gesture. She was not carelessly dressed, as she had been earlier in the day. From hair to silken hose and white kid shoes she was immaculate, and she wore rouge and powder now. In that yellow lamplight (carefully placed, no doubt) she was certainly good-looking. In fact, she was good-looking at any time, and only no longer able to face daylight with the tale of youth. Her eyes were weapons, nothing less. We remained standing.

"This gentleman will speak to you," she said, motioning to the Arab to commence, and he bowed—from the shoulders upward.

"I am from His Highness the Sultan of Zanzibar," he announced, a little pompously. "A minister from His Highness." (In announcing their own importance Arabs very seldom err in the direction of under-estimate.) "I speak about the ivory, which I am informed you propose to set out on a journey to discover."

"Where did you get your information?" Yerkes countered.

"Don't be absurd!" ordered Lady Saffren Waldon. "I gave it to him! Where else need he go to get it?"

"Where did you get it, then?" he retorted.

"Never mind! Listen to what Hamed Ibrahim has to say!"

The Arab bowed his head slightly a second time.

"The ivory you seek," he said, "is said to be Tippoo Tib's own, and he will not tell the hiding-places. It does not belong to him. Such little part of it as ever was his was long ago swallowed by the interest on claims against him. The whole is now in truth the property of His Highness the Sultan of Zanzibar, and whoever discovers it shall receive reward from the owner. His Highness is willing, through me his minister, to make treaty in advance in writing with suitable parties intending to make search."

"You mean the Sultan wants to hire me to hunt for ivory for him?" Will asked, and the Arab made a gesture of impatience. At that Lady Saffren Waldon cut in, very vinegary once more.

"You two men are prisoners! Show much more sense! Come to terms or take the consequences! Listen! Tippoo Tib buried the ivory. The Sultan of Zanzibar claims it. The German government, for reasons of its own, backs the Sultan's claim; ivory found in German East Africa will be handed over to him in support of his claim to all the rest of it. If you—Lord Montdidier and the rest of you—care to sign an agreement with the Sultan of Zanzibar you can have facilities. You shall be supplied with guides who can lead you to the right place to start your search from—"

"Thought you wanted Lord Montdidier to say in London that you know where it all is," Will objected.

She colored slightly, and glared.

"Perhaps I am one of the guides," she said darkly. "I know more than I need tell for the sake of this argument! The point is, you can have facilities if you sign an agreement with the Sultan. Otherwise, you will be dogged wherever you go! Whatever you should find would be claimed! Every difficulty will be made for you—every treachery conceivable practised on you. Lord Montdidier can get influential backing, but not influence among the natives! He can not get good men and true information by pulling wires in London. The British government once offered ten per cent. of the value of the ivory found. The Sultan of Zanzibar offers twenty per cent.—"

"Twenty-five per cent.," corrected Hamed Ibrahim.

"Yes, but I should want five per cent. for my commission!"

"This sounds like a different yarn to the one you told on the stairs this afternoon," said Will. "See Monty and tell it to him."

"It is for you to tell Lord Montdidier. He runs away from me!"

"I refuse to tell him a word!" said Will, with a laugh like that of a boy about to plunge into a swimming pool—a sort of "Here goes!" laugh.

"You are extremely ill advised!"

"Do your worst! Monty'll be hunting for us two in about a minute. We're prisoners, are we? Suit yourself!"

"You are prisoners while I choose! You could be killed in this room, removed in sacks, thrown to the sharks in the roadstead, and nobody the wiser! But I have no intention of killing you. As it happens, that would not suit my purpose!"

We both glanced behind us involuntarily. It may be that we both heard a footstep, but it is always difficult to say certainly after the event. At any rate, while in the act of turning our heads, two of the three Arabs, who had previously left the room, threw nooses over them and bound our arms to our sides with the jiffy-swiftness only sailors know. The third man put the finishing touches, and presently adjusted gags with a neatness and solicitude worthy of the Inquisition.

"Throw them!" she ordered, and in a second our heels were struck from under us and I was half stunned by the impact of my head against the solid floor (for all the floors of that great place were built to resist eternity).

"Now!" she said. "Show them knives!"

We were shown forthwith the ugliest, most suggestive weapons I have ever seen—long sliver-thin blades sharper than razors. The Arabs knelt on our chests (their knees were harder and more merciless than wooden clubs) and laid the blades, edge-upward, on the skin of our throats.

"Let them feel!" she ordered.

I felt a sharp cut, and the warm blood trickled down over my jugular to the floor. I knew it was only a skin-cut, but did not pretend to myself I was enjoying the ordeal.

"Now!" she said.

The Arabs stepped away and she came and stood between us, looking down at one and then the other.

"There isn't a place in Africa," she said, "that you can hide in where the Sultan's men can't find you! There isn't a British officer in Africa who would believe you if you told

what has happened in this room to-night! Yet Lord Montdidier will believe you—he knows you presumably, and certainly he knows me! So tell Lord Montdidier exactly what
has happened! Assure him with my compliments that his
throat and yours shall be cut as surely as you dare set out
after that ivory without signing my agreement first. Tell
Lord Montdidier he may be friends with me if he cares to.
As his friend I will help make him rich for life! As his
enemy, I will make Africa too hot and dangerous to hold him!
Let him choose!"

She stepped back and, without troubling to turn away, put
powder on her nose and chin.

"Now let them up!" she said.

The Arabs lifted us to our feet.

"Loose them!"

The expert of the three slipped the knots like a wizard
doing parlor tricks; but I noticed that the other two held their
knives extremely cautiously. We should have been dead men
if we had made a pugnacious motion.

"Now you may go! Unless Lord Montdidier agrees with
me, the only safety for any of you is away from Africa! Go
and tell him! Go!"

"I'll give you your answer now!" said Will.

"No, you don't!" said I, remembering Monty's urgent ad-
monition to tell her nothing and ask no questions. "Come
away, Will! There's nothing to be gained by talking back!"

"Right you are!" he said, laughing like a boy again—this
time like a boy whose fight has been broken off without his
seeking or consent. Like me, he pulled out a handkerchief
and wiped blood from his neck. The sight of his own blood
—even such a little trickle as that—has peculiar effect on a
man.

"By Jiminy, she has scratched the wrong dog's ear!" he
growled to me as we went to the door together.

"They're all in there!" I said excitedly, when the door
slammed shut behind us. "Hurry down and get me a gun!
I'll hold the door while you run for police and have 'em all
arrested!"

"Piffle!" he said. "Come on! Three Sultan's witnesses and two lone white women against us two—come away! Come away!"

Monty and Fred were still out, so we went to our own room.

"I'm wondering," I said, "what Monty will say."

"I'm not!" said Will. "I'm not troubling, either! I'm not going to tell Monty a blessed word! See here:—she thinks she knows where some o' that ivory is. Maybe the government of German East Africa is in on the deal, and maybe not; that makes no present difference. She thinks she's wise. And she has fixed up with the Sultan to have him claim it when found, so's she'll get a fat slice of the melon. There's a scheme on to get the stuff, when who should come on the scene but our little party, and that makes 'em all nervous, 'cause Monty's a bad man to be up against. Remember: she claimed that she knows Monty and he knows her. She means by that that he knows she's a desperado, and she thinks he'll draw the line at a trip that promises murder and blackmail and such like dirty work. So she puts a scare into us with a view to our throwing a scare into him. If I scare any one, it's going to be that dame herself. I'll not tell Monty a thing!"

"How about Coutlass the Greek?" said I. "D'you suppose he's her accomplice?"

"Maybe! One of her dupes perhaps! I suspect she'll suck him dry of information and cast him off like a lemon rind. I dare bet she's using him. She can't use me! Shall you tell Monty?"

"No," I said. "Not unless we both agreed."

He nodded. "You and I weren't born to what they call the purple. We're no diplomatists; but we get each other's meaning."

"Here come Monty and Fred," said I. "Is my neck still bloody? No, yours doesn't show."

We met them at the stairhead, and Monty did not seem to notice anything.

"Fred has composed a song to the moonlight on Zanzibar roadstead while you fellows were merely after-dinner mun-

dane. D'you suppose the landlord 'ud make trouble if we let
him sing it?"

"Let's hope so!" said Will. "I'm itching for a row like
they say drovers in Monty's country itch for mile-stones! Let
Fred warble. I'll fight whoever comes!"

Monty eyed him and me swiftly, but made no comment.

"Bill's homesick!" said Fred. "The U. S. eagle wants its
Bowery! We'll soothe the fowl with thoughts of other things
—where's the concertina?"

"No, no, Fred, that'll be too much din!"

Monty made a grab for the instrument, but Fred raised it
above his head and brought it down between his knees with
chords that crashed like wedding bells. Then he changed to
softer, languorous music, and when he had picked out an air
to suit his mood, sat down and turned art loose to do her
worst.

He has a good voice. If he would only not pull such faces,
or make so sure that folk within a dozen blocks can hear him,
he might pass for a professional.

"Music suggestive of moonlight!" he said, and began:

"The sentry palms stand motionless. Masts move against the
    sky.
With measured creak of curving spars dhows gently to the
    jeweled stars
Rock out a lullaby.

"Silver and black sleeps Zanzibar. The moonlit ripples croon
Soft songs of loves that perfect are, long tales of red-lipped
    spoils of war,
And you—you smile, you moon!
For I think that beam on the placid sea
That splashes, and spreads, and dips, and gleams,
That dances and glides till it comes to me
Out of infinite sky, is the path of dreams,
And down that lane the memories run
Of all that's wild beneath the sun!

"You fellows like that one? Anybody coming? Nobody for
Will to fight yet? Too bad! Well—we'll try again! There's

no chorus. It's all poetic stuff, too gentle to be yowled by three
such cannibals as you! Listen!

"Old as the moonlit silences, to-night's loves are the same
As when for ivory from far, and cloves and gems of Zanzibar
King Solomon's men came.

"Sinful and still the same roofs lie that knew da Gama's heel,
Those beams that light these sleepy waves looked on when men
          threw murdered slaves
To make the sharks a meal.
And I think that beam on the silvered swell
That spreads, and splashes, and gleams, and dips,
That has shone on the cruel and brave as well,
On the trail o' the slaves and the ivory ships,
Is the lane down which the memories run
Of all that's wild beneath the sun."

The concertina wailed into a sort of minor dirge and ceased.
Fred fastened the catch, and put the instrument away.
"Why don't you applaud?" he asked.
"Oh, bravo, bravo!" said Will and I together.
Monty looked hard at both of us.
"Strange!" he remarked. "You're both distracted, and
you've each got a slight cut over the jugular!"
"Been trying out razors," said Yerkes.
"Um-m-m!" remarked Monty. "Well—I'm glad it's no
worse. How about bed, eh? Better lock your door—that lady
up-stairs is what the Germans call *gefaehrlich!** Goo'night!"

___

*Gefaehrlich*, dangerous.

# THE NJO HAPA SONG

*Tongues! Oh, music of eastern tongues, harmonied murmur*
*of streets ahum!*
*Trade! Oh, frasila weights of clove—ivory—copra—copal*
*gum—*
*Rubber—vanilla and tortoise-shell! The methods change.*
*The captains come.*

*I was old when the clamor o' Babel's end*
*(All seas were chartless then!)*
*Drove forth the brood, and Solitude*
*Was the newest quest of men.*
*I lay like a gem in a silken sea*
*Unseen, uncoveted, unguessed*
*Till scented winds that waft afar*
*Bore word o' the warm delights there are*
*Where ground-swells sing by Zanzibar*
*Long rhapsodies of rest.*

*Wild, oh wilder than winter blasts my wet skies shriek when*
*the winds are freed.*
*Mild, oh milder than virgin mirth is the laugh o' the reefs*
*where sea-birds feed,*
*Screaming and skirling and down again. (Though the sea-*
*birds warn do captains heed?)*

# CHAPTER THREE

There is no public landing wharf at Zanzibar. Passengers have to submit their persons into the arms of loud-lunged Swahili longshoremen, who recognize one sole and only point of honor: neither passenger nor luggage shall be dropped into the surf.

Their invariable habit, the instant the view-halloa is raised, is to scamper headlong, pounce on the victim and pull him apart (or so it feels) until fortune, superior strength, or some such element decides the point; and then more often than not it is the victim's fate to be carried between two men, each hold of a thigh, each determined to get ashore or to the boat first, and each grimly resolved not to let go until three times the proper fee shall have been paid. Of only these two things let the passenger assure himself—fight how he may, he will neither escape their clutches nor get wet. Rather they will hold him upside-down until the contents of his pockets fall into the surf. Dry on the beach or into the boat they will dump him. And whatever he shall pay them will surely be insufficient.

But we had a privy councilor of England of our party, and favors were shown us that never fall to the lot of ordinary travelers. Opposite the Sultan's palace is the Sultan's private wharf, so royal and private that it is a prison offense to trespass on it without written permission. Because of his official call at the Residency, and of his card left on the Sultan, wires had been pulled, and a pompous individual whose black face sweated greasily, and whose palm itched for unearned increment, called on Monty very shortly after breakfast with intimation that the wharf had been placed at our disposal, since His Highness the Sultan desired to do us honor.

So when the B. I. steamer dropped anchor in the great roadstead shortly after noon we were taken to the wharf by

one of the Sultan's household—a very civil-spoken Arab gentleman—and three English officers met us there who made a
fuss over Monty and were at pains to be agreeable to the rest
of us. While we stood chatting and waiting for the boat that
should row us and belongings the mile-and-a-half or so to the
steamer, I saw something that made me start. Fred gazed
presently in the same direction.

"Johnson is number one!" he said, as if checking off my
mental processes. He meant Hassan. "Number two is Georges
Coutlass, our friend the Greek. Number three is—am I drunk
this early in the day?—what do you see?—doesn't she look
to you like?—by the big blind god of men's mistakes it's—
Monty! Didums, you deaf idiot, look! See!"

At that everybody naturally looked the same way. Everybody nodded. Coutlass the Greek, and Hassan, reputed
nephew of Tippoo Tib, were headed in one boat toward the
steamer, the worse for the handling, but right side up and
no angrier than the usual passenger. Following them was
another boat containing a motley assortment of Arabs and.
part-Arabs, who might, or might not be associated with them.

On the beach still, surrounded yet by a swarm of longshoremen who yelled and fought, Lady Isobel Saffren Waldon
and her Syrian maid stood at bay. Her two Swahili men-
servants were overwhelmed and already being carried to a
boat. Her luggage was being borne helter-skelter after them,
and another boat waited for her just beyond the belt of surf,
the rowers standing up to yell encouragement at the sweating
pack that dared not close in on its victims. Lady Isobel Saffren Waldon appeared to have no other weapon than a parasol,
but she had plainly the upper hand.

"She has a way with her with natives," said the senior officer present.

"It's a pity," said Monty. "I mean, one scarcely likes to
use this wharf and watch that."

"Quite so. Yet we daren't accord her official recognition.
She'd be certain to make capital out of it. We're awfully
glad she's going. The Residency atmosphere is one huge sigh
of relief. We would like to speed the parting guest, but it

mayn't be done. However, you'll see there are others not so particular. I imagine her friends are late for the appointment."

"Where's she going?" asked Monty.

"British East Africa."

"Mombasa?"

"And then on. She has drafts on a German merchant in Nairobi."

From. that moment until we were safely in our quarters on the steamer Monty's attitude became one of rigid indifference toward her or anything to do with her. The British officers went out to the steamer with us, but all the way Monty only talked of the climate, trade conditions, and the other subjects to which polite conversation of Africa's east coast is limited. Fred kept nudging him, but Monty took no notice. Yerkes whispered to Fred. Then I heard Fred whisper to Monty in one of those raucous asides that he perfectly well knows can be heard by everybody.

"Why don't you ask 'em about *her*, you ass?"

But Monty refused to rise. He talked of the bowed and ancient slaves of Zanzibar, who refused in those days to be set free and afforded prolific ground for attack on British public morals by people whose business it is to abuse England for her peccadillos and forget her virtues.*

We reached the ship, and were watching our piles of luggage arrive up the accommodation ladder when the solution of Lady Isobel Saffren Waldon's problem appeared. She arrived alongside in the official boat of the German consulate, a German officer in white uniform on either hand, and the German ensign at the stern.

"Pretty fair impudence, paying official honors to our undesirables, yet I don't see what we can do," said the senior from the Residency.

Yerkes drew me aside.

"Did you ever see anything more stupidly British?" he de-

---

*In 1914 there were still thousands of slaves in German East, although the German press and public were ever loudest in their condemnation of British conditions.

manded. "It's as obvious as the nose on your face that she's
up to some game. It's as plain as twice two that the Germans
are backing her whether the British like it or not. Look at
those two Heinies now!"

We faced about and watched them. After bowing Lady
Waldon to her cabin, they approached our party with brazen
claim to recognition—and received it. They were met, and
spoken to apparently as cordially as if their friendship had
been indisputable.

"Did you ever see anything to beat it? Why not kick 'em
into the sea? Either that woman's a crook or she isn't. If
she isn't, then the British have treated her shamefully, turning their backs on her. But we know she *is* a crook! And so
do they. The Germans know it, too, and they're flaunting her
under official British noses! They're using her to start something the British won't like, and the British know it! Yet
she's going to be allowed to travel to British territory on a
British ship, and the Heinies are shaken hands with! If
you complained to Monty I bet he'd say, 'Don't talk fight
unless you mean fight!'"

"Monty might also add, 'Don't talk—fight!'" said I.

"Oh, rot!" Will answered. "British individuals may bridle
a bit, but their government'll shut its eyes until too late,
whatever happens! You mark my words!"

We strolled back toward our party in great discontent, I
as much as he, never supposing there was another country
in the world that could so deliberately shut its eyes to dog's
work until absolutely forced to interfere, by a hair not quite
too late.

Coutlass and Hassan traveled second-class—the Arab and
half-Arab contingent third—and none of them troubled us
at present, except that Will swore at sight of Coutlass swaggering as if the ship and her contents were all his.

"To hear him brag you'd believe the British government
afraid of him!" he grumbled.

But an immediate problem drove Coutlass out of mind.
Lady Isobel Saffren Waldon had been given a cabin in line
with ours, at the end of our corridor. Her maid, and her

two Swahili servants were obliged to pass our doors to get to her cabin at all. As nearly all ships' cabins on those hot routes do, ours intercommunicated by a metal grill for ventilating purposes, and a word spoken in one cabin above a whisper could be heard in the next.

Fred was the first to realize conditions. He opened his door in his usual abrupt way to visit Monty's cabin and almost fell over the Syrian maid, her eye at Monty's key-hole —a little too early in the game to pass for sound judgment, as Fred was at pains to assure her.

The alarm being given, we locked our cabin doors, repaired to the smoking-room, and ordered drinks at a center table where no eavesdropper could overhear.

"It's one of two things," said Monty. He had his folding board out, and we did not doubt he would play chess from there to London. "Either they know exactly where that ivory is, or they haven't the slightest idea."

"My, but you're wise!" said Will.

Monty ignored him. "They suspect us of knowing. They mean to prevent our getting any of it. If they do know, they've some reason of their own for not getting it themselves at present. If they don't know, they suspect we know and intend to claim what we find."

"How should they think we know?" objected Will. "The first we ever heard of the stuff was in the lazaretto in Zanzibar."

"True. Juma told us. Juma probably told them that *we* told *him*. Natives often put the cart before the horse without the slightest intention of lying."

"All the same, why should they believe him?"

"Why not? Zanzibar's agog with the story—after all these years. The ivory must have been buried more than a quarter of a century ago. Some one's been stirring the mud. We arrive, unexpectedly from nowhere, ask questions about the ivory, make plans for British East Africa—and there you are! The people who were merely determined to get the stuff jump to the false conclusion that we really know where it is."

"Q. E. D.!" said Fred, finishing his drink.

"Not at all," said Monty. "There are two things yet to be demonstrated. They're true, but not proven. The German government is after the stuff. And the German government has very special reasons for secrecy and tricks."

"We four against the German government looks like longish odds," said I.

"Remains to be seen," said Monty. "If the German government's very special reasons were legal or righteous they'd be announced with a fanfare of trumpets."

"Where's all this leading us?" demanded Fred.

"To a slight change of plan," said Monty.

"Thank the lord! That means you don't go to Brussels —stay with us!"

"Nothing of the sort, Fred. But you three keep together. They're going to watch you. You watch them. Watch Schillingschen particularly closely, if you find him. The closer they watch you, the more likely they are to lose sight of me. I'll take care to have several red herrings drawn across my trail after I reach London. Perhaps I'll return down the west coast and travel up the Congo River. At any rate, when I do come, and whichever way I come, I'll have everything legal, in writing. Let your game be to seem mysterious. Seem to know more than you do, but don't tell anybody anything. Above all, listen!"

Fred leaned back in his chair and laughed.

"Didums!" he said. "This is the idioticest wild goose chase we ever started on! I admit I nosed it. I gave tongue first. But think of it—here we are—four sensible men—hitherto sensible—off after ivory that nobody can really prove exists, said to be buried somewhere in a tract of half-explored country more than a thousand miles each way—and the German government, and half the criminals in Africa already on our idiotic heels!"

"Yet the German government and the crooks seem convinced, too, that there's something worth looking for!" laughed Monty. And none of us could answer that.

For that matter, none of us would have been willing to withdraw from the search, however dim the prospect of success might seem in the intervals when cold reason shed its comfortless rays on us. Intuition, or whatever it is that has proved superior so often to worldly wisdom (temptation, Fred calls it!) outweighed reason, and Fred himself would have been last to agree to forego the search.

The voyage is short between Zanzibar and Mombasa, but there was incident. We were spied on after very thorough fashion, Lady Saffren Waldon's title and gracious bearing (when that suited her) being practical weapons. The purser was Goanese—beside himself with the fumes of flattery. He had a pass-key, so the Syrian maid went through our cabins and searched thoroughly everything except the wallet of important papers that Monty kept under his shirt. The first and second officers were rather young, unmarried men possessed of limitless ignorance of the wiles of such as Lady Waldon. It was they who signed a paper recommending Coutlass to the B. I. agents and a lot of other reputable people in Mombasa and elsewhere, thus offsetting the possibility that the authorities might not let him land. (Had we known all that at the time, Monty's word against him might have caused him to be shipped back whence he came, but we did not find it out until afterward; nor did we know the law.)

And at Mombasa we made our first united, serious mistake. It was put to the vote. We all agreed.

"I can come ashore," said Monty, "introduce you to officialdom, get you put up for the club, and be useful generally. That, though, 'll lend color to the theory that you're in league with me—whereas, if I leave you to your own resources, that may help lose my scent. When they pick it up again we'll be knowing better where we stand."

"If you came ashore for a few hours we'd have the benefit of your prestige," said I.

"I admit it."

"I suspect a title's mighty near as useful on British territory as in N'York or Boston," said Will. "We'd bask in smiles."

"Not wholly," said Monty. "There's another side to that. There's an English official element that would rather be rude to some poor devil with a title than draw pay (and it loves its pay, you may believe me!). You'd have friends in high places, but make enemies, too, if I go ashore with you."

"What's your own proposal?" Fred demanded.

"I've stated it. I want you fellows to choose. There's no need of me ashore—that's to say, I've a draft to bearer for the amount you three have in the common fund—here, take it. If you think you'll need more than that, then I'll have to go to the bank with you and cash some of my own draft. I think you'll have enough."

"Plenty," said Will.

"Let's send him home!" proposed Fred.

"How about communications?" We had contrived a code already with the aid of a pocket Portuguese-English dictionary, of which Fred and Monty each possessed a similar edition.

"The Mombasa Bank, Will. You keep them posted as to your whereabouts. When I write the bank manager I'll ask him to keep my address a secret."

So we said good-by to Monty and left him on board, and wished we hadn't a dozen times before noon next day, and a hundred times within the week.

The last sight we had of him was as the shore boat came alongside the wharf and the half-breed customs officials pounced smiling on us. My eyes were keenest. I could see Monty pacing the upper deck, too rapidly for evidence of peace of mind—a straight-standing, handsome figure of a man. I pointed him out to the others, and we joked about him. Then the gloom of the customs shed swallowed us, and there was a new earth and, for the present, no more sea.

The island of Mombasa is so close to the cocoanut-fringed mainland that a railway bridge connects them. Like Zanzibar, it is a place of strange delights, and bridled lawlessness controlled by the veriest handful of Englishmen. There are strange hotels—strange dwellings—streets—stores—tongues and faces. The great grim fort that brave da Gama built, and held against all comers, dominates the sea front and the lower town. The brass-lunged boys who pounce on baggage,

fight for it, and tout for the grandly named hotels are of as
many tribes as sizes, as many tongues as tribes.

Everything is different—everything strange—everything,
except the heat, delightful. And as Fred said, "some folk
would grumble in hell!" Trees, flowers, birds, costumes of
the women, sheen of the sea, glint of sun on bare skins of
every shade from ivory to ebony, dazzling coral roadway and
colored coral walls, babel of tongues, sack-saddled donkeys
sleepily bearing loads of coral for new buildings, and—winding in and out among it all—the narrow-gauge tramway on
which trolleys pushed by stocky little black men carry officialdom gratis, and the rest of the world and his wife according
to tariff; all those things are the alphabet of Mombasa's
charm. Arranged, and rearranged—by chance, by individual
perspective, and by point of view—they spell fascination, at-
tractiveness, glamour, mystery. And no acquaintance with
Mombasa, however intimate or old, dispels the charm to the
man not guilty of cynicism. To the cynic (and for him)
there are sin—as Africa alone knows how to sin—disease, of
the dread zymotic types—and death; death peering through
the doors of godowns, where the ivory tusks are piled; death
in the dark back-streets of the bazaar, where tired policemen
wage lop-sided warfare against insanitary habits and a quite
impracticable legal code; death on the beach, where cannibal
crabs parade in thousands and devour all helpless things;
death in the scrub (all green and beautiful) where the tiny
streets leave off and snakes claim heritage; death in the grim
red desert beyond the coast-line, where lean, hopeless jackals
crack to-day men's dry bones left fifty years ago by the slave
caravans—marrowless bones long since stripped clean by the
ants. But we are not all cynics.

Last to be cynic or pessimist was Louis McGregor Abraham, proprietor of the Imperial Hotel—Syrian by birth, Jew
by creed, Englishman by nationality, and admirer first, last
and all the time of all things prosperous and promising, except his rival, the Hotel Royal.

"You came to the right place," he assured us when the
last hot porter had dumped the last of our belongings on the

porch, had ceased from chattering to watch Fred's financial
methods, had been paid double the customary price, and had
gone away grumbling (to laugh at us behind our backs).
"They'd have rooked you at the other hole—underfed you,
overcharged you, and filled you full of lies. I tell the truth
to folk who come to my hotel."

And he did,-some of it. He was inexhaustible, unconquer-
able, tireless, an optimist always. He had a store that was
part of the hotel, in which he claimed to sell "everything the
mind of man could wish for in East Africa"; and the boast
was true. He even sold American dime novels.

"East Africa's a great country!" he kept assuring us.
"Some day we'll all be rich! Have to get ready for it! Have
to be prepared! Have to stock everything the mind of man
can want, to encourage new arrivals and make the old ones
feel at home. Lose a little money, but why grumble? Get
it back when the boom comes. As it will, mind you. As it
will. Can't help it. Richest country in the world—grow anything—find anything—game—climate—elevation—scenery—
natives by the million to do the work—all good! Only waiting for white men with energy, and capital to start things
really moving!"

But there were other points of view. We went to the bank,
and found its manager conservative. The amount of the draft
we placed to our credit insured politeness.

"Be cautious," he advised us. "Take a good look round
before you commit yourselves!"

He agreed to manage the interchange of messages between
us and Monty, and invited us all to dinner that evening at
the club; so we left the bank feeling friendly and more confident. Later, a chance-met English official showed us over
the old fort (now jail) where men of more breeds and sorts
than Noah knew, better clothed and fed than ever in their
lives, drew endless supplies of water in buckets from da
Gama's well.

"Some of them have to be kicked out when their sentences
expire!" he told us. "See you at the club to-night. Glad to
help welcome you."

But there was a shock in store, and as time passed the shocks increased in number and intensity. Our guns had not been surrendered to us by the customs people. We had paid duty on them second-hand at the rate for new ones, and had then been told to apply for them at the collector's office, where our names and the guns' numbers would be entered on the register—for a fee.

We now went to claim them, and on the way down inquired at a store about ammunition. We were told that before we could buy cartridges we would need a permit from the collector specifying how many, and of what bore we might buy. There was an Arab in the store ahead of us. He was buying Martini Henry cartridges. I asked whether he had a permit, and was told he did not need one.

"Being an Arab?" I asked.

"Being well known to the government," was the answer.

We left the store feeling neither quite so confident nor friendly. And the collector's Goanese assistant did the rest of the disillusioning.

No, we could not have our guns. No, we could have no permit for ammunition. No, the collector was not in the office. No, he would not be there that afternoon. It was provided in regulations that we could have neither guns, sporting licenses, nor permits for ammunition. The guns were perfectly safe in the government godown—would not be tampered with—would be returned to us when we chose to leave the country.

"But, good God, we've paid duty on them!" Oakes protested.

"You should not have brought the guns with you unless you desired to pay duty," said the Goanese.

"But where's the collector?" Yerkes demanded.

"I am only assistant," was the answer. "How should I know?"

The man's insolence, of demeanor and words, was unveiled, and the more we argued with him the more sullen and evasive he grew, until at last he ordered us out of the office. At that we took chairs and announced our intention of staying until

the collector should come or be fetched. We were informed
that the collector was the most important government official
in Mombasa—information that so delighted Fred that he grew
almost good tempered again.

"I'd rather twist a big tail than a little one!" he announced.
"Shall we sing to pass the time?"

The Goanese called for the *askari*,* half-soldier, half-police-
man, who drowsed in meek solitude outside the office door.

"Remove these people, please!" he said in English, and then
repeated it in Kiswahili.

The *askari* eyed us, shifted his bare feet uncomfortably,
screwed up his courage, tried to look stern, and said something in his own tongue.

"Put them out, I said!" said the Goanese.

"He orders you to put us out!" grinned Fred.

"The office closes at three," said the Goanese, glancing at
the clock in a half-hearted effort to moderate his own daring.

"Not unless the collector comes and closes it himself, it
doesn't!" Fred announced with folded arms.

Will pulled out two rupees and offered them to the sentry.

"Go and bring us some food," he said. "We intend to stay
in here until your *bwana makubwa*† comes."

The sentry refused the money, waving it aside with the air
of a Cæsar declining a crown.

"Gee!" exclaimed Will. "You've got to hand it to the
British if they train colored police to refuse money!"

The *askari*, it seemed, was a man of more than one kind
of discretion. Without another word to the Goanese he saluted
the lot of us with a sweep of his arm, turned on his heel and
vanished—not stopping in his hurry to put on the sandals
that lay on the door-step. We amused ourselves while he was
gone by firing questions at the Goanese, calculated to disturb
what might be left of his equanimity without giving him
ground for lawsuits.

"How old are you?"—"How much pay do you get?"—"How
long have you held your job?"—"Do you ever get drunk?"

---

*Askari*, soldier.
† *Bwana makubwa*, lit. big master, senior government officer.

—"Are you married?"—"Does your wife love you?"—"Do you keep white mice?"—"Is your life insured?"—"How often have you been in jail?"—"Are you honest?"—"Are you vaccinated against the jim-jams?"—"Why is your name Fernandez and not Braganza?"

The man was about distracted, for he had been unwise enough to try to answer, when suddenly the collector came in great haste and stalked through the office into the inner room.

"Fernandez!" he called as he passed, and the Goanese hurried after him, hugely relieved. There was five minutes' consultation behind the partition in tones too low for us to catch more than a word or two, and then Fernandez came out again with a "Now wait and see, my hearties!" smile on his face. He was actually rubbing his palms together, sure of a swift revenge.

"He says you are to go in there," he announced.

So we filed in, Fred Oakes first, and it seemed to me the moment I saw the collector's face that the outlook was not so depressing. He looked neither young nor incompetent. His jaw was neither receding nor too prominent. His neck sat on his shoulders with the air of full responsibility, unsought but not refused. And his eyes looked straight into those of each of us in turn with a frank challenge no honest fellow could resent.

"Take seats, won't you," he said. "Your names, please?"

We told him, and he wrote them down.

"My clerk tells me you tried to bribe the *askari*. You shouldn't do that. We are at great pains to keep the police dependable. It's too bad to put temptation in their way."

Will, with cold precision, told him the exact facts. He listened to the end, and then laughed.

"One more Goanese mistake!" he said. "We have to employ them. They mean well. The country has no money to spend on European office assistants. Well—what can I do for you?"

At that Fred cut loose.

"We want our guns before dark!" he said. "It's the first time my character has been questioned by any government, and I say the same for my friends!"

"Oh?" said the collector, eying us strangely.

"Yes!" said Fred.

"That is so," said I.

"Entirely so," said Will.

"I have information," said the collector, tapping with a pencil on his blotter, "that you men are ivory hunters. That you left Portuguese territory because the German consul there had to request the Portuguese government to expel you."

"All easily disproved," said Fred. "Confront us, please, with our accusers."

"And that Lord Montdidier, with whom you have been traveling, became so disgusted with your conduct that he refused to land with you at this port as he at first intended!"

We all three gasped. The first thing that occurred to me, and I suppose to all of us, was to send for Monty. His steamer was not supposed to sail for an hour yet. But the thought had hardly flashed in mind when we heard the roar of steam and clanking as the anchor chain came home. The sound traveled over water and across roofs like the knell of good luck—the clanking of the fetters of ill fate.

"Where's her next stop?" said I.

"Suez," Fred answered.

Simultaneously then to all three the thought came too that this interpretation of Monty's remaining on board was exactly what we wanted. The more people suspected us of acting independently of him the better.

"Confront us with our accusers!" Fred insisted.

"You are not accused—at least not legally," said the collector. "You are refused rifle and ammunition permits, that is all."

"On the ground of being ivory hunters?"

"Suspected persons—not known to the government—something rather stronger than rumor to your discredit, and nothing known in your favor."

"What recourse have we?" Fred demanded.

"Well—what proof can you offer that you are bona fide travelers or intending settlers? Are you ivory hunters or not?"

"I'll answer that," said Fred—dexterously I thought, "when I've seen a copy of the game laws. We're law-abiding men."

The collector handed us a well thumbed copy of the Red Book.

"They're all in that," he said. "I'll lend it to you, or you can buy one almost anywhere in town. If you decide after reading that to go farther up country I'm willing to issue provisional game licenses, subject to confirmation after I've looked into any evidence you care to submit on your own behalf. You can have your guns against a cash deposit—"

"How big?"

"Two hundred rupees for each gun."

Fred laughed. The demand was intended to be away over our heads. The collector bridled.

"But no ammunition," he went on, "until your claim to respectability has been confirmed. By the way, the only claim you've made to me is for the guns. You've told me nothing about yourselves."

"Two hundred a gun?" said Fred. "Counting a pistol or revolver as one? Three guns apiece—nine guns—eighteen hundred rupees' deposit?"

The collector nodded with a sort of grim pleasure in his own unreasonableness. Fred drew out our new check book.

"You fellows agreeable?" he asked, and we nodded.

"Here's a check on the Mombasa Bank for ten thousand, and your government can have as much more again if it wants it," he said. "Make me out a receipt please, and write on it what it's for."

The collector wrote. He was confused, for he had to tear up more than one blank.

"I suppose we get interest on the money at the legal local rate?" asked Fred maliciously.

"I'll inquire about that," said the collector.

"Excuse me," said Fred, "but I'm going to give you some advice. While you're inquiring, look into the antecedents of Lady Isobel Saffren Waldon! It's she who gave out the tip against us. Her tip's a bad one. So is she."

"She hasn't applied for guns or a license," the collector

answered tartly. "It's people who want to carry firearms—
people able and likely to make trouble whom we keep an
eye on."

"She's more likely to make trouble for you than a burning
house!" put in Will Yerkes. "If my partner hadn't paid you
that check I'd be all for having this business out! I'm going
to let them know in the States what sort of welcome people receive at this port!"

"You came of your own accord. You weren't invited," the
collector answered.

"That's a straight-out lie!" snapped Will. "You know
it's a lie! Why, there isn't a newspaper in South Africa that
hasn't been carrying ads of this country for months past.
Even papers I've had sent me from the States have carried
press-agent dope about it. Why, you've been yelling for settlers like a kid squalling for milk—and you say we're not invited now we've come here! I'm going to write and tell the
U. S. papers what that dope is worth!"

"Ivory hunters are not settlers," the collector inter-
jected.

"Who said we're ivory hunters?" Will was in a fine rage,
and Fred and I leaned back to enjoy the official's discomfort.
"Besides, your ads bragged about the big game as one of the
chief attractions! All the information you can possibly have
against us must have come from a female crook in the pay of
the German government! You're not behaving the way gentlemen do where I was raised!"

"There is no intention to offend," said the collector.

"Intention is good!" said Will, laughing in spite of himself. "There's another thing I want to know. What about
ammunition? We're to have our guns. They're useless without cartridges. What about it?"

"The guns shall be sent to your hotel to-night. The provisional sporting licenses—if you want them—will be ready
to-morrow morning—seven hundred and fifty rupees apiece—
I'll charge them against your deposit. If the licenses should
be confirmed after inquiry, I will send you permits through
the post for fifty rounds of ammunition each."

Will snorted. Fred Oakes yelled with laughter, and I gaped with indignation.

"I'm going into this to the hilt!" spluttered Fred. "I wouldn't have missed it for a fortune! We three are going to constitute ourselves a committee of inspection. We're going to wander the country over and report home to the newspapers —South African—British—U. S. A.—and any other part of the world that's interested! We won't worry about ammunition. Send us permits for whatever quantity seems to you proper, and we'll note it all down in our diaries!"

We all stood up, the collector obviously uncomfortable and we, if not at ease, at least happier than we had been.

Fred nodded to the collector genially, and we all walked out.

Mombasa is a fairly large island, but the built-over part of it is small, so it was not surprising that we should emerge from the office face to face with Lady Saffren Waldon. She was the one surprised, not we. She probably thought she had spiked our guns in that part of the world forever, and the sight of us coming laughing from the very office where we should have been made glum must have been disconcerting.

She was riding on one of the little trolley-cars, pushed by two boys in white official uniform, dressed in her flimsiest best, a lace parasol across her knee, and beside her an obvious member of the government—young, and so recently from home as not to have lost his pink cheeks yet.

Had there not been an awning over the trolley-car she might have used the parasol to make believe she had not seen us. But the awning precluded that, and we were not more than two or three yards away.

"Laugh!" whispered Fred.

So we crossed the track laughing and the trolley had to pause to let us by. We laughed as we raised our helmets to her—laughed both at her and at the pink and white puppy she had taken in leash. And then the sort of thing happened that nearly always does when men with a reasonable faith in their own integrity make up their minds to see opprobrium through. Fate stepped hard on our arm of the balance.

If built-over Mombasa is a small place, so is Africa. So is

the world. Striding down the hill from the other hotel, the rival one, the Royal, came a man so well known in so many lands that they talk of naming a tenth of a continent after him—the mightiest hunter since Nimrod, and very likely mightier than he; surely more looked-up to and respected—a little, wiry-looking, freckled, wizened man whose beard had once been red, who walked with a decided limp and blinked genially from under the brim of a very neat khaki helmet.

"Why, bless my soul if it isn't Fred Oakes!" he exclaimed, in a squeaky, worn-out voice that is as well known as his face, and quickened his pace down-hill.

"Courtney!" said Fred. "There's only one man I'd rather meet!"

The little man laughed. "Oh, you and your Montdidier are still inseparable, I suppose! How are you, Fred? I'm glad to see you. Who are your friends?"

At that minute out came the collector from his office— stood on the step, and stared. Fred introduced us to Court- ney, and I experienced the thrill of shaking hands with the man accounts of whose exploits had fired my schoolboy imagi- nation and made stay-at-home life forever after an impossi- bility.

"I missed the steamer, Fred. Not another for a week. Go- ing down now to see about a passage to Somaliland. I suppose you'll be at the club after dinner?"

"No," said Fred. "We've an invitation, but I think we'll send a note and say we can't come. We'll dine at our hotel and sit on the veranda afterward."

I wondered what Fred was driving at, and so did the col- lector who was headed across the street and listening with all ears.

"That so? Not a bad idea. They've very kindly made me an honorary member of the club, but I rather expect there's a string to that—eh, Fred, don't you? They'll expect stories —stories. I get tired of telling the same tales so many times over. Suppose I join you fellows, eh? I'm at the Royal. You at the other place? Suppose I join you after dinner, and we have a pipe together on the veranda?"

"Nothing I'd like better," said Fred, and I felt too pleased with the prospect to say anything at all. Growing old is a foolish and unnecessary business, but there is no need to forego while young the thrills of unashamed hero-worship; in fact, that is one of the ways of continuing young. It is only the disillusioned (poor deceived ones) and the cynics who grow old ungracefully.

We went up-street, through the shadow of the great grim fort. The trolley-car trundled down among the din, smells and colors of the business-end of town. Looking over my shoulder I saw Courtney talking to the collector.

"We're getting absolution, Fred!" said I.

"I'm not sure we need it," Fred answered. "I hope Courtney won't tell too much!" So quickly does a man jump from praying for friends at court to fearing them!

"Courtney looked to me," said Will, "like a man who would give no games away."

"Glad you think that of him," said Fred.

"Why?"

"Tell you later, maybe."

But he did not tell until after dinner. (It was a good dinner for East Africa. Shark steak figured in it, under a more respectable name; and there was zebu hump, guinea-fowl, and more different kinds of fruit than a man could well remember.) When it was over we sat in deep armchairs on the long wide veranda that fronts the whole hotel. The evening sea-breeze came and wafted in on us the very scents of Araby; the night sounds that whisper of wilderness gave the lie to a tinkling guitar that somewhere in the distance spoke of civilized delights. The surf crooned on coral half a mile away, and very good cigar smoke (from a box that Monty had sent ashore with our belongings) supplemented coffee and the other aids to physical contentment. Then, limping between the armchairs, and ashamed that we should rise to greet him—motioning us down again with a little nervous laugh—Courtney came to us. Within five minutes of his coming the world, and the clock, and the laws of men might have all reversed themselves for aught we cared. Without really being conscious he was doing it Courtney plunged into our problem, grasped it, sized it up, advised us, flooded us with priceless, wonderful advice, and did it with such almost feminine sympathy that I believe we would have been telling him our love-affairs at last, if a glance at the watch he wore in a case at his belt had not told him it was three A. M.

"There's trouble," he began when he had filled his pipe. "You boys are in trouble. What is it?" he asked, shifting and twitching in his seat—refusing an armchair—refusing a drink.

"Tell us first what's the matter with you," said Fred.

"Oh, nothing. An old wound. A lion once dragged me by this shoulder half a mile or so. At this time of year I get pains. They last a day or two, then pass. Go on, tell me."

He never sat really still once that whole evening, yet never once complained or made a gesture of impatience.

"I propose," said Fred, with a glance at Yerkes and me, "to tell Courtney everything without reserve."

The little old hunter nodded, watching us with bright blue eyes. I received the impression that he knew more secrets than he could tell should he talk down all the years that might be left him. He was the sort of man in whom nearly every one confides.

"We're after Tippoo Tib's ivory!" said Fred, plunging into the middle of things. "Monty has gone to drive a bargain with the King of Belgium. Do you think it's a wild goose chase?"

Courtney chuckled. "No," he said. "I wouldn't call it that. They've been killing elephants in Africa ever since the flood. Ivory must have accumulated. It's somewhere. Some of it must be so old and well seasoned as to be practically priceless, unless rats have spoiled it. Rats play old Harry with ivory, you know."

"Have you a notion where it is?" demanded Fred.

Courtney laughed. "Behold me leaving the country!" he said. "If I knew I'd look. If I saw I'd take!"

"Can you give us a hint?"

"There are caves near the summit of Mount Elgon that would hold the world's revenues. None of them have ever been thoroughly explored. Cannibals live in some of them. Cannibals and caverns is a combination that might appeal to Tippoo Tib, but there's no likelihood that he buried all that ivory in one place, you know. I suspect the greater part is in the Congo, and that the Germans know its whereabouts within a mile or two."

"How did they discover it?"

"Why don't they dig it out?"

"What keeps 'em from turning their knowledge into money?"

We had forgotten our own troubles. Courtney, too, seemed to forget for the moment that he had begun by asking us a question.

"Remember Emin Pasha? When was it—'87—'88—'89 that Stanley went and rescued him? Perhaps you recall what was then described as Emin's ingratitude after the event? British government offered him a billet. Khedive of Egypt cabled him the promise of a job, all on Stanley's recommendation. Emin turned 'em all down and accepted a job from the Germans. Nobody understood it at the time. My own idea is that Emin thought he knew more or less where that hoard is. He didn't really want to come away with Stanley, you know. Being a German, I suppose he preferred to share his secret with his own crowd. I dare say he thought of telling Stanley but judged that the 'Rock breaker' might demand a too large share. The value of the stuff must be so enormous that it's almost worth going to war about, from the point of view of a nation hungry for new colonies. Emin is dead, and it's likely he left no exact particulars behind him. To my personal knowledge the Germans have had a swarm of spies for a long time operating beyond the Congo border."

"Were you looking for the stuff yourself?" I asked.

"Oh, no," he laughed. "But when I'm hunting I look about me. I'll tell you where the stuff may possibly be. There's a section of country called the Bahr el Gazal that the Congo people claim, but that I believe will eventually prove to lie on the British side of the boundary. It was good elephant country—which is to say bad living and traveling for man—

since the earth took shape out of ooze. Awful swampy, malarious, densely wooded, dangerous country, sparsely inhabited by savages not averse to cannibalism when they've opportunity. The ivory may be there. If the Germans know it's there they're naturally afraid the British government would claim the whole district the minute the secret was out. Their plan may possibly be to wait until a boundary dispute arises in the ordinary course of time (keeping a cautious eye on the cache meanwhile, of course) and then take the Congo government side. If they can contrive to have it acknowledged as Congo territory, they might then pick a quarrel with the Congo government—or come to some sort of terms with them."

"They've patience," I said, "if they're playing that game."

Courtney raised his eyebrows until his forehead was a mass of deep wrinkles. Then he blew a dozen smoke rings.

"Patient—perhaps. It's my impression they're as remorseless and persistent as white ants—undermining, digging, devouring everywhere while the rest of the world sleeps. Do you remember there was a mutiny of native troops in Uganda not many years ago? Some said that was because the troops were being paid in truck instead of money, and like most current excuses that one had some truth in it. But the men themselves vowed they were going to set up an African Muhammedan empire."

"What had that to do with Germans?" asked Fred.

"Nothing that I can personally prove," said Courtney. "But I've a broad acquaintance among natives, and considerable knowledge of their tongues. Muhammedanism is spreading among them very rapidly. Over and over again, beside camp-fires, and in the dark when they thought I was not listening, I have heard them talk of missionaries from German territory who spread a doctrine of what you might call pan-Islam for lack of a better name. I said at the time of the Uganda mutiny that I believed Germans were behind it. I've seen no reason to change my opinion since. It's obvious that if the mutiny had by some ill chance succeeded Uganda would have been an easy prey for Karl Peters and his Germans. If that ivory of Tippoo Tib's is really in the Bahr el Gazal at the back of Uganda, then the German motive for stirring up the Uganda mutiny would be obvious."

"But doesn't our government know all this?" demanded Fred.

"That depends on what you mean by the word know," answered Courtney. "I've made no secret of my own opinion."

"But they wouldn't listen?"

"Some did, some didn't. The Home government—which was the India Office in those days—took no notice whatever. One or two men out here believed, but I think they're dead. When the Foreign Office took the country over I don't suppose they overhauled old reports very carefully. I dare say my letters on the subject lie inches deep in dust."

"England doesn't deserve to keep her colonies!" vowed Fred, caught in a sudden flood of indignation.

Courtney laughed.

"When you've seen as many of the other nations' colonies as I have you'll qualify that verdict! We do our best. God gave us our work to do, and the devil came and made us stupid! Take this country, for instance."

"Yes!" agreed Fred. "Take this country! We came ashore to-day—left Monty on board ship on his way to Europe. Nobody knew a thing about us. A female woman, known to the police in Zanzibar and so notorious in Europe that she's in no hurry to go home—said, too, on every hand to be in the pay of the German government—chose to tell lies about us to the chuckle-headed puppies in charge of Mombasa. Net result—what do you suppose?"

"I know," said Courtney. "I've been told this evening." His eyes changed, and his voice took on the almost feminine note of appeal that came strangely from a big game hunter. "You boys must overlook things. These boys you're angry with are younger than you, Fred. That collector you've contrived to pick a quarrel with has fought Arabs and cannibal troops— odds against him of fifty or a hundred to one, mind you—all across the Congo and back again. He fought in the Uganda mutiny. He's a man. He's a merchant, though, with a mer chant's education. He was taken over with the rest of the clerks when the British government superseded the British East Africa Trading Company. He has never had the advantage of legal training. Went to a common school. No advantages of any kind. Poorly paid and overworked. There's no money in the country yet. Nobody to tax. Salaries—expenses and so on come from home, voted by Parliament. As long as that condition lasts they're all going to feel nervous. They know they'll get the blame for everything that goes wrong, and precious little credit in any case. Parliament advertised the country in answer to their complaints of no revenue. Parliament called for settlers. But they're not ready for settlers. They don't know how to handle them. They've no troops—nothing but a handful of black police. How shall they keep in order colonials armed with repeating rifles? They're not ready. The Uganda Railway isn't finished yet; trains get through to Victoria Nyanza once a week, but there's endless work to be done yet on the line, and Parliament grudges them every penny they spend on it. Yet the railway was rushed through by order of Parliament to prevent Doctor Karl Peters and the Germans from claiming occupation of the head-waters of the Nile and so dominating Upper Egypt. You boys must be considerate."

"All right," said Fred. "I'll grant all that."

"But what gets me," Will interrupted, "is that they should condemn us out-of-hand—on sight—untried—on the say-so of this Lady Saffren Waldon. She carries German letters of credit. She's so notoriously in league with Germans that you'd think even these little Napoleons 'ud know it. I'm American myself, thank God, but these two men are their own kith and kin. Why should they judge their own countrymen unheard on the say-so of a woman like that? That's what rattles me!"

Courtney blew six smoke rings.

"You'll have to forgive them, lad. Too many of the Englishmen who have come here were bad hats from the South, so hot-footed that they burned the grass. Then—don't forget that the Germans have a military government to the south

of us—all experienced men—a great many of them unmiti-
gated rascals, but nearly all of them clever — students of
strategy and psychology and tactics—some of them brilliant
men who have had to apply for colonial service because of
debt or scandal. They're overmanned where we are under-
manned — backed up from home where our boys are only
blamed and neglected—well supplied with troops and ammunition, where our police are kept down to the danger point
and now and then even without cartridges. The Germans
have no railway yet, but they've a policy and they keep it
secret. We have a railway, and no policy except retrenchment
and economy. I'm convinced the German government has no
scruples. We have. So you must sympathize with our young
men, not quarrel with them."

"Believe me," I said, "we didn't start out to quarrel with
anybody. That woman lied about us. There's no excuse for
believing her without giving us a hearing."

"Oh, yes there is. I spoke with her myself this evening,"
said Courtney. "She's staying at my hotel, you know. She's
a match for much more experienced men than our young officials. They've been fighting Arabs, not flirting. She had
the impudence to try to flatter me. I don't doubt she's telling a crowd of men to-night that I'm in love with her—perhaps not exactly telling them that, but giving them to understand it. Why don't I stroll down to the club and deny it?
For the same reason that you don't openly denounce her!
It's semi- or wholly-sentimental chivalry—rank stupidity, if
you like to call it that, but it's national, I'm glad to say, and
I'm as proud of it as any one."

"Doesn't it look to you," said Fred, "that if she and the
German government are so infernally anxious to spoil our
chances — and they suspect what we're after, you know —
doesn't it look to you as if there may really be something
in this quest of ours?"

"Undoubtedly," said Courtney. "There's ivory in it, tons
and tons and tons of ivory. Somebody will find it some day."

"Join us then!" said Fred. "Cancel your trip to Somaliland and come with us! I can speak for Monty. I know he'll welcome you into the partnership!"

"I believe I could almost speak for Monty, too," laughed Courtney. "He and I were at Eton together, and we've never ceased being friends. But I can't come with you. No. I'm making a sort of semi-official trip. I shall hunt, of course, but there are observations to be made. The pan-Islamic theory is said to be making headway also in Somaliland."

"Do you feel you have any lien on the Elgon Caves and Bahr el Gazal clues?" Fred asked.

"No. I make you a present of those ideas. I'm sure I hope you find the stuff. I'm wondering, though—I'm wondering."

"I'll bet you a dollar I'm thinking of the same thing," said Will.

"Out with it, then."

"What's to prevent the Germans from making their own dicker with the King of the Belgians or with the Congo government, and rifling the hoard on a fifty-fifty or some such basis?"

"Correct," said Courtney. "I confess myself puzzled about that. But I know no European politics. There may be a thousand reasons. And then, you know, the King of the Belgians has the name of being a grasping dealer. The management of his private zone on the Congo is unspeakable. It's possible the Germans may prefer not to risk putting His Majesty on the scent."

"Well, we've our work cut out," said Fred, laughing and yawning. "That woman has started us off with a bad name."

"That is one thing I can really do for you," Courtney answered. "I've no official standing, but the boys all listen to me. I'll tell them—"

"For the love of God don't tell them too much!" Fred exclaimed.

"I'll tell them you're friends of mine," he went on. "I believe that will solve the sporting license and ammunition problem. As for the woman—if I were in your shoes I would steal a march on her. I wouldn't be surprised if your licenses and ammunition permits were here at the hotel by ten to-morrow morning. I see they've sent your guns already. Well, there's a train for Nairobi to-morrow noon, and not another for three days. I'd take to-morrow's train if I were you. I always find in going anywhere the start's the principal thing. You'll go?"

"We will," we answered, one after the other.

"Good night, then, boys; I'll be going."

But we walked with him down to his hotel—I, and I think the others, full to the teeth with the pleasure of knowing him, as well as of envy of his scars, his five or six South African campaigns, his adventures, and (by no means least) his un-blemished record as a gentleman. Merely a little bit of a man with a limp, but better than a thousand men who lacked his gentleness.

# THE NJO HAPA SONG

*Delights—ah, Ten are the dear delights (and the Book for-*
*    bids them, one by one)—*
*The broad old roads of a thousand loves—back turned to the*
*    Law—the lawless fun—*
*Old Arts for new—old hours reborn—and who shall mourn*
*    when the sands have run?*

*    I was old when they told the Syren Tales*
*    (All ears were open then!)*
*    And the harps were afire with plucked desire*
*    For the white ash oars again—*
*    For oars and sail, and the open sea,*
*    High prow against pure blue,*
*    The good sea spray on eye and lip,*
*    The thrumming hemp, the rise and dip,*
*    The plunge and the roll of a driven ship*
*    As the old course boils anew!*

*Sweetly I call, the captains come. The home ties draw at*
*    hearts in vain.*
*Potent the spell of Africa! Who East and South the course*
*    has ta'en*
*By Guardafui to Zanzibar may go, but he shall come again.*

# CHAPTER FOUR

Courtney proved better than his word. Our Big Game Licenses arrived after breakfast, and permits for five hundred rounds of rifle ammunition each. In an envelope in addition was Fred's check with the collector's compliments and the request that we kindly call and pay for the licenses. In other words we now had absolution.

We called, and were received as fellow men, such was the genius of Courtney's friendship. A railway man looked in. The collector's dim office became awake with jokes and laughter.

"Going up to-day?" he asked. "I'll see you get berths on the train."

We little realized at the moment the extent of that consideration; but understanding dawned fifteen minutes before high noon when we strolled to the station behind a string of porters carrying our luggage. Courtney was there to see us off, and he looked worried.

"I'm wondering whether you'll ever get your luggage through," he said with a sort of feminine solicitude. It was strange to hear the hero of one's school-days, mighty hunter and fearless leader of forlorn campaigns, actually troubled about whether we could catch our train. But so the man was, gentle always and considerate of everybody but himself.

There was law in this new land, at all events along the railway line. Not even handbags or rifles could pass by the barrier until weighed and paid for. Crammed in the vestibule in front of us were fifty people fretfully marshalling in line their strings of porters lest any later comer get by ahead of them; foremost, with his breast against the ticket window, was Georges Coutlass. Things seemed not to be proceeding as he wished.

There was one babu behind the window—a mild, unhappy-looking Punjabi, or Dekkani Mussulman. There was another

86

at the scales, who knew almost no English: his duty was to weigh—do sums—write the result on a slip, and then justify his arithmetic to office babu and passenger, before any sort of progress could be made. The fact that all passengers shouted at him to hurry or be reported to his superiors complicated the process enormously; and the equally discordant fact that no passenger—and especially not Georges Coutlass—desired or intended to pay one anna more than he could avoid by hook, crook, or argument, made the game amusing to the casual looker-on, but hastened nothing (except tempers). The temperature within the vestibule was 112° by the official thermometer.

"You pair of black murderers!" yelled Coutlass as we took our place in line. "You bloody robbers! You pickpockets! You train-thieves! Go out and dig your graves! I will make an end of you!"

"You should not use abusive language," the babu retorted mildly, stopping to speak, and then again to wipe his spectacles, and his forehead, and his hands, and to glance at the clock, and to mutter what may or may not have been a prayer.

Coutlass exploded.

"Shouldn't, eh? Who the hell are you to tell me what I shouldn't do? Sell me a ticket, you black plunderer, d'you hear! Look! Listen!"

He snatched a piece of paper from the babu's hand and turned to face the impatient crowd.

"This hell-cat—" (the unhappy babu looked less like a hell-cat than any vision of the animal I ever imagined)— "wants to make out that seventy-one times seven annas and three pice is forty-nine rupees, eleven annas! Oh, you charlatan! You mountebank! You black-blooded robber! You miscreant! Cut your throat, I order you!"

The babu expostulated, stammered, quailed. Coutlass drew in his breath for the gods of Greece alone knew what heights of fury next. But interruption entered.

"There, that's enough of you! Get to the back of the line!"

The man who had promised us berths came abruptly

through the barrier, and unlike the babu did not appear afraid of any one. The Greek let out his gathered breath with a bark of fury, like a seal coming up to breathe. Taking that for a symptom of opposition the newcomer, very cool in snow-white uniform and helmet, seized Coutlass by the neck and hustled him, arguing like a boiler under pressure, through the crowd. The Greek was three inches taller, and six or eight inches bigger round the chest, but too astonished to fight back, and perhaps, too, aware of the neighborhood of old da Gama's fort, where more than one Greek was pining for the grape and olive fields of Hellas. With a final shove the railway official thrust him well out into the road.

"If you miss the train, serve you right!" he said. "Babus are willing servants, to be treated gently!"

Then he saw us.

"You're late! Where's your luggage? These your porters? All right—put you on your honor. Go on through. Save time. Have your stuff weighed, and settle the bill at Nairobi. All of it, mind! Babu, let these people through!"

Followed by Courtney, who seemed to have right of way wherever it suited him to wander, we filed through the gate, crossed the blazing hot platform, and boarded a compartment labeled "Reserved." The railway man nodded and left us, to hurry and help sell tickets.

It was an Indian type railway carriage he left us in, a contraption not ill-suited to Africa—nor yet so comfortable as to diminish the sensation of travel toward new frontiers.

Each car was divided into two compartments, entirely separate and entered from opposite ends; facing ours was the rear end of a second-class car, into which we could look if the doors were open and we lay feet-foremost on the berths. The berths were arranged lengthwise, two each side, and one above the other.

It was what they called a mixed train, mixed that is of freight and passengers—third-class in front, second next, then first, and a dozen little iron freight cars of two kinds in front. In those days there were neither tunnels nor bridges on that railway, and there was a single seat on the roof at each end of first- and second-class compartments reached by a ladder, for any passenger enamored of the view. Even the third-class compartments (and they were otherwise as deliberately bare and comfortless as wood and iron could make them) had lattice-work shades over the upper half of the windows.

For the babu's encouragement, and to increase the panic of the ticketless, the engineer was blowing the whistle at short intervals. Passengers, released in quicker order now that a white official was lending the two babus a hand, began coming through the barrier in sudden spurts, baggage in either hand and followed hot-foot by natives with their heavier stuff. They took headers into the train, and the porters generally came back grinning.

"I see through the whistling stunt," Will announced. "My, but that fellow on the engine has faith; or else the system's down real fine in these parts! He won't be back for a week. Those woolly-headed porters are going to save up his commission and hand it to him when he brings the down-train in! The game's good: he whistles—passenger runs—can't make change—pays two, three, four, ten times what the job's worth—and the porters divvy up with the engineer. But good lord, the porters must be honest!"

Presently a pale white man in khaki with a red beard entered our compartment, and Courtney had to make room for him on the seat. He apologized with less conviction of real regret than I ever remember noticing, although the pouches under his eyes gave him a rather world-weary look.

"Not another first-class berth on the train—every last one engaged. Might be worse. Might have had to ride with Indians. Curse of this country, Indians are. I'd rid the land of 'em double-quick if government 'ud pay me a rupee a head —an' I'd provide cartridges! But government likes 'em! Ugh! Ever travel in one compartment with a dozen of 'em? Sleep in a tent with a score of 'em? Share blankets with a couple of 'em on a cold night? No? You be glad I'm not an Indian. One's enough!"

We made room for his belongings, and leaned from the window all on one seat together. The time to start arrived and passed; hot passengers continued spurting for the train at intervals—all sorts of passengers—English, Mauritius-French, Arab, Goanese, German, Swahili, Indian, Biluchi, one Japanese, two Chinamen, half-breeds, quarter-breeds of all the hues from ivory to dull red, guinea-yellow, and bleached out black; but the second-class compartment facing our door remained empty. There was a name on the card in the little metal reservation frame, and every passenger who could read English glanced at it, but nobody came to claim it even when the engine's extra shrill screaming and at last the ringing of a bell warned Courtney that time was really up, and he got out on the platform.

"Good-by," he said through the window. "I've done what I could to bring you luck. Don't be tempted to engage the first servants who apply to you at Nairobi. If you wait there a week I'll send my Kazimoto to you; he's a very good gun-bearer. He'll be out of a job when I'm gone. I shall give him his fare to Nairobi. Engage him if you want a dependable boy, but remember the rule about dogs: a good one has one master! I don't mean Kazimoto is a dog—far from it. I mean, treat him as reasonably as you would a dog, and he'll serve you well. He's a first-class Nyamwezi, from German East. Oh, and one more scrap of advice—":

He came close to the window, but at that moment the engine gave a final scream and really started. Passengers yelled farewells. The engine's apoplectic coughs divided the din into spasms, and there came a great bellowing from the ticket office. He could not speak softly and be heard at all. Louder he had to speak, and then louder, ending almost with a shout.

"The best way to Elgon is by way of Kisumu and Mumias, whatever anybody else may tell you. And if you find the stuff, or any of it,"—(he was running beside the train now) —"be in no hurry to advertise the fact! Go and make terms first with government—then—after you've made terms—tell 'em you've found it! Find the stuff—make terms—then produce what you've found! Get my meaning? Good-by, all. Good luck!"

We left him behind then, wiping the sweat from his wrinkled, freckled forehead, gazing after us as if we had all been lifelong friends of his. He made no distinction between us and Fred, but was equally anxious to serve us all.

"If that man isn't white, who is?" demanded Will, and then there was new interest.

We had left the ticket office far behind, but the train was moving slowly and there was still a good length of platform before our car would be clear of the station altogether. We heard a roar like a bull's from behind, and a dozen men—white, black and yellow—came careering down the platform carrying guns, baggage, bedding, and all the paraphernalia that travelers in Africa affect.

First in the van was Georges Coutlass, showing a fine turn of speed but tripping on a bed-sheet at every other step, with his uncased rifle in one hand, his hat in the other, an empty bandolier over one shoulder and a bag slung by a strap swinging out behind him. He made a leap for the second-class compartment in front of us, and landed on all fours on the platform. We opened the door of our compartment to watch him better.

Once on the platform he threw his rifle into the compartment and braced himself to catch the things his stampeding followers hurled after him—caught them deftly and tossed them in, yelling instructions in Greek, Kiswahili, Arabic, English, and two or three other languages. It may be that the engineer looked back and saw what was happening (or perhaps the guard signaled with the cord that passed through eyeholes the whole length of the train) for though we did not slow down we gained no speed until all his belongings had been hurled, and caught, and flung inside. Then came his traveling companions—caught by one hand and dragged on their knees up the steps. They were heavy men, but he snatched all three in like a boy pulling chestnuts from the fire.

The first was a Greek—evil-looking, and without the spirit that in the case of Coutlass made a stranger prone to overlook shortcomings—dressed in khaki, with rifle and empty bandolier. Next, chin, elbow, hand and knee up the steps came a fat, tough-looking Goanese, dressed anyhow at all in

pink-colored dirty shirt, dark pants, and a helmet, also with
rifle and empty bandolier. I judged he weighed about two
hundred and eighty pounds, but Coutlass yanked him in like
a fish coming overside. Last came a man who might be Arab,
or part-Arab, part-Swahili, whom I did not recognize at first,
fat, black, dressed in the white cotton garments and red fez
of the more or less well-to-do native, and voluble with rare
profanity.

"Johnson!" shouted Fred with almost the joy of greeting
an old acquaintance.

It was Hassan, sure enough, short-winded and afraid, but
more afraid of being left behind than of the manhandling.
Coutlass took hold of his outstretched arm, hoisted him,
cracked his shins for him against the top step, and hurled him
rump-over-shoulders into the compartment, where the other
Greek and the Goanese grabbed him by the arms and legs and
hove him to an upper berth, on which he lay gasping like a
fish out of water and moaning miserably. Their compartment
was a mess of luggage, blankets, odds-and-ends, and angry
men. Coutlass found a whisky bottle out of the confusion, and
swallowed the stuff neat while the other Greek and the Goanese waited their turn greedily. There was nothing much in
that compartment to make a man like Hassan feel at home.

"Those Greeks," said our red-bearded traveling companion
as we shut the door again, "are only one degree better than
Indians—a shade less depraved perhaps—a sight more dangerous. I sure do hate a Punjabi, but I don't love Greeks!
The natives call 'em *bwana masikini* to their faces—that means
Mister Mean White y'know. They're a lawless lot, the Greeks
you'll run across in these parts. My advice is, shoot first!
Walk behind 'em! If they ain't armed, hoof 'em till they cut
an' run! Greeks are no good!"

We introduced ourselves. He told us his name was Brown.

"There's three Browns in this country: Hell-fire Brown of
Elementaita, Joseph Henry Brown of Gilgil, and Brown of
Lumbwa. Brown of Lumbwa's me. Don't believe a word
either of the other two Browns tell you! Yes, we're all settlers. Country good to settle in? Depends what you call

good. If you like lots of room, an' hunting, natives to wait on you, an' your own house on your own square mile—comfortable climate—no conventions—nor no ten commandments, why, it's pretty hard to beat. But if you want to wear a white shirt, and be moral, and get rich, it's rotten! You've a chance to make money if you're not over law-abiding, for there's elephants. But if you're moral, an' obey the laws, you haven't but one chance, an' she's a slim one."

"Well," said Fred genially, "tell us about the only one. We're men to whom the ten commandments are—"

"You look it!" Brown interrupted. "Well, what's the odds? You'll never find it, an' anyhow, everybody knows it's Tippoo Tib's ivory. I mean to have a crack at spotting it myself, soon as I get my farm fenced an' one or two other matters attended to. Gov'ment offers ten per cent. to whoever leads 'em to it, but they can't believe any one's as soft as that surely! They'll be lucky if they get ten per cent. of it themselves! Man alive, but they say there's a whale of a hoard of it! Hundreds o' tons of ivory, all waiting to be found, and fossicked out, an' took! Say—if I was some o' those Greeks for instance, tell you what I'd do: I'd off to Zanzibar, an' kidnap Tippoo Tib. The old card's still living. I'd apply a red-hot poker to his silver-side an' the under-parts o' his tripe-casings. He'd tell me where the stuff is quicker'n winking! Supposin' I was a Greek without morals or no compunctions or nothin', that's what I'd do! I don't hold with allowin' any man to play dog in the manger with all that plunder!"

"Have you a notion where the stuff might be?" Fred wondered guilelessly.

"Ah! That 'ud be tellin'!"

We had crossed the water that divides Mombasa from the mainland. Behind us lay the prettiest and safest harbor on all that thousand-league-long coast; before us was the narrow territory that still paid revenue and owed nominal allegiance to the Sultan of Zanzibar, although really like the rest of those parts under British rule. We were bowling along beside plantations of cocoanut, peanut, plantain and pineapple, with here and there a thicket of strange trees to show what the aboriginal jungle had once looked like. When we stopped at wayside stations the heat increased insufferably, until we entered the great red desert that divides the coast-land from the hills, and after that all seemed death and dust, and haziness, and hell.

At first we passed occasional baobabs, with trunks fifteen or twenty feet thick and offshoots covering a quarter of an acre. Then the trees thinned out to the sparse and shriveled all-but-dead things that struggle for existence on the borderlines between man's land and desolation. At last we drew down the smoked panes over the window to escape the glare and sight of the depressing desolation.

The sun beat down on the iron roof. The heat beat up from the tracks. Red dust polluted the drinking water in the little upright tank. Dust filled eyes, nostrils, hair. Dust caked and grew stiff in the sweat that streamed down us. Yet we stopped once at a station, and humans lived there and a man got off the train. A lone lean babu and his leaner, more miserable native crew came out and eyed the train like vultures waiting for a beast to die. But we did not die, and the train passed on into illimitable dusty redness, leaving them to watch the hot rails ribbon out behind our grumbling caboose.

There began to be carousing in the second-class compartment next ahead of us. Our own Brown of Lumbwa produced a stone crock of Irish whisky from a basket, imbibed copiously, offered us in turn the glistening neck, looked relieved at our refusal, and grew voluble.

"Hear them Greeks an' that Goa. You'd think they were gentlemen o' breeding to hear 'em carryin' on! Truth is we've no government worth a moment's consid'ration, an' everybody knows it, Greeks included! You men lookin' for farms? Take your time! Once you get a farm, an' get your house built, an' stock bought, an' stuff planted—once you've got your capital invested so to speak, they've got you! Till then you're free! Till then they'll maybe treat you with consideration! Till then you leave the country when you like an' kiss yourselves good-by to them an' Africa. Till then they've got no hold! The courts can fine you, maybe, but can they make you pay?

It's none so easy if you're half awake! But take me: Suppose
I break a reggylation. What happens? They know where to
find me—how much I've got—where it is—an' if I don't pay
the fine, they come an' collar my cattle an' sticks! D'you notice any Greeks applyin' for farms? Not no crowds of 'em
you don't! I don't know one single Greek who has a farm in
all East Africa! Any Goas? Not a bit of it! Any Indians?
Not one! So when a few extry elephants get shot, I get the
blame—down at Lumbwa, where there ain't no elephants; an'
the Greeks, Goas, Arabs an' Indians get fat on the swag!
It's easy to keep track of a white man; the natives all know
him, an' his name, an' where he lives, an' report everything he
does to the nearest gov'ment officer. But Greeks an' Goas an'
Indians an' Arabs ain't white, so the natives make no mention
of 'em. They do the lootin'; we settlers get the blame; an'
the whole perishing country's going to blazes as fast as a lump
of ice melting in hell—but not so fast as I'd like to see it go.
Have some o' this whisky, won't you?"

I was scarcely listening to him, but he seemed to get drunk
just "so far and no further," and Fred found him worth attention. It happened that Fred, Will and I were all thinking of the same thing. Will put a hand to his neck and
stroked the little scar the Arab knife had made in Zanzibar.

"What sort of a country's this for women?" Fred demanded.

"Which women?" Brown asked in sort of mild amazement.

"White women?"

"Rotten! Leastwise, there aren't any. Yes, there's three.
Two officials' wives, an' Pioneer Jane French. Heard o' her?
Walked from South Africa, Jane did — hoofed it along o'
French, bossed his boys, drove the cattle, shot the meat, ran
the whole shootin' match, an' runs him, too, when he's sober
an' she's drunk. When they're both drunk everybody ducks.
She's scarcely a woman, she's sort of three-men-rolled-into-
one. Give her a horsewhip an' she'll manage the unruliest
crowd o' savages ever you or she set eyes on! Countin' her as
one, an' the two officials' wives, an' her on this train, there's
four."

Our eyes met. I awoke to sudden interest that startled our
informant and made him curious in turn.

"On this train?"

"On this train. Didn't you see her? She was watching
you chaps through the window slits like the Queen o' Sheba
keepin' tabs on Solomon. Say, what's she doing in this country anyhow? I made a try to get a seat in her carriage, but
she ordered me out like Aunt Jemima puttin' out the cat the
last thing. She's got a maid in with her, but the maid ain't
white—Jew—Syrian—Levantine—Dago—some such breed.
She's in this compartment next behind."

Our eyes met again. Fred laughed, and Will leaned forward to whisper to me: "She heard what Courtney said to
us about the way to Mount Elgon!"

"D'you know her name?" asked Brown.

"No!" we all three lied together with one voice.

"I do! I seen it on the reservation card. Lady Isobel Saffren Waldon! Pretty high-soundin' patronymic, what? Lady
Isobel Saffren Waldon!" He repeated the name over and
over, crescendo, with growing fervor. "What's a woman with
a title doin', d'you suppose? The title's no fake. She's got
the blood all right, all right! You ought to ha' heard her shoo
me out! Lummy! A nestin' hen giving the office to a snake
weren't in it to her an' me! Good looker, too! What's she
doin' in East Africa?"

We made no shift to answer.

"The officials' wives," he went on, "are keen after Tippoo's
ivory, but, bein' obliged to stay in the station except when
their husbands go on *safari,* an' then only go where their husbands go, they've no show to speak of. Pioneer Jane's nuts
on it, an' she's dangerous. Jane's as likely to find the stuff
as any one. She's independent—go where she blooming well
pleases—game as a lioness—looks like one, too, only a lioness
is kind o' softer an' not so quick in the uptake. My money's
on Jane for a place. But d'you suppose this Lady Saffren
Whatshername's another one? Them Greeks ahead of us I'm
sure of; all the Greeks in Africa are huntin' for nothin' else.
But what about the dame?"

"Going to join her husband, perhaps," suggested Fred to put him off.

"There's no man o' that name in British East or Uganda. I know 'em all—every one."

"Father—brother—uncle—nephew—oh, perhaps she's just traveling," said Fred.

"Just traveling my eye! Titled ladies don't come 'just traveling' in these parts—not by a sight, they don't—not alone!"

He helped himself to more whisky, but had reached the stage where it had no further visible effect on him.

"Anyhow," he said, wiping the neck of the jar with his hand, "if she kids herself she'll be let go where she pleases— why, she kids herself! It takes Pioneer Jane to trespass where writs don't run! Jane goes where her husband don't dare follow. The officials don't say a word. Y'see there's no jail where they could stow a white woman and observe the decencies. So she goes over the border-line whenever she sees fit. The king's writ runs maybe for thirty miles north o' this railway. Once over that they can't catch you. But unless you're a black man, or Pioneer Jane, the natives tip the gov'ment off an' gov'ment rounds you up afore you get two-thirds the way. They'll take less than half a chance with her ladyship or I'm a Dutchman. Why? How would it look to have to bring her back between two native policemen? She'll not be allowed five miles outside Nairobi township!"

He up-ended his whisky again, consumed about a pint of it, and settled down to sleep. We took him by the legs and arms and threw him on the upper berth to stew in the cabined heat under the roof.

"It's good Monty's not with us," said Fred. He sat down and laughed at our surprise that he should state such heresy. "Monty mustn't break laws, but who cares if we do?"

"Laws?" said Will disgustedly. "I don't care who makes or breaks the laws of this land! Let's beat it! Let's join Monty in London and make plans for some other trip. Everybody's after this ivory. We haven't a look-in. Even if we knew where to look for it we'd be followed. Let's take the next train back from Nairobi, and the next boat for Europe!"

Fred rubbed his hands delightedly, and stroked his beard into the neat point it refuses to keep for long at a time in very hot weather.

"Let's stay in Nairobi," he said, "at least until Courtney sends that boy he promised us. We can put in the time asking questions, and then—"

"What then?" grumbled Will.

"There may be truth in what Brown of Lumbwa says about a dead-line."

"Dead-line?"

"Beyond which the king's writ doesn't run."

"Betcherlife there's truth in it!" Brown mumbled from the upper berth.

Will exploded silently, going through the motions of reeling off all the bad language he knew—not an insignificant performance.

"He's really asleep now," I said, standing on the lower berth and lifting the man's eyelid to make sure.

"Who cares?" said Will. "He's heard. We've given the game away. The woman heard Courtney shout about how to reach Mount Elgon. So did this sharp. Now he hears Fred talk about dead-lines and the king's writ and breaking laws! The game's up! Me for the down-train and a steamer!"

We smoked in silence, rendered more depressing by the deepening gloom outside. With the evening it grew no cooler. What little wind there was followed the train, so that we traveled in stagnation. Utter darkness brought no respite, but the fascination of flitting shadows and the ever-new mystery of African night. The train drew up at last in a station in the shadow of great overleaning mountains, and the heat shut down on us like hairy coverings. We seemed to breathe through thicknesses of cloth, and the very trees that cast black shadow on the platform ends were stifling for lack of air.

"One hour for dinner!" called the guard, walking limply along the train. "Just an hour for dinner! Dinner waiting!"

He was not at all a usual-looking guard. He was dressed in riding breeches and puttee leggings, and wore a worn-out horsey air as if in protest against the obligation to work in a black man's land. In countries where the half-breed and the black man live for and almost monopolize government employment few white men take kindly to braid and brass buttons. That fellow's contempt for his job was equaled only by the babu station master's scorn of him and his own for the station master. Yet both men did their jobs efficiently.

"Only an hour for dinner, gents—train starts on time!"

"Guard!" called a female voice we all three recognized. "Guard! Come here at once, I want you!"

We left Brown of Lumbwa snoring a good imitation of the Battle of Waterloo on the upper berth, and filed out to the dimly-lighted platform. A space in the center was roofed with corrugated iron and under that the yellow lamplight cast a maze of moving shadows as the passengers swarmed toward the dining-room. The smell of greasy cooking blended with the reek of axle and lamp oil. At the platform's forward end shadowy figures were throwing cord-wood into the tender, and the thump-thump-thump of that sounded like impatience; everything else suggested lethargy.

"Guard!" called the voice again. "Come here, guard!"

He stopped in passing to close our windows and lock our compartment door against railway thieves.

"There's a man asleep in there," I said.

"The 'eat 'll sober 'im!" he grinned, slamming the last window down. "What'll you bet 'er 'ighness don't want me to fetch dinner to 'er? She was in the train in Mombasa two hours afore startin' time, an' the things she ordered me to do 'ud have made a 'alf-breed think 'e was demeaning of 'imself! I 'aven't seen the color of 'er money yet. If she wants dinner she gets out and walks or 'er maid fetches it—you watch!"

Coutlass, the other Greek and the Goanese staggered out beside us on to the platform, drunk enough not to know whether Hassan was with them or not. He came out and stood beside them in a sort of alert defensive attitude.

"Guard!" called the voice again. "Where is the man?"

We followed the last of the crowd through the screened doors, and took seats at a table marked "First Class Only." There were four men there ahead of us, two government officials disinclined to talk; a missionary in a gray flannel shirt, suffering from fever and too suspicious to say good evening; and a man in charge of that section of the line, who checked the station master's accounts and counted money in a tray between mouthfuls. Between us and the second-class tables was a wooden screen on short legs, and beyond that arose babel. Second-class is democratic always, and talks with its mouth full. In addition to our privilege of paying more for exactly the same food, we enjoyed exclusiveness, a dirty table-cloth, and the extra smell from the kitchen door. (The table-cloth was dirty because the barefoot Goanese waiters invariably stubbed their feet against a break in the floor and spilt soup exactly in the same place.)

We had scarcely taken our seats when Coutlass swaggered in, closely followed by his gang. Inside the door he turned on Hassan.

"Black men eat outside!" he snarled, and shoved him out again backward. Then he came over to us and stood leering at the framed sign, "First Class Only," avoiding our eyes, but plainly at war with us.

"Gassharamminy!" he growled. "You think you're popes or something! You three would want a special private piece of earth to spit on!" He raised his voice to a sort of scream. "I proclaim one class only!"

At that he lifted his foot about level with his chest and kicked the screen over. The crash brought everybody to his feet except the two officials and the railway man. They continued eating, and the railway man continued counting copper coins as if life depended on that alone.

"Sit down all!" yelled Coutlass. "You will eat with better appetite now that you can behold the blushes of these virgins!" Then he swaggered over to the long table, thrust the other Greek and the Goanese into chairs on either side of him, and yelled for food. It was the first time we had been referred to publicly as virgins, and I think we all three felt the strain.

The Goanese manager—a wizened old black man with perfectly white hair—came running from the kitchen in a state of near-collapse, the sweat streaming off him and his hands trembling.

"What shall I do?" he asked, almost upsetting the railway man's tray of money. "That man is crazy! He came in once before and broke the dishes! Twice he has come in here and eaten and refused to pay! What shall I do?"

"Nothing," said the railway man. "Go on serving dinner. Serve him too."

The manager hurried out again and the running to and fro resumed. Then in came the guard.

"First-class for two on trays!" he shouted.

The railway man beckoned to him and he winked as he passed by us.

"When you've seen to that, and had your own meal, I want you," said the railway man.

"Thought you said the lady's maid would have to come and fetch the food?" I said maliciously as the guard passed my chair a second time.

"So I did. But if you know how to refuse her, just teach me! I told her flat to have the maid fetch it. She let on they're both too frightened to cross the platform in the dark! Never saw anything like 'em! Tears! An' dignified! When I climbed down they was too afraid next to be left alone. Swore train-thieves 'ud murder 'em! I had to leave 'em my key to lock 'emselves in with until I come back with the grub! What d'you think of that?"

But our soup came, and one could not think and eat that stuff simultaneously. The railway man looked up for a moment, saw my face, and explained in a moment of expansiveness that meat would not keep in that climate but was "perfectly good" when cooked.

"Besides," he added, "you'll get nothing more until you reach Nairobi to-morrow noon!"

That turned out to be not quite true, but as an argument

it worked. We swallowed, like the lined-up merchant seamen taking lime-juice under the skipper's eye.

The guard grew impatient and went into the kitchen, but had scarcely got through the door when a scream came from the direction of the train that brought him back on the run. No black woman ever screams in just that way, and in a land of black and worse-than-black men imagination leaps at a white woman's call for help.

There was a stampede for the door by every one except the Greeks and Goanese and the railway man. (He had to guard the money.) We poured through the screen doors, the guard fighting to burst between us, and, because with a self-preserving instinct that I have never thought quite creditable to the human race, everybody ran toward his own compartment, it happened that we three and the two officials and the guard came first on the scene of trouble.

Brown of Lumbwa was still drunk—affectionate, it seemed, by that time.

"You've no call to be 'fraid of me, li'l sweetheart!" The door was open. Within the compartment all was dark, but every sound emerged. There came a stifled scream.

"Li'l stoopid! What d'you come in for, if you're 'fraid o' poor ole Brown? I won't hurt you."

The guard passed between us and went up the step. He listened, looked, disappeared through the open door, and there came a sound of struggling.

"Whassis?" shouted Brown. "An interloper? No you don't! This is my li'l sweetheart! She came in to see me—didn't you, Matilda Ann?"

The woman apparently broke free. The guard yelled for help. Fred and one of the government officials were nearest and as they entered they passed the woman coming out. I recognized Lady Saffren Waldon's Syrian maid, with the big railway key in her fist that the guard had left with her. By that time there was a considerable crowd about our car, unable to see much because it stood in the way of the station lamplight. She slipped through—to the right—not toward Lady Isobel's compartment, and I lost sight of her behind some men. I ran after her, but she was gone among the shadows, and although I hunted up and down and in and out I could find her nowhere.

When I returned to our car Brown of Lumbwa was out on the platform with his hair all tousled and a wild eye. The guard was wiping a bloody nose and everybody was inventing an account of what nobody had seen.

"Scrag him!" advised some expert on etiquette.

"What the hell right has anybody got," demanded Brown with querulous ferocity, "to interfere between me and a lady? Eh? Whose compartment was she in? Me in hers or her in mine? Eh? Me, I'm sleeping. Hasn't a gent a right to sleep? Next thing I know she's fingerin' my whiskers. How should I know she's not balmy on red beards an' makin' love to me? What right's she got in my compartment anyhow? Who let her in? Who asked her? What if I did frighten her? What then?"

"Who was she?" demanded the official. "Had anybody seen her before?"

"The maid attending the lady in the next compartment," said I.

"Are you sure?"

"Positive."

"Very well. Guard! See who is in there!"

The guard wiped blood from his nose and obeyed orders. We clustered round the steps to hear.

" 'Ow many's in here?" he demanded.

There was no answer. He tried the door and it opened readily.

" 'Scuse me, but is there two of you? I can't see in the dark."

"Oh, is that our dinner?" said Lady Saffren Waldon's voice.

"No ma'am, not the dinner yet."

"Why not, pray?"

"There's folks accusin' your maid o' enterin' the next compartment an'—an'—"

"Nonsense! My maid is here! You kept us so long waiting for dinner we were both asleep! Ah! There's light at last, thank heaven!"

Two native porters running along the roofs were dropping lamps into the holes appointed for them, and the train that had been a block of darkness hewn out of the night was now a monster, many-eyed.

"They're both in there, so 'elp me!" the guard reported, retreating backward through the door and leering at us.

There remained nobody, except the still indignant Brown of Lumbwa to levy charges, and the crowd remembered its dinner (not that anything could be expected to grow cold in that temperature).

"The train will start on time!" announced the babu station master, and everybody hurried to the dining-room. Brown came with us, bewildered.

"How did it happen?" he demanded. "When did we get here? Why wasn't I called for dinner? How did she get in? Where did she go to?"

"Oh, come and eat curried cow, it's lovely!" answered Will.

Fred overtook us at the door, and whispered:

"Our things have been gone through, but I can't find that anything's missing."

Within the dining-room was new ground for discontent. The British race and its offshoots wash, but disbelieve with almost unanimity in water as a drink. Every guest at either table had left at his place a partly emptied glass of beer, or brandy and soda, or whisky. Each looked for the glass on his return, and found it empty.

"Those Greeks!" exclaimed the Goanese manager, with a fearful air, and shoulders shrugged to disclaim his own responsibility.

Coutlass and the other Greek were sitting at a table with a gorged look, glancing neither to the right nor left, yet not eating. I looked at the railway official, who had not left his seat. It struck me he was laughing silently, but he did not look up. The crowd, after the manner of all crowds, stormed at the Goanese manager.

"What can I do? What shall I do?" wailed the unhappy little man. "They are bigger than I! They were greedy! They took!"

All those charges were evidently true, and stated mildly. Coutlass rose to his feet.

"Gassharamminy!" he thundered, and his stomach stuck out over the table it was so full of various drinks. "Why should we not take? Who isn't thirsty in this hell of a place? Who leaves good drink deserves to lose it!"

"What shall I do?" wailed the Goanese manager.

"Take the orders for drinks again," said the railway man, glancing up from his figures. "Bring the account to me."

The waiters ran to fill orders, and a babel of abuse at the second table was hurled at Coutlass and his friends; but they did not leave the table because there was another course to come, and, as the manager had said, they were greedy. Then in came the guard, his face a blood-and-smudgy picture of discontent.

"Say!" he yelled. "Ain't I goin' to get those two first-classes on trays?" He came and stood by us. "Did you ever 'ear the likes of it? They swear neither of 'em was out of the compartment. They call me a liar for askin' for my key back! They swear I never gave it to 'em, 'an they never asked for it, an' their door was never locked, nor nothin'!"

He passed on to the railway man.

"I'll have to borry your key, sir. Mine's lost. Can't open doors until I get one from somewhere."

The railway man passed him his key with a bored expression and no remark.

"Don't forget that I want you presently," he ordered. "Be quick and get your own dinner."

"I'm in love with this ivory hunt!" Fred whispered to us across the table. "If she's sure our pockets are worth going through, I'm sure there's something to look for!"

"Are you sure the maid went through our things?" asked Will.

"Quite. I left my shooting jacket hanging on a hook. Everything was emptied out of the pockets on to the berth."

"I think I'll make you a confession presently," said I, with a look at Will that just then he did not understand.

"Never confess before dessert and coffee!" advised Fred. "It spoils the appetite."

# THE SLAVE GANGS

*Our fathers praised the old accustomed things,*
  *The privilege of chiefs, the village wall*
*Within whose circling dark Monumme\* sings*
  *O' nights of belly-full and ease and all*
*They taught us we should prize and praise*
  *(Only of dearth and pestilence should be our fears;)*
*And now behind us are the green, regretted days.*
  *The water in the desert is our tears.*
          *Then ye, who at the waters drink*
          *Of Freedom, oh with Pity think*
          *On us, who face the desert brink*
          *Your fathers entered willingly.*

*Our fathers mocked the might of the Unseen,*
  *Teaching that only what we saw and felt*
*Was good to fight about—what aye had been,*
  *Old-fashioned foods that their forefathers smelt,*
*Old stars each night illuming the old sky,*
  *The warm rain softening ere women till the ground,*
*The soft winds singing, only ask not why!*
  *And now our weeping is the desert sound.*
          *Oh ye, who gorge the daily good,*
          *Unquestioned heirs of all ye would,*
          *Spare not too timidly the blood*
          *Your fathers shed so willingly.*

*Our fathers taught us that the village good was best.*
  *Later we learned the red, new tribal creed*
*That our place was the sun—night owned the rest*
  *Unless their treasure profited our greed!*
*But now we gather nothing where our fathers sowed,*
  *For harvest grim the vultures wait in rows*
*As, urged by greedier than us with gun and goad,*
  *Yoked two by two the slave safari goes.*

---

\* *Monumme* (Kiswahili)—Lit. male—man in his prime.

*Oh ye, who from true judgment shrink,*
*Nor gentleness with courage link,*
*Be thoughtful when the cup ye drink*
*Your fathers spilled so willingly.*

# CHAPTER FIVE

THE guard procured his trays at last, delivered them at a run, returned in a hurry and swallowed his own meal at a side-table. Then, with his mouth full, he reported for orders to the railway official, who was still checking figures. The room was beginning to grow empty. Coutlass and his Greek friend and the Goanese sat almost alone at the far end of the other table, finishing their pudding. I had not noticed until then that the guard was a singularly little man. He stood very few inches taller than the seated official. I suppose that hitherto in some way his energy had seemed to increase his inches.

"Are there handcuffs in the caboose?"

"Yes, sir."

"Fetch them."

In spite of Brown of Lumbwa's protests, who wept at the notion of having to eat alone, we were in the act of settling our bills and going. But mention of handcuffs suggesting entertainment, we lit cigars and, imagining we stayed for love of him, Brown cooed at us.

"I've the darbies in my pocket, sir!"

I thought the guard looked more undersized than ever. He would have made a fair-sized middle-weight jockey.

"Tell that Greek—Coutlass his name is—to come here."

With his tongue stuck into his cheek and a wink at us the guard obeyed.

"He says for you to go to 'ell, sir!" he reported after a moment's interview.

"Very well. Arrest him!"

"He'll need help," I interrupted. "My two friends and I—"

"Oh, dear no," said the official. "He is fully up to his work."

So we moved our chairs into position for a better view.

109

The guard advanced fox-terrierwise to within about six paces of Coutlass.

"Up with both your 'ands, Thermopylæ!" he snapped. "Your bloomin' reckonin's come!"

Coutlass showed tobacco-stained teeth for answer, and his friends rutched their chairs clear of the table, ready for action. Yet they were taken unawares. With a terrier's speed the guard pounced on Coutlass, seized him by the hair and collar, hurled him, chair and all, under a side-table, and was on the far side of the table kicking his prostrate victim in the ribs before either Greek or Goanese—likewise upset in the sudden onslaught—could gather themselves and interfere.

The Goanese was first on his feet. He hurled a soda-water bottle. The guard ducked and the bottle smashed into splinters on the wall. Before the sound of smashing glass had died the Goanese was down again, laid out by blows on the nose and jugular. Then again the guard kicked Coutlass, driving him back under the table from which he was trying to emerge on all fours.

The second Greek looked more dangerous. His face grew dark with rage as the lips receded from his yellow teeth. He reached toward his boot, but judged there were too many witnesses for knife work and rushed in suddenly, yelling something in Greek to Coutlass as he picked up a chair to brain the guard with. He swung the chair, but the guard met it with another one, dodged him, and tripped him as he passed. In another second it was his turn to be kicked in the ribs until he yelled for mercy. (An extra large dinner and all those assorted drinks in addition to what they had had in the train made neither man's wind good.)

No mercy was forthcoming. He was kicked, more and more violently, until the need of crawling through the door to safety dawned on his muddled wits and he made his exit from the room snake fashion. By that time Coutlass was on his feet, and he too elected to force the issue with a chair. The guard sprang at the chair as Coutlass raised it, bore it down, and drove his fist hard home into the Greek's right eye three times running.

"'Ave you 'ad enough?" he demanded, making ready for another assault. The Goanese had recovered and staggered to his feet to interfere, but Coutlass yielded.

"All right," he said, "why should I fight a little man? I surrender to save bloodshed!"

"Put your 'ands out, then!"

Coutlass obeyed, and was handcuffed ignominiously.

"Outside, you!"

A savage kick landed in exactly the place where the Goanese least expected and most resented it. He flew through the door as if the train had started, and then another kick jolted Coutlass.

"Forward, march! Left—right—left—right!"

With hands manacled in front and the inexorable bantam guard behind, Coutlass came and stood before the railway official, who at last condescended not to seem engrossed in his accounts.

"'Ere he is, sir!"

"I suppose you know, my man, that I have magisterial powers on this railway?" said the official.

Coutlass glowered but said nothing.

"This is not the first time you have made yourself a nuisance. You broke dishes the last time you were here."

"That is long ago," Coutlass objected. "That was on the day the place was first opened to the public. There was a celebration. Every one was drunk."

"You broke plates and refused to pay the damage."

"Officials were drunk. I saw them!"

"The damage amounted to seventeen rupees, eight annas."

"Gassharamminy! All the crockery from Mombasa to Nairobi isn't worth that amount! I shall not pay!"

"Now there's another bill for those drinks you and your friends stole when passengers' backs were turned. I saw you do it!"

"Why didn't you object at the time?" sneered Coutlass.

"Here is the bill: twenty-seven rupees, twelve annas. Total, forty-five rupees, four annas. You may make the manager a present of the odd sum for his injured feelings, and call it an even fifty. Settle now, or wait here for the down-train and go to jail in Mombasa!"

"Wait in this place?" asked Coutlass, aghast.

"Where else? There'll be a down passenger train in a week."

"I pay!" said the Greek, with a hideous grimace.

"Take the irons off him, then."

The guard unlocked the handcuffs and Coutlass began to fumble for a money-bag.

"Give me a receipt!" he demanded, thumbing out the money.

"You are the receipt!" said the official. "An Englishman would have been sent to jail with a fine, and have paid the bill into the bargain. You're treated leniently because you can't be expected to understand decent behavior. You're expected to learn, however. Next time you will catch it hot!"

"All aboard!" called the guard cheerfully. "All aboard!"

"Tears, idle tears!" said Brown of Lumbwa, taking my arm and Fred's. "Thass too true—too true! They'd have jailed an Englishman—me, f'rinstance. One little spree, an' they'd put me in the Fort! One li'l indishcresshion an' they'd jug me for shix months! Him they let go wi' a admonisshion! It's 'nother case o' Barabbas, an' a great shame, but you can't change the English. They're ingcorridgible! Brown o' Lumbwa's my name," he added by way of afterthought.

"Take advice and get under blankets afore you go to sleep, gents!" warned the guard. All windows were once more opened wide, and every one was panting.

"A job on this 'ere line's a circus!" he grinned. "I'm lucky if there's only one fight before Nairobi! 'Ave your blankets ready, gents! Cover yourselves afore you sleep!"

That sounded like a joke. The sweat poured from every one in streams. The hot hair cushions were intolerable. The dust gathered from the desert stirred and hung, and there was neither air to breathe nor coolness under all those overhanging mountains.

"Get under your blankets, gents!" advised the guard, passing down the train; and then the train started.

I had the upper berth opposite Brown's, where it was hottest of all because of the iron roof. Drunk though he was, I noticed that the first thing Brown did after we had hoisted him aloft was to dig among the blankets like a dog and make the best shift he could of crawling under them. With one blanket twisted about his neck and shoulders and the other tangled about his knees he remarked to the roof that his name was Brown of Lumbwa, and proceeded to sob himself to sleep. He had made the journey a dozen times, so knew what he was doing. I drew on my own blankets, and stifling, blowing out red dust, remembered a promise.

"Will!" I said. "Tell Fred what happened to us in Zanzibar while he and Monty viewed the moon!"

"We agreed not to," he answered, but it seemed to me he might arouse his own enthusiasm if he did tell.

"Who's afraid of Fred?" said I.

That settled it.

"One of you shall tell before you sleep!" Fred announced, sitting up. "Who feareth not God nor regardeth me will blench before the prospect of a sleepless night! Speak, America!"

He took out a cleaning rod from his gun-case, and proceeded to stir Will's ribs and whack his feet. In a minute there was a rough-house—panting, and bursts of laughter—cracks of the cleaning rod on Will's bare legs—the sound of hands slipping on sweaty arms—and

"Murder!" yelled Brown of Lumbwa, waking up. "Murder! Oh, mur-durrr!"

"Shut up, you fool!" I shouted at him. But he only yelled the louder.

"I knew these tears were not for nothing!" he wailed. "It was premonition!. Pass me the whisky! Pass it up here! Oh, look! They're at each other's throats! Murder! Oh, mur-durrr! Pass the whisky or I'll come down and kill everybody in self-defense! Murrrrr-durrr!"

They stopped fooling because his idiotic screams could be heard all down the train.

"There," said Brown, "you see, I've saved two worthless

lives! Very foolish of me! Pass the whisky! See that I save
a little for the morning!"

At that he fell asleep again; and because Fred threatened
to start new commotion and wake him unless Will or I confessed at once, Will took up the tale, I leaning over the edge of
my berth to prompt him. Fred laughed all through the story,
and finally crawled under his blanket again to lie chuckling
at the underside of Brown of Lumbwa's berth.

"I don't see what we've scored by telling him," said Will
to me. "We've merely given him a peg to hang jokes on!"

But I knew that now Will had told the story he would not,
for very shame, withdraw from the venture until we should
have demonstrated that no Lady Saffren Waldon, nor Sultan
of Zanzibar, nor Germans, nor Arabs could make us afraid.
And it seemed to me that was sufficient accomplishment for
one night.

The train's progress slowed and grew slower. The panting
of the engine came back to us in savage blasts. We were climbing by curves and zigzags up the grim dark wall of mountains. And as we mounted inch by inch, foot by foot, the air
freshened and grew cooler—not really cool yet by a very Ja-
cob's ladder of degrees, but delectable by comparison.

There was something peacefully exhilarating in the thought
of rising from the red dead level of that awful plain, littered
with the bones of camels and the slaves whom men pinned into
the yokes to perish or survive in twos.* As we mounted foot
by foot we fell asleep. Later, as we mounted higher, we shiv-
ered under blankets. There is a spirit and a spell of Africa
that grip men even in sleep. The curt engine blasts became in
my dreams the panting of enormous beasts that fought. A
dream-continent waged war on itself, and bled. I saw the
caravans go, thousands long, the horsed and white-robed Arab
in the lead—the paid, fat, insolent *askaris,* flattering and flog-

---

*It was the cheerful Arab rule never to release one slave from
the yoke if the other failed on the journey, on the principle that
then the stronger would be more likely to care for, encourage,
and drive the weaker.

ging—slaves burdened with ivory, and other, naked, new ones, two in a yoke, shivering under the *askaris'* lash, the very last dogged by vultures and hyenas, lean as they, ill-nourished on such poor picking.

Then I saw elephants in herds five thousand strong that screamed and stormed and crashed, flattening out villages in rage that man should interfere with them—in fear of the ruthless few armed men with rifles in their rear. Whole herds crashed pell-mell through artfully staged undergrowth into thirty-foot-deep pits, where they lingered and died of thirst, that Arabs (who sat smoking within hail until they died) might have the ivory.

And all I saw in my dream was as nothing to the things I really was to see. None of the cruelty of man, none of the rage and fear of animal have vanished yet from Africa. Some of the cruelty is more refined; some of the herds are smaller; some good is making headway but Africa is unchanged on the whole. It is a land of nightmares, with lovely oases and rare knights errant; a land whose past is gloom, whose present is twilight and uncertainty, but whose future under the rule of humane men is immeasurable, unimaginable.

In my dream din followed crash and confusion until the engine's screaming at last awoke me. My blanket had fallen to the floor and I was shivering from cold. I jumped down to recover it and realized it was dawn already. We were bowling along at a fine pace past green trees and undulating veld, and I wondered why the engine should keep on screaming like a thing demented. I knelt on Fred's berth to lean from the window and look ahead. We were going round a slight curve and I could see the track ahead for miles.

Three hundred yards away a full-grown rhinoceros stood planted on the track, his flank toward us and his interest fixed on anything but trains. He was sniffing the cool morning, looking the other way.

"Wake up, you fellows!" I yelled, and Fred and Will put their heads through the window beside me just in time to see the rhino take notice of the train at last. When the engine was fifty yards from him he wheeled, took a short-sighted squint at it, sniffed, decided on war, and charged. The engineer crowded on steam.

"He's a game enough sport!" chuckled Fred.

"He's a fool!" grinned Will.

He was both, but he never flinched. He struck the cow-catcher head-on and tried to lift it sky-high. The speed and weight of the engine sent him rolling over and over off the track, and the shock of the blow came backward along the train in thunderclaps as each car felt the check. The engineer whistled him a requiem and a cheer went up from fifty heads thrust out of windows. But he was not nearly done for.

He got up, spun around like a polo pony to face the train, deliberately picked out level going, and charged again. This time he hit the car we were in, and screams from the compartment behind us gave notice that Lady Saffren Waldon's maid was awake and looking through a window too. He hit the running-board beside the car, crumpled it to matchwood, lifted the car an inch off the track, but failed to disrail us. The car fell back on the metal with a clang, and the rhino recoiled sidewise, to roll over and over again. This time the impetus sent him over the edge of a gully and we did not doubt he was dead at the bottom of it.

The guard stopped the train and came running to see what the damage amounted to.

"Any gent got his rifle handy?" he shouted. "The train's ahead o' time. There's twenty minutes for sport!"

We dived for our rifles, but Coutlass had his and was on the track ahead of us, his eye a ghastly sight from the guard's overnight attentions, his face the gruesome color of the man who has eaten and drunk too much, but his undamaged eye ablaze, and nothing whatever the matter with his enthusiasm.

"Give me a cartridge—a cartridge, somebody!" he yelled. "Gassharamminy! He's not dead! I saw him kick as he went over the edge legs upwards! Give me one cartridge and I'll finish him!"

By that time every male passenger was out on the track, some in night-shirts, some in shirts and pants, some with next-to-nothing at all on, but nearly all with guns. Somebody gave Coutlass a handful of cartridges that fitted his Mauser rifle and he was off in the lead like a hero leading a forlorn hope, we after him. We searched high and low but lost all trace of the rhino, and at the end of half an hour the engine's whistle called us back. There were blood and hair all over the engine —blood and hair on our car, but the rhino had been as determined in defeat as in attack, and if he died of his wounds he contrived to do it alone and in dignity.

"That leaves Coutlass with six cartridges," said I, overtaking Fred. "Let's hope their owner asks for them back."

The owner did ask for them. He stood with his hand out by the door of the Greek's compartment.

"You didn't use those cartridges," he said.

"But I will!" sneered Coutlass. "Out of my way!"

He sprang for his door and slammed it in the man's face, and the other Greek and the Goanese jeered through the window. I caught sight of Hassan beside them looking gray, as unhappy black men usually do. Will saw him too.

"The cannibal's ours," he said, "supposing we want him and play our cards kind o' careful."

The next thing to delay the train was an elephant, who walked the track ahead of us and when the engine whistled only put on speed. Hypnotized by the tracks that reached in parallel lines to the horizon, with trunk outstretched, ears up, and silly tail held horizontally he set himself the impossible task of leaving us behind. The more we cheered, the more the engine screamed, the fiercer and less dignified became his efforts; he reached a speed at times of fourteen or fifteen miles an hour, and it was not until, after many miles, he reached a culvert he dared not cross that he switched off at right angles. Realizing then at last that the train could not follow him to one side he stood and watched us pass, red-eyed, blown and angry. He had only one tusk, but that a big one, and the weight of it caused him to hold his head at a drunken-looking angle.

"Stop the train!" yelled Coutlass, brandishing his rifle as he climbed to the seat on the roof. But the guard, likewise on the roof at his end of the train, gave no signal and we speeded on. We were already in the world's greatest game reserve, where no man might shoot elephant or any other living thing.

We began to pass herds of zebra, gnu, and lesser antelope—more than a thousand zebra in one herd—ostriches in ones and twos—giraffes in scared half-dozens—rhinoceros—and here and there lone lions. Scarcely an animal troubled to look up at us, and only the giraffes ran.

Watching them, counting them, distinguishing the various breeds we three grew enormously contented, even Will Yerkes banishing depression. Obviously we were in a land of good hunting, for the strictly policed reserve had its limits beyond which undoubtedly the game would roam. The climate seemed perfect. There was a steady wind, not too cold or hot, and the rains were recent enough to make all the world look green and bounteous.

To right and left of us—to north and south that is—was wild mountain country, lonely and savage enough to arouse that unaccountable desire to go and see that lurks in the breast of younger sons and all true-blue adventurers. We got out a map and were presently tracing on it with fingers that trembled from excitement routes marked with tiny vague dots leading toward lands marked "unexplored." There were vast plateaus on which not more than two or three white men had trodden, and mountain ranges almost utterly unknown—some of them within sight of the line we traveled on. If the map was anything to go by we could reach Mount Elgon from Nairobi by any of three wild roads. Fred and I underscored the names of several places with a fountain pen.

"And say!" said Will. "Look out of the window! If we once got away into country like that, who could follow us!"

"But you can't get away!" said a weary voice from the upper berth. "I'm Brown of Lumbwa. That's my name, gents, and I know, because I tried! Thought I was sound asleep, didn't you! Well, I weren't! Listen to me, what happens. You start off. They get wind of it. They send the police helter-skelter hot-foot after you—native police—no officer—Masai they are, an' I tell you those Masai can make their sixty miles a day when they're minded an' no bones about it either! Maybe the Masai catches you and maybe not. S'posing they do they can't do much. They've merely a letter with 'em commanding you to return at once and report at the gov'ment office. And o' course—bein' ignorant, same as me, an' hotheaded, an' eager—you treat that contumelious an' tip the Masai the office to go to hell. Which they do forthwith. They're so used to bein' told to go to hell by wishful wanderers that they scarcely trouble to wait for the words. Presently they draw a long breath an' go away again like smoke being blowed down wind. An' you proceed onward, dreamin' dreams o' gold an' frankincense an' freedom."

"Well, what next?" said I, for he made a long pause, either for reminiscence or because of headache.

"Whisky next!" he answered. "I left a little for the morning, didn't I? I almost always do. Hold the bottle up to the light—no, no, you'll spill it!—pass it here! Ah-h-h-gug-gug!"

He finished what was left and tried to hurl the empty bottle through the window, but missed and smashed it against the woodwork.

"'Sapity!" he murmured. "Means bad luck, that does! Poor ole Brown o' Lumbwa—poor ole fella'. Pick up the pieces, boys! Pick 'em up quick—might get some o' poor ole Brown's bad luck—cut yourselves or what not. Pick 'em up careful now!"

We did, and it took ten minutes, for the splinters were scattered everywhere.

"Next time you do a thing like that you shall get out an' walk!" announced Fred.

"That 'ud be only my usual luck!" he answered mournfully. "But I was tellin' how you notify the Masai police to go to hell, an' they oblige. It's the last obligin' anybody does for you. Every native's a bush telegraph—every sleepy-seemin' one of 'em! They know tracks in an' out through the scrub that ain't on maps, an' they get past you day or night wi'out you knowin' it, an' word goes on ahead o' you—precedes you as the sayin' is. You come to a village. You need milk, food,

porters maybe, an' certainly inf'mation about the trail ahead.
You ask. Nobody answers. They let on not to sling your
kind o' lingo. Milk—never heard o' such stuff—cows in them
parts don't give milk! Food? They're starving. It isn't
overeating makes their bellies big, it's wind. Porters? All the
young men are lame, an' old 'uns too old, an' the middle 'uns
too middle-aged—an' who ever heard of a native woman
workin' anyhow. Who tills the *mtama* patch, then? It don't
get tilled, or else the women only 'tend to it at tillin' time.
Nobody works at anythin' about the time you come on the
scene, for work ain't moral, pleasin' nor profitable, an' there
you are! As for the trail ahead, lions an' cannibals are the
two mildest kind of calamities they guarantee you'll meet."

"You don't have to believe them," I argued. "No man in
his senses would start without porters of his own—"

"Who *never* run away, an' *never, oh never* go lame o'
course!" said Brown.

"Porters enough and to spare," I continued. "And food
for a month or two—"

"How are you going to get away right under their noses
with food for a month or two?" demanded Brown. "You've
got to live off the country after a certain distance. The further you go, the worse for you, for they'll sell you nothing
and give you less. By and by your porters get tipped off by
the natives of some village you spend a night at. You look
for 'em next mornin' and where are they? Gone! There are
their loads, an' no one to carry 'em! You've got to leave your
loads an' return, an' the police you told so stric'ly to go to
hell meet you with broad grins and lead you to the gov'ment
office. There the collector, or, what's worse, the 'sistant collector, gives you a lecture on infamy an' the law of doin' as
you'd be done by. You ask for your loads back, an' he laughs
at you. An' that's all about it, excep' that next time you happen to want a favor done you by gov'ment you get a lecture instead! No, you can't get away, an' it's no use tryin'! If you
was Greeks maybe, or Arabs, yes. Bein' English, the Indian
Penal Code, which is white man's law in these parts, 'll get
you sure!"

Brown of Lumbwa sighed at recollection of his wrongs, turned over, and went to sleep again. The train bowled along over high veld, cutting in half magnificent distances and stopping now and then at stations whose excuse for existence was unimaginable. We stopped at a station at last where the Hindu clerk sold tea and biscuits. The train disgorged its passengers and there was a scramble in the tiny ticket office like the rush to get through turn-stiles at a football game at home, only that the crowd was more polyglot and less good-natured.

Coutlass, his Greek friend and the Goanese being old travelers on that route were out of the train first, first into the room, and first supplied with breakfast. Fred and I were nearly last. Brown of Lumbwa refused to leave his berth but lay moaning of his wrongs, and the iniquity of drink not based on whisky. I missed Will in the scramble, and although it was nearly half an hour before I got served I did not catch sight of him in all that time.

I counted eleven nations taking tea in that tiny room and there were members of yet other tribes strolling the platform, holding themselves aloof with the strange pride of the pariah the wide world over.

When Will came in he was grinning, and his ears seemed to stick out more than usual, as they do when he is pleased with himself.

"Didn't I say fat Johnson was ours if we'd play our cards right?" he demanded.

"You mean Hassan?"

"He'd had no breakfast. He'd had no supper. He had no money. The Greeks took away what little money he did have on the pretext that he might buy a return ticket and desert them. They seem to think that a day or two's starvation might make him good and amenable. I found him trying to beg a bite from a full-blooded Arab, and say! they're a loving lot. The Arab spat in his eye! I offered to buy him eats but he didn't dare come in here for fear the Greeks 'ud thrash him, so I slipped him ten rupees for himself and he's the gratefulest fat black man you ever set eyes on. You bet it takes food and lots of it to keep that belly of his in shape. There's a back door to this joint. He slipped round behind and bribed the babu to feed him on the rear step, me standing guard at the corner to keep Greeks at bay. He's back in the car now, playing possum."

"Let's trade him for Brown of Lumbwa," suggested Fred genially. "Call him into our car and kick Brown out!"

"Trade nothing! I tell you the man is ours! Call him, and he'll bargain. Let him be, and the next time the Greeks ill-treat him he'll come straight to us in hope we'll show him kindness."

"Swallow your tea quickly, Solomon!" Fred advised him. "There goes the whistle!"

It was fresh tea, just that minute made for him. Will gulped down the scalding stuff and had to be thumped on the back according to Fred. With eyes filled with water he did not see what I did, and Fred was too busy guarding against counter-blows. The most public place and the very last minute always suited those two best for playing horse.

"Thought you said Johnson was asleep," said I.

"Possuming," coughed Will. "Shamming sleep to fool the Greeks."

"Possuming, no doubt," I answered, "but the Greeks are on. He has just come scurrying out of Lady Saffren Waldon's compartment. The Greeks watched him and made no comment."

We piled into our own appointed place and sat for a while in silence.

"All right," said Will at last, lighting his pipe. "I own I felt like quitting once. I'll see it through now if there's no ivory and nothing but trouble! That dame can't thimblerig me!"

"We're supposed to know where the ivory is," grinned Fred. "Keep it up! They'll hunt us so carefully that they'll save us the trouble of watching them!"

"I'm beginning to think we do know where the ivory is," said I. "I believe it's on Mount Elgon and they mean to prevent our getting it."

"If that turns out true, we'll have to give them the slip,

that's all," said Fred, and got out his concertina. Just as Monty always played chess when his brain was busy, Fred likes to think to the strains of his infernal instrument. One could not guess what he was thinking about, but the wide world knew he was perplexed, and Lady Saffren Waldon in the next compartment must have suffered.

After a while he commenced picking out the tunes of comic songs, and before long chanced on one that somebody in the front part of the train recognized and began to sing. In ten minutes after that he was playing accompaniments for a full train chorus and the scared zebra and impala bolted to right and left, pursued by Tarara-boom-de-ay, Ting-a-ling-a-ling, and other non-Homeric dirges that in those days were dying an all-too-lingering death.

It was to the tune of *After the Ball* that the engine dipped head-foremost into a dry watercourse, and brought the train to a jaw-jarring halt. The tune went on, and the song grew louder, for nobody was killed and the English-speaking races have a code, containing rules of conduct much more stringent than the Law of the Medes and Persians. Somebody—probably natives from a long way off, who needed fuel to cook a meal—had chopped out the hard-wood plate on which the beams of a temporary culvert rested. Time, white ants, gravity and luck had done the rest. It was a case thereafter of walk or wait.

"Didn't I tell you?" moaned Brown of Lumbwa. "Didn't I say walkin' 'ud be only just my luck?"

So we walked, and reached Nairobi a long way ahead of Coutlass and his gang, whose shoes, among other matters, pinched them; and we were comfortably quartered in the one hotel several hours before the arrival of Lady Saffren Waldon and those folk who elected to wait for the breakdown gang and the relief train.

It was a tired hotel, conducted by a tired once-missionary person, just as Nairobi itself was a tired-looking township of small parallel roofs of unpainted corrugated iron, with one main street more than a mile long and perhaps a dozen side-streets varying in length from fifty feet to half a mile.

He must have been a very tired surveyor who pitched on that site and marked it as railway headquarters on his map. He could have gone on and found within five miles two or three sightlier, healthier spots. But doubtless the day's march had been a long one, and perhaps he had fever, and was cross. At any rate, there stood Nairobi, with its "tin-town" for the railway underlings, its "tin" sheds for the repair shops, its big "tin" station buildings, and its string of pleasant-looking bungalows on the only high ground, where the government nabobs lived.

The hotel was in the middle of the main street, a square frame building with a veranda in front and its laundry hanging out behind. Nairobi being a young place, with all Africa in which to spread, town plots were large, and as a matter of fact the sensation in our corner room was of being in a wilderness—until we considered the board partition. Having marched fastest we obtained the best room and the only bath, but next-door neighbors could hear our conversation as easily as if there had been no division at all. However, as it happened, neither Coutlass and his gang nor Lady Saffren Waldon and her maid were put next to us on either side. To our right were three Poles, to our left a Jew and a German, and we carried on a whispered conversation without much risk.

She and her maid arrived last, as it was growing dusk. We had already seen what there was to see of the town. We had been to the post-office on the white man's habitual hunt, for mail that we knew was non-existent. And I had had the first adventure.

I walked away from the post-office alone, trying to puzzle out by myself the meaning of Lady Saffren Waldon's pursuit of us, and of her friendship with the Germans, and her probable connection with Georges Coutlass and his riff-raff. I had not gone far either on my stroll or with the problem—perhaps two hundred yards down a grassy track that they had told me led toward a settlement—when something, not a sound, not a smell, and certainly not sight, for I was staring at the ground, caused me to look up. My foot was raised for a forward step, but what I saw then made me set it down again.

To my right front, less than ten yards away, was a hillock about twice my own height. To my left front, about twelve yards away was another, slightly higher; and the track passed between them. On the right-hand hillock stood a male lion, full maned, his forelegs well apart and the dark tuft on the end of his tail appearing every instant to one side or the other as he switched it cat-fashion. He was staring down at me with a sort of scandalized interest; and there was nothing whatever for me to do but stare at him. I had no weapon. One spring and a jump and I was his meat. To run was cowardice as well as foolishness, the one because the other. And without pretending to be able to read a lion's thoughts I dare risk the assertion that he was puzzled what to do with me. I could very plainly see his claws coming in and out of their sheaths, and what with that, and the switching tail, and the sense of impotence I could not take my eyes off him. So I did not look at the other hillock at first.

But a sound like that a cat makes calling to her kittens, only greatly magnified, made me glance to the left in a hurry. I think that up to that moment I had not had time to be afraid, but now the goose-flesh broke out all over me, and the sensation up and down my spine was of melting helplessness.

On the left-hand hillock a lioness stood looking down with much intenser and more curious interest. She looked from me to her mate, and from her mate to me again with indecision that was no more reassuring than her low questioning growl.

I do not know why they did not spring on me. Surely no two lions ever contemplated easier quarry. No victim in the arena ever watched the weapons of death more helplessly. I suppose my hour had not come. Perhaps the lions, well used to white men who attacked on sight with long-range weapons, doubted the wisdom of experiments on something new.

The lioness growled again. Her mate purred to her with an uprising reassuring note that satisfied her and sent my heart into my boots. Then he turned, sprang down behind the hillock, and she followed. The next I saw of them they

were running away like dogs, jumping low bushes and heading
for jungle on the near horizon faster than I had imagined
lions could travel.

That ended my desire for further exercise and solitude. I
made for the hotel as fast as fear of seeming afraid would let
me, and spent fifteen aggravating minutes on the veranda
trying to persuade Fred Oakes that I had truly seen lions.

"Hyenas!" he said with the air of an old hunter, to which
he was quite entitled, but that soothed me all the less for that.

"More likely jackals," said Will; and he was just as much
as Fred entitled to an opinion.

While I was asserting the facts with increasing anger, and
they were amusing themselves with a hundred-and-one ridiculous reasons for disbelieving me, Lady Saffren Waldon came.
She had, as usual, attracted to herself able assistance; a settler's ox-cart brought her belongings, and she and her maid
rode in hammocks borne by porters impressed from heaven
knew where. It was not far from the station, but she was the
type of human that can not be satisfied with meek beginnings.
That type is not by any means always female, but the women
are the most determined on their course, and come the biggest
croppers on occasion.

She was determined now, mistress of the situation and of
her plans. She left to her maid the business of quarreling
about accommodations; (there was little left to choose from,
and all was bare and bad); dismissed the obsequious settler
and his porters with perfunctory thanks that left him no excuse for lingering, and came along the veranda straight toward
us with the smile of old acquaintance, and such an air of being
perfectly at ease that surprise was disarmed, and the rudeness
we all three intended died stillborn.

"What do you think of the country?" she asked. "Men like
it as a rule. Women detest it, and who can blame them? No
comforts—no manners—no companionship—no meals fit to
eat—no amusement! Have you killed anything or anybody
yet? That always amuses a man!"

We rose to make room for her and I brought her a chair.
There was nothing else one could do. There is almost no twi-

light in that part of East Africa; until dark there is scarcely a hint that the day is waning. She sat with us for twenty or thirty minutes making small talk, her maid watching us from a window above, until the sun went down with almost the suddenness of gas turned off, and in a moment we could scarcely see one another's faces.

Then came the proprietor to the door, with his best ex-missionary air of knowledge of all earth's ways, their reason and their trend.

"All in!" he called. "All inside at once! No guest is allowed after dark on the veranda! All inside! Supper presently!"

"Pah!" remarked Lady Saffren Walden, rising. "What is it about some men that makes one's blood boil? I suppose we must go in."

She came nearer until she stood between the three of us, so close that I could see her diamond-hard eyes and hear the suppressed breathing that I suspected betrayed excitement.

"I must speak with you three men! Listen! I know this place. The rooms are unspeakable—not a bedroom that isn't a megaphone, magnifying every whisper! There is only one suitable place—the main dining-room. The proprietor leaves the oil-lamp burning in there all night. People go to bed early; they prefer to drink in their bedrooms because it costs less than treating a crowd! I shall provide a light supper, and my maid shall lay the table after everybody else is gone upstairs. Then come down and talk with me. It's important! Be sure and come!"

She did not wait for an answer but led the way into the hotel. There was no hall. The door led straight into the dining-room, and the noisy crowd within, dragging chairs and choosing places at the two long tables, made further word with her impossible, even if she had not hurried up-stairs to her room.

"What do you make of it—of her? Isn't she the limit?"

The words were scarcely out of Will's mouth when a roar that made the dishes rattle broke and echoed and rumbled in the street outside. The instant it died down another followed it—then three or four—then a dozen all at once. There came the pattering of heavy feet, like the sound of cattle coming homeward. Yet no cattle—no buffaloes ever roared that way.

"Now you know why I ordered you all inside," grinned the ex-missionary owner of the place. I divined on the instant that this was his habit, to stand by the door before supper and say just those words to the last arrivals. I had a vision of him standing by his mission door aforetime, repeating one jest, or more likely one stale euphuism night after night.

"Lions?" I asked, hating to take the bait, yet curious beyond power to resist.

"Certainly they're lions! Did you think you were dreaming? Are you glad you came in when I called you? Would you rather go out again now? Make a noise like a herd of cattle, don't they! That's because they're bold. They don't care who hears them! The day is ours. It used to be theirs, but the white man has come and broken up their empire. The night is still theirs. They're reveling in it! They're boasting of it! Every single night they come swaggering through like this just after sunset. They'll come again just before dawn, roaring the same way. You'll hear them. They'll wake you all right. No trouble in this hotel about getting guests downstairs for early breakfast!"

"I'll get my rifle and settle the hash of one or two of them before I eat supper!" announced Will, turning away to make good his words. But the proprietor seized him by the arm.

"Don't be foolish! It has been tried too often! I never allowed such foolishness at my place. A party up-street fired from the windows. Couldn't see very well in the dark, but wounded two or three lions. What happened, eh? Why the whole pack oₓ lions laid siege to the house! They broke into the stable and killed three horses, a donkey, and all the cows and sheep. There weren't any shutters on the house windows —nothing but glass. It wasn't long before a young lion broke a window, and in no time there were three full-grown ones into the house after him. They injured one man so severely that he died next day. They only shot two of the lions that got inside. The other two got safely away, and since that time people here have known enough not to interfere with them ex-

cept by daylight! They'll do no harm to speak of unless you
fire and enrage them. They'll kill the stray dogs, or any other
animal they find loose; and heaven help the man they meet!
But the place to be after six P. M. in Nairobi is indoors. And
it's the place to stay until after sunrise! Hear them roar!
Aren't they magnificent? Listen!"

The noise that twenty or thirty lions can make, deliberately
bent on making it and roaring all at once, is unbelievable.
They throw their heads up and glory in strength of lungs
until thunders take second place and the listener knows why
not the bravest, not the most dangerous of beasts has managed to impose the fable of his grandeur on men's imagination.

We were summoned to the table by the din of Georges
Coutlass rising to new heights of gallantry.

"Gassharamminy!" he shouted, thumping with a scarred
fist. With a poultice on his eye he looked like a swashbuckler
home from the wars; and as he had not troubled to shave
himself, the effect was heightened. "What sort of company
sits when a titled lady enters!" He seized a big spoon and
rapped on the board with it. "Blood of an onion! Rise, every
one!"

Everybody rose, although there were men in the room in
no mind to be told their duty by a Greek. Lady Saffren
Waldon walked to a place near the head of the table with a
chilling bow. As usual when night and the yellow lamplight
modified merciless outlines, she looked lovely enough. But
she lacked the royal gift of seeming at home with the vulgar
herd. She could make men notice her—serve her, up to a
certain point—and feel that she was the center of interest
wherever she might choose to be; but because she was everlastingly on guard, she lacked the power to put mixed company at ease.

Only the ex-missionary at the head of the table seemed to
consider himself socially qualified to entertain her. She was
at no pains to conceal contempt for him.

"You honor my poor hotel!" he assured her.

"It is certainly a very poor hotel," she answered.

"Do you expect to remain long, may I ask?"

"What right have you to ask me questions? Tell that native to go away from behind my chair. My own maid will wait on me."

Whether purposely or not, she cast such a chill upon the company that even Georges Coutlass subsided within himself, and, though he ate like a ravening animal, did not talk. Almost the only conversation was between the owner and the native servants, who waited at table abominably and were noisily reprimanded, and argued back. Each reprimand increased their inefficiency and insolence. Natives detest a fussy, noisy white man.

Bad food, indifferent cooking, and no conversation worthy of the name produced gloom that drove every one from table as soon as possible. Even the proprietor, with unsatiable curiosity exuding from him, but no spirit for forcing issues, departed to a sanctum of his own up somewhere under the roof. The boys cleared the tables. The smell of food spread itself and settled slowly. A half-breed butler served countless orders of drinks on trays, and sent them up-stairs to bedrooms. Presently we three sat alone in the long bare room.

"Shall we wait for her?" I asked. "Haven't we had enough of her?"

Fred laughed. "She can scarcely cut the throats of all three of us!"

"I said we'd never hear the last of it!" said Will, with a scowl at me.

"Shall we wait for her?" I repeated.

My own vote would have been in favor of going up-stairs and leaving her to her own devices. I could see that Fred was afire with curiosity, but guessed that Will would agree with me. However, the point was settled for us by the arrival of her maid, who smiled with unusual condescension and produced from a basket an assortment of drinks, nuts, cigarettes and sandwiches. She spread them on the table and went away again.

We sat and smoked for an hour after that, imagining every moment that Lady Saffren Waldon would be coming. Whenever we yawned in chorus and rose to go up-stairs, a footstep seemed to herald her arrival. To have passed her on the stairs would have been too awkward to be amusing.

At last we really made up our minds to go to bed; and then she really came, appearing at the bend in the stairs just as I set my foot on the lower step, so we trooped back to our chairs by the window. She was dressed in a lacy silk negligee, and took pains this time to appear gracious.

"I waited until I felt sure we should not be disturbed," she said, smiling. "Won't you come and sit down?"

We brought our chairs to the table, she sitting at one end and we together at one side, Fred nearest her and I farthest away. She made a sign toward the wine and sandwiches, and offered us cigarettes of a sort I had never seen. Without feeling exactly like flies in a spider's web, we were nervous as schoolboys.

"What do you want with us?" asked Will at last.

She laughed and took a cigarette.

"Don't let us talk too loud. You three men are after the Tippoo Tib ivory. So is the Sultan of Zanzibar. So is the German government. So am I!"

She gave the statement time to do its own work, and smoked a while in silence. The strength of her position, and our weakness, lay in there being three of us. Any one of us might let drop an ill-considered word that would commit the others. I think we all felt that, for we sat and said nothing.

"You answer her, Fred," I said at last, and Will nodded agreement.

So Fred got up and sat on the other side of the table, where we could see his face and he ours.

"You haven't answered Mr. Yerkes' question," he said. "What do you want with us, Lady Saffren Waldon?"

"I want an understanding with you. I will be plain to begin with. We all know you know where the ivory is. Lord Montdidier is not the man to connect himself with any wild goose chase. We don't pretend to know how you came by the secret or why he has gone to London, but we are sure you know it—perfectly sure, and for five or six reasons. We are willing to buy the secret from you at your own price."

"Who are 'we'?" asked Fred pointedly, helping himself to nuts.

"The German government, the Sultan of Zanzibar, and myself."

Fred smiled. "Between you you probably could pay," he remarked.

"I will tell you a few hard facts," she said, "now that the ice is broken. You will never be allowed to make full use of your own secret. You have arrived at an inopportune moment, for you and for us. Our plans have been on foot a long time. Our search has been systematic, and it is a mathematical certainty we shall find what we look for in time. We do not propose to let new arrivals on the scene spoil all our plans and disappoint us just because they happen to have information. If you go ahead you will be watched like mice whom cats are after. If you find the ivory, you will be killed before you can make the discovery known!"

"We seem up against it, don't we!" smiled Fred.

"You are! But you can save us trouble, if you will. Name your price. Tell me your secret. Go your way. If your story proves true you shall be paid by draft on London."

"Are you overlooking the idea," asked Fred, "that we might tell the secret to the British government, and be contented with our ten per cent. commission?"

"I am not. You are expressly warned against any such foolishness. In the first place, you will be killed at once if you dare. In the second place, how do you know the British government would pay you ten per cent.?"

"I've had dealings with the English!" laughed Fred.

"Bah! Do you think this is Whitehall? Do you think the officials here are proof against temptation? When I tell you that in Whitehall itself I can bribe two officials out of three, perhaps you'll understand me when I say that all these people have their price! And the price is low! Tell them where the ivory is—lead them to it—and they'll swear they found it themselves, so as to keep the commission themselves! And as for you—you three"—she sneered with the most sardonic, thin-lipped smile I ever saw—"there are lions out here, and buffalo, snakes, fevers, native uprisings—more ways of being rid of you than by choking you to death with butter!"

"Do you suppose," asked Fred, "that Lord Montdidier has no influence in London, that he—"

"I know he *had* influence. I should have told you first, perhaps. Lord Montdidier was murdered on board ship. A telegram reached Mombasa yesterday at ten A. M. from up-coast saying that the body of an unknown Englishman had been picked up at sea by an Arab dhow, with the face too badly eaten by fish to be recognizable. You may take it from me, that is Lord Montdidier's corpse."

The calm announcement was intended to surprise us, and it did, but the result surprised her.

"You she-devil!" said Will. "If you and your gang have murdered that fine fellow I'll turn the tables on you! You go up-stairs, and pray he isn't dead! Pray that corpse may prove to be some one's else! If he's dead I'll guarantee you it's the worst day's work you ever had a hand in! Go up-stairs!"

He flung away the cigarette she had given him and knocked his chair away.

"Sit down, you young fool!" she said. "Don't make all that noise!"

But Will had none of the respect for titles acquired by marriage that made most men an easy mark for her.

"Leave the room!" he ordered. "Go away from us! Just you hope that's a lie about Monty, that's all!"

"Sit down!" she repeated. "I admit I am a little previous. The story is unconfirmed yet. Sit down and be sensible! Something of the sort will happen to all of you unless you three men get religion!"

But Will began to pace the floor noisily, stopping to glare at her each time he turned.

"Is there any sense in protracting the scene?" asked Fred.

"No," she admitted. "I see you are too hot-headed to be reasoned with. But it makes little difference! Fever—ani-

mals—climate—sun—flood—accident—natives—there are excuses in plenty—explanations by the dozen! I will say good
night, then—and good-by!"

"Yes, good-by!" growled Will, facing her with his back
to the stairs. "You take us for men with a price, do you?"

"All men have a price," she smiled bitterly. "Only it is
no use offering flowers to pigs! We must treat pigs another
way—pigs, and young fools! And fools old enough to know
better!" she added with a nod toward Fred, who bowed to
her in mock abasement—too politely, I thought.

Will got out of her way and she went up-stairs with the
manner of an empress taking leave of subjects. Fred swept
her food and wine from the table and stowed it in a corner,
and we sat down at the table again.

"The whole thing's getting ridiculous," he said.

"Why don't we hunt up some official in the morning," I
proposed, "and simply expose her?"

"No use," said Will. "She never followed us up here and
tried that game without being sure of her pull. Besides—
what kind of a tale could we tell without letting on we're
after the ivory? I vote we see the game through to a finish."

"Good!" said Fred. "I agree!"

"The only clue we've got," said I, "is Courtney's advice
about Mount Elgon."

"And what Coutlass said in Zanzibar about German East,"
added Will.

"Tell you what," said Fred, rapping the table excitedly.
"Instead of falling foul of this government by slipping over
the dead-line, why not run down to German East—pretend to
search for the stuff down there—and go from German East
direct to Mount Elgon, giving 'em all the slip. Who's got the
map?"

"It's up-stairs," I said. "I'll fetch it."

There was nothing like silence in the rooms above. Men
were smoking and drinking in one another's rooms. Some
doors were open to make conversation easier across the landing, and nobody was asleep. But I was surprised to see
Georges Coutlass leaning against the door-post of the room

he shared with the other Greek and the Goanese, obviously on guard, but against whom and on whose behalf it was difficult to guess.

"Are you off to bed?" he asked, piercing me with his unbandaged eye. "Why don't the others go, too?"

It dawned on me what he was after.

"Take the wine if you want it," I said. "None of us will prevent you."

He went down-stairs in his stocking feet, leaving his own door wide. I glanced in. The other Greek and the Goanese were asleep. Hassan lay on the floor on a mat between their cots. He looked up at me. I did not dare speak, but I smiled at him as friendly as I knew how and made a gesture I hoped he would interpret as an invitation to come and attach himself to our party. Then I hurried on, for Coutlass was coming back with a bottle of wine in each hand.

I was five minutes in our bedroom. In a minute I knew what had happened. We had left the door locked, but the lock was a common one; probably the keys of other doors fitted it, and there was not one thing in the room placed exactly where we had left it. Everything was more or less in place, but nothing quite.

I returned empty-handed down-stairs, locking the bedroom door behind me.

"Listen, you chaps!" I said. "While we waited for that woman she and her maid went through our things again!"

"How d'you know it was she?" asked Fred.

"No mistaking the scent she uses. Where's our money?"

"Here in my pocket."

"Good. The map's gone, though!"

Will showed his teeth in the first really happy smile for several days.

"Good enough!" he said. "Let's go to bed now. I'll bet you my share of the ivory they're poring over the map with a magnifying-glass! D'you remember the various places we underscored? They'll think it's a cryptogram and fret over it all night! Come on—come to bed!"

# THE SONG OF THE GREAT GAME RESERVE

*Noah was our godfather, and he pitched and caulked a ship*
*With stable-room for two of each and fodder for the trip,*
*Lest when the Flood made sea of earth the animals should die;*
*And two by two he stalled us till the wrath of God was by.*
*But who in the name of the Pentateuch can the paleface peo-*
*ple be*
*Who ha' done on the plains of Africa more than he did at sea?*

*A million hoofs once drummed the dust (Kongoni led the*
*way!)*
*From river-pool to desert-lick we thundered in array*
*Until the dark-skin people came with tube and smoke and*
*shot,*
*Hunting and driving and killing, and leaving the meat to rot.*
*And we didn't know who the hunters were, but we saw the*
*herds grow thin*
*That used to drum the dust-clouds up with thousand-footed*
*din.*

*We were few when the paleface people came—scattered and*
*few and afraid.*
*Fewer were they, but they brought the law, and the dark-skin*
*men obeyed.*
*The paleface people drew a line that none by dark or day*
*Might cross with fell intent to hunt—capture or drive or slay.*
*But who can the paleface people be with red-meat appetites*
*Who ruled anew what Noah knew—that animals have rights?*

*And now in the Athi Game Reserve—in a million-acre park*
*A million creatures graze who went by twos into the Ark.*
*We sleep o' nights without alarm (Kongoni, prick your ear!)*
*And barring the leopard and lion to watch, and ticks, we've*
*nought to fear,*
*Zebra, giraffe and waterbuck, rhino and ostrich too—*
*But who can the paleface people be who know what Noah*
*knew?*

# CHAPTER SIX

THE lions awoke us a little before dawn as the proprietor had promised. They seemed to have had bad hunting, for their boastfulness was gone. They came in twos and threes, snarling, only roaring intermittently—in a hurry because the hated daylight would presently reverse conditions and put them at disadvantage.

I grew restless and got up. The air being chilly, I put my clothes on and sat for a while by the window. So it happened I caught sight of Hassan, very much afraid of lions, but obviously more afraid of being seen from the hotel windows. He was sneaking along as close to the house as he could squeeze, his head just visible above the veranda rail.

For no better reason than that I was curious and unoccupied, I slipped out of the house and followed him.

Once clear of the hotel he seemed to imagine himself safe, for without another glance backward he ran up-street in the direction of the bazaar. I followed him down the bazaar—a short street of corrugated iron buildings—and out the other end. Being fat, he could not run fast, although his wind held out surprisingly. If he saw me at all he must have mistaken me for a settler or one of the Nairobi officials, for he seemed perfectly sure of himself and took no pains whatever now to throw pursuers off the track.

It soon became evident that he was making for an imposing group of tents on the outskirts of the town. As he drew nearer he approached more slowly.

It now became my turn to take precautions. There was no chance of concealment where I was—nothing but open level ground between me and the tents. But now that I knew Hassan's destination, I could afford to let him out of sight for a minute; so I turned my back on him, walked to where a sort of fold in the ground enabled me to get down unseen into a shallow nullah, and went along that at right angles to Hassan's course until I reached the edge of some open jungle, about half a mile from the tents. I noticed that it came to an end at a spot about three hundred yards to the rear of the tents, so I worked my way along its outer edge, and so approached the encampment from behind.

I had brought a rifle with me, not that I expected to shoot anything, but because the lion incident of the previous afternoon had taught me caution. It had not entered my head that in that country a strange white man without a rifle might have been regarded as a member of the mean white class; nor that anybody would question my right to carry a rifle, for that matter.

The camp was awake now. There were ten tents, all facing one way. Two of them contained stores. The central round tent with an awning in front was obviously a white man's. One tent housed a mule, and the rest were for native servants and porters. The camp was tidy and clean—obviously belonging to some one of importance. Fires were alight. Breakfast was being cooked, and smelled most uncommonly appetizing in that chill morning air. Boys were already cleaning boots, and a saddle, and other things. There was an air of discipline and trained activity, and from the central tent came the sound of voices.

I don't know why, but I certainly did not expect to hear English. So the sound of English spoken with a foreign accent brought me to a standstill. I listened to a few words, and made no further bones about eavesdropping. Circumstances favored me. The boys had seen I was carrying a rifle and was therefore a white man of importance, so they did not question my right to approach. The tent with the mule in it and the two store tents were on the right, pitched in a triangle. I passed between them up to the very pegs of the central tent from which the voices came, and discovered I was invisible, unless some one should happen to come around a corner. I decided to take my chance of that.

The first thing that puzzled me was why a German (for it was a perfectly unmistakable German accent) should need to talk English to a native who was certainly familiar with both Arabic and Kiswahili. When I heard the German addressed as *Bwana* Schillingschen I wondered still more, for from all accounts that individual could speak more native tongues than most people knew existed. It did not occur to me at the time that if he wished not to be understood by his own crowd of boys he must either speak German or English, and that Hassan would almost certainly know no German.

"A good thing you came to me!" I heard. The accent was clumsy for a man so well versed in tongues. "Yes, I will give you money at the right time. Tell me no lies now! There will be letters coming from people you never saw, and I shall know whether or not you lie to me! You say there are three of the fools?"

"Yes, *bwana*. There were four, but one going home—big lord gentleman, him having black m'stache, gone home."

There was no mistaking Hassan's voice. No doubt he could speak his mother tongue softly enough, but in common with a host of other people he seemed to imagine that to make himself understood in English he must shout.

"Why did he go home?"

"I don't know, *bwana*."

"Did they quarrel?"

"*Sijui*."*

"Don't you dare say '*sijui*' to me!"

"Maybe they quarrel, maybe not. They all quarreling with Lady Saffunwardo—staying in same hotel, Tippoo Tib one time his house—she wanting maybe go with him to London. He saying no. Others saying no. All very angry each with other an' throwing *bwana masikini*, Greek man, down hotel stairs."

"What had he to do with it?"

"Two Greek man an' one Goa all after ivory, too. She —Lady Saffunwardo afterwards promising pay them three if they come along an' do what she tell 'em. They agreeing

---

*Sijui*, I don't know: the most aggravating word in Africa, except perhaps *bado kidogo*, which means "presently," "bye and bye," "in a little while."

quick! Byumby Tippoo Tib hearing bazaar talk an' sending me along too. She refuse to take me, all because German consul man knowing me formerly and not making good report, but Greek *bwana* he not caring and say to me to come along. Greek people very bad! No food—no money—nothing but swear an' kick an' call bad names—an' drunk nearly all the time!"

"What makes you think these three men know where the ivory is?" said the German voice. It was the voice of a man very used to questioning natives—self-assertive but calm—going straight each time to the point.

"They having map. Map having marks on it."

"How do you know?"

"She—Lady Saffunwardo go in their bedroom, stealing it last night."

"Did you see her take it?"

"Yes, *bwana.*"

"Did you see the marks on it?"

"No, *bwana.*"

"Then how do you know the marks were on it? Now, remember, don't lie to me!"

"Coutlass, him Greek man, standing on stairs keeping watch. Them three men you call fools all sitting in dining-room waiting because they thinking she come presently. She send maid to their room. Maid, fool woman, upset everything, finding nothing. 'No,' she say, 'no map—no money—no anything in here.' An' Lady Saffunwardo she very angry an' say, 'Come out o' there! Let me look!' And Lady Saffunwardo going in, but maid not coming out, an' they both search. Then Lady Saffunwardo saying all at once, 'Here it is. Didn't you see this?' An' the maid answering, 'Oh, that! That nothing but just ordinary pocket map! That not it!' But Lady Saffunwardo she opening the map, an' make little scream, an' say, 'Idiot! This is it! Look! See! See the marks!' So, *bwana,* I then knowing must be marks on map!"

"Good. What did she do with it?"

"*Sijui.*"

"I told you not to dare say *'sijui'* to me!"

"How should I know, *bwana,* what she doing with it?"

"Could you steal it?"

"No, *bwana!*"

"Why not?"

"You not knowing that woman! No man daring steal f'm her! She very terrible!"

"If I offered you a hundred rupees could you steal it?"

"*Sijui, bwana.*"

"I told you not to use that word!"

"*Bwana,* I—"

"Could you steal it?"

"Maybe."

"That is no answer!"

"Say that again about hundred rupees!"

"I will give you a hundred rupees if you bring me that map and it proves to be what you say."

"I go. I see. I try. Hundred rupees very little money!"

"It's all you'll get, you black rascal! And you know what you'll get if you fail! You know me, don't you? You understand my way? Steal that map and bring it here, and I shall give you a hundred rupees. Fail, and you shall have a hundred lashes, and what Ahmed and Abdullah and Seydi got in addition! The hundred lashes first, and the ant-hill afterward! You're not fool enough to think you can escape me, I suppose?"

"No, *bwana.*"

"Then go and get the map!"

"But afterward, what then? She very *gali* * woman."

"Nonsense! Steal the map and bring it here to me. Then I've other work for you. Are you a renegade Muhammedan?"

"No, *bwana!* No, no! Never! I'm good Moslem."

"Very well. Back to your old business with you! Preach Islam up and down the country. Go and tell all the tribes in British territory that the Germans are coming soon to establish an empire of Islam in Africa! Good pay and easy living! Does that suit you?"

---

*Gali,* same as Hindustani *kali*—cruel, hard, fierce, terrible.

"Yes, *bwana*. How much pay?"

"I'll tell you when you bring the map. Now be going!"

Hassan went, after a deal of polite salaaming. Then boys began bringing the German's breakfast, and unless I chose to confess myself an eavesdropper it became my business to be in the tent ahead of them. So I strode forward as if just arrived and purposely tripped over a tent-rope, stumbling under the awning with a laugh and an apology.

"Who are you?" demanded the German without rising. He had the splay shovel beard described to us in Zanzibar —a big dark man, sitting in the doorway of a tent all hung with guns, skins and antlers. He was in night-shirt and trousers—bare feet—but with a helmet on the back of his head.

"A visitor," I answered, "staying at the hotel—out for a morning shot at something—had no luck—got nothing—saw your tents in the distance, and came out of curiosity to find out who you are."

"My name is Professor Schillingschen," he answered, still without getting up. There was no other chair near the awning, so I had to remain standing. I told him my name, hoping that Hassan had either not done so already, or else that he might have so bungled the pronunciation as to make it unrecognizable. I detected no sign of recognition on Schillingschen's face.

The boys reached the tent with his breakfast, and one of them dragged a chair from inside the tent for me. I sat down on it without waiting for the professor to invite me.

"I'm tired," I said, untruthfully, minded to refuse an invitation to eat, but interested to see whether he would invite me or not.

"Have you any friends at the hotel?" he asked, looking up at me darkly under the bushiest eyebrows I ever saw.

"I've got friends wherever I go," I answered. "I make friends."

"Are you going far?" he demanded, holding out a foot for his boy to pull a stocking on.

"That depends," I said.

"On what?"

"On whether I get employment."

I said that at random, without pausing to think what impression I might create. He pulled the night-shirt off over his head, throwing the helmet to the ground, and sat like a great hairy gorilla for the boy to hang day-clothes on him. He had the hairiest breast and arms I ever saw, hung with lumpy muscles that heightened his resemblance to an ape.

"I might give you work," he said presently, beginning to eat before the boy had finished dressing him.

"I want to travel," I said. "If I could find a job that would take me up and down the length and breadth of this land, that would suit me finely."

"That is the kind of a man I want," he said, eying me keenly. "I have a German, but I need an Englishman. Do you speak native languages?"

"Scarcely a word."

To my surprise he nodded approval at that answer.

"I have parties of natives traveling all over the country gathering folk lore, and ethnographical particulars, but they get into a village and sit down for whole weeks at a time, drawing pay for doing nothing. I need an Englishman to go with them and keep them moving."

"All well and good," I said, "but I understand the government is not in favor of white men traveling about at random."

"But I am known to the government," he answered. "I have been accorded facilities because of my professional standing. Have you references you can give me?"

"No," I said. "No references."

I thought that would stump him, but on the contrary he looked rather pleased.

"That is good. References are too frequently evidence of back-stairs influence."

All this while he kept eying me between mouthfuls. Whenever I seemed to look away his eyes fairly burned holes in me. Whenever food got in his beard (which was frequently) he used the napkin more as a shield behind which to take stock

of me than as a means of getting clean again. By the time
his breakfast was finished his beard was a beastly mess, but
he probably had my features from every angle fixed indelibly
in his memory. The sensation was that I had been analyzed
and card indexed.

"I pay good wages," he remarked, and then stuck his face,
beard and all, into the basin of warm water his boy had
brought. "Where did you get that rifle?" he demanded, spluttering, and combing the beard out with his fingers.

It was on the tip of my tongue to say "At Zanzibar," but
as that might have started him on a string of questions as to
how I came to that place and whom I knew there, I tem-
porized.

"Oh, I bought it from a man."

"That is no answer!" he retorted.

If I had been possessed of much inclination to play deep
games and match wits with big rascals I suppose I would
have answered him civilly and there and then learned more
of his purpose. But I was not prepossessed by his charms or
respectful of his claim to superiority. The German type of
super-education never did impress me as compatible with
good breeding or good sense, and it annoyed me to have to
lie to him.

"It's all the answer you'll get!" I said.

"Where is your license for it?" he growled.

The game began to amuse me.

"None of your business!" I answered.

"How long have you been in the country?"

"Since I came," I said.

"And you have no license! You have been out shooting. A
lucky thing you came to my camp and not to some other
man's! The game laws are very strict!"

He spoke then to a boy who was standing behind me, giving
him very careful directions in a language of which I did not
know one word. The boy went away.

"The last man who went shooting near Nairobi without a
license," he said, "tried to excuse himself before the magis-

trate by claiming ignorance of the law. He was fined a thousand rupees and sentenced to six months in jail!"

"Very severe!" I said.

"They are altogether too severe," he answered. "I hope you have killed nothing. It is good you came first to me. You would better stand that rifle over here in the corner of my tent. To walk back to the hotel with it over your shoulder would be dangerous."

"I've taken bigger chances than that," said I.

"If you have shot nothing, then it is not so serious," he said, disappearing behind a curtain into the recesses of his tent.

He stayed in there for about ten minutes. I had about made up my mind to walk away when four of his boys approached the tent from behind, and one of them cried *"Hodi!"* The boy to whom he had given directions across my shoulder was not among them.

They threw the buck down near my feet, and he came out from the gloomy interior and stared at it. He asked them questions rapidly in the native tongue, and they answered, pointing at me.

"They say you shot it," he told me, stroking his great beard alternately with either hand.

"Then they lie!" I answered.

"Let me see that rifle!" he said, reaching out an enormous freckled fist to take it.

I saw through his game at last. It would have been the easiest thing in the world to extract a cartridge from the clip in the magazine and claim afterward that I had fired it away. Evidently he proposed to get me in his power, though for just what reason he was so determined to make use of me rather than any one else was not so clear.

"So I shot the buck, did I?" I asked.

"Those four natives say they saw you shoot it."

"Then it's mine?"

He nodded.

"It's heavy," I said, "but I expect I can carry it."

I took the buck by the hind legs and swung myself under it.

It weighed more than a hundred pounds, but the African climate had not had time enough to sap my strength or destroy sheer pleasure in muscular effort.

"What's mine's my own!" I laughed. "You gave me something to eat after all! Good day, and good riddance!"

The boys tried to prevent my carrying the buck away.

"Come back!" growled the professor. "I will take responsibility for that buck and save you from punishment. Bring it back! Lay it down!"

But I continued to walk away, so he ordered his boys to take the carcass from me. I laid it down and threatened them with my butt end. He brought his own rifle out and threatened me with that. I laughed at him, bade him shoot if he dared, offered him three shots for a penny, and ended by shouldering the buck again and walking off.

Meat was cheap in Nairobi in those days, so the owner of the hotel was not so delighted as I expected. He reprimanded me for being late for breakfast, and told me I was lucky to get any. Fred and Will had waited for me, and while we ate alone and I told them the story of my morning's adventure a police officer in khaki uniform tied up his mule outside and clattered in.

"Whose buck is that hanging outside the kitchen?" he demanded.

"There's some doubt about it," I said. "I've been accused of being the owner."

"Then you're the man I want. The court sits at nine. You'd better be there, or you'll be fetched!"

He placed in my hand what proved to be a summons to appear before the district court that morning on the charge of carrying an unregistered rifle and shooting game without a license. Two native policemen he had with him took down the buck from the hook outside the kitchen door and carried it off as evidence.

We finished our breakfast in great contentment, and strode off arm-in-arm to find the court-house, feeling as if we were going to a play—perhaps a mite indignant, as if the subject of the play were one we did not quite approve, but perfectly certain of a good time.

The court was crowded. The bearded professor, his four boys, and two other natives were there, as well as several English officials, all apparently on very good terms indeed with Schillingschen.

As we entered the court under the eyes of a hostile crowd I heard one official say to the man standing next him:

"I hope he'll make an example of this case. If he doesn't every new arrival in this country will try to take the law in his own hands. I hope he fines him the limit!"

"Give me your hunting-knife, Fred!" said I, and Fred laughed as he passed it to me. For the moment I think he thought I meant to plunge it into the too talkative official's breast.

First they called a few township cases. A drunken Muhammedan was fined five rupees, and a Hindu was ordered to remove his garbage heap before noon. Three natives were ordered to the chain-gang for a week for fighting, and a Masai charged with stealing cattle was remanded. Then my case was called, very solemnly, by a magistrate scarcely any older than myself.

The police officer acted as prosecutor. He stated that "acting on information received" he had proceeded to the hotel, outside of which he saw a buck hanging (buck produced in evidence) ; that he had entered the hotel, found me at breakfast, and that I had not denied having shot the buck. He called his two colored *askaris* to prove that, and they reeled off what they had to say with the speed of men who had been thoroughly rehearsed. Then he put the German on the stand, and Schillingschen, with a savage glare at me, turned on his verbal artillery. He certainly did his worst.

"This morning," he announced, after having been duly sworn on the Book, "that young man whose name I do not know approached my tent while I was dressing. The sound of a rifle being fired had awakened me earlier than usual. He carried a rifle, and I put two and two together and concluded he had shot something. Not having seen him ever before, and he standing before my tent, I asked him his name. He refused to tell me, and that made me suspicious. Then came my four boys carrying a buck, which they assured me they had seen him shoot. I asked him whether he had a license to shoot game, and he at once threatened to shoot me if I did not mind my own business. Therefore, I sent a note to the police at once."

His four boys were then put on the stand in turn, and told their story through an interpreter. Their words were identical. If the interpreter spoke truth one account did not vary from the next in the slightest degree, and that fact alone should have aroused the suspicion of any unprejudiced judge.

Having the right to cross-examine, I asked each in turn whether the rifle I had brought with me to court was the same they had seen me using. They asserted it was. Then I recalled the German and asked him the same question. He also replied in the affirmative. I asked him how he knew. He said he recognized the mark on the butt where the varnish had been chafed away.

Then I handed the hunting knife I had borrowed from Fred to the police officer and demanded that he have the bullet cut out of the buck's carcass. The court could not object to that, so under the eyes of at least fifty witnesses a flattened Mauser bullet was produced. I called attention to the fact that my rifle was a Lee-Enfield that could not possibly have fired a Mauser bullet. The court was young and very dignified—examined the bullet and my rifle—and had to be convinced.

"Very well," was the verdict on that count, "it is proved that you did not shoot this particular buck, unless the police have evidence that you used a different rifle."

The policeman confessed that he had no evidence along that line, so the first charge was dismissed.

"But you are charged," said the magistrate, "with carrying an unregistered rifle, and shooting without a license."

For answer I produced my certificate of registration and the big game license we had paid for in Mombasa.

"Why didn't you say so before?" demanded the magistrate.

"I wasn't asked," said I.

"Case dismissed!" snapped his honor, and the court began to empty.

"Don't let it stop there!" urged Will excitedly. "That Heinie and his boys have all committed perjury; charge them with it!"

I turned to the police officer.

"I charge all those witnesses with perjury!" I said.

"Oh," he laughed, "you can't charge natives with that. If the law against perjury was strictly enforced the jails wouldn't hold a fiftieth of them! They don't understand."

"But that blackguard with a beard—that rascal Schillingschen understands!" said I. "Arrest him! Charge him with it!"

"That's for the court to do," he answered. "I've no authority."

The magistrate had gone.

"Who is the senior official in this town?" I demanded.

"There he goes," he answered. "That man in the white suit with the round white topee is the collector."

So we three followed the collector to his office, arriving about two minutes after the man himself. The Goanese clerk had been in the court, and recognized me. He had not stayed to hear the end.

"Fines should be paid in the court, not here!" he intimated rudely.

We wasted no time with him but walked on through, and the collector greeted us without obvious cordiality. He did not ask us to sit down.

"My friend here has come to tell you about that man Schillingschen," said Fred.

"I suppose you mean Professor Schillingschen?"

The collector was a clean-shaven man with a blue jowl that suffered from blunt razors, and a temper rendered raw by native cooking. But he had photos of feminine relations and a little house in a dreary Midland street on his desk, and was no doubt loyal to the light he saw. I wished we had Monty with us. One glimpse of the owner of a title that stands written in the Doomsday Book would have outshone the halo of Schillingschen's culture.

I rattled off what I had to say, telling the story from the moment I started to follow Hassan from the hotel down to the end, omitting nothing.

"Schillingschen is worse than a spy. He's a black-hearted schemer. He's planning to upset British rule in this Protectorate and make it easy for the Germans to usurp!"

"This is nonsense!" the collector interrupted. "Professor Schillingschen is the honored friend of the British government. He came to us here with the most influential backing —letters of introduction from very exalted personages, I assure you! Professor Schillingschen is one of the most, if not the most, learned ethnologists in the world to-day. How dare you traduce him!"

"But you heard him tell lies in court!" I gasped. "You were there. You heard his evidence absolutely disproved. How do you explain that away?"

"I don't attempt to! The explanation is for you to make!" he answered. "The fact that he did not succeed in proving his case against you is nothing in itself! Many a case in court is lost from lack of proper evidence! And one more matter! Lady Isobel Saffren Waldon is staying—or rather, I should say, was staying at the hotel. She is now staying at my house. She complains to me of very rude treatment at the hands of you three men—insolent treatment I should call it!. I can assure you that the way to get on in this Protectorate is not to behave like cads toward ladies of title! I understand that her maid is afraid to be caught alone by any one of you, and that Lady Saffren Waldon herself feels scarcely any safer!"

Fred and I saw the humor of the thing, and that enabled us to save Will from disaster. There never was a man more respectful of women than Will. He would even get off the sidewalk for a black woman, and would neither tell nor laugh at the sort of stories that pass current about women in some smoking-rooms. His hair bristled. His ears stuck out on either side of his head.. He leaned forward—laid one strong brown hand on the desk—and shook his left fist under the collector's nose.

"You poor boob!" he exploded. Then he calmed himself. "I'm sorry for your government if you're the brightest jewel it has for this job! That Jane will use everything you've got except the squeal! Great suffering Jemima! Your title is collector, is it? Do you collect bugs by any chance? You act like it! So help you two men and a boy, a bughouse is where I believe you belong! Come along, fellows, he'll bite us if we stay!"

"Be advised," said the collector, leaning back in his chair and sneering. "Behave yourselves! This is no country for taking chances with the law!"

"Remember Courtney's advice," said Fred when we got outside. "Suppose we give him a few days to learn the facts about Lady Isobel, and then go back and try him again?"

"Say!" answered Will, stopping and turning to face us. "What d'you take me for? I like my meals. I like three squares a day, and tobacco, and now and then a drink. But if this was the Sahara, and that man had the only eats and drinks, I'd starve."

"Telling him the truth wouldn't be accepting favors from him," counseled Fred.

"I wouldn't tell him the time!"

That attitude—and Will insisted that all the officials in the land would prove alike—limited our choice, for unless we were to allay official suspicion it would be hopeless to get away northward. Southward into German East seemed the only way to go; there was apparently no law against travel in that direction. On our way to the hotel we passed Coutlass, striding along smirking to himself, headed toward the office from which we had just come.

"I'll bet you," said Will, "he's off to get an ammunition permit, and permission to go where he damned well pleases! I'll bet he gets both! This government's the limit!"

We laughed, but Will proved more than half right. Coutlass did get ammunition. Lady Saffren Waldon's influence was already strong enough for that. He did not ask for leave to go anywhere for the simple reason that his movements depended wholly on ours—a fact that developed later.

At the hotel there was a pleasant surprise for us. A squarely-built, snub-nosed native, not very dark skinned but very ugly —his right ear slit, and almost all of his left ear missing— without any of the brass or iron wire ornaments that most of the natives of the land affect, but possessed of a Harris tweed shooting jacket and, of all unexpected things, boots that he carried slung by the laces from his neck—waited for us, squatting with a note addressed to Fred tied in a cleft stick.

It does not pay to wax enthusiastic over natives, even when one suspects they bring good news. We took the letter from him, told him to wait, and went on in. Once out of the man's hearing Fred tore the letter open and read it aloud to us.

"Herewith my Kazimoto," it ran. "Be good to him. It occurred to me that you might not care after all to linger in Nairobi, and it seemed hardly fair to keep the boy from getting a good job simply because he could make me comfortable for the remainder of a week. So, as there happened to be a special train going up I begged leave for him to ride in the caboose. He is a splendid gun-bearer. He never funks, but reloads coolly under the most nerve-trying conditions. He has his limitations, of course, but I have found him brave and faithful, and I pass him along to you with confidence.

"And by the way: he has been to Mount Elgon with me. I was not looking for buried ivory, but he knows where the caves are *in which anything might be!*

"Wishing you all good luck,          Yours truly,
                                        "F. COURTNEY."

For the moment we felt like men possessed of a new horse apiece. We were for dashing out to look the acquisition over. But Will checked us.

"Recall what Courtney said about a dog?" he asked. "We can't all own him!"

Fred sat down. "Ex-missionaries own dice," he announced. "That's how they come to be ex! You'll find them in the little box on the shelf, Will. We'll throw a main for Kazimoto!"

"I know a better gamble than that."

"Name it, America."

"Bring the coon in and have him choose."

So I went out and felt tempted to speak cordially to the homeless ugly black man—to give him a hint that he was welcome. But it is a fatal mistake to make a "soft" impression on even the best natives at the start.

"*Karibu!*"* I said gruffly when I had looked him over, using one of the six dozen Swahili words I knew as yet.

He arose with the unlabored ease that I have since learned to look for in all natives worth employing; and followed me indoors. Will and Fred were seated in judicial attitudes, and I took a chair beside them.

"What is your name?" demanded Fred.

"Kazimoto."

"Um-m! That means 'Work-like-the-devil.' Let us hope you live up to it. Your former master gives you a good character."

"Why not, *bwana?* My spirit is good."

"Do you want work?"

"Yes."

"How much money do you expect to get?"

"*Sijui!*"

"Don't say '*sijui*'!" I cut in, remembering Schillingschen's method.

"Six rupees a month and *posho*," he said promptly. *Posho* means rations, or money in lieu of rations.

"Don't you rather fancy yourself?" suggested Fred with a perfectly straight face.

"Say two dollars a month all told!" Will whispered to me behind his hand.

"I am a good gun-bearer!" the native answered. "My spirit is good. I am strong. There is nobody better than me as a gun-bearer!"

"We happen to want a headman," answered Fred. "Have you ever been headman?"

---

*Karibu, enter, come in.

"No."

"Would you like to be?"

"Yes."

"Are you able?"

"Surely."

"Choose, then. Which of us would you like to work for?"

"You!" he answered promptly, pointing at Fred.

It was on the tip of the tongue of every one of us to ask him instantly why, but that would have been too rank indiscretion. It never pays to seem curious about a native's personal reasons, and it was many weeks before we knew why he had made up his mind in advance to choose Fred and not either of us for his master.

His choice made, and the offer of his services accepted, he took over Fred forthwith—demanded his keys—found out which our room was—went over our belongings and transferred the best of our things into Fred's bag and the worst of his into ours—remade Fred's bed after a mysterious fashion of his own, taking one of my new blankets and one of Will's in exchange for Fred's old ones—cleaned Fred's guns thoroughly after carefully abstracting the oil and waste from our gun-cases and transferring them to Fred's—removed the laces from my shooting boots and replaced them with Fred's knotted ones—sharpened Fred's razors and shaved himself with mine (to the enduring destruction of its once artistic edge)—and departed in the direction of the bazaar.

He returned at the end of an hour and a half with a motley following of about twenty, arrayed in blankets of every imaginable faded hue and in every stage of dirtiness.

"You wanting cook," he announced. "These three making cook."

He waved three nondescripts to the front, and we chose a tall Swahili because he grinned better than the others. "Although," as Fred remarked, "what the devil grinning has to do with cooking is more than anybody knows." The man, whose name was Juma, turned out to be an execrable cook, but as he never left off grinning under any circumstances (and it would have been impossible to imagine circumstances worse than those we warred with later on) we never had the heart to dismiss him.

After that, Will and I selected a servant apiece who were destined forever to wage war on Kazimoto in hopeless efforts to prevent his giving Fred the best end of everything. Mine was a Baganda who called himself Matches, presumably because his real name was unpronounceable. Will chose a Malindi boy named Tengeneza (and that means arrange in order, fix, make over, manage, mend—no end of an ominous name!). They were both outclassed from the start by Kazimoto, but to add to the handicap he insisted that since he was a headman he would need some one to help look after Fred at times when other duties would monopolize his attention. He himself picked out an imp of mischief whose tribe I never ascertained, but who called himself Simba (lion), and there and then Simba departed up-stairs to steal for Fred whatever was left of value among Will's effects and mine.

We had scarcely got used to the idea of once more having a savage apiece to wait on us when Kazimoto turned up at the door with a string of porters and a Goanese railway clerk. We had left our tents and heavy baggage checked at the station, but had said nothing about them to our new headman; however, he had made inquiries and worked out a plan on his own account. The railway clerk asked to know whether he should let Kazimoto have our things.

"Why?" demanded Fred.

"This hotel no good!" announced Kazimoto. "No place for boys. Heap too many plenty people. Pitching camp, that good!"

"All right," said Fred, and then and there paid our baggage charges.

Presently Brown of Lumbwa, who had spent most of the daylight hours in the little corrugated iron bar run by a Goanese in the bazaar, came lurching past the township camping ground, and viewed Kazimoto with his gang pitching our tents. He asked questions, but could get no information, so came along to us.

"Where you schaps going?" he demanded, leaning against

the wall. Fred took advantage of the opportunity and examined him narrowly as to his knowledge of German East and ways of getting there. He was in an aggravating mood that made at one moment a very well of information of him, and at the next a mere garrulous ass.

"Come along o' me t' Lumbwa," was his final word on the matter. "I'll put you on a road nobody knows an' nobody uses!"

We spent that night under canvas and talked the matter out. The usual way to reach Lumbwa was to wait for a freight or construction train and beg leave to ride on that, for as yet no passenger trains were running regularly on the western section of the line. But there was no rule against traveling anywhere south of the equator, and it was our purpose to march down into German East without any one being the wiser.

The next morning we imagined Brown was sober and sorry enough to hold his tongue, so, without going into details with him, we agreed to go with him "some of the way," and Fred spent the whole of that morning in the bazaar buying loads of food and general supplies. Will and I engaged porters, and with Kazimoto's aid as interpreter, had fifty ready to march that afternoon.

The whole trick of starting on a journey is to start. If you only make a mile or two the first day you have at least done better than stand still; loads have been apportioned and porters broken in to some extent; you have broken the spell of inertia, and hereafter there is less likely to be trouble. We made up our minds to get away that afternoon, and I was sent back to the hotel to find Brown, who had gone for his belongings.

If Brown had stayed sober all might have been well, but his headache and feeling of unworthiness had been too much for him and I found him with a straw in the neck of a bottle of whisky alternately laying down law to Georges Coutlass and drinking himself into a state of temporary bliss.

"You Greeks dunno nothin'!" he asserted as I came in. "You never did know nothin', an' you're never goin' to know

nothin'! 'Cause why? I'll tell you. Simply because I ain't
goin' to tell! I'm mum, I am! When s'mother gents an' me
have business, that's our business—see! None o' your business—'ss our business, an' I'm not goin' to tell you Greeks
nothin' about where we're off to, nor why, nor when. An' you
put that in your pipe an' smoke it!"

I sat in the dining-room for a while, hoping that the Greek
would go away; but as Brown was fast drinking himself into
a condition when he could not have been moved except on a
stretcher, and was momentarily edging closer to an admission
of all he knew or guessed about our intention, I took the bull
by the horns at last—snatched away his whisky bottle, and
walked off with it.

He came after me swearing like a trooper, and his own porters, who had been waiting for more than an hour beside his
loads, trailed along after him. Once in our camp we made a
hammock for him out of a blanket tied to a pole, and made
him over to two porters with the promise that they would get
no supper if they lost him. Then we started—uphill, toward
the red Kikuyu heights, where settlers were already trying to
grow potatoes for which there was no market, and onions that
would only run to seed.

To our left rear and right front were the highest mountain
ranges in Africa. Before us was the pass through which the
railway threaded over the wide high table-land before dipping
downward to Victoria Nyanza. On our left front was all Kikuyu country, and after that Lumbwa, and native reserves,
and forest, and swamp, and desert, and the German boundary.

We made a long march of it that first day, and camped after
dark within two miles of Kikuyu station. Most of the scrub
thereabouts was castor oil plant, that makes very poor fuel;
yet there were lions in plenty that roared and scouted around
us even before the tents were pitched.

Nobody got much sleep that night, although the porters
were perfectly indifferent to the risk of snoozing on the watch.
Kazimoto produced a thing called a *kiboko*—a whip of hippo-
potamus-hide a yard and a half long, and with the aid of that
and Will's good humor we constituted a yelling brigade, whose

business was to make the welkin ring with godless noises whenever a lion came close enough to be dangerous.

I made up a signal party of all our personal boys with all our lanterns, swinging them in frantic patterns in the darkness in a way to terrify the very night itself. Fred played his concertina nearly all night long, and when dawn came, though there were tracks of lions all about the camp we were only tired and sleepy. Nobody was missing; nobody killed.

We never again took lions so seriously, although we always built fires about the camp in lion country when that was possible. Partly by dint of carelessness that brought no ill results, and partly from observation we learned that where game is plentiful lions are more curious than dangerous, and that unless something should happen to enrage them, or the game has gone away and they are hungry, they are likely to let well alone.

If there are dogs in camp—and we bought three terrier pups that morning from a settler at Kikuyu—leopards are likely to be more troublesome than lions. The leopards seemed to yearn for dog-meat much as Brown of Lumbwa yearned for whisky.

The journey to Lumbwa is one of the pleasantest I remember. We took Brown's supply of whisky from him, locked it up with our own, sent him ahead in the hammock, and kept him at work as guide by promises of whisky for supper if he did his duty, and threats of mere cold water if he failed.

"But water rots my stomach!" he objected.

"Lead on, then!" was the invariable, remorseless answer. So Brown led.

Until we reached Naivasha with its strange lake full of hippo at an elevation so great that the mornings are frosty (and that within sight of the line) there was never a day that we were once out of sight of game from dawn to dark. When we awoke the morning mist would scatter slowly and betray sleepy herds of antelope, that would rise leisurely, stand staring at us, suddenly become suspicious, and then gallop off until the whole plain was a panorama of wheeling herds, reminding one of the cavalry maneuvers at Aldershot when the

Guards regiments were pitted against the regular cavalry—all riding and no wits.

Although we had to shoot enough meat for ourselves and men, we never once took advantage of those surprise parties in the early morning, preferring to stalk warier game at the end of a long march. The rains were a thing of the past, and we seldom troubled to pitch tents but slept under the stars with a sensation that the universe was one vast place of peace.

Occasionally we reached an elevation from which we could look down and see men toiling to build the railway, that already reached Nyanza after the unfinished fashion of work whose chief aim is making a showing. Profits, performances were secondary matters; that railway's one purpose was to establish occupation of the head waters of the Nile and refute the German claim to prior rights there. At irregular intervals trains already went down to the lake, and passengers might ride on suffrance; but we deluded ourselves with the belief that by marching we threw enemies off the scent. It was pure delusion, but extremely pleasant while it lasted. Where Africa is green and high she is a lovely land to march across.

Brown grew sober on the trip, as if approaching his chosen home gave him a sense of responsibility. His own reason for preferring the march to a ride in a construction train was simple:

"Every favor you ask o' gov'ment, boys, leaves one less to fall back on in a pinch! Ask not, and they'll forget some o' your peccadillos. Ask too often, and one day when you really need a kindness you'll find the Bank o' Good Hope bu'sted! And, believe me, boys, that 'ud be a hell of a predicament for a poor sufferin' settler to find himself in!"

The approach to Lumbwa was over steep hilly grass land, between forests of cedar—perfect country, kept clean by a wind that smelt of fern and clover.

"You can tell we're gettin' near my place," said Brown, "by the number o' leopards that's about."

We had to keep our three pups close at heel all the time, and even at that we lost two of them. One was taken from between Will's feet as he sat in camp cleaning his rifle. All he heard was the dog's yelp, and all he saw was a flash of yellow as the leopard made for the boulders close at hand. The other was taken out of my tent. I had tied it to the tent pole, but the stout cord snapped like a hair and the darkness swallowed both leopard and its prey before I could as much as reach my rifle to get a shot.

"Splendid country for farmin'," Brown remarked. "Splendid. On'y you can't keep sheep because the leopards take 'em. An' you can't keep hens for the same reason. Nor yet cows, because the leopards get the calves—leastways, that's to say unless you watch out awful cautious. Nor yet you can't keep pigeons, 'cause the leopards take them too. I sent to England for fancy pigeons—a dozen of 'em. Leopards got all but one, so I put him in the loft above my own house, where it seemed to me 'tweren't possible for a leopard to get, supposin' he'd dared. Went away the next day for some shootin', an' lo and behold!—came back that evenin' to discover my cook an' three others carryin' on as if Kingdom Come had took place at last. Never heard or saw such a jamboree. The blamed leopard was up in the loft; and had eaten the pigeon, feathers and all, but couldn't get out again!

"What happened? Nothin'! I was that riled I didn't stop to think—fixed a bayonet on the old Martini the gov'ment supplies to settlers out of the depths of its wisdom an' generosity—climbed up by the same route the leopard took— invaded him—an' skewered him wi' the bayonet in the dark! I wouldn't do it again for a kingdom—but I won't buy more pigeons either!"

"What do you raise on your farm, then—pigs?" we asked.

"No, the leopards take pigs."

"What then?"

"Well—as I was explainin' to that Greek Georges Coutlass at Nairobi—there's a way of farmin' out your cattle among the natives that beats keepin' 'em yourself. The natives put 'em in the village pen o' nights; an' besides, they know all about the business.

"All you need do is give 'em a heifer calf once in a while, and they're contented. I keep a herd o' two hundred cows in a native village not far from my place. The natural increase o' them will make me well-to-do some day."

The day before we reached Brown's tiny homestead we heard a lot of shooting over the hill behind us.

"That'll be railway men takin' a day off after leopards," announced Brown with the air of a man who can not be mistaken.

Nevertheless, Fred and I went back to see, but could make out nothing. We lay on the top of the hill and watched for two or three hours, but although we heard rifle firing repeatedly we did not once catch sight of smoke or men. We marched into camp late that night with a feeling of foreboding that we could not explain but that troubled us both equally.

Once or twice in the night we heard firing again, as if somebody's camp not very far away was invaded by leopards, or perhaps lions. Yet at dawn there were no signs of tents. And when that night we arrived at Brown's homestead we seemed to have the whole world to ourselves.

Brown's house was a tiny wooden affair with a thick grass roof. It boasted a big fireplace at one end of the living-room, and a chimney that Brown had built himself so cunningly that smoke could go up and out but no leopards could come down.

He got very drunk that night to celebrate the home-coming, and stayed completely drunk for three days, we making use of his barn to give our porters a good rest. By day we shot enough meat for the camp, and at night we sat over the log fire, praying that Brown might sober up, Fred singing songs to his infernal concertina, and all the natives who could crowd in the doorway listening to him with all their ears. Fred made vast headway in native favor, and learned a lot of two languages at once.

Every day we sent Kazimoto and another boy exploring among the Lumbwa tribe, gathering information as to routes and villages, and it was Kazimoto who came running in breathless one night just as Brown was at last sobering up, with the news that some Greeks had swooped down on Brown's cattle, had wounded two or three of the villagers who herded them, and had driven the whole herd away southward.

That news sobered Brown completely. He took the bottle of whisky he had just brought up from the cellar and replaced it unopened.

"There's on'y one Greek in the world knew where my cattle were!" he announced grimly. "There's on'y one Greek I ever talked to about cattle. Coutlass, by the great horn spoon! The blackguard swore he was after you chaps—swore he didn't care nothing about me! What he did to you was none o' my business, o' course—an' I figured anyway as you could look out for yourselves! Not that I told the swine any o' your business, mind! Not me! I was so sure he was gunnin' for you that I told him my own business to throw him off your track! And now the devil goes an' turns on me!"

He got down his rifle and began overhauling it, feverishly, yet with a deliberate care that was curious in a man so recently drunk. While he cleaned and oiled he gave orders to his own boys; and what with having servants of our own and having to talk to them mostly in the native tongue, we were able to understand pretty well the whole of what he said.

"You're not going to start after them to-night?" Fred objected. But he and Will were also already overhauling weapons, for the second time that evening. (It is religion with the true hunter never to eat supper until his rifle is cleaned and oiled.) I got my own rifle down from the shelf over Brown's stone mantelpiece.

"What d'you take me for?" demanded Brown. "There's one pace they'll go at, an' that's the fastest possible. There's one place they'll head for, an' that's German East. They can't march faster than the cattle, an' the cattle'll have to eat. Maybe they'll drive 'em all through the first night, and on into the next day; but after that they'll have to rest 'em an' graze 'em a while. That's when we'll begin to gain. The tireder the cattle get, the faster we'll overhaul 'em, for we can eat while we're marchin', which the cattle can't! You chaps just stay here an' look after my farm till I come back!"

"You mean you propose to go alone after them?" asked Fred.

"Why not? Whose cattle are they?"

He was actually disposed to argue the point.

"Man alive, there'll be shootin'!" he insisted. "If they once get over the border with all those cattle, the Germans'll never hand 'em over until every head o' cattle's gone. They'll fine 'em, an' arrest 'em, an' trick 'em, an' fine 'em again until the Germans own the herd all legal an' proper—an' then they'll chase the Greeks back to British East for punishment same as they always do. What good 'ud that be to me? No, no! Me— I'm going to catch 'em this side o' the line, or else bu'st—an' I won't be too partic'lar where the line's drawn either! There's maybe a hundred miles to the south o' their line that the Germans don't patrol more often than once in a leap-year. If I catch them Greeks in any o' that country, I'm going to kid myself deliberate that it's British East, and act accordin'!"

At last we convinced him, although I don't remember how, for he was obstinate from the aftermath of whisky, that we would no more permit him to go alone than he would consider abandoning his cattle. Then we had to decide who should follow with our string of porters, for if forced marching was in order it was obvious that we should far outdistance our train.

We invited Brown to follow with all the men while we three skirmished ahead, but he waxed so apoplectically blasphemous at the very thought of it that Fred assured him the proposal was intended for a joke. Then we argued among ourselves, coaxed, blarneyed, persuaded, and tried to bribe one another. Finally, all else failing, we tossed a coin for it, odd man out, and Fred lost.

So Brown, Will Yerkes and I, with Kazimoto, our two personal servants, and six boys to carry one tent for the lot of us and food and cooking pots, started off just as the moon rose over the nearest cedars, and laughed at Fred marshaling the sleepy porters by lamplight in the open space between the house and barn. He was to follow as fast as the loaded porters could be made to travel, and with that concertina of his to spur them on there was little likelihood of losing touch.

But the rear-guard, when it comes to pursuing a retreating enemy, is ever the least alluring place.

"You've got all the luck," he shouted. "Make the most of it or I'll never gamble on the fall of a coin again!"

That pursuit was a journey of accidents, chapter after chapter of them in such close sequence that the whole was a nightmare without let-up or reason. I began the book by falling into an elephant pit.

Before we had gone a mile in the dark we stood in doubt as to whether the most practicable trail went right or left. Brown set his own indecision down frankly to the whisky that had muddled him. Even Kazimoto, who had passed that way three times, did not know for certain. So I went forward to scout—stepped into the deep shadow of some jungle—trod on nothing—threw the other foot forward to save myself—and fell downward into blackness for an eternity.

I brought up at last unhurt in the trash and decaying vegetation at the bottom of a pit, and looked up to see the stars in a rough parallelogram above me, whose edge I guessed was more than thirty feet above my head. I started to dig my way out, but the crumbling sides fell in and threatened to bury me alive unless I kept still. So I shouted until my lungs ached, but without result. I suppose the noise went trumpeting upward out of the hole and away to the clouds and the stars. At any rate, Will and Brown swore afterward they never heard it.

I was fifteen minutes in the hole that very likely had held many an elephant with his legs wedged together under him until the poor brute perished of thirst, before it occurred to me to fire my rifle. I fired several shots when I did think of it; but we had agreed on no system of signals, and instead of coming to find me at once, the other two cursed me for wasting time shooting at leopards in the dark instead of scouting for the track. I used twenty cartridges before they came to see what sort of battle I was waging, and with the last shot I nearly blew Brown's helmet off as he stooped over the hole to look down in.

Then there were more precious minutes wasted while someone cut a long pole for me to swarm up, and at the end of that time, when I stood on firm ground at last and wiped the blood from hands and knees, we were no wiser about the proper direction to take.

The next accident was a little before midnight. Will Yerkes was leading, I following, next the boys, and Brown bringing up the rear (for in those wild hills there is never a good track wide enough for two men to march abreast. Even the cattle proceed in single file unless driven furiously.) Will came on a leopard devouring its kill, a fat buck, in the midst of the track in the moonlight, and the brute resented the interruption of his meal. It slunk into the shadows before Will could get a shot at it, and for the next two hours followed us, slinking from shadow to shadow, snarling and growling. It plainly intended murder, but which of us was to be the victim, and when, there was no means of guessing, so that the nerves of all of us were tortured every time the brute approached.

We wasted at least thirty cartridges on futile efforts to guess his whereabouts in velvet black shadows, and Brown went through all the stages from simple nervousness to fear, and then to frenzy, until we feared he would shoot one of us in frantic determination to ring the leopard's knell.

At last the brute did rush in, and of course where least expected. He seized one of our porters by the shoulder, his claws doing more damage than his teeth. I shot him by thrusting my rifle into his ear, and although that dropped him instantly his claws, in the dying spasm and by the weight of his fall, tore wounds in the man's arm eighteen or twenty inches long.

One of the things we did have with us was bandages. But it took time to attend to the man's wounds properly by lamp and moonlight, and after that he could neither march fast, nor was there anywhere to leave him.

So just before dawn Fred came up with us, and was more pleased at our discomfiture than sympathetic. He told off two men to carry the injured porter to a mission station more than a day's march away, and redistributed the loads. Then we went on again, once more placing rock, hill, and cedar forest between us and our supply column, this time with Fred's counsel ringing in our ears.

"Better send for nursemaids and perambulators, and have yourselves pushed!"

At noon that day we found the track of the driven cattle, and soon after that came on the half-devoured carcass of a heifer that the Greeks had shot, presumably because it could not march, and perhaps with the added reason that freshly-killed meat would draw off leopards and hyenas and provide peace for a few miles.

Once on the trail it would not have been easy to lose it, except in the dark, for the Greek marauders were bent on speed and the driven cattle had smashed down the undergrowth in addition to leaving deep hoof-prints at every water-course.

The first suspicion that dawned on me of something more than mere freebooting on the part of Coutlass, was due to the discovery of hoof-prints of either mules or horses. I was marching alone in advance, and came on them beside a stream that was only apparently fordable in that one place. After making sure of what they were I halted to let Will and Brown catch up.

"Did Coutlass have money enough to buy mules for himself and gang?" wondered Will.

"That robber?" snorted Brown. "When Lady Saffren Waldon refused him tobacco money in the hotel he tried to borrow from me!"

"Where could he steal mules?" Will asked.

"Nowhere. Aren't any!"

"Horses, then?"

"He'd never take horses. They'd die."

"What are they riding, then?"

"Unless he stole trained zebras from the gov'ment farm at Naivasha," said Brown, "an' they're difficulter to ride 'an a greasy pole up-ended on a earthquake, he must ha' bought mules from the one man who has any to sell. And he lives t'other side o' Nairobi. There are none between there and here—none whatever. Zachariah Korn—him who owns mules —is too wide awake to be stolen from. He bought 'em, you take it from me, and paid twice what they were worth into the bargain."

"Then he bought them with her money!" said Will.

"If not Schillingschen's," said I.

"Or the Sultan of Zanzibar's," said Will, "or the German government's."

"But why? Why should she, or they, conspire at great expense and risk to steal Brown's cattle?"

"They'll figure," said Will, "that Brown is helping us, and therefore, Brown is an enemy. Prob'ly they surmise Brown is in league with us to show us a short cut to what we're after. If that's how they work it out, then they wouldn't need think much to conclude that putting Brown on the blink would hoodoo us. Maybe they allow that that much bad luck to begin with would unsettle Brown's friendly feelings for us. Anyway—somebody bought the mules—somebody stole the cattle—cattle are somewhere ahead. Let's hurry forward and see!"

We did hurry, but made disgustingly poor time. Once a dozen buffalo stampeded our tiny column. Our five porters dropped their loads, and the biggest old bull mistook our only tent for our captain's dead body and proceeded to play ball with it, tossing it and tearing it to pieces until at last Will got a chance for a shoulder shot and drilled him neatly. Two other bulls took to fighting in the midst of the excitement and we got both of them. Then the rest trotted off; so we packed the horns of the dead ones on the head of our free porter (for the tent he had carried was now utterly no use) and hastened on.

Once, in trying to make a cut that should have saved us ten or fifteen miles between two rivers, we fell shoulder-deep into a bog and only escaped after an hour's struggle during which we all but lost two porters. We had to retrace our steps and follow the Greek's route, only to have the mortification of seeing Fred and our column of supplies coming over the top of a rise not eight miles behind us.

Determined not to be overtaken by him a second time and treated to advice about nursemaids, we dispensed with sleep altogether for that night, and nearly got drowned at the second river.

We found a native who owned a thing he called a *mtungi*—a near-canoe, burned out of a tree-trunk. He assured us the ford was very winding (he drew a wiggly finger-mark in the mud by way of illustration) but that his boat would hold twice our number, and that he could take us over easily in the dark. In fact he swore he had ferried twice our number over on darker nights more than twenty or thirty times. He also said that he had taken the cattle over by the ford early that morning, and then had crossed over in the boat with two Greeks and a *bwana* Goa. He showed us the brass wire and beads they gave him in proof of that statement, and we began to put some faith in his tale.

So we all piled into his crazy boat with our belongings, and he promptly lost the way amid the twelve-foot grass—papyrus mostly—that divided the river into narrow streams and afforded protection to the most savagely hungry mosquitoes in the world. Our faces and hands were wet with blood in less than two minutes.

Presently, instead of finding bottom for his pole, he pushed us into deep water. The grass disappeared, and a ripple on the water lipping dangerously within three inches of our uneven gunwale proved that we were more or less in the main stream. We had enjoyed that sensation for about a minute, and were headed toward where we supposed the opposite bank must be, when a hippo in a hurry to breathe blew just beside us—saw, smelt, or heard us (it was all one to him)—and dived again.

I suppose in order to get his head down fast enough he shoved his rump up, and his great fat back made a wave that ended that voyage abruptly. Our three inches of broadside vanished. The canoe rocked violently, filled, turned over, and floated wrong side up.

"All the same," laughed Will, spluttering and spitting dirty water, "here's where the crocks get fooled! They don't eat me for supper!"

He was first on top of the overturned boat, and dragged

me up after him. Together we hauled up Brown, who could not swim but was bombastically furious and unafraid; and the three of us pulled out the porters and the fatuous boat's owner. The pole was floating near by, and I swam downstream and fetched it. When they had dragged me back on to the wreck the moon came out, and we saw the far bank hazily through mist and papyrus.

The boat floated far more steadily wrong side up, perhaps because we had lashed all our loads in place and they acted as ballast. Will took the pole and acted the part of Charon, our proper pilot contenting himself with perching on the rear end lamenting the ill-fortune noisily until Kazimoto struck him and threatened to throw him back into the water.

"They don't want a fool like you in the other world," he assured him. "You will die of old age!"

The papyrus inshore was high enough to screen the moon from us, and we had to hunt a passage through it in pitch darkness. Then, having found the muddy bank at last (and more trillions of mosquitoes) we had to drag the overturned boat out high and dry to rescue our belongings. And that was ticklish work, because most of the crocodiles, and practically all the largest ones, spend the night alongshore.

Matches were wet. We had no means of making a flare to frighten the monsters away. We simply had to "chance it" as cheerfully and swiftly as we could, and at the end of a half-hour's slimy toil we carried our muddied loads to the nearest high ground and settled down there for the night.

It would be mad exaggeration to say we camped. Wet to the skin—dirty to the verge of feeling suicidal—bitten by insects until the blood ran down from us—lost (for we had no notion where the end of the ford might be)—at the mercy of any prowling beasts that might discover us (for our rifle locks were fouled with mud)—we sat with chattering teeth and waited for the morning.

When the sun rose we found a village less than four hundred yards away and sent the boys down to it to unpack the loads and spread everything in the sun to dry, while we went down to the river again and washed our rifles. Then we dried and oiled them, and without a word of bargain or explanation, invaded the cleanest looking hut, lay down on the stamped clay floor, and slept. It was only clean-looking, that hut. It housed more myraids of fleas than the air outside supported "skeeters"; but we slept, unconscious of them all.

At four that afternoon we had the mortification of being roused by Fred's voice, and the dumping of loads as his sixty porters dropped their burdens inside the village stockade. He had scorned the ferry and crossed the ford on foot, making a prodigious splash to keep crocodiles away, and was as full of life and fun as a schoolboy on vacation.

"Wake up, you vorloopers!" he shouted. "Wake up! Shake off the fleas and come, and I'll show you something!"

He had already had the tale of our night's misfortune in detail from the owner of the only canoe (who claimed double pay on the ground that we had lost no loads in spite of overturning. "The last really white man who crossed lost *all* his loads!" he explained.)

"Come and I'll show you something you never saw before, you scouts!—you advance guard!—you line of skirmishers!"

Will hurled a lump of earth at him, and chased him to the river, where they wrestled, trying to throw each other in, until both were breathless. Then, when neither could make another effort:

"Look!" gasped Fred.

There was an island in mid-stream below where we must have crossed. The stream was straight, and from where we stood we could see more than half a mile of alluvial mud with an arm of the river on either side. The mud was white, not black—so white that it dazzled the eyes to look at it.

"Know what it is?" Fred panted.

We did not know, and it was no use guessing. It looked like burned lime, or else the secretions of about a billion birds; and there were no birds to speak of.

"Crocodile eggs!" said Fred.

We did not believe that. Even Brown did not believe it. There was no time to spare, but Brown out of curiosity agreed, so we took the absurd canoe and poled down to investigate. As we came nearer the solid white broke up into a myriad dots, and Fred's tale stood confirmed.

They were as long as two hens' eggs laid end to end, or longer. They lay in the sun in batches in every stage of incubation, and from almost every batch there were little crocodiles emerging, that made straight for the water. What worse monster preyed on them to keep their numbers down, or what disease took care of their prolixity we could not guess. Perhaps they ate one another, or just died of hunger. The owner of the boat vowed there were no fish left in the river, and that the crocodiles did not eat hippo unless it were first dead.

We took another tent from among Fred's loads, changed two of our porters for stronger ones, and went forward that evening; for it began to be obvious that the speed had been telling on the cattle. We passed two more dead heifers within a few miles of the river bank, and there were other signs that for all our long sleep we were gaining on them.

Perhaps the Greeks thought they had shaken off pursuit. Judging by the compass they were headed for the shore of Victoria Nyanza, where the grazing would be better, food for men would be purchaseable, and the number of villages closely spaced would make the task of night-herding vastly easier. There isn't a village in that part of Africa that is not proud to be a host to anybody's cattle, if only because the ownership of so much living wealth casts glory on all who come in contact with it.

There was no means of telling whether or not we were over the German border. The boundary-line had not been surveyed yet, and on the map the part where we were was set down as "unexplored," although that was scarcely accurate; the route was well enough known to Greeks and Arabs, and other bad characters bent on smuggling or in some other way defeating the ends of justice.

We marched that night until midnight, slept until dawn, and were off again. At noon we reached rising ground, and Kazimoto ran ahead of us to the summit. We saw him standing at gaze for three or four minutes with one hand shading his eyes before he came scampering back, as excited as if his own fortune were in the balance.

"*Hooko-chini!*" he shouted. "*Hooko-chini — mba-a-a-li sana!*"—(They're down below there, very far away!)

We hurried up-hill, but for many minutes could see nothing except a plain of waving grass higher than a man's head and almost as impenetrable as bamboo—country that carried small hope in it for man or beast, that would be a holocaust in the dry season when the heat set fire to the grass, and was an insect-haunted marsh at most other times. However, path across it there must be, for the Greeks had driven Brown's cattle that way that very morning, and Kazimoto swore he could see them in the distance, although Brown, and Will, and I—all three keen-sighted—could see nothing whatever but immeasurable, worthless waving grass.

At last I detected a movement near the horizon that did not synchronize with the wind-blown motion of the rest. I pointed it out to the others, and after a few minutes we agreed that it moved against the wind.

"They're hurrying again," said Brown, peering under both hands. "There's no feed for cattle on all this plain. They're racing to get to short grass before the cattle all die. Come on—let's hurry after 'em!"

For the second time on that trip we essayed a short cut, making as straight as a bee would fly for the point on the horizon where we knew the Greeks to be. And for the second time we fell into a bog, nearly losing our lives in it. We had to pull one another out, using even our precious rifles as supports in the yielding mud, and then spending equally precious time in cleaning locks and sights again.

After that we hunted for the cattle trail and followed that closely; and that was not so easy as it reads, because the trampled grass had risen again, and cattle and mounted men can cross easily ground that delays men on foot.

The heat was that of an oven. The water—what there was of it in the holes and swampy places—stank, and tasted acrid. The flies seemed to greet us as their only prospect of food that year. The monotony of hurrying through grass-stems that cut off all view and only showed the sky through a waving curtain overhead was more nerve-trying than the physical weariness and thirst.

We slept a night in that grass, burning some of it for a smudge to keep mosquitoes at bay, and an hour after dawn, reaching rising ground again, realized that we had our quarry within reach at last.

They were out in the open on short good grazing. The Greeks' tent was pitched. We could see their mules, like brown insects, tied under a tree, and the cattle dotted here and there, some lying down, some feeding.

"At last!" said Brown. "Boys, they're our meat! There's a tree to hang the Greeks and the Goa to! When we've done that, if you'll all come back with me I'll send to Nairobi for an extra jar of Irish whisky, and we'll have a spree at Lumbwa that'll make the fall of Rome sound like a Sunday-school picnic! We're in German territory now, all right. There's not a white man for a hundred miles in any direction —except your friend that's coming along behind. There's nobody to carry tales or prevent! I'm no savage. I'm no degenerate. I don't hold with too much of anything, but—"

"There'll be no dirty work, if that's what you mean," said Will quietly.

Brown stared hard at him.

"D'you mean you'll object to hanging 'em?"

"Not in the least. We hang or shoot cattle thieves in the States. I said there'll be no dirty work, that's all."

"Shall we rest a while, and come on them fresh in the morning?" I proposed.

"Forward!" snorted Brown. "Why d'you want to wait?"

"Forward it is!" agreed Will. "When we get a bit closer we'll stop and hold council of war."

"One minute!" said I. "Tell me what that is?"

I had been searching the whole countryside, looking for some means of stealing on the marauders unawares and finding none. They had chosen their camping place very wisely from the point of view of men unwilling to be taken by sur-

prise. Far away over to our right, appearing and disappearing as I watched them, were a number of tiny black dots in
a sort of wide half-moon formation, and a larger number of
rather larger dots contained within the semicircle.

"Cattle!" exploded Brown.

"And men!" added Will.

"Black men!" said I. "Black men with spears!"

"Masai!" said Kazimoto excitedly. He had far the keenest
eyes of all of us.

We were silent for several minutes. The veriest stranger
in that land knows about the feats and bravery of the Masai,
who alone of all tribes did not fear the Arabs, and who ter-
rorized a quarter of a continent before the British came and
broke their power.

"*Mbaia cabisa!*" muttered Kazimoto, meaning that the development was very bad indeed. And he had right to know.

He explained it was a raid. The Masai, in accordance with
time-honored custom, had come from British East to raid
the lake-shore villages of German territory, and were driving
back the plundered cattle. None can drive cattle as Masai
can. They can take leg-weary beasts by the tail and make
them gallop, one beast encouraging the next until they all
go like the wind. For food they drink hot blood, opening a
vein in a beast's neck, and closing it again when they have
had their fill. Their only luggage is a spear. Their only
speed-limit the maximum the cattle can be stung to. On a
raid three hundred and sixty miles in six days is an ordinary
rate of traveling.

Just now they did not seem in much hurry. They had
probably butchered the fighting men of all the villages in
their rear, and were well informed as to the disposition of
the nearest German forces. There were probably no Germans
within a hundred miles. There was no telegraph in all those
parts. To notify Muanza by runner and Bagamoyo on the
coast from there by wire would take several days. Then Bagamoyo would have to wire the station at Kilimanjaro, and
there was no earthly chance of Germans intercepting them
before they could reach British East.

Nor was there any treaty provision between British and German colonial governments for handing over raiders. The Germans had refused to make any such agreement for reasons best known to themselves. The fact that they were far the heaviest losers by the lack of reciprocal police arrangements was due to the fact that most of the Masai lived in British East. The Masai would have raided across either border with supreme indifference.

"Masai not talking. Masai using spear and kill!" remarked Kazimoto.

"One good thing our gov'ment's done," said Brown. "Just one. It has kept those rascals from owning rifles! But lordy! They've got spears that give a man the creeps to see!"

He began looking to his rifle. So did Will and I.

"Now this here is my fight," he explained. "Them's my cattle. They're all the wealth I own in the world. If I lose 'em I'm minded to die anyhow. There's nothing in life for a drunkard like me with all his money gone and nothing to do but take a mean white's job. You chaps just wait here and watch while I 'tend to my own affairs."

"Exactly!" Will answered dryly. "I've a hundred rounds in my pockets. That ought to be enough."

While we made ready, leaving our loads and porters in a safe place and giving the boys orders, I saw two things happen. First, the Masai became aware of the little Greek encampment and the two hundred head of cattle waiting at their mercy; and second, the Greeks grew aware of the Masai.

The Greeks had boys with them; I saw at least half a dozen go scattering to round up the cattle. The tents began to come down, and I saw three figures that might be the Greeks and the Goanese holding a consultation near the tree.

"And now," remarked Will, "I begin to see the humor in this comedy. Which are we—allies of the Greeks or of the Masai? Are we to help the Greeks get away with Brown's cattle, or help the Masai steal 'em from the Greeks? Are your cattle all branded, Brown?"

"You blooming well bet they are!"

"Masai know enough to alter a brand?"

"Never heard o' their doing it."

"Then if the Masai get away with them to British East, if you can find 'em you can claim 'em, eh?"

"Claim 'em in court wi' the whole blooming tribe o' Masai —more'n a quarter of a million of 'em—all on hand to swear they bought 'em from me; an' the British gov'ment taking sides with the black men, as it always does? Oh, yes! That sounds easy, that does!"

"But if the Greeks get away with 'em," argued Will, "you've no chance of recovering at all."

"I'll not take sides with Masai—even against Greeks!" Brown answered grimly, and Will laughed.

"If we attack the Greeks first," I said, "perhaps they'll run. We're nearer to them than the Masai are. The Masai will have to corral their own cattle before they can leave them to raid a new lot. We can open fire at long range to begin with. If that scares the Greeks away, then we can round up Brown's cattle and drive them back northward. We may possibly escape with them too quickly for the Masai to think it worth while to follow."

Brown laughed cynically.

"We can try it," he said. "An' if the Greeks don't run pretty quick they'll never run again—I'll warrant that!"

Nobody had a better plan to propose, so we emptied our pockets of all but fifty rounds of ammunition each, and gave the rest to Kazimoto to carry, with orders to keep in hiding and watch, and run with cartridges to whoever should first need them.

Then, because instead of corraling their cattle the Masai were already dividing themselves into two parties, one of which drove the cattle forward and the other diverged to study the attack, we ducked down under a ridge and ran toward the Greeks. The sooner we could get the first stage of the fighting off our hands the better.

It proved a long way—far longer than I expected, and the going was rougher. Moreover, the Greeks' boys were losing no time about rounding up the cattle. By the time they were ready to make a move we were still more than a mile away, and out of breath.

"If they go south," panted Brown, throwing himself down by a clump of grass to gasp for his third or fourth wind, "the Masai'll catch 'em sure, an' we'll be out o' the running! Lord send they head 'em back toward British East!"

He was in much the worst physical condition because of the whisky, but his wits were working well enough. The Greeks on the other hand seemed undecided and appeared to be arguing. Then Brown's prayer was answered. The Greeks' boys decided the matter for them by stampeding the herd northward toward us. They did not come fast. They were lame, and bone-weary from hard driving, but they knew the way home again and made a bee line. Within a minute they were spread fan-wise between us and the Greeks, making a screen we could not shoot through.

"Scatter to right and left!" Brown shouted. "Get round the wings!"

But what was the use? He was in the center, and short-winded. I climbed on an ant-hill.

"The Greeks are on the run!" I said. "They are headed southward! They've got their boys together, and have abandoned the cattle! They're off with their tent and belongings due south!"

"The cowards!" swore Brown, with such disappointment that Will and I laughed.

"Laugh all you like!" he said. "I've a long job on my hands! I'll have revenge on 'em if it takes the rest o' my life! I'll follow 'em to hell-and-gone!"

"Meanwhile," I said, still standing on the ant-hill, "the Masai are following the cattle! They're smoking this way in two single columns of about twenty spears in each. The remainder are driving their own cattle about due eastward so as to be out of the way of trouble."

"All right," said Brown, growing suddenly cheerful again. "Then it'll be a rear-guard action. Let the cattle through, and open fire behind 'em! Send that Kazimoto o' yours to

warn our boys to round 'em up and drive 'em slow and steady
northward !"

Kazimoto ran back and gave the necessary orders. He lost
no time about it, but returned panting, and lay down in a
hollow behind us with cartridges in either fist and a grin on
his face that would have done credit to a circus clown. I
never, anywhere, saw any one more pleased than Kazimoto
at the prospect of a fight.

We let the cattle through and lay hidden, waiting for the
raiders. They were in full war dress, which is to say as nearly
naked as possible except for their spears, a leg ornament made
from the hair of the colobus monkey, a leather apron hung
on just as suited the individual wearer's fancy, a great shield,
and an enormous ostrich-feather head-dress. They seemed in
no hurry, for they probably guessed that the cattle would
stop to graze again when the first scare was over; yet they
came along as smoke comes, swiftly and easily, making no
noise.

Suddenly those in the lead caught sight of our boys getting
behind the cattle to herd them northward. They halted to
hold consultation—apparently decided that they had only
unarmed natives to deal with—and came on again, faster
than before.

"Better open fire now !" said Brown, when they were still
a quarter of a mile away.

"Wait till you can see their eyes !" Will advised. "An unexpected volley at close quarters will do more havoc than
hours of long-range shooting."

"This ain't a long range !" Brown objected. "As for unexpected—just watch me startle 'em ! My sight's fixed at four
hundred. Watch !"

He fired—we wished he had not. The leading Masai of the
right-hand column jerked his head sidewise as the whistling
bullet passed, and then there was nothing for it but to follow
his lead and blaze away for all we were worth. If Brown had
been willing to accept Will's advice there is nothing more
likely than that the close-quarter surprise would have won
the day for us. We would have done much more execution

with three volleys at ten-yard range. As it was, we all missed
with our first shots, and the Masai took heart and charged
in open order.

The worst of it was that, although we dropped several of
them, now the others had a chance to discover there were
only three of us. Their leader shouted. The right-hand column continued to attack, but changed its tactics. The left-
hand party made a circuit at top speed, outflanked us, and
pursued the cattle.

Supposing my count was right, we had laid out, either
wounded or dead, seven of the crowd attacking us. This left
perhaps fourteen against us, to be dealt with before the others
could come back with the cattle and take us in the rear.

Will brought another man down; I saw the blood splash
on his forehead as the bullet drilled the skull cleanly. Then
one man shouted and they all lay prone, beginning to crawl
toward us with their shields held before, not as protection
against bullets (for as that they were utterly worthless) but
as cover that made their exact position merest guesswork.

I fell back and took position on the ant-hill from which
I had first seen them, thus making our position triangular
and giving myself a chance to protect the other two should
they feel forced to retire. The extra height also gave me a
distinct advantage, for I could see the legs of the Masai over
the tops of their shields, and was able to wound more than
one of them so severely that they crawled to the rear.

But the rest came on. Kazimoto began to be busy supplying cartridges. In that first real pinch we were in he certainly lived up to all Courtney had said of him, for without
the stimulus of his proper master's eye he neither flinched
nor faltered, but crawled from one to the other, dividing the
spare rounds equally.

The Masai began to attempt to outflank us, but my position
on the ant-hill to the rear made that impossible; they found
themselves faced by a side of the triangle from whichever
side they attacked. But in turning to keep an eye on the flank
I became aware of a greater danger. The cattle were coming
back. That meant that the other Masai were coming, too,

and that in a few moments we were likely to be overwhelmed. I shouted to Will and Brown, but either they did not hear me, or did not have time to answer.

I fired half a dozen shots, and then distinctly heard the crack of a rifle from beyond the cattle. That gave matters the worst turn yet. If one of the raiders had a rifle, then unless I could spot him at once and put him out of action our cause was likely lost. I stood up to look for him, and heard a wild cheer, followed by three more shots in quick succession. Then at last I saw Fred Oakes running along a depression in the ground, followed at a considerable distance by the advance-guard of his porters. He was running, and then kneeling to fire—running, and kneeling again. And he he was not wasting ammunition. He was much the best shot of us all, now that Monty was absent.

The terrified cattle stampeded past us, too wild to be checked by any noise. Seeing them, and sure now of their booty, the party attacking us hauled off and took to their heels. Will and Brown were for speeding them with bullets in the rear, but I yelled again, and this time made myself heard. Those who had got behind the cattle and were driving them were coming on with spears and shields raised to slay us in passing. The other two joined me, and we stood on the ant-hill three abreast. They charged us—seven or eight of them. Three bit the dust, but the rest came on, and if it had not been for two swift shots from Fred's rifle in the very nick of time we should have all been dead men.

As it was, one seized me by the knees and we went over together, rolling down the ant-hill, he slashing at me with his great broad-bladed spear, I ahold of his wrist with one hand, and with the other fist belaboring him in the face. He was stronger than I—greasier—sweatier—harder to hold. He slipped from under me, rolled on top, wrenched his wrist free, and in another second grinned in my face as, with both knees in my stomach, he raised the spear to kill. I shut my eyes. I had not another breath left, nor an effort in me, but I thought I would deny him the pleasure of watching my death agony. But I could not keep my eyes shut. Opening

them to see why he did not strike, I saw Kazimoto with my
rifle in both hands swing for his skull with the full weight
of the butt and all his strength. Kazimoto grunted. The Masai half turned his head at the sound. The butt hit home—
broke off—and my face and breast were deluged with blood
and brains.

When I had wiped off that mess with Kazimoto's help I
saw Fred and Will and Brown pursuing the retreating Masai,
kneeling to shoot every few yards, at every other shot or so
bringing down a victim, but being rapidly out-distanced.
Cattle are all the Masai care about. They had the cattle.
They had hold of tails and were making the whole herd
scamper due east, where they no doubt knew of a trail not
in maps. They made no attempt to defend themselves—left
their dead lying—and ran. I saw two or three wounded ones
riding on cows, and no doubt some of those who ran holding
to the cows' tails were wounded, too.

I was useless now, as far as fighting was concerned, for
the butt of my rifle was broken clean off at the grip, but I
ran on, and heard Brown shout:

"Shoot cattle! Don't let the brutes get away with them
all!"

He was shooting cows himself when I came up, but it was
Fred who stopped him.

"Never mind that, old man. We'll follow 'em up! Our
time's our own. We'll get your cattle back, never fear. Dead
ones are no use."

Brown stopped shooting and began to blubber. Whisky
had not left him manhood enough to see his whole available
resources carried away before his eyes, and he broke down as
utterly as any child. It was neither agreeable nor decent to
watch, and I turned away. I was feeling sick myself from
the pressure of the Masai's knees in my stomach. That, and
the sun, and the long march, and hunger (for we had not
stopped to eat a meal that day) combined in argument, and I
hunted about for a soft place and a little shade. It happened
that Fred Oakes was watching me, although I did not know
it. He suspected sunstroke.

I saw a clump of rushes that gave shade enough. I could crush down some, and lie on those. I hurried, for I was feeling deathly sick now. As I reached the grass my knees began giving under me. I staggered, but did not quite fall.

That, and Fred's watchfulness, saved my life; for at the moment that my head and shoulders gave the sudden forward lurch, a wounded Masai jumped out of the rushes and drove with his spear at my breast. The blade passed down my back and split my jacket.

He sprang back, and made another lunge at me, but Fred's rifle barked at the same second and he fell over sidewise, driving the spear into my leg in his death spasm.

The twenty minutes following that are the worst in memory. Kazimoto broke the gruesome news that the spear-blade was almost surely poisoned—dipped in gangrene. The Masai are no believers in wounded enemies, or mercy on the battlefield.

We doubted the assertion for a while—I especially, for none but a hypochondriac would care to admit without proof that gangrene had been forced into his system. Kazimoto grew indignant, and offered to prove the truth of his claim on some animal. But there was no living animal in sight on which to prove it. We asked him how long gangrene, injected in that way, took to kill a man.

"Very few minutes!" he answered.

Then it occurred that none of us knew what to do. Kazimoto announced that he knew, and offered to make good at once if given permission. He demanded permission again and again from each one of us, making me especially repeat my words. Then he gathered stems of grass a third of an inch thick from the bed of the tiny watercourse, and proceeded to make a tiny fire, talking in a hurry as he did it to several of Fred's string of porters, who were now arriving on the scene.

While I watched with a sort of tortured interest what he was doing at the fire, five of the largest boys with whom he had been speaking rushed me from behind, and before I could struggle, or even swear, had me pinned out on my back

on the ground. One sat on my head; one on my poor bruised
stomach; the others held wrists and ankles in such way that
I could not break free, nor even kick much, however hard I
tried.

Then Kazimoto came with glowing ends of grass from the
fire, blowing on them to keep them cherry-red, and inserted
one after another into the open spear-wound. I could not cry
out, because of the man sitting on my face, but I could bite.
And to the everlasting glory of the man—Ali bin Yema, his
name was—be it written that he neither spoke nor moved a
muscle, although my front teeth met in his flesh.

I do not know how long the process lasted, or how many
times Kazimoto returned to the fire for more of his sizzling
sticks, for I fainted; and when I came round the agony was
still too intense to permit interest in anything but agony.
They had my leg bandaged, how and with what I neither knew
nor cared. And it was evident that unless they chose to leave
me in camp where I was they would have to abandon all
thought of pursuing Masai for the present. Even Brown
saw the force of that, and he was the first to refuse flatly to
leave me there.

For a while they hunted through the grass for more
wounded men, but found none. There must have been several, but they probably feared the sort of mercy from us that
they habitually gave to their own enemies, and crawled away
—in all likelihood to die of thirst and hunger, unless some
beast of prey should smell them out and make an earlier end.

Then there was consultation. It was decided a doctor for
me was the most urgent need; that Muanza, the largest German station on Victoria Nyanza, was probably as near as
anywhere, and that German East being our immediate destination anyway, the best course to take was forward, roughly
south by west. So I was slung in a blanket on a tent-pole,
and we started, I swearing like a pirate every time a boy
stumbled and jolted me. (There is something in the nature
of a burn that makes bad language feel like singing hymns.)

Our troubles were not all over, for we passed through a
country where buck were fairly plentiful, and that meant

lions. They did no damage, but they kept us awake; and one night, near the first village we came to, where our porters all quartered themselves with the villagers for sake of the change from their crowded tents, the fires that we made went out, and five lions (we counted their foot-prints afterward) came and sniffed around the pegs of the tent in which Fred and I lay, we lying still and shamming dead. To have lifted a rifle in the darkness and tried to shoot would have been suicide.

Then there were trees we passed among—baobabs, whose youngest tendrils swung to and fro in the evening breeze like snakes head-downward. And taking advantage of that natural provision, twenty-foot pythons swung among them, in coloring and marking aping the habit of the tree. One of them knocked Fred's helmet off as he marched beside me. They are easy to kill. He shot it, and it dropped like a stone, three hundred pounds or more, but the sweat ran down Fred's face for half an hour afterward.

(Since then I have seen pythons kill their prey a score of times. I never once saw one kill by crushing. The end of their nose is as hard as iron, and they strike a terrific blow with that, so swift that the eye can not follow it. Then, having killed by striking, they crawl around their prey and crush it into shape for swallowing.)

But the worst of the journey was the wayside villages— dirty beyond belief, governed in a crude way by a' headman whom the Germans honored with the title of sultani. These wayside beggars (for they were no better)—destitute paupers, taxed until their wits failed them in the effort to scrape together surplus enough out of which to pay—were supplied with a mockery of a crown apiece, a thing of brass and imitation plush that they wore in the presence of strangers. To add to the irony of that, the law of the land permitted any white man passing through to beat them, with as many as twenty-five lashes, if they failed to do his bidding.

On arriving at such a village, the first thing we did was to ask for milk. If they had any they brought it, not daring to refuse, for fear lest a German sergeant-major should be

went along to wreak vengeance later. But it was always too
dirty to drink.

That ceremony over, the headman retired and the village
sick were brought for our inspection. Gruesome sores, running ulcers, wounds and crippled limbs were stripped and ex-
posed to our most reluctant gaze. There was little we could
do for them. Our own supply of medicines and bandages was
almost too small for our own needs to begin with. By the
time we passed three villages we scarcely had enough lint and
liniment left to take care of my wound; but even that scant
supply we cut in half for a particularly bad case.

"Don't the Germans do anything for you?" we demanded,
over and over again.

The answer was always the same.

"*Germani mbaia!*" (The Germans are bad!)

They were lifeless—listless—tamed until neither ambition
nor courage was left. When their cattle had brought forth
young and it looked as if there might be some profit at last,
the Masai came and raided them, taking away all but the very
old ones and the youngest calves. The Germans, they said,
taxed them and took their weapons away, but gave them no
protection.

At one place we passed a rifle, lying all rusted by the track.
At the next village we asked about it. They told us that a
German native soldier had deserted six months before and had
thrown his rifle away. Since that day no one had dared touch
it, and they begged us to send back and lay it where we found
it, lest the Germans come and punish them for touching it.
So we did that, to oblige them, and they were grateful to the
extent of offering us one of their only two male sheep.

I forget now for how many days we traveled across that sad
and saddening land, Fred always cheerful in spite of everything, Will more angry at each village with its dirt and sores,
Brown moaning always about his lovely herd of cows, and I
groaning oftener than not.

My leg grew no better, what with jolting and our ignorance
of how to treat it. Sometimes, in efforts to obtain relief, I
borrowed a cow at one village and rode it to the next; but a

cow is a poor mount and takes as a rule unkindly to the business. Now and then I tried to walk for a while, on crutches that Fred made for me; but most of the time I was carried, in a blanket that grew hotter and more comfortless as day dragged after day.

At last, however, we topped a low rise and saw Muanza lying on the lake-shore, with the great island of Ukerewe to the northward in the distance. From where we first glimpsed it it was a tidy, tree-shaded, pleasant-looking place, with a square fort, and a big house for the commandant on a rise overlooking the town.

"Now we'll wire Monty at last!" said Fred.

"Now we'll shave and wash and write letters!" said Will.

"Now at last for a doctor!" said I.

But Brown said nothing, and Kazimoto wore a look of anxious discontent.

# THE DARKNESS COMPREHENDED IT NOT

*When Kenia's peak glows gold and rose*
*A dawn breeze whispers to the plain*
*With breath cooled sweet by mountain snows—*
*"The darkness soon shall come again!"*
*Stirs then the sleepless, lean Masai*
*And stands o'er plain and peak at gaze*
*Resentful of the bright'ning sky,*
*Impatient of the white man's days.*

*Oh dark nights, when the charcoal glowed and falling hammers rang!*
*When fundis\* forged the spear-blades, and the warriors danced and sang!*
*When the marriageable spearmen gathered, calling each to each*
*Telling over proverbs that the tribal wisemen teach,*
*Brother promising blood-brother partnership in weal and woe—*
*Nightlong stories of the runners come from spying on the foe—*
*Nights of boasting by the thorn-fire of the coming tale of slain—*
*Oh the times before the English! When will those times come again!*

*Oh the days and nights of raiding, when the feathered spearmen strode*
*With the hide shields on their forearms, and the wild Nyanza road*
*Grew blue with smoking villages, grew red with flaring roofs,*
*Grew noisy with the shouting and the thunder of the hoofs*
*As we drove the plundered cattle—when we burned the night with haste—*
*When we leapt at dawn from ambush—when we laid the shambas waste!*

---

\* *Fundis*—skilled workmen.

*Oh the new spears dipped in life-blood as the women shrieked
    in vain!*
*Oh the days before the English! When will those days come
    again!*

*Oh the homeward road in triumph with the plunder borne
    along*
*On the heads of taken women! Oh the laughter and the song!*
*Oh the tusks of yellow ivory—the frasilas of beads—*
*And, best of all, the heifers that the marriageable needs!*
*The yells when village eyes at last our sky-line feathers see*
*And the maidens run to count how many marriages shall be—*
*Ten heifers to a maiden (and the chief's girl stands for
    twain)—*
*Oh the days before the English! When will those days come
    again!*

*Now the fat herds grow in number, and the old are rich in
    trade,*
*Now the grass grows green and heavy where the six-foot spears
    were made.*
*Now the young men walk to market, and the wives have beads
    and wire—*
*Brass and iron—glass and cowrie—past the limit of desire.*
*There is peace from lake to mountain, and the very zebra
    breed*
*Where a law says none may hurt them (and the wise are they
    who heed!)*
*Yea—the peace lies on the country as our herds o'erspread the
    plain—*
*But the days before the English—when shall those days come
    again!*

> *When Kenia's peak glows gold and rose*
>   *A dawn breeze whispers to the plain*
> *With breath cooled sweet by mountain snows—*
>   *"The darkness soon shall come again!"*
> *Stirs then the sleepless, lean Masai*
>   *And stands o'er plain and peak at gaze*
> *Resentful of the bright'ning sky,*
>   *Impatient of the white man's days.*

# CHAPTER SEVEN

WHAT first looked like a pleasant place dwindled into charmlessness and insignificance as we approached. There was neatness — of a kind. The round huts were confined to certain streets, and all inhabited by natives. Arabs, Swahili, Indians, Goanese, Syrians, Greeks and so on had to live in rectangular huts and keep to other streets. On one street, chiefly of stores, all the roofs were of corrugated iron. And all the streets were straight, with shade trees planted down both sides at exactly equal intervals.

But the German blight was there, instantly recognizable by any one not mentally perverted by German teaching. The place was governed—existed for and by leave of government. The inhabitants were there on suffrance, and aware of it—not in the very least degree enthusiastic over German rule, but awfully appreciative.

The first thing we met of interest on entering the township was a chain-gang, fifty long, marching at top speed in step, led by a Nubian soldier with a loaded rifle, flanked by two others, and pursued by a fourth armed only with the hippo-hide whip, called *kiboko* by the natives, that can cut and bruise at one stroke. He plied it liberally whenever the gang betrayed symptoms of intending to slow down.

Those Nubians, we learned later, were deserters from British Sudanese regiments, and runaways from British jails, afraid to take the thousand-mile journey northward home again, scornful of all foreign black men, fanatic Muhammedans, and therefore fine tools in the German hand. They worked harder than the chain-gang, for they had to march with it step for step and into the bargain force it to do its appointed labor. The chain-gang kept the township clean—very clean indeed, as far as outward appearance went.

The boma, or fort, was down by the water-front and its high eastern wall, pierced by only one gate, formed one boun-

189

dary of the drill-ground that was also township square. Facing the wall on the eastern side of the square was a row of Indian and Arab stores. At the north end was the market building—an enormous structure of round stucco pillars supporting a great grass roof; and facing that at the southern end were the court-house, the hospital, and a store owned by the Deutch Oest Africa Gesellschaft, known far and wide by its initials—a concern that owned the practical monopoly of wholesale import and export trade, and did a retail business, too.

We went first to the hospital. Fred and Will lifted me out of the hammock, for my wound had grown much worse during the last few days, and the door being shut they set me down on the step. Then we sent Kazimoto into the fort with a note to the senior officer informing him that a European waited at the hospital in need of prompt medical treatment.

The sentry admitted Kazimoto readily enough, but he did not come out again for half-an-hour, and then looked glum.

"*Habanah!*" he said simply, using the all-embracing native negative.

"Isn't any one in there?" we demanded all together.

"Surely."

"How many?"

"Very many."

"Officers?"

He nodded.

"Is a doctor there?"

He told us he had asked for the doctor. A soldier had pointed him out. He had placed the note in the doctor's hand.

"Did he read it?" we asked.

"Surely. He read it, and then showed it to the other officers."

"What did they say?"

"They laughed and said nothing."

It seemed pretty obvious that Kazimoto had made a mistake in some way. Perhaps he had visited the non-commissioned officers' mess.

"I'll go myself," announced Will. "I can sling the German language like a barkeep. Bet you I'm back here with a doctor inside of three minutes !"

He strode off like Sir Galahad in football shorts, and was passed through the gate by the sentry almost unchallenged. But he was gone more than fifteen minutes, and came back at last with his ears crimson. Nor would he answer our questions.

"Shall I go?" suggested Fred.

"Not unless you like insolence! We passed the camping-ground, it seems, on our way in. We've leave to pitch tents there. We'd better be moving."

So we trailed back the way we had come to a triangular sandy space enclosed by a cactus hedge at the junction of three roads. There were several small grass-roofed shelters with open sides in there, and two tents already pitched, but we were not sufficiently interested just then to see who owned the other tents. We pitched our own—stowed the loads in one of the shelters—gave our porters money for board and rations—and sent them to find quarters in the town. Another of the shelters we took over for a kitchen, and while our servants were cooking a meal we four gathered in Fred's tent and began to question Will again.

"They've got a fine place in there," he said. "Neat as a new pin. Officers' mess. Non-commissioned officers' quarters. Stores. Vegetable garden. Jail—looks like a fine jail—hold a couple of hundred. Government offices. Two-story buildings. Everything fine. The officers were all sitting smoking on a veranda.

" 'Is one of you the doctor?' I asked in German, and a tall lean one with a mighty mean face turned his head to squint at me: but he didn't take his feet off the rail. He looked inquisitive, that's all.

" 'Are you the doctor?' I asked him.

" 'I am staff surgeon,' he answered. 'What do you want?'

"I told him about your wound, and how we'd marched about two hundred miles on purpose to get medical assistance. He listened without asking a question, and when I'd done he said curtly that the hospital opens for out-patients at eight in the morning.

"Well, I piled it on then. I told him your leg was so rotten that you might not be alive to-morrow morning. He didn't even look interested. I piled it on thicker and told him about the poisoned spear. He didn't bat an eyelid or make a move. So I started in to coax him.

"I did some coaxing. Believe me, I swallowed more pride in five minutes than I guessed I owned! A ward-heeler cadging votes for a Milwaukee alderman never wheedled more gingerly. I called him 'Herr Staff Surgeon' and mentioned the well-known skill of German medicos, and the keen sense of duty of the German army, and a whole lot of other stuff.

"'To-morrow morning at eight!' was all the answer I got from him.

"I reckon it was somewhere about that time I began to get rattled. I pulled out money and showed it. He looked the other way, and when I went on talking he turned his back. I suspect he didn't dare keep on lookin' at money almost within reach. Anyhow, then I opened on him, firin' both bow guns. I dared him to sit there, with a patient in need of prompt attention less than two hundred yards away. I called him names. I guaranteed to write to the German government and the United States papers about him. I told him I'd have his job if it cost me all my money and a lifetime's trouble. He was just about ready to shoot—I'd just about got the red blood rising on his neck and ears—when along came the commandant—der Herr Capitain—the officer commanding Muanza— a swag-bellied ruffian with a beard and a beery look in his eye, but a voice like a man falling down three stories with all the fire-irons.

"'What do you want?' he demanded in English, and I thanked him first for not having mistaken me for one of his own countrymen. Then I told him what I'd come for.

"'To-morrow at eight o'clock!' he snapped, after he'd had a word with the medico. 'Meanwhile, make yourself scarce out of here! There is a camping-ground for the use of for-

eigners. You and your party go to it! If you do any damage
there you will hear from me later !'

"I didn't come as easy as all that. I stood there telling
him things about Germany and Germans, and what I'd do to
help his personal reputation with the home folks, until I
guessed he had his craw as near full as he could stand it without having me arrested. Then I did come—whistling
*Yankee-doodle*. And say—Fred! Where's that concertina of
yours?"

Fred patted it. His beloved instrument was never far from
hand.

"Why don't you play all the American and English tunes
you know to-night? Play and sing 'em, *Britannia Rule the
Waves — Marching Through Georgia — My Country 'tis of
Thee—The Marseillaise—The Battle Hymn of the Republic*
—and anything and everything you know that Squareheads
won't like. Let's make this camp a reg'lar—hello—see who's
here !"

Fred had begun fingering the keys already and the first
strains of *Marching Through Georgia* began to awake the
neighborhood to recognition of the fact that foreigners were
present who held no especial brief for German rule. The
tent-door darkened. Brown leapt to his feet and swore.

"Gassharamminy!" said a voice we all recognized instantly.
"That tune sounds good! I've lived in the States! I'm a
United States citizen! A man can't forget his own country's
tunes so easily !"

Cool and impudent, Georges Coutlass entered and, without
waiting for an invitation, took a seat on a load of canned food.
Brown grabbed the nearest rifle (it happened to be Fred's)—
snapped open the breach—discovered it was loaded—and took
aim. Coutlass did not even blink. He was either sure Fred
and Will would interfere, or else at the end of his tether and
indifferent to death.

"Don't be an ass, Brown !"

Fred knocked the rifle up. Will took it away and returned
it to the corner.

"All very easy for you men to take high moral ground and

all that sort of rot," Brown grumbled. "It's my cattle he took! It's me he's ruined! What do I care if the Germans hang me? Let me have a crack at him—just one!"

"Use your fists all you care to!" grinned Will.

But Brown was no match for the Greek without weapons—very likely no match for him with them. Coutlass sat still and grinned, while Brown remained in the back of the tent, glaring.

"Bah!" sneered Coutlass. "Of what use is being sulky? I found cattle in a village. How should I know whose cattle they were? Why blame me? The Masai got the cattle, not I! They took them from me, and they'd have taken them from you just the same! You lost nothing by my lifting them first! Gassharamminy! By blazes! We're all in the same boat! Let's be friendly, and treat one another like gentlemen! We're all in the power of the Germans, unless we can think of a way to escape! I and my party are under arrest. So will you be by to-morrow! I shall tell a tale to-morrow that will keep you by the heels for a month at least while they investigate! Wait and see!"

"Get out of this tent!" growled Fred in the dead-level voice he uses when he means to brook no refusal.

"Presently!"

Fred made a spring at him, but Coutlass was on his feet with the speed of a cat, and just outside the tent in time to avoid the swing of Fred's fist. He withdrew about two yards, and stood there grinning maliciously.

"You'll be glad to make terms with me by this time to-morrow!" he boasted. "By James, you'll be glad to have me for a friend! Listen, you fools! Make terms with me now; let us all go together and unearth that Tippoo Tib ivory, and I can arrange with these Germans to let us go away! Otherwise, you shall see how long you stop here! By the Twelve Apostles! You shall rot in a German jail until your joints creak!"

His Greek friend and the Goanese, supposing him in trouble perhaps, came and stood in line with him. Very comfortless they looked, and of the three only Coutlass had courage of a kind.

"They stole the cattle on the British side of the border," Will said sotto voice. "No earthly use threatening them with German law."

"Keep away from our camp," Fred ordered them, "or take the consequences! Mr. Brown here is in no mood for pleasantries!"

"That drunkard Brown?" roared Coutlass. "He is in no mood for—oh, haw-hah-hee-ho-ha-ha-ha-ha! Drunkard Brown of Lumbwa wants to avenge himself, and his friends won't let him! Oh, isn't that a joke! Oh, ha-ha-ha-hee-hee-ha-ho-ho!"

His two companions made a trio of it, yelling with stage laughter like disgusting animals. Fred took a short quick step forward. Will followed, and Brown reached for the rifle again. But I stopped all three of them.

"Come back! Don't let's be fools!" I insisted. "I never saw a more obvious effort to start trouble in my life! It's a trap! Keep out of it!"

"Sure enough," Will admitted. "You're right!"

He returned into the tent and the Greeks, perhaps supposing he went for weapons, retreated, continuing to shout abuse at Brown who, between a yearning to get drunk and sorrow for his stolen cattle, was growing tearful.

"They got here first," I argued. "They've had time to tell their own story. That may account for our cold reception by the Germans. He says they're under arrest. That may be true, or it may be a trick. It's perfectly obvious Coutlass wanted to start a fight, and I'm dead sure he wasn't taking such a chance as it seemed. Who wants to look behind the cactus hedge and see whether he has friends in ambush?"

"Drunkard Brown is on the town—on the town—on the town!" roared Coutlass and his friends from not very far away.

"Oh, let me go and have a crack at 'em!" begged Brown. "I tell you I don't care about jail! I don't care if I do get killed!"

Fred kept a restraining hand on him. Will left the tent and walked straight for the gap in the cactus hedge by which we had entered the enclosure. It was only twenty yards away.

Once through the gap he glanced swiftly to right and left— laughed—and came back again.

"Only six of 'em!" he grinned. "Six full-sized Nubians in uniform, with army boots on, no bayonets or rifles, but good big sticks and handcuffs! If we'd touched those Greeks they'd have jumped the fence and stretched us out! What the devil d'you suppose they want us in jail for?"

"D'you suppose they think," I said, "that if they had us in jail in this God-forsaken place we'd divulge the secret of Tippoo's ivory?"

"Why don't we tell 'em the secret!" suggested Will, and that seemed such a good idea that we laughed ourselves back into good temper—even Brown, who had no notion whether we knew the secret, being perfectly sure we would not be such fools as to tell the true whereabouts of the hoard in any case.

"I want to get even with all Africa!" he grumbled. "I want to make trouble that'll last! I'd start a war this minute if I knew how! If it weren't for those bloody Greeks laughing at me I'd get more drunk to-night than any ten men in the world ever were before in history! Yes, sir! And my name's Brown of Lumbwa to prove I mean what I say!"

After a while, seeing that no trouble was likely, the Nubian soldiers came out of ambush and marched away. We ate supper. The Greeks and the Goanese subsided into temporary quiet, and our own boys, squatting by a fire they had placed so that they could watch the Greeks' encampment, began humming a native song. Their song reminded Fred of Will's earlier suggestion, and he unclasped the concertina.

Then for three-quarters of an hour he played, and we sang all the tunes we knew least likely to make Germans happy, repeating *The Marseillaise* and *Rule Britannia* again and again in pious hope that at least a few bars might reach to the commandant's house on the hill.

Whether they did or not—whether the commandant writhed as we hoped in the torture of supreme insult, or slept as was likely from the after-effect of too much bottled beer with dinner—there were others who certainly did hear, and made no secret of it.

To begin with, the part of the township nearest us was the quarter of round grass roofs, where the aborigines lived; and the Bantu heart responds to tuneful noise, as readily as powder to the match. All that section of Muanza, man, woman and child, came and squatted outside the cactus hedge. (It was *streng politzeilich verboten* for natives to enter the European camping-ground, so that except when they wanted to steal they absolutely never trespassed past the hedge.)

Enraptured by the unaccustomed strains they sat quite still until some Swahili and Arabs came and beat them to make room. When the struggle and hot argument that followed that had died down, Indians began coming, and other Greeks, until most of the inhabitants of the eastern side of town were either squatting or standing or pacing to and fro outside the camping-ground.

At last rumor of what was happening reached the D. O. A. G.—the store at the corner of the drill-ground, where it seemed the non-commissioned officers took their pleasure of an evening. Pleasure, except as laid down in regulations, is not permitted in German colonies to any except white folk. No less than eight German sergeants and a sergeant-major, all the worse for liquor, turned out as if to a fire and came down-street at a double.

They had *kibokos* in their hands. The first we heard of their approach was the crack-crack-crack of the black whips falling on naked or thin-cotton-clad backs and shoulders. There was no yelling (it was not allowed after dark on German soil, at least by natives) but a sudden pattering in the dust as a thousand feet hurried away. Then, in the glow of our lamplight, came the sergeant-major standing spraddle-legged in front of us.

He was a man of medium height, in clean white uniform. The first thing I noticed about him was the high cheek-bones and murderous blue eyes, like a pig's. His general build was heavy. The fair mustache made no attempt to conceal fat lips that curled cruelly. His general air was that most offensive one to decent folk, of the bully who would ingratiate by seeming a good fellow.

*" 'nabnd, meine Herren!"* he said aggressively, with a smile more than half made up of contempt for courtesy. *"Ich heisse* Schubert—Feldwebel Hans Schübert."

*"Wass wollen Sie?"* Will asked. He was the only one of us who knew German well.

But Schubert, it seemed, knew English and was glad to show it off.

"You make fine music! *Ach!* Up at the D. O. A. G. very near here we *Unteroffitzieren* spend the evening, all very fond of singing, yet without music at all. Will you not come and play with us?"

"I only know French and English tunes!" lied Fred.

*"Ach!* I do not believe it! *Kommen Sie!* There is beer at the D. O. A. G.—champagne—brandy—whisky—rum—"

"I'm going, then, for one!" announced Brown, getting up immediately.

"Cigars—cigarettes—tobacco," the sergeant-major continued. "There is no closing time." He saw that the line of argument was not tempting, and changed his tactics. "Listen! You gentlemen have not too many friends in Muanza! I speak in friendship. I invite you on behalf of myself and other *Unteroffitzieren* to spend *gemuthlich* evening with us. That can do you no harm! In the course of friendly conversation much can be learned that official lips would not tell! *Kommen Sie nun!"*

"Let's go!" I said. "My leg hurts like hell. If I stay here I can't sleep. Anything to keep from thinking about it! Besides, some one must go and look after Brown!"

"Who'll watch those Greeks?" Fred demanded. "They'd as soon steal as eat!"

"We'd better all stay here together," said Will, "and take turns keeping watch till morning." He said it with a straight face, but I did not think he was in earnest.

*"Ach!"* exclaimed Schubert. "That is all *ganz einfach!* You shall have *askaris!"*

He turned and shouted an order. A non-commissioned officer went running back up-street.

"You shall have three *askaris* to guard your camp. So

nothing whatever shall be stolen! Then come along and make music—*seien Sie gemuthlich!* Yah?"

Brown had already gone, jingling money in his pocket. We waited until the Nubian soldiers came—saw them posted—and then walked up-street behind the sergeants, Schubert leading us all, and I limping between Fred and Will. They as good as carried me the last half of the way.

The sergeants marched with the air peculiar to military Germans, of men who are going to be amused. They said nothing—did not smile—but strode straight forward, three abreast, swinging their *kibokos* with a sort of elephantine sporty air. They were men of all heights and thicknesses, but each alike impressed me with the Prussian military mold that leaves a man no imagination of his own, and no virtue, but only an animal respect for whatever can make to suffer, or appease an appetite.

The D. O. A. G. proved a mournful enough lounging place in which to spend convivial evenings. However, it seemed that when the sergeant-major had decreed amusement the non-commissioned officers' mess overlooked all trifles in brave determination to obey. They marched in, humming tunes (each a different one, and nearly all high tenor) and took seats in a room at the rear of the building with their backs against a mud-brick wall that was shiny from much rubbing by drill tunics.

Down the center was a narrow table, loaded with drinks of all sorts. A case of bottled beer occupied the place of pride at one end; as Schubert had boasted, nothing was lacking that East Africa could show in the way of imported alcohol. Under the table was an unopened case of sweet German champagne, and on a little table against one wall were such things as absinth, chartreuse, peppermint, and benedictine. Soda-water was slung outside the window in a basket full of wet grass where the evening breeze would keep it cool.

"Now for *Gesang!*" shouted Schubert, knocking the neck off a bottle of beer, and beginning to sing like a drunken pirate.

A man whom he introduced as "a genuine Jew from Jerusalem" came out from a gloomy recess filled with tusks and sacks of dried red pepper, and watched everything from now on with an eye like a gimlet, writing down in a book against each sergeant's name whatever he took to drink. They appeared to have no check on him. Nobody signed anything. Nobody as much as glanced at his account.

"What is the use?" said Schubert, noticing my glance and interpreting the unspoken question. "There is just so much drink in the whole place. We shall drink every drop of it! All that matters is, who is to pay for the champagne? That stuff is costly."

They all took beer to begin with, knocking the necks from the bottles as if that act alone lent the necessary air of deviltry to the whole proceedings. A small, very black Nyamwesi came with brush and pan and groped on the floor all night for the splinters of glass, sleeping between times in a corner until a fresh volley of breaking bottle necks awoke him to work again.

"*Die Wacht am Rhein!*" yelled Schubert. "Start it up! Sing that first!" He began to sing it himself, all out of tune.

Fred cut the noise short by standing up to play something nobody could sing to—a jangling clamor of chords and runs on which he prides himself, that he swears is classical, but of which neither he nor anybody knows the name. Then he drank some beer and sang a comic song or two in English, we joining in the choruses.

Meanwhile, Brown was soaking away steadily, taking whatever drink came first to hand, and having no interest whatever in anything but the task of assuaging the thirst he had accumulated in the course of all that long marching since he left home. He had forgotten his cattle already—the Greeks who stole them—the Masai who stole from the Greeks. He paid for all he took, to the Jew's extreme surprise and satisfaction, and grumbled at the price of everything, to the Jew's supremest unconcern.

"An' my name's Brown o' Lumbwa, just in proof of all I say!" he informed the room at large at intervals.

When Will had exhausted all the American songs he knew,

and Fred had run through his own long list there was nothing left for it but to make up accompaniments to the songs the sergeants had been raised on. Fred made the happy discovery that none of them knew *The Marseillaise,* so he played that as an antidote each time after they had made the hardwood rafters ring and the smoke-filled air vibrate with Teutonic jingoism. The Jew, who probably knew more than he cared to admit, grew more and more beady-eyed each time *The Marseillaise* was played.

There was a pause in the proceedings at about ten o'clock, by which time all the sergeants except Schubert were sufficiently drunk to feel thoroughly at ease. Schubert was cold-eyed sober, although scarcely any longer thirsty.

A native was brought in by two *askaris* and charged before Schubert with hanging about the boma gate after dark. He was asked the reason. The Jew, sitting beside me with his book of names and charges, poured cool water over my bandages and translated to me what they all said. He spoke English very well indeed, but in such low tones that I could scarcely catch the words, drawing in his breath and not moving his lips at all.

The native explained that he had waited to see the *bwana makubwa*—the commandant. He had nowhere to go and no money with which to pay for lodging, so he proposed to wait outside the gate and watch for the coming of the commandant next morning. He would intercept him on his way down from the white house on the hill.

He was asked why. To beg a favor. What favor? Satisfaction. For what? For his daughter. He was the father of the girl whom the commandant had favored with attentions. She had been a virgin. Now she was to have a child. It would be a half-black, half-white child. Who would now marry a woman with such a child as that? Yet nothing had been given her. She had been simply sent back home to be a charge on her parents and an already poverty-stricken village. Therefore he had come to ask that justice be done, and the girl be given at least a present of money.

The sergeants roared with laughter, all except Schubert,

who seemed only appalled by the impudence of the request. He sat back and ordered the story repeated.

"And you dare ask for money from the *bwana makubwa?*" he demanded. "You dog of a Nyamwesi! Is the honor not sufficient that your black brute of a daughter should have a baby by such a great person? You cattle have no sense of honor! You must learn! Put him down! Beat him till I say stop!"

There was no need to put him down, however. The motion of the hand, voice inflection, order were all too well understood. The man lay face-downward on the floor without so much as a murmur of objection, and buried his face in both hands. The *askaris* promptly stripped him of the thin cotton loin-cloth that constituted his only garment, tearing it in pieces as they dragged it from him.

"Go on!" ordered Schubert. "Beat him!"

Both the *askaris* had *kibokos*. The longest of the two was split at the nether end into four fingers. The shortest was more than a yard long, tapering from an inch and a half where the man's fist gripped it to half an inch thick at the tip. They stood one each side of their victim and brought the whips down on his naked skin alternately.

"Slowly!" ordered Schubert. "Slowly, and with all your strength! The brute doesn't feel it when you beat so fast! Let him wait for the blow! Don't let him know when it's coming! So—so is better!"

Not every blow drew blood, for a native's skin is thick and tough, especially where he sits. But the blows that fell on the back and thighs all cut the skin, and within two minutes the native's back was a bloody mass, and there was blood running on the floor, and splashes of blood on the whitewashed wall cast by the whips as they ascended.

I made up my mind the man was going to be killed, for Schubert gave no order and the *askaris* did not dare stop without one. The victim writhed, but did not cry out, and the writhing grew less. Even Brown sobered up for a time at the sight of it. He came and sat between me and the Jew.

"It's a shame!" he grumbled. "Up in our country twenty-five lashes is the masshimum, an' only to be laid on in the presence of a massishtrate. *You* beat a black man an' they'll fine you first offense, jail you second offense, an' third offense God knows what they'll do! Poor ole Brown o' Lumbwa! They fined me once a'ready. Nessht time they'll put me in jail! Better get quite drunk an' be blowed to it!"

He staggered back to his chair by the farther wall, leering at Schubert as he passed.

"You're no gentleman!" he asserted aggressively. "You're no better 'n a black man yourself! You ought-to-be-on-floor 'stead o' him! Dunno-how-behave-yourself! Take your coat off, an' come outside, an' fight like a man!"

Schubert gave the order to stop at last. The *askaris* stood aside, panting from the effort.

"Get up!" ordered Schubert.

The miserable Nyamwesi struggled to his feet and stood limply before Schubert, his back running blood and his face drawn with torture.

"Don't you know how to behave!" demanded Schubert.

The native made no answer.

"If you don't salute properly I'll order you thrown down and thrashed again!"

The native saluted in a sort of imitation of the German military manner.

"Now, will you lie in wait for the *bwana makubwa* to trouble him with your pig's affairs again?"

"No."

"Will you go back home?"

"Yes."

"You've learned a lesson, eh?"

"Yes."

"Then say thank you!"

"Thank you!"

"*Rrruksa!*"*

The poor wretch turned and went, staggering rather than

---

*Ruksa, you have leave to go.

walking, to the door and disappearing into outer darkness without a backward glance.

"Now for some more songs and a round of drinks!" Schubert shouted.

But Fred was no longer in mood to make music, or even to be civil. He shut the concertina up, and asked the Jew how much he owed. The sergeants went on singing without music, and while we waited for the Jew to reckon up Fred's score Schubert came over to us, sat down between me and Fred, and proceeded to deal with the new situation in proper German military manner, by direct assault.

"Always you English criticize!" he began. "Can you never travel without applying your cursed standards to everything you behold? I tell you, we Germans know how to rule these black people! We understand! We employ no sickly sentiment! We give orders—they obey, or else suffer terribly and swiftly! In that manner we arrive at knowing where we are!"

"Are you well loved by the people?" Fred asked him politely.

"Bah! *Sie wollen wohl beliebt werden!*\* Not I! Not we! Of what value is the love of such people? Their fear is what we cultivate! Having made them afraid of us, we successfully make them work our will! But why should I trouble to explain? In a few years there will only be one government of Africa! One, I tell you, and that German! You English are not fit to govern colonies! You are mawkishly sentimental! You think more of the feelings of a black man and of the rights of his women than of progress—advancement—*kultur!* Bah! I tell you they have no feelings a real man need consider! They are only fit for furthering the aims of us Germans! And their women have no rights! None whatever! You know, I suppose, that it is the policy of the German government to encourage the spread of Muhammedanism in Africa? Well, under the Muhammedan law as given in the Koran women have no souls! That is good! That is as it should be! No women have souls!"

---

\*You want to be popular, don't you!

"How about your own mother?" Fred suggested.

"She was a good Prussian! She was a super-woman! Not to be mentioned in the same breath with women of any other race! Yet even she—the good Prussian mother—could not hold a candle to a man! Her business was to raise sons for Prussia, and she did it! I have eight brothers, all in the army, and only one sister; she has four sons already!"

"Strange that your nation should breed like that!" said Fred.

"Not strange at all!" answered Schubert. "We are needed to conquer the world! Think, for instance, when we have conquered the Congo Free State, and taken away East and South Africa from England—to say nothing of Egypt and India!—how many Prussian sergeant-majors we shall want! *Donnerwetter!* Do you think we Germans will long be satisfied with this miserable section of East Africa that was all the English left to us on this coast? We use this for a foothold, that is all! We use this to gain time and get ready! You think perhaps I do not know, eh? I am only *feldwebel* —non-commissioned officer, you call it. Well and good. I tell you our officers talk all the time of nothing else! And they don't care who hears them!"

The Jew gave Fred his bill, scrawled on a piece of wrapping paper. Schubert snatched it away and crumpled it into a ball.

"*Kreutzblitzen!* You are my guests to-night! I invited you!"

"Thanks," Fred answered, "but we don't care to be your guests. Here," he said, turning to the Jew, "take your money!"

Schubert said nothing, but eyed the Jew with a perfectly blank face, as if he watched to see whether the man would damn himself or not.

"Take your money!" repeated Fred. But the Jew turned his back and busied himself with bottles at the side-table.

"He knows better!" Schubert laughed. "He understands by this time our German hospitality!"

"All right," answered Fred. "We'll go out without paying!"

"Not at all," retorted Schubert. "The mess shall pay the bill in full! You stay here until I have said what I have to say to you! The rest of your party may go, but you stay! You can explain to the others afterward."

He leaned forward, reached a bottle of beer off the table, knocked off the neck, and emptied the contents down his throat at a draught. Behind his back we exchanged glances

"I'll listen," said Fred.

"You alone?"

"No, we all stay. All or none!"

Schubert made a contemptuous gesture with his thumb toward Brown, who had fallen dead drunk on the floor.

"Will that one stay, too?"

"He is not of our party really," Fred answered. "He knows nothing of our affairs."

"You men are in trouble—worse trouble than you guess!"

Schubert looked with his cruel blue eyes into each of ours in turn, then stared straight in front of him and waited.

"I don't believe it," Fred answered. "We have done nothing to merit trouble."

"Merit in this world is another name for chance!" said Schubert.

"What are we supposed to have done?" demanded Fred.

Schubert at once assumed what was intended to be a sly look, of uncommunicable knowledge.

"None of my business to tell what my officers know," he answered. "As for that, time will no doubt disclose much. The point is—trouble can be forestalled."

"Aw—show your hand!" cut in Will, leaning in front of Fred. "I've seen you Heinies fishing for graft too often in the States not to recognize symptoms! Spill the bait can! There's no other way to tell if we'll bite! Tell us what you're driving at!"

"Ivory!" said Schubert savagely and simply, shutting his jaws after the word like a snap with a steel spring. It would have broken the teeth of an ordinary human.

"What ivory?"

We all did our best to look blank.

"You know! Tippoo Tib's ivory! It belongs to the German government! Emin Pasha, whom that adventurer Stanley rescued against his will, agreed to sell the secret to us, but we never agreed on a price and he died without telling. *Gott!* He would have told had I had the interviewing of him! It was known in Zanzibar that you and a certain English lord shared the secret. You have been watched. You are known to be in search of the stuff."

"The deuce you say!" Fred murmured, with a glance to left and right at us.

"If you were to go to the office to-morrow, and tell our commandant what you know," said Schubert, "you might be suitably compensated. You would certainly be given facilities for leaving the country in comfort at your leisure."

"Who told you to promise us that?" Fred demanded, turning on him.

The *feldwebel* did not answer, but sat with his legs straight out in front of him, his heels together, and the palms of his hands touching between his knees. The sergeants were all singing, smoking and drinking. The Jew was back at his old post, watching every one with gimlet eyes.

"Think it over!" said Schubert, getting up. "There is time until morning. There is time until you leave this building. After that—" He shrugged his square shoulders brutally.

There was no sense in going out at once, as we had intended, with that combination of threat and promise hanging over us.

"Why not do what we said—admit that we know what we don't know—and put 'em on the wrong scent?" Will whispered.

"I wish to God Monty were here!" groaned Fred.

"Rot!" Will answered. "Monty is all you ever said of him and then some; but we're able to handle this ourselves all right without him. Tell 'em a bull yarn, I say!"

Fred relapsed into a sort of black gloom intended to attract the Muse of Strategy. He was always better at swift action in the open and optimism in the face of visible danger than at matching wits against something he could not see beginning or end of.

"Tell 'em it's in German East!" urged Will. "Offer to lead them to it on certain conditions. Think up controversial proposals! Play for time!"

Fred shook his head.

"What if it turns out true? Monty's in Europe. Suppose he should learn while he's there that the stuff is really in German East—we'd have spoiled his game!"

"If the stuff should really be in German East," Will argued, "we've no chance in the world of getting even a broker's share of it, Monty or no Monty! Take my advice and tell 'em what they want to know!"

Meanwhile an argument of another kind had started across the room. Schubert had related with grim amusement to Sergeant Sachse, who was sitting next him, our disapproval of the flogging of the father of the the commandant's abandoned woman.

"At what were they shocked?" wondered Sachse. "At the flogging, or the intercourse, or because he sent the female packing when she proposed to have a child? Do they not know that to have children about the premises would be subversive of military excellence?"

"They were shocked at all three things," grinned Schubert, "but chiefly, I think, at the flogging."

"Bah! Such a tickling of a native's hide doesn't hurt him to speak of! Wait until they see our court in the morning!"

It was that that raised the clamor. Even Schubert, who might be supposed to have won promotion because he could stay sober longer than the others, was beginning to grow noisy in his speech and to laugh without apparent reason. The rest were all already frankly drunk, and any excuse for dispute was a good one. They one and all, including Schubert, denied Sachse's contention that a flogging did not hurt enough to matter.

"I bet I could take one without winking!" Sachse announced.

Schubert's little bright pig-eyes gleamed through the smoke at that.

"*Kurtz und gut!*" he laughed. "There is a case of champagne unopened. I bet you that case of champagne that you lie! That you can not take a flogging!"

There was an united yelp of delight. The sergeants rose and gathered round Sachse. Schubert cursed them and drove them to the chairs again.

"Open that case of champagne!" he roared, and the Jew obeyed, setting the bottles on the table in two rows.

"I bet you those twelve bottles you dare not take a regular flogging, and that you can not endure it if you dare try!"

"I can stand as much as you!" hedged Sachse.

"Good! We will see! We will both take a flogging—stroke for stroke! Whoever squeals first shall pay for the champagne!"

Sachse could not back out. His cheeks grew whiter, but he staggered to his feet, swearing.

"I will show you of what material a German sergeant is made!" he boasted. "It is not only Prussians who are men of metal! How shall it be arranged?"

The arrangement was easy enough. Schubert shouted for an *askari,* and the corporal who was doing police duty outside in the street came running. He had a *kiboko* in his hand almost a yard and a half long, and Schubert examined it with approval.

"How would you like to flog white men?" he demanded.

"I would not dare!" grinned the corporal.

"Not dare, eh? Would you not obey an order?"

"Always I obey!" the man answered, saluting.

"Good. I shall lie here. This other *bwana* shall lie there beside me. You shall stand between. First you shall strike one, then the other—turn and turn about until I give the order to cease! And listen! If you fail once—just one little time!—to flog with all your might, you shall have two hundred lashes yourself; and they shall be good ones, because I will lay them on! Is it understood?"

"Yes," said the corporal, the whites of his eyes betraying

doubt, fear and wonder. But he grinned with his lips, lest the *feldwebel* should suspect him of unwillingness.

"Are the terms understood?" demanded Schubert, and the sergeants yelped in the affirmative.

"Then choose a referee!"

One of the sergeants volunteered for the post. Schubert lay down on the floor, and Sachse beside him about four feet away. The corporal took his stand between. He was an enormous Nubian, broad of chest, with the big sloping shoulder muscles that betray double the strength that tailors try to suggest with jackets padded to look square.

"*Nun—recht feste schlagen!*"* ordered Schubert. Then he took the sleeve of his tunic between his teeth and hid his face.

"One!" said the referee. Down came the heavy black whip with a crack like a gun going off. Schubert neither winced nor murmured, but the blood welled into the seat of his pants and spread like red ink on blotting-paper.

"One!" said the referee again. The corporal faced about, and raised his weapon, standing on tiptoe to get more swing. Sachse flinched at the sound of the whip going up, and the other sergeants roared delight. But he was still when it descended, and the crack of the blow drew neither murmur nor movement from him either. Like the *feldwebel*, he had his sleeve between his teeth.

"Two!" said the referee, and the black whip rose again. It descended with a crack and a splash on the very spot whence the blood flowed, this time cutting the pants open, but Schubert took no more notice of it than if a fly had settled on him. There was a chorus of applause.

"Two!" said the referee. Again the corporal faced about and balanced himself on tiptoe. Sachse was much the more nervous of the two. He flinched again while waiting for the blow, but met it when it did come without a tremor of any kind. He was much the softer. Blood flowed from him more

---

*Now, hit good and hard!

freely, but his pants seemed to be of sterner stuff, for they did not split until the eight-and-twentieth lash, or thereabouts.

From first to last, although the raw flesh lay open to the lash, and the corporal, urged to it by the united threats and praise of all the other sergeants, wrought his utmost, Schubert lay like a man asleep. He might have been dead, except for the even rise and fall of his breathing, that never checked or quickened once. Nine-and-forty strokes he took without a sign of yielding. At the eight-and-fortieth Sachse moaned a little, and the referee gave the match against him.

Schubert rose to his feet unaided, grinning, red in the face, but without any tortured look.

"Now you can say forever that you have flogged two white men!" he told the *askari*.

"Who will believe me?" the man answered.

Sachse had to be helped to his feet. He was pale and demanded brandy.

"What did I tell you?" laughed Schubert. "A Prussian is better than any man! Look at him, and then at me!"

He shouted for his servant, who had to be fetched from the boma—a smug-faced little rascal, obviously in love with the glory reflected on the sergeant-major's servant. He was made to produce a basin and cold water—he discovered them somewhere in the dim recesses of the store—and sponge his master's raw posterior before us all. Then he was sent for clean white pants and presently Schubert, only refusing to sit down, was quite himself again.

Sachse on the other hand refused the ministrations of the boy—was annoyed by the chaff of the other sergeants—refused to drink any of the sweet champagne he would now have to pay for—and went away in great dudgeon, murmuring about the madness that takes hold of men in Africa.

Meanwhile, while Schubert strutted and swaggered, making jokes more raw and beastly than his own flogged hide, the Jew came and poured more cool water on my hot bandages, touching them with deft fingers that looked like the hairy legs of a huge spider—his touch more gentle—more fugitive than any woman's.

"You should not tell zat dam *feldwebel* nozink!" he advised in nasal English. "Nefer mind vat you tell heem he is all ze same not your frien'. He only obey hees officers. Zey say to cut your t'roat—he cut it! Zey say to tell you a lot o' lies—he tell! He iss not a t'inker, but a doer: and hees faforite spectacle iss ze blood of innocence! Do not effer say I did not tell you! On ze ozzer hand, tell no one zat I did tell! Zese are dangerous people!"

He resumed business with his account book, and I whispered to Fred and Will what advice he had given. Seeing us with our heads together, Schubert crossed the room, beginning to get very drunk now that the shock of the flogging had had time to reinforce the alcohol. (The blows had sobered him at first.)

"What have you decided?" he asked, standing before us with his legs apart and his hands behind him in his favorite attitude—swaying gently back and forward because of the drink, and showing all his teeth in a grin.

"Nothing," Fred answered. "We'll think it over."

"Too late in the morning!" he answered, continuing to sway. "I can do nothing for you in the morning."

"What can you do to-night?" Fred asked.

He shrugged his shoulders. "I can report. The report will go in at dawn."

"You may tell your superiors," Fred answered, rising, "that if they care to make us a reasonable offer, I don't say we won't do business!"

Schubert leered.

"To-morrow will be too late!" he repeated.

It was Fred's turn to shrug shoulders, and he did it inimitably, turning his back on Schubert and helping Will support me to the door. The *feldwebel* stood grinning while I held to the door-post and they dragged Brown to his feet. He made no offer to help us in any way at all, nor did any of the sergeants.

There was no getting action from Brown. He was as dead to the world as a piece of wood, and there being no other obvious solution of the problem, Will hoisted him upon his back and carried him, he snoring, all the way home to camp. Fred hoisted and carried me, for the pain of my wound when I tried to walk was unbearable.

We reached camp abreast and were challenged by the sentries, who made a great show of standing guard. They took Brown and threw him on the bed in his own tent—accepted Fred's offer of silver money—and departed, marching up-street in their heavy, iron-bound military boots with the swing and swagger only the Nubian in all the world knows just how to get away with.

I lay on the bed in Fred's tent, and then Kazimoto came to us, hugely troubled about something, stirring the embers of the fire before the tent and arranging the lantern so that its rays would betray any eavesdropper. He searched all the shadows thoroughly, prodding into them with a stick, before he unburdened his mind.

"Those *askaris* were not put here to guard our tents," he told us. (The really good native servant when speaking of his master's property always says our, and never your.) "As soon as you were gone the Greeks and the Goa came. They and the *askaris* questioned me. It was a trick! You were drawn away on purpose! One by one—two by two—they questioned us all, but particularly me."

"What about?" Fred demanded.

"About our business. Why are we here. What will we do. What do we know. What do I know about you. What do you know about me. Why do I serve you. How did I come to take service with you. To what place will we travel next, and when. How much money have we with us. Have we friends or acquaintances in Muanza. Do you, *bwana,* carry any letters in your pockets. Of what do you speak when you suppose no man is listening. *Bwana,* my heart is very sad in me! Those Greeks tell lies, and the Germans stir trouble in a big pot like the witches! I know the Germans! I am Nyamwezi. I was born not far from here, and ran away as soon as I was old enough because the Germans shot my father and let my mother and brothers starve to death. I did not starve, because one of them took me for a servant; but I ran away from him. My heart is very sad to be in this place! They ask what of a hoard of ivory. I tell them I do not know, and they threaten to beat me! This place is bad! Let us go away to-night!"

There was no sleep that night for any of us. My wound hurt too much. The others were too worried. By the light of the lantern in Fred's tent we cooked up a story to tell that we hoped would induce the Germans to let us wander where we chose.

"Sure, they'll watch us!" Will admitted. "But as our only real reason for coming down here—leaving Brown's cattle out of the reckoning—was to throw people off the scent, in what way are we worse off? The lake is big enough to lose ourselves in! What is it—two hundred and fifty miles long by as many broad? D'you mean we can't give their sleuths the slip? We can't beat that for a plan: let 'em keep on thinking we know where Tippoo hid the stuff. If we succeed in losing 'em they'll think we're at large in German East and keep on hunting for us—whereas we'll really be up in British East. Let's send a telegram in code to Monty!"

Then Fred thought of an idea that in the end solved our biggest problem, although we did not think much of it at the time.

"They may refuse to take a telegram in code," he said. "It's likely they'll open letters. (We can try the code, of course. They'll probably take our money, and put their experts on deciphering the message. They'll say it was lost if there are any inquiries afterward.) I propose we send a straight-out cablegram advising Monty of our whereabouts (they'll let that go through) and warning him to ask for letters at the Bank in Mombasa before he does anything else."

"Yes, but—" Will objected.

"Wait!" said Fred. "I haven't finished. Then write two letters: one full of any old nonsense, to be sent in the regular way by mail. They'll open that. The other to go by runner. Kazimoto can find us a runner. He knows these Wanyamwezi. He can pick a man who'll get through without fail."

We could think of nothing to say against the plan. The argument that the German government would scarcely stoop to opening private mail did not seem to hold water when we examined it, so we wrote as Fred suggested—one letter telling Monty that we hoped to make some arrangement with the Germans, and at all events to wait in German East until he could join us—and the other telling him the real facts at great length, laboriously set out in the code we had agreed upon.

We sealed the second letter in several wrappers, and sewed it up finally in a piece of waterproof silk. Then we sent for Kazimoto and ordered him to find the sort of messenger we needed.

"Send me!" he urged. "I will start now, before it is light! I will hide by day and travel by night until I reach the British border! Give me only enough cooked food and my pay, and I will take the letter without fail!"

We refused, for he was too useful to us. He begged again and again to be sent with the letter, promising faithfully to wait for us afterward on the British side of the border at any place we should name. But we upbraided him for cowardice, ordered him to find another messenger, and promised him he need have no fear of Germans as long as he remained our servant.

Before high noon we would each have given many years of Kazimoto's pay if only we could have recalled that decision and have known that he was speeding away from Muanza toward a border where white men knew the use of mercy.

Just as the first peep of dawn began to color the sky Schubert came swaggering down-street to us, wiping his mouth with the back of his hand.

"How have you slept?" he asked us, laughing.

We answered something or other.

"I did not trouble to sleep! I stayed and finished the drinks. I have just swallowed the last of the beer! Whoever wants a morning drink must wait for it now until the overland *safari* comes!"

We displayed no interest. Brown, the only one likely

to yearn for alcohol before breakfast, snored in his tent still.

"What of it now? I go drill my troops. Parade is at six sharp! There remain twenty minutes. Come with me and tell your secret at the boma now, before it is too late!"

"Explain why it would be too late after breakfast!" demanded Fred.

"All right," said Schubert. "I will tell you this much. There will come a launch this morning from Kisumu in British East. There will be people on that launch, one of whom has authority that overrides that of the commandant of this place. The commandant desires to know your information—and get the credit for it—before that individual, whose authority is higher, comes. Is that clear?"

"Perfectly," Fred answered.

"See if this is clear, too!" cut in Will. "You go and ask your commandant what price he offers for the secret! Nothing for nothing! Tell him we're not afraid of him!"

"It is none of my business to tell him anything," sneered Schubert, spitting and turning on his heel. He swaggered out of the camping-ground and up-street again, leaving the clear impression behind him that he washed his hands of us for good and all.

"Let's watch him drill his men," said I. "I'll wait on the hospital steps until they open the place."

So we ate a scratch breakfast and Fred and Will helped me up-street, past where the Jew stood blinking in the morning sun on the steps of the D. O. A. G. He seemed to be saying prayers, but beckoned to us.

"Trouble!" he said. "Trouble! If you have any frien's fetch them—send for them!"

"Can you send a letter for us to British East?" Fred asked him.

"God forbid!" He jumped at the very thought, and shrugged himself like a man standing under a water-spout. "What would they do to me if I were found out?"

"What is the nature of the trouble?" Fred asked him.

"Ah, who should tell! Trouble, I tell you, trouble! Zat

cursed Schubert sat here drinking until dawn. I heard heem
say many t'ings! Send for your frien's!"

He turned his back on us and ran in. There was a lieutenant arrayed in spotless white with a saber in glittering
scabbard watching us all from the boma gate. A little later
that morning we knew better why the Jew fled indoors at
sight of him.

Schubert was standing in mid-square with a hundred *askaris* lined up two-deep in front of him. There were no other
Germans on parade. The corporals were Nubians, and the
rest of the rank and file either Nubian or some sort of Sudanese. He was haranguing them in a bastard mixture of
Swahili, Arabic, and German, they standing rigidly at attention, their rifles at the present.

Not content with the effect of his words, he strode up presently to a front-rank man and hit him in the face with
clenched fist. In the effort to recover his balance the man
let his rifle get out of alignment. Schubert wrenched it from
him. It fell to the ground. He struck the man, and when he
stooped to pick the rifle up kicked him in the face. Then
he strode down the line and beat two other men for grinning. All this the lieutenant watched without a sign of disapproval, or even much interest.

Meanwhile the chain-gang emerged from the boma gate,
going full-pelt, fastened neck to neck, the chain taut and
each man carrying a water-jar. The minute they had crossed
the square Schubert commenced with company drill, and for
two hours after that, with but one interval of less than five
minutes for rest, he kept them pounding the gravel in evolution after evolution—manual exercise at the double—skir-
mishing exercise—setting up drill—goose-step, and all the
mechanical, merciless precision drill with which the Germans
make machines of men.

His debauch did not seem in the least to have affected him,
unless to make his temper more violently critical. By seven
o'clock the sun was beating down on him and dazzling his
eyes from over the boma wall. The dust rose off the square.
The words of command came bellowing in swift succession

from a throat that ought to have been hard put to it to whisper. If anything, he grew more active and exacting as the *askaris* wearied, and by the time the two hours were up they were ready to a man to drop.

But not so he. He dismissed them, and swaggered over to the market-place to hector and bully the natives who were piling their wares in the shade of the great grass roof. Then he went into the boma to breakfast just as a sergeant in khaki came over and unlocked the hospital door. I followed the sergeant in, but he ordered me out again.

"I have come to see the doctor," I said. "I need attention."

He was not one of the sergeants who had been drunk in the D. O. A. G. the night before, but a man of a higher mental type, although no less surly.

"It will be for the doctor to say what you need when he has seen you!" he answered, turning his back and busying himself about the room. Will translated, and I limped out again.

By and by the doctor came, and passed me sitting on the steps amid a throng of natives who seemed to have all the imaginable kinds of sores. He took no notice of me, but sent out the sergeant to inquire why I had not stood up as he passed. I did not answer, and the sergeant went in again.

Fred by that time was simply blasphemous, alternately threatening to go in and kick the doctor, and condemning Will's determination to do the same thing. Finally we decided to see the matter through patiently, and all sat together on the steps watching the activity of the square. There was a lot going on—bartering of skins and hides—counting of crocodile eggs, brought in by natives for sake of the bounty of a few copper coins the hundred—a cock-fight in one corner—the carrying to and fro of bunches of bananas, meat, and grain in baskets; and in and out among it all full pelt in the hot sun marched the chain-gang, doing the township dirty work.

By and by Schubert emerged from the boma gate followed by natives carrying a table and a soap-box. He set these under a limb of the great baobab that faced the boma gate not far from the middle of the square. I noticed then for the first time that a short hempen rope hung suspended from the largest branch, with a noose in the end. The noose was not more than two feet below the branch.

Schubert's consideration of the table's exact position, and the placing of the soap-box on the table, was interrupted by the arrival of Coutlass, his Greek companion and the Goanese arm in arm, followed closely by two *askaris* who shouted angrily and made a great show of trying to prevent them. One of the *askaris* aimed his rifle absurdly at Coutlass, both Greeks and the Goanese daring him gleefully to pull the trigger.

They purposely came close to us, not that we showed signs of meaning to befriend them. They were simply unable to understand that there are degrees of disgrace. To Coutlass all victims of government outrage ought surely to be more than friendly with any one in conflict with the law. Personal quarrels should go for nothing in face of the common wrong.

"There is going to be a hanging!" Coutlass shouted to us. "They thought we would remain quietly in camp with that going on! Give us chairs!" he called to Schubert. "Provide us a place in the front row where we may see!"

Schubert grinned. He returned to the boma yard and presumably conferred with an officer, for presently he came out again and gave the Greeks leave to stand under the tree, provided they would return to camp afterward. Later yet, Brown came along and joined us on the steps, looking red-eyed and ridiculous.

"Goin' to be a hangin'," he announced. "I been askin' natives about it. Black man stole the condemned man's daughter an' refused to pay cows for her accordin' to custom or anythin'—said he could do what the white men did an' help himself. Father of the girl took a spear and settled the thief's hash with it — ran him through — did a clean job. Serve him right—eh—what? Germans went an' nabbed him, though—tried him in open court—goin' to hang him this mornin' for murder! How does it strike you?"

We were not exactly in mood to talk to Brown—in fact,

we wished him anywhere but with us, but he thought himself perfectly welcome, and rambled on:

"Up in British East we don't hang black men for murder unless it's what they call an aggravated case—murder an' robbery—murder an' arson—murder an' rape. Hang a white man for murderin' a black sure as you're sitting here, an' shoot a black man for murderin' a white; but the blacks don't understand, so when they kill one another in such a case as this, why we give 'em a short jail sentence an' a good long lecture, an' let 'em go again. These folks have it t'other way round. They never hang a German, whether he's guilty or not, but hang a poor black man, what doesn't understand, for half o' nothin'!"

A great crowd began gathering about the tree, and was presently driven by *askaris* with whips into a mass on the far side of the tree from us. Whether purposely or not, they left a clear view from the hospital steps of all that should happen. Evidently warning had been sent out broadcast, for the inhabitants of village after village came trooping into town to watch, each lot led by its sultani in filthy rags and the foolish imitation crown his conquerors had supplied him at several times its proper price. The square was a dense sea of people before nine o'clock, and the *askaris* made the front few hundreds lie, and the next rows squat, in order that the men and women behind might see.

Then at last out came the victim with his hands tied behind him and a bright red blanket on his loins. He was a proud-looking fellow. He halted a moment between his guard of German sergeants and eyed the crowd, and us, and the tree, and the noose. Then he looked down on the ground and appeared to take no further interest.

The sergeants took him by the arms and led him along to the table between them. Out came the commandant then, in snow-white uniform, with his saber polished until it shone —all spruced up for the occasion, and followed by a guard of honor consisting of lieutenant, two sergeants, and six black *askaris*.

There was a chair by the table. At sight of the commandant the sergeants made their victim use that as a step by which to mount the table and soap-box, and there he stood eying his oppressors as calmly as if he were witnessing a play. A murmur arose among the crowd. A number of natives called to him by name, but he took no notice after that one first steady gaze.

"They're sayin' good-by to him," said Brown, breathing in my ear. "They're telling him they won't forget him!"

The crack of *askaris'* whips falling on head and naked shoulders swiftly reduced the crowd to silence. Then the commandant faced them all, and made a speech with that ash-can voice of his—first in German, then in the Nyamwezi tongue. Will translated to us sentence by sentence, the doctor standing on the top step behind us smiling approval. He seemed to think we would be benefited by the lecture just as much as the natives.

It was awful humbug that the commandant reeled off to his silent audience—hypocrisy garbed in paternal phrases, and interlarded with buncombe about Germany's mission to bring happiness to subject peoples.

"Above all," he repeated again and again, "the law must be enforced impartially—the good, sound, German law that knows no fear or favor, but governs all alike!"

When he had finished he turned to the culprit.

"Now," he demanded, "do you know why you are to be hanged?"

There was a moment's utter silence. The crowd drew in its breath, seeming to know in advance that some brave answer was forthcoming. The man on the table with his hands behind him surveyed the crowd again with the gaze of simple dignity, looked down on the commandant, and raised his voice.

It was an unexpected, high, almost falsetto note, that in the silence carried all across the square.

"I am to die," he said, "because I did right! My enemy did what German officers do. He stole my young girl. I killed him, as I hope all you Germans may be killed! But hope no longer gathers fruit in this land!"

"Ah-h-h-h!" the crowd sighed in unison.

"Good man!" exploded Fred, and the doctor tried to kick him from behind—not hard, but enough to call his attention to the proprieties. His toe struck me instead, and when I looked up angrily he tried to pretend he was not aware of what he had done.

Under the trees the commandant flew into a rage such as I have seldom seen. Each land has a temper of its own, and the white man's anger varies in inverse ratio with his nearness to the equator. But *furor teutonicus* transplanted is the least controllable, least dignified, least admirable that there is. And that man's passion was the apex of its kind.

His beard spread, as a peacock spreads its tail. His eyes blazed. His eyebrows disappeared under the brim of his white helmet, and his clenched fists burst the white cotton gloves. He half-drew his saber—thought better of that, and returned it. There was an *askari* standing near with *kiboko* in hand to drive back the crowd should any press too closely. He snatched the whip and struck the condemned man with it as high up as he could reach, making a great welt across his bare stomach. The man neither winced nor complained.

"For those words," the commandant screamed at him in German, "you shall not die in comfort! For that insolence mere hanging is too good!"

Then he calmed himself a little, and repeated the words in the native tongue, explaining to the crowd that German dignity should be upheld at all costs.

"Fetch him down from there!" he ordered.

Schubert sprang on the table and knocked the condemned man off it with a blow of his fist. With hands bound behind him the poor fellow had no power of balance, and though he jumped clear he fell face-downward, skinning his cheek on the gravel. The commandant promptly put a foot on his neck and pinned him down.

"Flog him!" he ordered. "Two hundred lashes!"

It was done in silence, except for the corporal's labored breathing and the commandant's incessant sharp commands to beat harder—harder—harder. A sergeant stood by counting.

The crack of the whip divided up the silence into periods of agony.

When the count was done the victim was still conscious. Schubert and a sergeant dragged him to his feet, and hauled him to the table. Four other men—two sergeants and two natives—passed a rope round the table legs. Schubert lifted the victim by the elbows so that his head could pass through the noose, and when that was accomplished the man had to stand on tiptoe on the soap-box in order to breathe at all.

"All ready!" announced Schubert, and jumped off with a laugh, his white tunic bloody from contact with the victim's tortured back.

"*Los!*" roared the commandant

The men hauled on the rope. Table and soap-box came tumbling away, and the victim spun in the air on nothing, spinning round, and round, and round—slower and slower and slower—then back the other way round faster and faster.

They say hanging is a merciful death—that the pressure of rope on two arteries produces anesthesia, but few are reported to have come back to tell of the experience. At any rate, as is not the case with shooting, it is easy to know when the victim is really dead.

For seconds that seemed minutes—for minutes that seemed hours the poor wretch spun, his elbows out, his knees up, his tongue out, his face wrinkled into tortured shapes, and his toes pointed upward so sharply that they almost touched his shins. Then suddenly the toes turned downward and the knees relapsed. The corpse hung limp, and the crowd sighed miserably, to the last man, woman and child, turning its back on what to them must have symbolized German rule.

They left the corpse hanging there. It was to be there until evening, some one said, for an example to frequenters of the market-place. The crowd trailed away, none glancing back. The pattering of feet ceased. The market-place across the square resumed its hum and activity. Then a native orderly came down the steps and touched me on the elbow. I struggled to my feet and limped after him up the steps.

Practically at the mercy of the doctor, I made up my mind

to be civil to him whether that suited me or not. I rather expected he would come to meet me, perhaps help me to a chair, and I wondered how, in my ignorance of German, I should contrive to answer his questions.

But I need not have worried. I did not even see him. He had left by the back door, and the orderly washed the wound and changed my bandages. That was all. There was no charge for the bandages, and the orderly was gentle now that his master's back was turned.

"Didn't he leave word when he would see me?" I asked.

*"Habanah!"* he answered—meaning, "He did not—there is not—there is nothing doing!"

# IPSOS CUSTODES

*We were an ignorant people. Out of a gloom we came*
*Hungering, striving, feasting—vanishing into the same.*
*Came to us your foreloopers, told us the gloom was bad,*
*Spoke of the Light that might be—simply it could be had—*
*Knowledge and wealth and freedom, plenty and peace and*
*  play,*
*And at all the price of obedience. "Listen and learn and*
*  obey,"*
*We were told, "and the gloom shall be lifted. Ignorance surely*
*  is shame."*
*We listened to your foreloopers, till presently Cadis\* came.*

*We were an ignorant people. Our law was "an eye for an eye,"*
*And he who wronged should right the wrong, and he who stole*
*  should die—*
*Bad law the Cadis told us, based on the fall of man;*
*And they set us to building law-courts on the Pangermanic*
*  plan—*
*Courts where the gloom of ages should be pierced, said they,*
*  with Light*
*And scientific theory displace wrong views of Right.*
*The Cadis' law was writ in books that only they could read,*
*But what should we know of the strings to that? 'Twas gloom*
*  when we agreed.*

*We were an ignorant people. The Offizieren came*
*To lend to law eye, tooth, and claw and so enforce the same.*
*Now nought are the tribal customs; free speech is under ban;*
*Displaced are misconceptions that were based on fallen man,*
*And our gloom has gone in darkness of the risen German's*
*  night,*
*Nor is there salt of mercy lest it sap the hold of Might.*
*They strike—we may not answer, nor dare we ask them why.*
*We sold ourselves to supermen. If we rebel, we die.*

---

\* *Cadi*—judge.

# CHAPTER EIGHT

I sat down once more on the hospital steps, and listened while Fred and Will relieved themselves of their opinions about German manners. Nothing seemed likely to relieve me. I had marched a hundred miles, endured the sickening pain, and waited an extra night at the end of it all simply on the strength of anticipation. Now that the surgeon would not see me, hope seemed gone. I could think of nothing but to go and hide somewhere, like a wounded animal.

But there were two more swift shocks in store, and no hiding-place. The path to the water-front led past us directly along the southern boma wall. Before Fred and Will had come to an end of swearing they saw something that struck them silent so suddenly that I looked up and saw, too. Not that I cared very much. To me it seemed merely one last super-added piece of evidence that life was not worth while.

Plainly the launch had come from British East, of which Schubert had spoken. Hand in hand from the water-front, followed by the obsequious Schubert, all smiles and long black whip (for the chain-gang trailed after with the luggage, and needed to be overawed), walked Professor Schillingschen and Lady Isobel Saffren Waldon. They seemed in love—or at any rate the professor did, for he ogled and smirked like a bearded gargoyle; and she made such play of being charmed by his grimaces that the Syrian maid fell behind to hide her face.

None of us spoke. We watched them. Personally I did not mind the feeling that the worst had happened at last. I was incapable of sounding further depths of gloom—too full of pain bodily to suffer mentally from threats of what might yet be. But the other two looked miserable—more so because Fred's bearded chin perked up so bravely, and Will set his jaw like a rock.

Not one of us had said a word when the biggest *askari*

we had seen yet strode up to us—saluted—and gave Fred a
sealed envelope. It was written in English, addressed to us
three by name (although our names were wrongly spelled).
We were required to present ourselves at the court-house at
once, reason not given. The letter was signed "Liebenkrantz
—Lieutenant."

The *askari* waited for us. I suppose it would not be correct to say we were under arrest, but the enormous black man
made it sufficiently obvious that he did not intend returning
to the court without us. The court-house was not more than
two hundred yards away. As we turned toward it we saw
Lady Saffren Waldon being helped into the commandant's
litter, borne by four men, the commandant himself superintending the ceremony with a vast deal of bowing and chatter,
and Professor Schillingschen looking on with an air of owning litter, porters, township, boma, and all. As we turned
our backs on them they started off toward the neat white
dwelling on the hill.

The court was a round, grass-roofed affair, with whitewashed walls of sun-dried brick. For about four-fifths of the
circumference the wall was barely breast-high, the roof being supported on wooden pillars bricked into the wall, as well
as by the huge pole that propped it up umbrella-wise in the
center.

The remaining fifth of the wall continued up as high as
the roof, forming a back to the platform. Facing the platform was the entrance, and on either side benches arranged
in rows followed the curve of the wall. There was a long
table on the platform, at which sat the lieutenant who had
summoned us, with a sergeant seated on either hand. The
sergeants were acting as court clerks, scribbling busily on
sheets of blue paper, and in books.

Behind the lieutenant, in a great gilt frame on the whitewashed wall, was a full-length portrait of the Kaiser in general's uniform. The Kaiser was depicted scowling, his gloved
hands resting on a saber almost as ferocious-looking as the
one the lieutenant kept winding his leg around.

All the benches were crowded with spectators, prisoners,

witnesses, and litigants. Outside, at least two hundred Arabs, Indians, and natives leaned with elbows on the wall and gazed at the scene within. The lieutenant glared, but otherwise took no notice of our entry; he gave no order, but one of the two sergeants came down from the platform and kicked half a dozen natives off the front bench to make room for us.

We were mistaken in supposing our case would be called first, or even among the first. The floor in the midst of the court was clear except for a long single line of natives and six *askari* corporals, each with a whip in his hand. It was evident at once that these natives were all ahead of us, even if those on the benches were not to be heard and dealt with before our turn came.

"Look at the far end of the line!" whispered Fred.

Lo and behold Kazimoto, looking rather drawn and gray, but standing bravely, looking neither to the right nor left. I judged he knew we were in court—he could hardly have failed to notice our coming in—but he sturdily refused to turn his head and see us.

"What has he done?" I wondered.

"Nothing more than told some Heinie to go to hell—you can bet your boots!" said Will.

The lieutenant was in no hurry to enlighten us. Our boy stood at the wrong end of the line to be taken first. The lieutenant called a name, and two great *askaris* pounced on the trembling native at the other end and dragged him forward, leaving him standing alone before the desk.

"Silence!" the lieutenant shouted, and the court became still as death.

He had a voice as mean as a hyena's—a voice that matched his face. The insolent, upturned twist of his fair mustache showed both corners of a thin-lipped mouth. He had the Prussian head, shaped square whichever way you viewed it. There was strength in the jaw-bones—strength in the deep-set bright eyes—strength in the shoulders that were square as box-corners without any padding—strength in the lean lithe figure; but it was always brute strength. There was no moral strength whatever in the restless fidgeting—the savage winding and unwinding of his left foot around the saber scabbard, or the attitude, leaning forward over the table, of petulant pugnacity. And the cruel voice was as weak as the hand was strong with which he rapped on the table.

He questioned the boy in front of him sharply—told him he stood charged with theft—and demanded an answer.

"With theft of what thing, and whose thing?"

The answer was bold. The trembling had ceased. Now that he faced nemesis the strength of native fatalism came to his rescue, bolstering up the pride that every uncontaminated Nyamwezi owns. He was not more than seventeen years old, but he stood there at last like a veteran at bay.

"Put him down and beat him!" ordered the lieutenant. "Impudent answers to this court shall always be soundly punished! Call the next case while that one is being taught good manners!"

A woman was stood in front of the line, fidgety with fear, in doubt whether to lay her suckling baby on the bench before she faced military justice. She laid it on the floor at her feet, hesitated, and then picked it up again and wrapped it in a corner of the red blanket that constituted her only dress.

"Take that brat away from her!" the lieutenant ordered. "She must pay attention to me. With that in her arms she will only think of mothering!"

An *askari* seized the baby by the arm and leg and gave it with a laugh to another woman to hold, its mother whimpering with fright until she saw it safely nestled.

"Quick, now! What about this one?"

It seemed there was no charge against her. The two sergeants searched through the piles of blue sheets in vain.

"Then what the devil is she here for? What do you want, you?"

The trembling woman pointed to her baby, but was dumb. It needed courage to answer that lieutenant, and the crack —crack—crack of a thick *kiboko* descending at measured intervals on the naked back of the boy who had answered boldly was no help toward reassurance.

"Speak!" the lieutenant ordered, "or I shall have you compelled to speak!"

She burst into sudden volubility. The dam once down, she poured forth a catalogue of wrongs that seemed endless, switching off from one dialect to another and at intervals inserting, apropos apparently of nothing, the few words of German she had picked up. The lieutenant yelled for an interpreter, and a Nyamwezi who knew German rose from the front bench and came and stood beside her.

"That baby is a white man's," he explained.

"What does she want?"

"She says the white man is the *bwana dakitari* (the doctor!)."

"Oh! Then I am glad she came here. It is time these loose women were taught a lesson! They tell the same tale. They say a white man passed through the village, gave their father a present, and carried them off. Is that her tale, too?"

"Yes."

"Well—what of it? The father agreed at the time when he accepted the present, didn't he? The consequence is a baby—not for the first time! Instead of going back to her village, she comes here and tries to blackmail the officer! She is young. It's the first time she has been in this court. This time I will be lenient. One hundred lashes!"

The interpreter translated, and the woman screamed. An *askari* seized her by the shoulders. She clung to him, but he threw her to the ground, and another one tore off the blanket that would have deadened the blows to some extent. She begged, and clung to their feet, but the blows began to rain on her, and presently she lay still, her breasts flattened against the earth floor, her mouth full of dust, and her naked body paralyzed by fear of the descending lash.

"Now bring up number one again!" the lieutenant ordered.

The *askaris* ceased from flogging him. One of them kicked him to his feet, and he resumed his stand in front of the lieutenant, looking up at him as proudly as ever, for all that his back was bruised and bloody.

"Did you steal or did you not?" asked the lieutenant.

"Steal what from whom?"

"Oh, go on beating him! Next case!"

The next man escaped the whip, but his witnesses were less fortunate. He brought two men and a woman with him to prove an alibi on a charge of attempted theft, and the glibness of their answers convinced the lieutenant they were lying. In the absence of all evidence for the prosecution except the unsupported word of a police *askari* who admitted a personal grudge against the defendant, the lieutenant resorted to the whip to change the witnesses' convictions, but without avail. The woman yelled under the lash like a demented thing, but, far from withdrawing her statements, tried to spit in the lieutenant's face when jerked to her feet and stood again before him—an impossible feat because the platform on which he sat at the table was too high. He had her beaten a second time for spitting.

The next man was a fat Baganda from British territory, charged with trading without a license. He pleaded ignorance of the law, and denied having traded. He was flogged for telling lies in court, and changed his testimony under the lash, whereat he was promptly sentenced to a hundred and fifty lashes and a month on the chain-gang. Under the lash a second time, he recanted—swore that his first statements had been true and that he had done no trading—a mistake in tactics that only caused the tale of lashes to be increased by fifty and the term on the chain-gang to be doubled.

"You must learn that the methods taught you on British territory are of no use here!" remarked the lieutenant.

By the time Kazimoto was called and stood out alone in front of him the lieutenant was in a boiling rage, and the floor of the court was actually crowded by prone natives being beaten. Extra *askaris* had been sent for in order that proceedings might not be delayed, and the audience could scarcely hear the evidence and sentences because of the crack of whips and the moans of victims. (Not that they all moaned by any means. By far the most of them submitted to the torture in grim proud silence: but the few who did make a noise—especially the women—made lots of it.)

As Kazimoto faced the lieutenant he turned once and looked at us. His eyes sought Fred's.

"Oh, *bwana!*" he said — and now for the first time we learned why he had chosen Fred to be his particular master. "I have been faithful! Stroke, then, that beard of yours as *Bwana* Courtney, my former master, used to stroke his. Then we shall both know what to do!"

Fred stroked his beard promptly, for the man needed comfort, not ridicule: but the concession to his superstition did none of us any good.

"Face this way!" the lieutenant shouted at him. "You are charged with being a deserter from German service. Also with giving information to foreigners. Also with serving foreigners in their effort to exploit the country, and with refusing to give proper answers when questioned by those in authority. Do you understand?"

"No," said Kazimoto in the most melancholy tone I ever heard from him.

"Are you a Nyamwezi? Now don't dare to lie to me!"

"Yes."

"You were born in this country?"

"Yes."

"Then you belong in this country!"

"I belong where my master takes me. My spirit is good. I am a true man," Kazimoto answered.

"Your spirit is rotten! You are a traitor! What do you mean by talking to me of your master, you reptile! Your master is the German government, of which His Majesty the Kaiser is supreme overlord! There is a picture of your master!" He pointed with a thumb over his shoulder to the full-length atrocity in oils behind him. "Salute it!"

The boy obeyed.

"Answer now! Who is your master?"

Kazimoto hesitated.

"Answer, I order you!"

He turned and pointed a finger at Fred, who nodded.

"That English *bwana* is my master," he said stoutly. It

was a forlorn hope, though. He did not seem to believe that
the statement of fact would do him any good.

Fred jumped to his feet.

"That is perfectly correct," he said in English. "The boy
is my servant, engaged on British territory, under a contract
for wages to be paid in English money. He is to be paid off
in British East at the end of my journey."

"Who asked you to speak?" demanded the lieutenant angrily, sitting up like a startled scorpion. "Do you not know
this is a court?"

"It looks like a shambles!" Fred answered, glancing to right
and left and indicating the victims of the whip writhing in
the name of German justice.

"Shut up, you fool!" counseled Will in a stage whisper, but
either Fred did not hear him, or was too worked up to care.

"Silence! Sit down!"

"I warn you!" Fred answered. "That boy has claimed
British protection. I shall see he has it!"

Then he sat down. The lieutenant glared at Kazimoto, the
glare changing to a cold grin as he realized how fully we were
all at his mercy for the moment.

"You are sentenced," he said, "to two hundred lashes for
making impudent answers to the court, and to six months on
the chain-gang for deserting from this country and entering
foreign service. Further evidence against you will be assem-
bled in the meanwhile, and other charges against you will be
tried on completion of the chain-gang sentence!"

"I protest!" shouted Fred, jumping up again. "I give notice of appeal to whatever higher court there is. I am ready
to give bonds!"

"What does this delay mean?" snapped the lieutenant. "Put
him down at once and lay the lashes on!"

The unfortunate Kazimoto was pounced on by two *askaris*
and thrown face-downward on the floor. One of them tore
off his clothes, ripping up his good English jacket.

"Did you hear my protest?" shouted Fred. "Did you hear
my notice of appeal?"

"I did," said the lieutenant. "Appeals are heard at the coast. You must give notice by mail, and receive an acknowledgment from the higher military court before I grant stay of execution. Lay on the lashes!"

"I will hold you personally liable for this outrage," Fred told him, "if it costs me all my money and all the rest of my years! I defy you to continue!"

"You have yourself to blame!" the lieutenant grinned. "But for your uninvited interruption the Nyamwezi would have had a better hearing! Lay those lashes on harder and more slowly!"

Kazimoto was taking his gruel like a man. Two *askaris* were beating him. The blows fell at random anywhere below the neck and above the heels, raising a great welt where they did not actually cut the skin. He had buried his face in his forearms, and Will had gone to stand near him, stooping down to encourage him with any words at all that might seem to serve.

"Stick it out, Kazi! We'll stand by! We won't leave you down here! Remember you've got friends who won't desert you!"

Probably in his agony Kazimoto did not understand a word of it, but the lieutenant did, and swiftly took steps to interfere.

"Call the Europeans' cases next!" he shouted, and promptly the German sergeants stepped down from the platform to marshal us in line. The lieutenant went through the form of studying the blue papers, and called out our names. That of Brown was included, but Brown was not in court and we were kept standing there until he had been fetched from his tent. He had retired immediately after the hanging to sleep off the effects of his debauch, and being now deprived of that luxury arrived between two *askaris* in a volcanic temper. He insulted the lieutenant to begin with.

"A diet o' beer an' sausage don't seem to have filled you full o' good manners, do it?"

The lieutenant scowled, but for the moment chose to ignore the pleasantry.

"You people are charged," he said, "with entering German territory otherwise than by a regular road and without reporting at a customs station. Further, with intending to defraud the customs—with carrying and possessing arms without a license—with being in possession of ammunition without a permit—with shooting game without a license—with filibustering—with intentional homicide, in that you shot and killed certain men of the Masai tribe within German territory—with wandering at large without permits and with felonious intent; and last, and this is the most serious charge, with being spies within the military meaning of that term. Do you plead guilty or not guilty?"

We were dumb. Even the crack of the heavy whips on poor Kazimoto's skin ceased to make impression on us. Suffering already from my wound to the point of nausea, I actually reeled before this new deluge of trouble, and had to hold on to Fred and Will. They each put an arm under mine. It was Brown who spoke and stole from our sails what little wind there might have been.

"Decline to plead!" he shouted boisterously. "You're no judge, you're a pirate! You're not fit to try natives, let alone white men! You're a disgrace, that's what you are! All you're fit for is to make a decent fellow glad he needn't know you!"

"Silence!" roared the lieutenant, banging on the table with his open palm—then with his fist—then with a mallet.

"Silence yourself!" retorted Brown as soon as the hammering ceased. "You ought to be ashamed o' yourself! Your court's a bally disgrace, an' you're the worst thing in it! You and your Kaiser can go to hell, and be damned to both of you!"

"One month in jail for contempt of court and *Majestaetsbeleidigung!*" snapped the lieutenant. "Take him away!"

Quite clearly that was not the first time that a white man had been imprisoned in Muanza. There was no hesitation about the way in which an *askari* seized Brown's wrists or a sergeant snapped the handcuffs. He was hustled out expostulating, kicked on the shins by the sergeant when he faced about to argue, and shoved into a run by both sergeant and *askari*.

"You others would better be careful what you say!" said the lieutenant.

"I've a mind to share Brown's cell!" said Will, but the lieutenant affected not to hear that.

"Since you refuse to plead in this court, you shall be held until the arrival of Major Schunck from the coast. Your arms and ammunition are to be handed over to the *askaris,* who will be sent to the rest-camp to receive them. The *askaris* will search your belongings thoroughly to make sure they have all your weapons. You are ordered confined within the limits of this township, and if you are detected making any attempt to trespass outside township limits you will be confined as the Greeks are within the rest-camp under observation. The porters you brought into the country are all to be paid their full wages by you until Major Schunck shall have dealt with you; the porters are refused permission to leave Muanza, being needed as witnesses. Next case!"

He scrawled his signature at the foot of each sheet of blue paper, and made a motion with his arm that we should leave court. But we sat down and waited until the two Nubian giants had finished flogging Kazimoto, and when they dragged him to his feet Will and Fred walked over to give him a few words of comfort. That act of ordinary kindness threw the lieutenant into another fury.

"Bring the Nyamwezi here!" he ordered, and the *askaris* hustled him up in front of the table.

"What do you do? Have you no manners? Return proper thanks for the lesson you have received!"

Kazimoto stood silent.

"For God's sake——" Will began.

"Say 'Thank you' to him, Kazimoto!" Fred whispered.

There is no native word for "Thank you"—only a bastard thing introduced by tyrants from Europe who never understood the African contention that the giver rewards himself if his gift is worth anything at all.

"*Asente,*" said Kazimoto meekly.

"Why don't you salute? Don't you know where you are?"

"For the love of God salute him!" Will almost shouted.

Kazimoto obeyed.

"Take him and put him on the chain-gang!" ordered the lieutenant. "You Europeans leave the court!"

"I'm no European!" Will shouted back. "Thank the Lord I was born in a country you'll never set foot in!"

"Take them away before I have to make an example of them!" the lieutenant ordered.

Obediently the *askaris* gathered about us and hustled us out into the open, poking at my bandaged wound to get swifter action, and going as far as to threaten us with their hippo-hide whips. I trod on the naked toe of one of them with sufficient suddenness and weight to deprive him of the use of it for all time, and luckily for me he did not see who did it. The *askari* next to him had boots on, and got the blame.

The black men who were to search our belongings tried to induce us to hurry, but we insisted on seeing the iron ring riveted to Kazimoto's neck. The ring had a shackle on it, and through that they passed the long chain that held him prisoner in the midst of a gang of forty men. Nobody washed the wounds on his back. We bought water from a woman who was passing with a great jar on her head, and did that much for him. He was naked. His clothes that the *askaris* had torn from him had been thrown outside the court, and some one had stolen them. Later they gave him a piece of cheap calico to bind round his waist, but during all that hot afternoon he had nothing to keep the sun from his tortured back; nor would they permit us to give him anything.

The mortification of having one's private belongings gone through by black men in uniform was made more exasperating still by the fact that Coutlass and the other Greek and the Goanese were spectators, amusing themselves with comments that came nearer to causing murder than they guessed.

The real motive of the search was evident within two minutes from the commencement. The *askaris* could not read, but they showed a most remarkable affinity for paper that had been written on. They took the guns and ammunition first, but after that they emptied everything from our bags and boxes on to the sand, and confiscated every scrap of paper, shaking our books to make sure nothing was left between the leaves.

They even took away our writing material in their zeal to find information likely to prove useful to their masters. But they forgot to search our pockets, so that they overlooked the letter we had written in code to Monty and had not yet sent away by messenger.

That letter became our most besetting problem. How to find a runner who would take it to British East and mail it for us up there without betraying us first to the Germans was something we could not guess. Even Fred grew gloomy when we realized there was probably not a native on the whole countryside with sufficient manhood left in him to dare make the attempt. The first overture we might make would almost certainly be reported to the commandant at once.

"What fools we were not to send Kazimoto with it when he begged us to!"

"What worse than fools!"

"What brutes! Think what we might have saved him!"

We were unanimous as to that, but unanimity brought no comfort, until we all together hit on a notion that did ease our feelings a trifle. Coutlass and his two friends were sitting on camp-stools in the open where they could have a full view of our doings. Assuming the camping-ground to be equally divided between their party and ours, they were well within our portion. We decided their curiosity was insolent, declared inexorable war, and there and then felt better.

Fred went out with a tent-peg and scored in the sand a deep line to denote our boundary, the Greeks watching, all eyes and guesswork.

"Over the other side with you!" Fred ordered when he had finished.

They refused. He charged at them, and they ran.

"Whichever of you, man or servant, sets foot on our side of that line shall be a dead-sure hospital case!" Fred announced. "We'll reciprocate by leaving your side of the camp to you!"

"Who made you men rulers of this rest-camp?" Coutlass demanded.

"We did," Fred answered. "We've lost our rifles just as you have. We'll fight you with bare hands and skin you alive if you trespass!"

"Gassharamminy!" shouted Coutlass. "By hell and Waterloo, you mistake me for a weakling! Wait and see!"

We had to wait a very long and weary time, but we did see. In the days that followed, when my wound festered and I grew too ill to drag myself about, Fred and Will were able to leave me alone in the camp without any fear of a visit from the Greeks. It was not that there was much left worth stealing, but a mere visit from them might have had consequences we could never have offset. Alone, unable to rise, I could not have forced them to leave, and their lingering would surely have been interpreted by the guard, who always watched them from the corner of the road, as evidence of collusion of some sort between them and us.

Just at that time Coutlass, as it happened, would have liked nothing better in the world than the chance to persuade the Germans that he was in our councils. Fred's mere irritable determination to divide the camp in halves saved us in all human probability from a trap out of which there would have been no escape.

## "SPEAK YE, AND SO DO"

*Oh Thou, who gavest English speech*
  *To both our Anglo-Saxon breeds,*
*And didst adown all ages teach*
    *That Art of crowning words with **deeds**,*
*May we, who use the speech, be blest*
  *With bravery, that when shall come*
*In thy full time our hour of test—*
    *That promised hour of Christendom,*
*We may be found, whate'er our need,*
  *How grim soe'er our circumstance,*
*Unwilling to be fed or freed,*
  *Or fame or fortune to enhance*
*By flinching from the good begun,*
  *By broken word or serpent plan,*
*Or cruelty in malice done*
    *To helpless beast or subject man.*

**Amen.**

# CHAPTER NINE

THERE was method, of course, behind the difference in treatment extended to us and to the Greeks. The motive for making Coutlass sell his mules and stay within the miserable confines of the rest-camp was to make sure he had money enough to feed himself, and to cut off all opportunity for swift escape. Not for a second were the Germans sufficiently unwary to admit collusion with him.

The real ownership of the three mules was left in little doubt when they were sold at public auction and bought in by Schillingschen. Fred and Will attended the auction the day following our scene in court, and extracted a lot of amusement from bidding against Schillingschen, compelling him finally to pay a good sum more than the mules were worth.

Coutlass was in a strange predicament. The looting of Brown's cattle had been a bid for fortune on his own account. Yet by causing us to give chase he had brought us into the German net more handily than ever they had hoped. So it was reasonable on his part to suppose that if he could betray us more completely still, he might get rewarded instead of treated as a broken tool.

Yet he did not dare to approach our camp, for fear lest Fred should carry out his threat and fight. The fight would certainly be reported by the *askari* on watch at the crossroads, and that would destroy his chance of making believe to be in our confidence. So he kept sending notes to me when the others were absent, even the native boy who brought them not daring to enter our camp, but fastening the message to a stone and throwing it in through the tent door.

They were strange, illiterate messages, childishly conceived, varying between straight-out offers to help us escape and dark insinuations that he knew of something it would pay us well to investigate.

It was an English missionary spending three days in Mu-

241

anza on his way to Lake Tanganika, who came to see what he could do for my wound and cleared up the mystery quite a little by reporting what he had heard in the non-commissioned mess, where he had been invited to eat a meal.

"The Greek," he said, "is trying to curry favor by pretending he knows your plans. If he succeeds in worming into your confidence and persuading you to make plans to escape with him, they will feel justified in putting you in jail—and that, I understand, is where they want you."

"Will you do me a favor?" I asked.

He hesitated. It was kindness that had sent him down to ease my pain, if possible, not anti-Germanism; it was part of German policy to pose as the friend of all missionaries, and if anything he was prejudiced against us—particularly against Brown, whom he had visited in jail, and who assured him the only hymn he ever sang was "Beer, glorious beer!"

"That depends," he answered.

"We are quite sure any letters we write will be opened," J said.

He answered that he could hardly believe that.

"If we could send a letter unopened to British East it would solve our worst problem," I told him. "If you know of a dependable messenger who would carry our letter, I would contribute fifty pounds out of my own pocket to the funds of your mission."

I made a mistake there, and realized it the next moment.

"What kind of letter is worth fifty pounds?" he asked me. "Isn't it something illegal that you fear might get you into worse trouble if opened and read?"

I argued in vain, and only made my case worse by citing as an instance of German official turpitude the staff surgeon's neglect of me.

"But he tells me you refuse to be treated by him!" he answered. "He says you enter his hospital and are insolent if he happens to be too busy to attend to you at once. He says you refuse to let a native orderly dress your wound!"

He had been entertained to one meal at the commandant's house on the hill, and regaled by awful accounts of our fe-

rocity. I did not succeed in inserting as much as the thin end
of a different view until he asked me how a man's name could
be Professor Schillingschen and his wife's Lady Isobel Saffren Waldon.

"I don't understand about titles," he said. "Shouldn't she
take his name, or else he hers, or something?"

I assured him that marriage had never as much as entered
the head of either of them.

"They're simply living together," I said. "He's a cynical
brute. She's a designing female!"

The missionary mind recoiled and refused to believe me.
But after he had thought the matter over and seen the probability, he swung over to a sort of lame admission that a few
more of my statements might perhaps be true.

"I will take your letter and guarantee its delivery in British East, provided I may read it and do not disapprove of its
contents," he volunteered.

"That's not unreasonable," I said, "but the letter is in code."

"I should have to see it decoded."

I told him to find Fred and Will. He came on them sitting
smoking under the great rock near the water-front that had
been inset with a bronze medallion of Bismarck, and startled
them almost into committing an assault on him, by saying that
he wanted our secret code at once. They had been trying to
get tobacco to Brown, and sweetmeats to Kazimoto, had failed
in both efforts and were short-tempered. He explained after
they had insulted him sufficiently, and they walked down to
the camp one on either hand, apologizing all the way. I imagine they had criticized missions of all denominations pretty
thoroughly.

In the end he decided not to read the letter at all.

"I have reached the conclusion you three men are gentlemen," he said, "and would not take advantage of me. I will
take your letter to Ujiji, and send it to the south end of Lake
Tanganika, to be put in the British mail bag for Mombasa by
way of Durban. It will take a long time to reach its destination—perhaps two months; but I will have it registered, and
it will undoubtedly get there."

That he kept his word and better we had ample proof later
on, but I did not bless him particularly fervidly at the time,
for he went straight to the doctor and repeated my complaints.
He left for Ujiji the next day, and the net result of his
friendly interference was that the doctor refused me any sort
of attention at all—even a change of bandages.

Fred and Will did their best for me, but it was little. I
read in their faces, and in their studied cheerfulness when
speaking in my presence, that they had made up their minds
I was going to lose the number of my mess. They went to
the commandant and the lieutenant besides the doctor in efforts to secure for me some sort of consideration, but without
result; and they wrote at least six letters to the British East
African Protectorate government that we ascertained afterward never reached their destination. They tried to register
one letter, but registration was refused.

"Why don't they jail us simply, and have done with it?"
Will kept wondering aloud.

"They will when it suits their books," said I. "For the present they scarcely dare. Word might reach the British government. They're breaking no international law by holding us
here and keeping tabs on us."

Before many days I grew unable to leave the hard cork
mattress on the camp-bed in Fred's tent. They went again to
the commandant, this time determined to force the issue.

"I will send some one," he told them, and they came away
delighted that strong language should succeed where politeness formerly had failed.

But all the commandant did send was an *askari* twice a day,
to lean on his rifle in the tent door, leer at me, and march
away again.

"He comes to see if I'm dead," said I. "It would be incon-
venient to have me die in jail; there might be inquiries afterward from British East. After I'm dead and buried they'll
jail you two healthy ones, and keep you until you 'blab'!"

"Why don't we straight out tell 'em we don't know a thing
about the ivory?" wondered Will.

"Because they wouldn't believe us!" Fred answered.

Seven days after the sentry's first call the doctor took to coming in person to look at me. He never except once stepped inside the tent, but was satisfied to give me a glance of contempt and go away again, once or twice taking pains to inspect the Greeks' camp before leaving. He usually had Schubert trailing in his wake, and gave him stern orders about sanitation which nobody ever carried out. The sanitary conditions of that rest-camp were simply non-existent until we came there, and we had gone to no pains on the Greeks' account.

But the Greeks did us an unexpected good turn, though it looked like making more trouble for us at the time. They began to complain of lack of exercise, and to grow actually sick for want of it. Because of that, and jealousy, they raised a clamor about our freedom to go anywhere within township limits as against their strict confinement to the camp. The commandant came down to the camp in person to hear what they had to say, and being in a good humor saw fit to yield a point. Being a military German, though, he could not do it without attaching ignominious conditions.

There was a band attached to the local company of Sudanese—an affair consisting of four native war-drums and two fifes. They knew eight bars of one tune, and were proud of it, the fifers blowing with beef and pluck and the drummers thundering native fashion, which means that the only difference between their noise and a thunder-storm was in the tempo.

Day after day, twice a day, whether it rained or shone, it seemed to be the law that this "band" should patrol the whole township limits, playing its only tune, lifting the tops of men's heads with its infernal drumming, and delighting nobody except the players and the township urchins, who marched in its wake rejoicing.

The Greeks and the Goanese were given leave to march with the band twice a day for the sake of exercise. They refused indignantly. The commandant flew into the rage that is the birthright of all German officials, but suddenly checked himself; he had a brilliant idea.

He withdrew the permission and changed it to an order

that Coutlass and his two friends should march with the band twice daily for the sake of their health, on pain of imprisonment should they refuse.

"And I will prove to you," he said, "that the good German rule is impartial. All aliens awaiting trial and confined within the township limits shall march with the band if they are able!" As an afterthought he added magnanimously: "Those in the jail, too, provided they have not been sentenced for serious crimes!"

So Coutlass, his Greek friend, the Goanese, Fred, Will, and Brown of Lumbwa marched about the town twice daily, at seven in the morning and three in the afternoon, a journey of five miles, Fred and Will making no objection because it gave them a chance to talk with Brown. There were strict orders against talking, and four *askaris* armed with rifles marched behind to enforce the rule as well as keep guard over Brown. But the drums were so thunderous and the shrill fifes so lusty that the *askaris* could not hear conversation pitched in low tones.

"Brown says," said Fred, returning from the first march, "that he sleeps with only a sheet of corrugated iron between him and the ward where the chain-gang lies. He can talk with Kazimoto when he happens to be at that end of the chain. They've nothing but planks to lie on, any of them. He says Kazimoto seems determined to kill the lieutenant who sentenced him, and as soon as he's off the chain we'd better grab him and hurry him out of the country."

"Six months!" said I. "Splendid advice! How many of us will be alive or at liberty six months from now? Not I, at any rate!"

"How d'you suppose they discipline the chain-gang?" Fred asked, ignoring my growing hopelessness.

"With the lash," said I. "I've seen!"

"That's by day," said Fred. "They've better ways at night. One plan is no supper or breakfast; but the champion scheme is the doctor's. On complaint by the *askaris* that a man on the chain has shirked his work, or answered back, or been obstreperous, the doctor serves him out a handful of strong pills

and sees him swallow them. They don't unchain them at
night. D'you get the idea?"

"Not yet."

"Every time the man has to go outside he must wake the
whole gang and take them with him! They're weary after
working twelve hours at a stretch. After the second or third
time up they begin to object pretty strenuously. After the
third or fourth time he's so unpopular that he'd almost rather
die than wake them. Imagine the result, and what he suffers!"

Despondency began to have hold of me, and I no longer
wished to live. The doctor's momentary daily visits increased
my loathing for the crew who tyrannized there in the name of
Progress, and I could see no way of retaliating. I became
seized with a sort of delirious conviction that if only I could
die and be out of the way my friends would be far better able
to contrive without me. There is no convalescence in a mood
of that sort, and each morning found me nearer death than
the last. Then malaria developed, to give me the finishing
touch, and although strangely enough I grew less instead of
more delirious, Fred and Will at last made no secret of their
belief that I was doomed.

I myself was as sure of death as they were of dinner, and
had better appetite for my fate than they for the meal, when
one morning the doctor came earlier than usual. He had
Schubert with him, and they both peered through the tent
door. I was alone, for Fred and Will were in the other tent.
The doctor stepped inside and examined me closely, drawing
up the mosquito net to see my face. I did not trouble to speak
to him, or even to open my eyes after the first glimpse. He
spoke to Schubert in German, let the net fall again, and went
away. Schubert spat and rubbed his hands, and swung along
after him.

Then I heard Will and Fred arguing.

"Don't be a fool!" That was Fred's voice.

"I tell you I'll tell him!"

"Fine thing to tell a poor devil that's dying! Let him die
in peace!"

"No. He has guts, for I've seen him use 'em. I shall tell him. You wait here!"

But they both came in, and sat one on either side of my bed.

"Did you hear what that doctor person said to the sergeant-major?" asked Will.

"I don't talk his beastly language," I answered.

"He said you'll be dead by this evening! He told Schubert to go and get the chain-gang and have them dig your grave at noon instead of laying off for dinner. He added they'll have you buried and out of the way by four or five o'clock. Then Schubert asked him—"

"No need to tell him that!" Fred objected. But Will was watching my face keenly, and went on.

"Schubert asked him who was to say whether you are dead or not. What d'you suppose the answer was?"

Fred objected again, but Will waved him aside.

"The answer he gave Schubert was: 'Once he is covered with two meters of earth, I shall not hesitate to sign a certificate!'—So now you know what to expect!"

Will smiled as he watched me. His face was as keen and calm as Fred's was troubled.

"Take more than his guesswork to put you where he'd like to have you—eh?" he laughed. And I sat up.

Fred began to grin too. "You were right, Will!" he admitted.

It was not anger that swept over me and gave me new strength. Anger, I think, would have hastened the end. It was sudden recognition of my own superiority to the devils who knew so little mercy. It was simple inability in the last recourse to admit myself able to be their victim. Even my leg felt better. I demanded food; and by the time they returned from their morning march around the township I had made my boy dress me and was sitting up.

We dated the turn of the tide of our fortunes from that hour. Certainly from that day we began to prosper—at first gradually, but after a while in the old swift way that had made all our ventures with Monty such amazingly amusing work.

We saw the chain-gang—Kazimoto last, with a shovel over his shoulder—march away at noon to dig me a grave in the sand close to where they burned the township refuse. Fred and Will went and watched them a while, contriving to slip a paper of snuff into Kazimoto's hand while he rested and let the pick-men labor. (Snuff to a Nyamwezi is as comforting as an old sweet pipe to nine white men out of ten.)

When Schubert came that evening at five with an old sack to put my body in, and plenty of *askaris* to help decide disputes, I was standing up. He could not very well make even himself believe that a man who could speak and walk was dead, but he could be immensely enraged by what he was pleased to call my *schweinspiel*.* He cursed me in every language he knew, including several native ones, and ended by threatening to make sure of me before going to so much trouble a second time.

We enraged him still further by laughing at him, and Fred got out his concertina that for many days past had lain idle. The first few notes of it made me realize more than any other thing could have done what depths of despondency we must have plumbed, for hitherto, for as long as I had known Fred, he had always been able with that weird instrument of his to rouse his own spirits and so stir the rest of us. He resumed old habits now, and gloom departed.

That evening I went to bed like a new man, and for the first night for long weeks slept until dawn, awaking hungry. My leg began to mend. We all saw the absurdity, if nothing else, of the treatment meted out to us, based on no better grounds than our supposed possession of a secret. Laughter brought good hope. Hope gave us courage, and courage set Fred and Will hunting for a means of escape. We decided there and then that to wait for this Major Schunck to come from the coast and pass judgment on us was a ridiculous waste of time as well as highly dangerous.

The first discovery Fred and Will made was that there were footholds cut in the great granite rock in which the Bismarck medallion was set. They climbed it, and discovered that from

*Literally, pig-play.

the summit they could see all Muanza harbor from the shore-
line to the island in the distance. Sitting up there, they presently spotted a native dhow drawn up with bow to the beach
with the indefinable, yet unescapable air of rather long dis-
use.

Resisting the first temptation to hurry along the shore and
examine it, they returned to camp to tell me of the find, and
sent Simba, Kazimoto's understudy, to find out whose the
dhow was and why it lay there. They explained it was a fairly
big dhow, and might be laid up there on account of leakiness.

But Simba came back grinning with the news that the dhow
belonged to an Indian from British East who had been jailed
for smuggling. The dhow had been sold to pay his court fine,
and was now owned by a Punjabi who had bought it as a spec-
ulation and repented already of his bargain, because the Germans would grant him no license to use it and nobody else
would buy.

They went off again to have another distant view of it and
to try and invent some means of inspecting it closely without
betraying their purpose. I was already able to walk with the
aid of a stick, although not fast enough to keep up with them,
and curiosity taking hold of me I called two of our servants
to give me a supporting arm and limped off to see the grave
the chain-gang had recently dug for me.

It was a struggle to get there, but it seemed to me the trip
was worth it. I found the grave about a foot too short, but
otherwise commensurate, and sat down on a stone beside it to
consider a number of things. A convalescent man sitting beside his own grave may be forgiven for amusing himself with
a lot of near-philosophy, and if I trespassed over the borders
of common sense on that occasion I claim it was not without
excuse.

My meditations were disturbed by the arrival on the scene
of the very last man I expected. We had been told that Professor Schillingschen had gone off on a journey, leaving his
"wife" in the care of the commandant; yet I looked up suddenly to see him standing on the other side of the grave with
both hands in the pockets of his knickerbockers and a grin of

malevolent amusement showing through the tangled mass of hair that hid his lower face.

"Yours?" he asked.

I nodded.

"A close call! I have seen closer! I have stood so close to the brink of death that the width of an eyelash would have damned me!"

"Piffle!" I answered rudely. "How can the already damned be damned again?"

He laughed.

"You are sick still. You are petulant. Never mind. I was coming to call on you. I watched you leave the camp from the top of that hill behind you, and followed. It is better. We can talk here without being overheard. Send those natives away!"

"Certainly not!" I answered, but I reckoned without the professor and the fear his hairy presence instilled in them.

"Go!" he said simply in the native tongue; and although I ordered them at once to stay by me they ran back to the camp as fast as their legs could carry them.

"How do you feel now?" the professor asked.

I stared at him, wondering just what he meant.

"I mean, without a pistol!"

I saw the point. The rest-camp was not far away, but as far as I could judge we were quite out of sight from it, and unless there should happen to be some one hiding among the rocks at the foot of the hill behind me we were quite alone, unless, as was probable, he had placed one or two of his own hangers-on in hiding within call.

"This grave should be a lesson to you!" he grinned.

"It has been," I answered.

"An illustration," he suggested.

"A period," said I.

"To your youth?" he asked maliciously. "To the age of folly?"

"To the time," I said, "when any man could blackmail me. I would go into that grave ten times rather than tell you what you want to know!"

"There are worse places than the grave!" he said, beginning to leer savagely. His eyes glittered. He could scarcely find patience for argument. The thin veneer of his first mock-friendliness was gone utterly.

"I imagine that German colonial life is far worse than death," said I.

"German will be the only rule in Africa," he answered. "You fools of English have set your hopes on the Christian missionary. No weaker-backed camel could exist! The German Michael is wiser! Islam is the key to the native mind—Islam and the lash—they understand that! In a few years there will be nothing in Africa that is not German from core to epidermis! As to whether you shall live to see that day or not depends on yourself, my young friend!"

Being quite sure that he had a plan in mind that nothing would prevent him from unfolding, I did not waste effort or words on prompting him, but sat still. My silence and apparent lack of curiosity disturbed him; there is nothing your bully likes better than to force his victim into a war of words.

"I will be short and blunt with you!" he began again. "I know your history! You were in Portuguese Africa with Lord Montdidier. There he came in possession of the secret of Tippoo Tib's ivory; how, I do not yet know, but you shall tell me that presently! You and your friends came with him to Zanzibar, where you made certain inquiries—sufficient to set the Sultan of Zanzibar by the ears. You left Zanzibar for Mombasa, and for some reason that you shall also tell me presently, Lord Montdidier did not leave the ship at Mombasa but continued the voyage toward London. Certain individuals decided that it would be better not to permit Lord Montdidier to reach Europe alive. There were agents charged with the duty of attending to that. It was considered safest to throw him overboard into the Mediterranean; men were ordered by cable to board the ship at Suez. Yet when the ship reached Suez nobody knew anything about him! Tell me where he left the ship, and why!"

He glared with eyes accustomed to extorting facts from savages, depending on physical weakness so to undermine my

will that I would give my secret away, perhaps without knowing it.

I lowered my eyes, not being minded to match the strength
of my eye-muscles against his. The news that Monty had not
reached Suez as a matter of fact made me feel physically sick.
If it were true, it meant most likely that he had been the victim of foul play, for that steamer was not scheduled to stop
anywhere before reaching the Suez Canal. As for the people
on the ship knowing nothing about him they no doubt preferred not to talk to strangers. That sort of news is easily
kept under cover for a while. Schillingschen grew angry at
my silence, and changed his tactics.

"Where did he leave the ship?" he shouted—suddenly—
savagely.

I did not answer. He came round to my side of the grave,
and laid a heavy clenched fist on my shoulder. It seemed to
weigh like lead in the weak condition I was in.

"You shall tell me what Lord Montdidier is doing now, or
that grave shall resemble in your imagination a bed of roses!"

He seized my neck in a grasp like iron, and squeezed it. I
rose suddenly and struck him in the stomach with my elbow.
Strength had returned more swiftly than I had guessed, or
perhaps it was indignation at the touch of his fingers. At any
rate he staggered clear of me, and I thought he would assault
me now in real earnest; but perhaps he suspected me of
having weapons concealed somewhere. Instead of rushing at
me like an angry bull he calmed himself and laughed.

"You are strong for a man they thought of burying!" he
said. "Never mind! You shall see reason presently! It is
well understood that you and your friends know where Tippoo
Tib's ivory is hidden. You imagine you can keep the secret.
If you keep it, you shall never make use of it, my young
friend! If you choose to tell, you shall be suitably rewarded!
Come now—I thought you were going to look for it down in
these parts. I admit you fooled me. You simply made a false
move to draw attention off from Lord Montdidier. Tell me
where he is and what he does—and—or—"

"And what? Or what?" I demanded, as insolently as I knew how. I saw no sense in answering him gently.

"I will show you!"

I had begun to feel weak again, but he offered me an arm, and since he seemed in no hurry I was able to struggle along beside him. We took to the main road, and when we reached the D. O. A. G. he called for a hammock and some porters. Being carried in that way was sheer luxury after the walk in my weak state, and I lay back feeling like a tripper on vacation. I saw Fred and Will climbing down from their observation post on top of the Bismarck monument, but he did not notice them.

Every German sergeant, and every *askari* we passed saluted us with about twice as much respect as I had ever seen them show the commandant; and Schillingschen returned salutes much less carefully than he, merely by a curt nod, or one raised finger. Apparently the military feared him, for when we passed the commandant, who was personally superintending the flogging of two natives in the market-place for not saluting himself, he took several paces forward to make sure Schillingschen should see his act of homage. The professor merely nodded in return, and I began to wonder whether there was a rift in the lute of Muanza's official good relations. Surely I hoped so. Anything calculated to set the Germans' garrison life at odds looked to me like the gift of heaven!

Schillingschen, striding beside the hammock, directed our course along the shore-front under palm-trees, planted in stately rows with meticulous precision. He kept far enough to one side to avoid the charge of being seen walking with me, but from time to time tossed me remarks calculated to keep my nerves on edge.

"What I shall show you is by way of warning!" was a remark he repeated two or three times. Then: "A native can always be made to talk by flogging him. Some white men need sterner measures!"

We left the commandant's house on the hill far behind and followed the curve of the lake shore, toward a rocky promontory with a clump of thick jungle behind it. Fear began to

get its work in, until the thought came that what he most
desired was to make me afraid; then I managed to summon
sufficient contempt for him and his tribe to regain my nerve
and once more almost enjoy the promenade.

He halted the hammock bearers at a spot about three hundred yards away from the promontory and, leaving them
standing there, turned inland with a hand on my arm to give
me support and direction. We followed a path that was fairly
well marked out and trodden, but rough, and several times I
should have fallen but for his help. My legs still refused
any sort of strenuous duty.

"The staff surgeon at this station is a man of ideas," he
announced as we rounded a big rock and passed down a narrow glade in the jungle. "He is original. He is not like
some of our official fools. He studies."

I refused to seem curious, and walked beside him in silence.

"He studies sleeping sickness. If he can find the key to
the solution of that scourge it will mean promotion for him.
He has noticed that the sleeping sickness is always at its worst
beside the lake, and putting two and two together like a sensible man has reached the conclusion that the disease may
be propagated in some way in the blood of these things."

We emerged into a clearing in which a pool more than a
hundred yards long and nearly as many wide was formed naturally by a hollow in the surface of a great sheet of granite.
The pool was fed by a trickle of water from a jumble of rocks
at one end. At the other end the bottom of the pond sloped
upward gradually, so that a ramp of smooth rock was formed,
emerging out of shallow water. A stone wall had been built
about three feet high to enclose that end of the pond, and all
the way along both sides the granite had been broken and
chipped until the edges were sheer and unclimbable.

"Look!" he said, pointing.

I looked and grew sick. On the ramp, half in the water
and half out lay about a hundred crocodiles basking in the
sun, their yellow eyes all open. They were aware of us, for
they began to move slowly higher out of water as if they expected something.

"You see that post?" asked Schillingschen.

The stump of a dead tree that he referred to stood up nearly straight out of a crack in the rock, and a few yards above water level. The crocodiles all lay nose toward it, some of them twelve or fourteen feet long, some smaller, and some very small indeed, all interested to distraction in the dead tree-trunk.

"That is where he feeds them," Schillingschen announced. "He has tested them for hearing, smell, and eyesight. By making fast a living animal to that post he has been able to convince himself that from about nine in the morning until five in the afternoon their senses are limited. Only occasionally do they come and take the bait between those hours. They are hungriest in the early morning just before daylight. Recently a large ape tied to the post at midday was not killed and eaten until four next morning, and that is about the usual thing, although not the rule. Now my proposal is—"

He stepped back and eyed me with the coldest look of appraisal I ever sickened under. I blenched at last—visibly suffered under his eye, and he liked it.

"—that you tell your secret or be fastened to that post from noon, say, until the crocodiles make an end of you!"

He stepped back a pace farther, perhaps to gloat over my discomfort, perhaps from fear of some concealed weapon.

"You have not much time to arrive at your decision!"

He took another pace backward. It occurred to me then that he was looking for some one he expected. Nobody turning up, he began to gather loose stones and throw them at the reptiles, driving them down into deep water, first in ones and twos and then by dozens. Most of them swam away to the far side of the pool, and hid themselves where it was deep.

Then, panting with having run, there came a native who looked like a Zulu, for he had enormous thighs and the straight up and down carriage, as well as facial characteristics.

"You are late!" shouted Schillingschen in German, "*Warum?* What d'ye mean by it?"

The man opened his mouth wide and made grimaces. He had no tongue. Schillingschen laughed.

"This is a servant who does no tattling in the market-place!" he said, turning again toward me. "He and I can tie you to that post easily. What do you say?"

There was nothing whatever to say, or to do except wonder how to circumvent him, and nothing in sight that could possibly turn into a friend—except a little tuft of faded brown that out of the corner of my eye I detected zigzagging toward me in the direction from which we had come. A moment later I knew it really was a friend. "Crinkle," a mongrel dog that Fred had adopted the day after our arrival, breasted the low rise, saw me, gave a yelp of delight and came scampering.

The dog sniffed my knee to make sure of me, and then trotted over to sniff Schillingschen. The professor stooped down to pat him, rubbed his ear a moment to get the dog's confidence, and then seized him suddenly by both hind legs. I saw what he intended too late.

"Stop, or I'll kill you!" I shouted, and made a rush at him. But he swung the yelping dog and hurled him far out into the pool.

A second later my fist crashed into his face and he staggered backward. A second later yet the dumb Zulu pinned my elbows from behind and set his knee into the small of my back with such terrific force that I yelled with pain. Then Schillingschen approached me and began to try to drive my teeth in with unaccustomed fists. He loosened my front teeth, but cut his own knuckles, so began looking about for a stick.

Strangely enough my own attention was less fixed on Schillingschen than on the wretched "Crinkle" swimming frantically for shore. Dog-like he was making straight for me, and there was no possibility whatever of his being able to scramble up the steep side. I shouted to call his attention, and tried to motion to him to swim toward shallow water, but the Zulu would not let my arms free, and the dog only thought I was urging him to hurry.

Schillingschen found a stick and came back to give me a hammering with it just at the moment when a crocodile saw "Crinkle." A blow landed on my head, cut my forehead, and sent the blood down into my eyes at the same moment that I heard the dog's yelp of agony; and next time I looked at the pond there was a tiny whirlpool on the surface, slightly tinged with red.

"You swine!" I shouted at Schillingschen, trying to break loose and attack him. For answer he raised his cudgel in both hands and stood on tiptoe to get leverage. If that blow had landed it must have broken something, for he was strong as a gorilla; but somebody shouted—I recognized Fred's voice, and in another second he and Will charged down on us. Schillingschen turned about to strike Fred instead of me, but Will's fist hit him on the ear and split it. The professor staggered backward, and a moment later Fred had felled the Zulu.

I reeled from weakness and excitement, and nearly fell down.

"Throw him to the crocks, you men!" I urged madly. "He threw Crinkle in. Throw him! Nobody'll ever know! He'd have dared throw me in! Nobody comes here! Throw him in and trust the crocks to leave no trace!"

"Shut up, you fool!" growled Fred.

"Did you see him throw that dog in?" I retorted.

"No," he answered, "but I saw him strike you. That's enough! I'll deal with him!"

I suppose Fred intended to knock the professor down and belabor him with the same stick he had used on me, but the plan died stillborn. Schillingschen bethought him of his hip-pocket, produced a repeating pistol, and leveled it.

"Any nonsense, and I shoot you all!" he announced.

That ended the battle as far as we were concerned. We had no firearms. Schillingschen wasted no time on explanations, but beckoned his Zulu and walked off, striding at a great pace and only looking back over his shoulder once or twice to make sure we were not in pursuit.

Fred and Will lent me an arm apiece and we followed slowly, I recounting as fast as I could all that had happened, and they trying to chaff me back into a sensible frame of mind.

"That was a decent dog!" I insisted. "He slept on my bed those nights when I had fever!"

"I know it," Fred answered. "Will and I lay and scratched,

while you rested, with proper flea-food for protection! Don't worry, we'll find you another dog!"

Schillingschen's consideration for my wound had vanished with the chance of making use of me. As we emerged into the open we saw him in the distance lolling in the hammock he had brought me in.

"Never mind!" grinned Will. "I'll bet the brute has an earache!"

"And teeth-ache!" added Fred.

"And I'll bet he has gone to prepare us a hot reception!" said I. "He owns this town!"

But nothing happened immediately on our return into the town. Actually Fred and Will had been outside township limits and could be arrested; suspecting foul play as soon as they saw me with Schillingschen, they had followed at once. They were as mystified as I when no swift vengeance lit on them. We saw Schillingschen carried in the hammock up the steep path leading to the commandant's house; but no one came down again. After we got back to camp we spent all the rest of the day waiting for the vengeance we felt sure was overdue, but none came. Toward evening we even began to grow hopeful again and to talk about the dhow. Fred and Will had examined it through field-glasses from the top of the rock, and were optimistic regarding its size and general condition.

"Even if it leaks rather badly," said Will, "we could reach some island, and beach it there, and caulk it."

"How about that launch, that brought the professor and Lady Saffren Waldon?" I asked.

"What about it?"

"Couldn't they follow us with that?"

"You bet they could!" said Will. "We've either got to spike the launch's boilers, or give them the complete slip on a dark night!"

"We might steal the launch!" suggested Fred, but that was too wild a proposal to be taken seriously. The launch was the apple of the German governmental eye, and the engine crew slept on it always.

The prospect was unpromising as ever, yet I went to bed

and listened to the strains of Fred's concertina in the next tent with less foreboding than at any time since reaching Muanza, and fell asleep to the tune of *Silver Hairs among the Gold,* a melancholy piece that Will liked to sing when hope or courage stirred him.

I was awakened near midnight of a moonless black night by a hand on my bedclothes and the light of a lantern in my eyes.

"Hus-s-s-h!" said some one. "Don't speak yet! Listen!"

It was a woman's voice, and it puzzled me indescribably, for a sick man's wits don't work swiftly as a rule when he lies between sleeping and waking.

"Listen!" said the voice again. "I must come to terms with you three men! You are the only hope left me! I have no friends in Muanza—and none whom I trust! Those Greeks and that Goanese would sell me to the first bidder, and these Germans are worse than dogs!"

"But who are you?" I asked stupidly.

For answer she held the lantern so that I could see her face. Her hand trembled, and the unsteady light threw baffling shadows, but even so I could see she looked drawn and aged.

"Where is your maid, then, Lady Waldon?" I asked, for it seemed to me that was one friend who had served her through thick and thin.

"Ask the commandant!" she answered. "The poor fool thinks he will marry her! Little she knows of the German method! I am alone! I have not even a servant any longer! I have walked through the shadows from the commandant's house, only lighting this lantern after I was inside the hedge. Nobody knows I am here. One watchman was asleep; the others did not see me. All you need fear is those Greeks. As long as they don't suspect I am here we can talk safely."

I tumbled out of bed on the far side, and went to waken the other two. After a hurried consultation we decided my tent was the best for the interview, because of the light that had burned in it nearly always while I was so deathly ill. We wrapped ourselves in blankets, and Fred went and shook Simba awake.

"Watch those Greeks!" he ordered him. "If they show signs of life, come and give the alarm!"

Then we set Lady Waldon's lantern on the ground in the back of my tent, closed the tent up, and foregathered. There was one chair. We three sat on the bed.

"Before we begin," said Fred, "we'd like some kind of proof, Lady Waldon, that your overture is honest! I've no need to labor the point. Until now you have been our implacable enemy. Why should we believe you are our friend to-night?"

She sighed. "I don't expect friendship," she answered. "You and I are in deep water, and must find a straw that may float us all! If I can help you to escape out of the country I will. If you can help me, you must! If you don't escape there are worse things in store for you than you imagine! If you tell your secret now, they intend to prevent your telling it to any one else afterward! And unless you tell they intend to take terrible steps to compel you! As for me—they have discovered that after all I know nothing, and am of no further use to them! They have not said so, but it is very clear to me how the land lies. Professor Schillingschen is drunk to-night; he came home with his ear and mouth bleeding, and has plied the whisky bottle freely ever since until he fell asleep an hour and a half ago. He boasted over his cups. They are simply using this long wait for Major Schunk, who is supposed to be coming from the coast, to gather additional evidence against you. They have men out following your trail back by the way you came, and if they can find no genuine evidence they will invent what they need; the purpose is to get you legally behind the bars; and if you ever come out again alive that would not be their fault!"

"What do you propose?" asked Fred.

"Escape!" she answered excitedly. Then another thought made her clench her fists. "Is it possible you told Professor Schillingschen your secret to-day? Did one of you tell him? Is that why he is drunk?"

She saw by our faces that that fear was groundless, but a greater one, that she might not be able to convince us, seized

her next and she made such an excited gesture that the shawl
she wore over her head and shoulders fell away and her long
hair came tumbling down like a witch's.

"Listen! There is nothing that you men from your point of
view could say too bad about me! I know! I have been in the
pay of Germany for many years, but what you don't know is
how they got me in the toils and kept me in, dragging me
down from one degradation to another! They have dragged
me down so far at last that I am not much more use to them.
If we were in British territory they would simply expose me
to the British government and save themselves the trouble
of ending my career. They did that to Mrs. Winstin Willoughby, and Lord James Rait, and fifty others; it was so
easy to put incriminating evidence against them in the hands
of the public prosecutor. Lord James Rait died in Dartmoor
Prison—a common felon. I shall not! But believe me—I am
certain as I sit here that they only wait for my return to British East! To have me murdered here might start incon-
venient rumors that would lead to unanswerable questions! It
was proposed to me to-day that I should return to British East
on the launch!"

"Then why talk about escaping?" Fred wondered. "Why
not go?"

"Because," she hissed emphatically, "don't you see, you
stupid!—if they send me back it will be to my doom! My one
chance is to escape from their clutches—get into touch with
British officials—and save the situation by telling my own
tale first!"

Fred was in no hurry to be convinced. I was already for
accepting her story and helping her out; but that was perhaps because I was a sick man, too recently recovered from
the gates of death to care to be hard on any one.

"I still don't see your danger," Fred told her. "In all my
life I fail to recall a single instance of the British courts passing a severe sentence on a spy. If you'll excuse my saying so,
your story about Lord James Rait is incorrect. I recall the
case well. He got a twenty-year sentence for forgery."

"True!" she answered. "And Mrs. Winstin Willoughby was
sentenced to fifteen years for theft! Lord James did forge
—in the way of business for the German government! Jane
Winstin Willoughby did steal—for the same blackguard masters! Do you think they will expose me as a spy? That
would be too clumsy, even for such bullies as they are! Do
you suppose they could have dragged me down to this without
some sword held over me? They can prove that I committed
a crime in England several years ago. Oh, yes, I am a criminal! I raised a check. It was a check on a German bank,
given to me by a German on behalf of a countryman of his.
I needed money desperately, and the man who brought the
check to me suggested I should raise it! Since then I have
tried to repay that money with interest a dozen times, but
they have always laughed and told me they preferred to leave
matters as they are."

"What would be the use of returning to British territory,
then?" asked Fred. "If they hold that over you, they can
denounce you at any time."

"Not they!" she answered. "Not if I get there first! I
know too much! I can tell too much! I can prove too much!
If I were once arrested on the charge of raising that check,
no government in the world would listen to me. But if I
can tell my story first, and confess about the check, and explain why the charge is likely to be brought against me, then
there will be Downing Street officials who know how to whisper to the German Embassy words that will frighten them
into silence! I can prove too much against the German government, if only I can tell my tale before they crush me!"

"Why not write it?" asked Fred, and it seemed to me
there was humor in his eye, but she only detected stubborn-
ness, and laughed scornfully.

"My own maid even gave them the letters written to me
by my sister! If I should be suspected of writing they would
never rest until they had the letter!"

"Give me your letter to mail!" suggested Fred maliciously.

"Deluded man!" she sneered. "All the letters you have

written since you came to Muanza lie in a drawer in the commandant's desk! I myself have read them!"

In the dark, with shifting shadows thrown by the cheap trade lantern, it was difficult to judge what was going on behind that beard of Fred's. I had begun to suspect he was coming over to my way of thinking and would yield to her presently, but he returned to the attack—very directly and abruptly.

"What is it you know against the German government?" he demanded, and sat with his jaw in the palm of his hand waiting for her answer.

"Why should I tell you? Why should I put myself completely in your power?"

"Why not?" asked Fred.

"What would prevent you from stealing my thunder, and telling my story as your own—leaving me at the Germans' mercy?"

"Something very potent that I think you would not understand if I talked of it," Fred answered. "Listen to me now a minute. I haven't conferred with my friends here, as you know. Whatever I tell you is subject to their agreeing with me. The only condition on which I, for one, would consent to taking part with you in anything—after all our experience of you!—would be that you should put yourself so completely in our power that we could feel we had your safekeeping. On those terms I would be willing to do my best to help you out."

"I agree to that like a shot!" said Will; and I nodded.

"You mean—?"

"All or nothing!" Fred insisted.

"You mean that you also, just like these Germans, must have a sword to hold over me?"

"I thought you wouldn't understand!" Fred answered. "What we demand, Lady Saffren Waldon, is proof that you really do give us your confidence. Without that we have nothing to say to you, and nothing to do with you!"

She broke down then and cried a little, tearing herself with sobs she hated to release. Suddenly she raised her head and

glared at us wildly, dry-eyed; not a tear had accompanied
the sobbing.

"If I tell you—if you fail me after that—I shall kill
myself in such way that you shall know my blood is on your
heads!"

Fred laughed. It was no doubt the best thing to do, but
I wondered how he managed it.

"Suppose you begin by telling us," he said. "We can discuss
the blood-stains afterward!"

Then she suddenly burst into her tale, as if she had rehearsed it a hundred times in readiness to pour into the
ears of the first British official who had power enough to
shield her. She told it dramatically, in few words, wasting no
breath on side-issues, and without once pausing to explain,
letting her words smash down the barriers of unbelief and
pave their own way for explanations afterward.

"Germany is planning to conquer the world!—not now,
but ten or a dozen years from now! She is getting ready
ceaselessly! Part of the plan is to undermine British rule in
Africa by means of a religious influence among the natives.
That is the special duty of Professor Schillingschen. As soon
as possible a great native army is to be trained, and thoroughly schooled in the fanatical precepts of Islam. But the
German people are too heavily taxed already, and refuse to
vote money for this miserable colony, where the great beginning must be made because it is only here that they can
work unsuspected. So funds must be found in some other
way!"

She paused for breath. No woman pleading at the bar of
justice could have seemed more in earnest. Of one thing I
was quite sure: she had found it worth her while to convince
us if that were possible. She was playing no half-hearted
game.

"Do you begin to see now why the Germans are so set on
finding Tippoo Tib's hoard of ivory? Do you begin to understand why they are determined, not only to prevent your
finding it, but to learn your secret? If rumor is one-half
true, the Arab buried somewhere enough ivory to finance this

plan of theirs! They have been going about the search systematically, and sooner or later they feel they must stumble on it. They will not let you forestall them!"

She paused again. Her very earnestness exhausted her more than the walk through the dark in danger had done.

"Take your time," Fred advised her. "We're all listening!"

"When I told you in Nairobi that Lord Montdidier had been murdered, I believed I was so near the truth that you would never know the difference. I knew the order had been given to have him killed on board ship—given by men who are accustomed to be obeyed—who do not excuse failure on any ground. They feared he might be going to divulge the secret of the ivory to his government in London. Oh, I tell you they stop at nothing! To-day London is the ivory market of the world, but they have their arrangements made for transferring that center of trade to Hamburg! They mean first to crush competitors, and then monopolize! They hope the ivory is in this country. In that case their task will be easy. But if it should be found in British East, they are all ready with the necessary men of influence to apply for a mining or agricultural concession, and they will fence that place off so thoroughly that no one will ever be the wiser until they have carried the ivory out of the country!"

"They could never get it out of British East without the government knowing," objected Fred; but she laughed at him.

"If worse came to the worst, they are ready with an offer to exchange ten times the territory elsewhere for just that small section of the country. They would give up German New Guinea, or Southwest Africa—anything! They have fooled the French and Russian governments until they are ready to bring pressure to bear on England diplomatically to induce her to make almost any bargain of that kind that the Germans want. They are even willing to concede to England the whole of Abyssinia, which nobody owns yet, and to back her up against the claims of France and Italy! Why should they not be willing to make temporary concessions, when all Africa is to be theirs in ten years' time! They will give to-day, and with the help of the money that ivory will bring they will create an army that shall take away to-morrow!"

"But how can you prove all this?" Fred asked her.

"How? I know the names of the men who are preaching Germany's sermons all through British East! I know all Schillingschen's secrets! Why should I not? I have suffered enough! He is a drunken brute nearly always after the sun goes down, and his caresses are disgusting; I have endured them until I know all he knows! Now he realizes that I know his secrets and have none of my own to tell, so he hopes to send me to my doom at the hands of the government I have betrayed too many times! What is the use of my pretending to be better than I am? I am a spy—a traitress—a divorced woman with worse than no reputation! I am not a person likely to be shown much mercy! I never would have recanted unless the end of my rope had come! Now I know I must buy my pardon—I must earn it—I must pay for it with solid value! Luckily I can do that! I do not ask you men for mercy. I know what is in store for you if you do not escape! I offer to help you to escape, in exchange for helping me!"

"Better be more precise!" suggested Fred. "Exactly what is in store for us?"

She pointed her finger at me. "You went out of bounds to-day with Schillingschen! Well and good; he was with you. But you, and you—" She pointed at Fred and Will. "—went without permission. Why do you suppose they overlooked such a splendid chance of jailing you legally? Schillingschen came up to the commandant's house in a towering passion, demanding the immediate arrest and close confinement of all three of you. He was only persuaded to wait a few days longer because a runner has come in with word that the bodies of several Masai whom you shot on this side of the German border have been found! The bones—the bullets found among the bones—and cartridge cases that will fit your rifles are being brought to Muanza! After that— the deluge, my friends! That is why Professor Schillingschen gets drunk and sings himself to sleep in spite of your being still at liberty! Either escape before that evidence reaches Muanza, or make up your minds for the worst! It is growing late—answer me—do you agree?"

Fred glanced once at each of us. We both nodded.

"We agree with reservations," he said.

"What are they? Man—don't be a fool! Don't fritter the lives of all of us away!"

"They're simple. We've a friend in the jail here. His name's Brown."

"That drunkard? Leave him! He's worthless!"

"We've a servant on the chain-gang. His name is Kazimoto."

"A nigger? You'd risk another day in this place for a nigger? How absurd! They're never grateful. They don't see things from the white man's standpoint. They don't expect ideal treatment. Leave him his wages and tell him to follow when they let him off the chain!"

"And we have a string of porters," Fred continued. "We will not leave Muanza without the porters, our man Kazimoto, and Mr. Brown of Lumbwa!"

"You are mad! You are crazy!"

"We are the men you have invited to trust you," Fred answered kindly. "Those are our conditions. We will not 'bate one iota! Take 'em or leave 'em, Lady Waldon!"

## IN HOC SIGNO VADE

*Lean, loveless, hungry lanes are these?*
  *The longest has an end.*
*Ill luck tasted to the bitter lees*
  *Soonest shall mend.*
*From out the foe's ranks if Heaven please*
  *Shall come your friend.*

# CHAPTER TEN

WE came to no fixed decision that night, although we knew there was no alternative. She held out, in the vain hope of making us agree to leave Kazimoto and Brown behind. The porters, she agreed, might come in very handy, although it was at least doubtful that we should be able to slip out of Muanza by land. The Germans had taken latterly to counting our porters every morning, to supplying them with ration money once every day, and to sending the bill to us by an *askari,* who waited for the cash. At any rate, she conceded the porters, provided we would leave the two others behind. And of course we were adamant.

She left us an hour and a half before dawn, we letting her return alone because of the greater danger of detection if we had tried to escort her. It was after she had gone, while we sat listening for the sound of a challenge that would have ruined all her hopes, if not ours, that Will conceived the bright idea which finally saved us.

"The Heinies don't know that we're wise to their game," he said cheerfully. His ears were sticking out from his head and he had the naughty boy look that always presaged wisdom. "Why don't we play that card for all it's worth?"

"We need five cards to make even a poker hand," Fred objected.

"Will a full house suit you—aces and queens?" he answered. "I've named you one ace already. Ace number two is the fact that these German officials are brutes pure and simple—brutes who don't understand how to be anything else, with brutal low cunning and no other cleverness."

"That sounds like the joker!" said Fred.

"It's ace number two, I tell you! The third is the fact that Brown of Lumbwa can talk with Kazimoto in the night through that corrugated iron partition! Three aces—count

270

'em—one, two, three! Queens? One of 'em left this tent a few minutes ago! The other's the dhow! We'll call that blessed boat the Queen of Sheba for luck! The Queen of Sheba got to her journey's end, and found more than she expected, and by the lights of little old Broadway, so shall we! I've dealt the cards—is it up to me to play them?"

"Your hand, America! Talk it over first, though! There's an awful lot hangs on the game!" said Fred.

I fell asleep while they argued over the points of Will's strategy. Africa is a land of sudden death and swift recoveries, but for a convalescent man I had been through a strenuous day and had right to be tired out. It was broad daylight when I awoke, and breakfast was ready. Fred and Will had returned from their march around the township with the native band, and to my surprise the commandant was standing in front of their tent, talking with them. I threw on a jacket and joined them at table.

"I don't understand you," said the commandant. "Either talk German or speak more slowly!"

Will took a purchase on his stock of patience and began again.

"If our porters run away, you'll blame us. We don't care to be blamed for what is none of our fault. So if you don't put 'em all on a chain and lock 'em up nights, we're going to discontinue paying for their keep. That's flat! You can work 'em if you like. Let 'em help keep the township clean. We'll pay their board and wages as long as you're responsible for their not escaping! And say! If you want to get real work out of 'em I'll give you a tip. There never was a savage like that Kazimoto of ours for getting results out of that gang. Put him on the same chain with the lot of 'em, and we'll all be satisfied! I don't presume to be running your jail, but I'm telling you facts that'll hurt nobody. Those porters 'ud be a darn sight better off with plenty of exercise."

"Do I understand you to ask that your porters be made prisoners?" asked the commandant.

"You get me exactly!" said Will.

The commandant grunted, nodded, waited for us to get

up and salute him, grunted again with disgust when we did nothing of the sort, turned on his heel, and walked off. We spent an hour on tenterhooks, and I began to believe the German had simply become more suspicious than ever and would keep closer watch on us without troubling at all about the men. But at the end of an hour we saw the porters rounded up, and a chain fetched out that was long enough to hold them all. They disappeared within the boma wall. Ten minutes later suddenly Will pointed toward the southward.

"Look! See what happens when the roofs of shanty-town take fire!"

Flames went up from the dry grass roof of one of the rectangular Swahili huts. Within thirty seconds the *askaris* on guard at the boma began firing their rifles in the air as fast as they could pull the trigger and reload. Within two minutes the chain-gang was headed for jail, where it was locked behind doors, in order that every *askari* in Muanza might be free to pile arms and hurry to the fire.

It was not only *askaris;* the whole township turned out as to the circus, with Schubert and his long *kiboko* ruling the riot. The other sergeants were in evidence, but quiet, imperturbable men compared to their *feldwebel,* plying their *kibokos* without wasting words, stirring the whole world within their reach into action—if not orderly and purposeful, action, at least.

Schubert climbed on a roof well to windward and safe from the sparks, and directed proceedings in a voice that out-thundered the mob's roar and crackling flames. To illustrate his meaning he seized handsful of the thatch on which he stood and tore them out, to the huge discontent of the owner. The crowd saw what he wanted and began at once tearing off roofs in a wide circle around the fire so as to isolate it, Schubert demonstrating until scarcely a handful of thatch remained on the roof he honored and he had to stand awkwardly on the crisscross poles, while the owner and his women wept.

Within ten minutes after the commencement of the fire there was under way a regular orgy of roof pulling. Whoever had an enemy ran and tore his roof off, and there were several instances of reciprocity, two families tearing off each other's roofs, each believing the other to be at the fire.

Muanza was a furious place—a riot—a home of din and tumult while the fire lasted, and when it was put out it took another hour to stop the fights between victims of the flames and unofficial salvage-men.

"D'ye get the idea of it?" asked Will. "D'ye see the Achilles heel?"

In that second, I believe, Fred Oakes and I betrayed ourselves genuine adventurers. Any fool could have talked glibly about setting the town on fire; any coward could have yelped about the danger of it, and improbability of success. It needed adventurers to size up instantly all the odds against the idea, recognize the one infinitesimal chance, and plump for it. And we were there!

"It's the only chance we've got!" agreed Fred. "I'm for it! Lead on, America!"

"I believe we can pull it off!" said I. "I'm game!"

After that it seemed like waste of time to talk, yet every single detail of our plan had to be thought out beforehand and mentally rehearsed, if we hoped to have even the one slim chance we built on. Luckily Professor Schillingschen continued drunk, which meant that he would sleep early and give Lady Waldon another chance to pay us a nocturnal visit. One of our boys told us that according to market gossips the commandant was drinking with him and the two of them were watching a sort of prolonged native nautch they had staged in seclusion on the hill.

The next day we learned there was to be a murder trial of no less than nine men—an event likely to keep the whole garrison's attention drawn away from us. And after the trial would come the hanging (it would have been impossible to convince any one, German or native, that the verdict and sentence were not foregone conclusions). The stars in their courses appeared to be on our side. For several nights to come the worst the moon could do would be to show a sliver of silver crescent for an hour or two.

Lady Waldon came earlier that night. When we outlined

our plan to her roughly she argued against it at first—said it was impossible—far-fetched—ridiculous. She insisted again on our simply sneaking away by night with her. But Fred wasted no time on argument, and took the upper hand.

"Take us or leave us, Lady Waldon, as we are! We've an unwritten rule that none of us has ever thought of breaking, that binds us to obey the member of the party whose plan we have adopted. On this occasion we have agreed to Mr. Yerkes' plan, and you've got to obey him implicitly if you want to have part with us! We will not leave our men or Brown of Lumbwa behind, and we will not change the plan by a hair's breadth! Will you or won't you obey?"

She yielded then very quickly. It seemed a relief to her at last to subject her views to those of men whose purpose was merely honest. Will took up the reins at once.

"We've talked over buying the boat," he said, "but that's hopeless. The more we paid for it the louder the owner would brag. The Germans would be 'on' in a minute. We've simply got to steal it. It's up to you to find out the man's proper name and address, and we'll send him the money from the first British post-office we reach."

"Don Quixote de la Mancha!" she said critically. "Well— we steal the boat and you pay for it afterward. The owner will think you are crazy, and if the Germans ever discover it they will take the money away from him by some legal process. But go on!"

"We've plenty of money," said Will, "so there's no need to worry about too many supplies to begin with. But we'll need scant rations for ourselves and all our men until we reach some place where more are to be bought. And we've got to get them on board the dhow secretly. The first question is, how to do that."

She told us at once of a path going round by the back of the hill behind us, that would make the trip to the dhow in the dark a matter of over two miles, but that avoided all sentries and habitations. We agreed that all three of us should climb to the top of the hill, which was not out of bounds, and study the track next morning. On the fateful night we must take our chance, just as she had done, of avoiding the sleepy-eyed sentry who kept watch over the Greeks.

"We'll talk to Brown of Lumbwa on the morning and afternoon march around the township," Will went on. "Brown must whisper to Kazimoto through the corrugated iron partition in the jail at night, and have them all ready to break loose at the signal and bring him along with them. We must be careful to show Brown just where the dhow is. He has been sober quite a while. Maybe he'll remember if we direct him carefully."

"What is to be the signal?" she asked.

"Just what I'm coming to," said Will. "A fire-alarm on the first windy night! The next question is, who is to start the fire? We'll need a good one! Yet if we do it, we're likely to be caught by the crowd coming running to deal with it."

"Coutlass!" she answered suddenly. "Coutlass and his two friends!"

"You'll perhaps pardon me," Fred answered, "but none of us would trust those Greeks as far as a hen could swim in alcohol!"

"Yet you must! Leave them to me! They don't know that the sand in my glass has run down. Let me go to them presently, pretending that I went direct to them and am afraid of being seen by you. I will tell them that the Germans want a good excuse for putting you three men in jail and that they will be sent away free as a reward if they will start a fire and charge you afterward with arson! I will tell them to choose the first windy night, so as to have a really spectacular blaze worth committing perjury about!"

"Better arrange a signal," Will advised. "They might otherwise fire before we were ready!"

"Very well. You men give me the word at midday of the day of the start, and I will spread red, white and blue laundry on the roof of the commandant's house for the Greeks to see."

"Good enough!" agreed Will. "Now one more stunt! We simply must have firearms. The Germans have taken ours away and locked them up. At a pinch I suppose we could manage with one rifle, provided we had lots of ammunition. We would rather have one each. In fact, the more the merrier. One we must have! What about it?"

She thought for several minutes. At last she told us that one of the commandant's rifles and one of Schillingschen's stood leaning in a corner of the living-room beside a bookcase. Whether she could make away with one or both of those without detection she did not know, and she would have to use her wits regarding ammunition. It was always kept locked up.

"Why not kill an *askari* and take his rifle and cartridges?" she asked. "The sentry on duty watching the Greeks will be in the way. Knock him on the head from behind!"

"Thank you!" grinned Will, exchanging glances with us. "We shall have about enough on our consciences setting fire to half the township. We'll not kill except in self-defense."

"But you won't set the town on fire! The Greeks will do that!"

"Don't let's argue ethics!" Fred interrupted, for Will's ears were getting red. "Can you tell us for certain, Lady Waldon, whether *all* the *askaris* and German sergeants really run to a fire? Or do a certain number remain in the boma?"

"Oh, I know about that," she answered. "Until the prisoners are all locked in—that is to say, in case of fire in the daytime—six or eight *askaris* remain inside the boma. The minute they are locked in, if the fire is serious, and in case of fire by night, they all go except two, who stand on the eastern boma wall, one at each corner. From there they are supposed to be able to see on every side except the water-front. Nobody guards the water-front; I don't know why, unless it is that the gate on that side is kept locked almost always and the wall runs along the water's edge."

"As a matter of fact," said I, "those two sentries on the wall will be too busy staring at the fire, if the Greeks really make a big one, to see anything else unless we march by under their noses with a brass band."

"Bah!" sneered Lady Waldon. "If I get that rifle I would dare shoot them both for you myself!"

"If you overstep one detail of Will's plan, I guarantee to
put you ashore on the first barren island we come to!" said
Fred. "Leave shooting to us!"

The next problem was to draw away from the Greeks the
attention of the *askari* at the cross-roads. We could not see
him, for it was one of those black African nights when the
stars look like tiny pin-pricks and there are no shadows because all is dark. To go out and look what he was doing
would have been to arouse his suspicion. Yet there was always a chance that he might be patrolling down near the
Greek camp; doubtless acting on orders, he had a trick of
approaching their tents very closely once in a while.

So when Lady Waldon had slipped out into the darkness
we lit half a dozen lamps and started a concert, Fred playing
and we singing the sort of tunes that black men love. He
took the bait, hook, sinker, and all; in the silence at the end
of the first song we heard his butt ground on the gravel just
beyond the cactus hedge in front of us; and there he stayed,
we entertaining him for an hour. By that time we were
quite sure that Lady Waldon had passed along the road behind him; so Fred went out and gave him tobacco.

"It's time you went and looked at those Greeks again!"
he advised him. "You would be in trouble if they slipped
away in the night!"

Now that a plan of campaign was finally decided on, there
seemed much less to do than we had feared. Mapping out in
our minds the way round the back of the hill to the dhow
was perfectly simple; we went and smoked on the hilltop,
and within an hour after breakfast had every turn and twist
memorized. Fred drew a chart of the track for safety's sake.

Persuading Brown of Lumbwa proved unexpectedly to be
much the most difficult task. Added to the fact that the
*askaris* who marched behind and the Greeks who marched
in front were unusually inquisitive, Brown himself was afraid.

"We'll all be shot in the dark!" he objected.

"Would you rather," Will asked, "be shot in the dark with a
run for your money, or fed to the crocks in the doctor's pond?"
And he told him about the crocodiles to encourage him.

"They'll have to let me out of jail at the end of the month," Brown argued.

"Don't you believe it! In less than a week from now we'll all be in on one and the same charge of filibustering! They'll not let you go back to British East to tell tales about their treatment of the rest of us," Will assured him.

But Brown proved tinged with a little streak of yellow somewhere. It was not until the afternoon march that Fred and Will, one on either side of him, by appeals to his racial instinct and recalling the methods of the military court, induced him to do his part. Once having promised he vowed he would see the thing through to the end; but he was the weak link; he was afraid; and he disbelieved in the wisdom of the attempt.

It was Kazimoto in the end who kept Brown up to the mark, and shamed him into action by superior courage. Fred found a chance to speak to him as the long string rested at noon under the narrow shade of a cactus hedge, and warned him in about fifty words of what was intended. (The *askaris*, almost as leg-weary as the gang, were sprawling at the far end of the line, gambling at pitch-and-toss.)

"Be sure you sleep as near to the partition as you can. Get details of the plan from Mr. Brown, and then drill the porters one by one! Don't let them tell one another. You tell each one of them yourself!"

Then he walked down the line and ordered the porters in a loud voice to obey the *askaris* implicitly, and to work harder in return for the good food and care they were getting, winking at the same time very emphatically, with the eye the *askaris* could not see.

The night work was the hardest, because, although we were quite sure about direction, even in the dark, it was another matter to feel our way and carry unaccustomed loads. By day we decided what to take and what to leave behind, and we cut down what to take with us to the irreducible, dangerous minimum. Then we broke that up into thirty- or forty-pound packages, so that when we all three made the trip to the dhow the most we took at one time was about a hundred pounds' weight. In the condition I was in I could take not more than one trip to the others' two; after the first it was agreed that I would better stay behind and keep an eye on the *askari*. The minute he showed symptoms of becoming inquisitive I was to invent some way of keeping his attention; so all unsuspected by him I lay in the sand by the roadside within three yards of him, while the ants crawled over me and he dozed leaning on his rifle. Once a long snake crawled over my wrist and my very marrow curdled with fear and loathing; but except for mosquitoes, who were legion and sucked their fill, there was no other contretemps. I don't know what I would have done if the *askari* had taken alarm and set off to investigate. I trusted to intuition should that happen.

The work of arranging the stuff in the dhow was the most difficult of all, because we dared not light a lantern, yet we also dared not stow things carelessly for fear of confusion when the hour of action came. The space was ridiculously small for ourselves and all those men, and every inch had to be economized. In addition to that the dhow had to be worked backward off the mud far enough to be shoved off easily, and then made fast by a rope to the bushes in such way as not to be noticeable. Most of the ropes turned out to be rather rotten, and we could only guess at the condition of the sails; the feel of them in the dark gave us small assurance. But fortunately we had a couple of hundred feet of good half-inch manila in camp with us, and that Fred and Will took out and stowed in the hold the night following.

We bought such things at the D. O. A. G. as we could without arousing suspicion, as, for instance, a quantity of German dried pea-soup—not that the porters would take to it kindly, but it would go a long way among them at a pinch. Live stock we did not dare buy, for fear of the noise it would make; but we laid in some eggs and bananas. Most of the thirty-pound loads were rice.

It troubled us sorely to leave our good tents, beds, and equipment behind, yet all we could take was the blankets and one gladstone bag packed with clothes for us all. Kettles and pots and pans were a noisy nuisance, yet we had to have them, and blankets for all those porters, who would escape from jail practically naked, were an essential; but fortunately we had a sixty-pound bale of trade-blankets among our loads.

Not one word did we exchange all this while with Coutlass and his friends. Not one overture did we make to them, or they to us. But there was no doubt of their intention to do their worst. They gloated over us—eyed us with lofty disdain and scornful superior knowledge. They were so full of the notion of having us jailed for their misdeed that they positively ached to come and jeer at us, and I believe were only saved from doing that by the shortness of the time.

At last, three days after decision had been reached, we threw our blankets with a red one uppermost over the top of both tents in the sun; and within thirty minutes after that Lady Saffren Waldon had spread on the commandant's roof a blue cotton dress, a white petticoat, and a blazing red piece of silken stuff. There and then the Greeks and the Goanese pledged one another out in the open with copious draughts in turn from the neck of one whisky bottle, and we began to pray they might not get too drunk before night. Judging by their meaning glances at us, they considered us their mortal and cruel enemies whom it would be an act of sublime virtue to bring to book.

The trial of the natives for murder had taken place, accompanied by the usual amount of thrashing of witnesses and the usual stir throughout the countryside. These were charged with having murdered an *askari* near their village —a big bully sent to arrest a man, who had taken leave to help himself to more than rations, and had made a lot too free with the village women. So German military honor had to be upheld exemplarily. Condign vengeance was sure and swift. The execution was to take place on the drill-ground on the day we chose for our departure.

There was no risk of investigations that day. Had we known it, we could have gone away in all likelihood in broad daylight, so busy was the garrison in marshaling into place and policing the swarms of villagers brought in from as far as sixty miles away to witness German justice. Even the customary parade of the band was canceled for that occasion, and that was our only real ground for uneasiness, for it prevented our having a last talk with Brown of Lumbwa and assuring ourselves that courage would not fail him in the pinch.

We worried in plenty without cause, as it seems that humans must do on the eve of putting plans, however well laid, to the test. We had a thousand scares—a thousand doubts—and overlooked at least a thousand evidences that fortune favored us. Toward the end our hearts turned to water at the thought that Kazimoto would probably fail to do his part, although why we should have doubted him after his faithful record, and knowing his hatred of German rule, we would have found it hard to say.

Several times that morning we showed ourselves about the town, with the purpose of allaying any possible suspicion and saving the authorities the trouble of asking what we were up to. With the same end in view we attended the execution in the afternoon, and sincerely wished before it was over that we had stayed away.

On this occasion even the chain-gangs were included among the spectators, in the front row, on the ground that, being proved criminals, they needed the lesson more than the hempen-noose-food not yet caught and tried and brought to book.

The same sort of sermon, only this time more fiery and full of ranting humbug about German righteousness, was preached by the commandant. The miserable victims had received a simple death sentence, but he explained that in virtue of his superior office he had seen fit to add to it. "Death," he explained, "would certainly rid the German protectorate of such conscienceless scalawags as these, but might not be enough to discourage the bad element that disliked German rule. Natives must be taught that the very name of all that is German must be reverenced, and that German punishment is as terrible and sure as the German arm is long! And be sure of this!" he continued. "The ear of the German government is as far-reaching as its arm! In your villages—in

your homes—in your families—there is always an agent of the
government listening! Your own brother—your wife—your
child may be that agent of the government! Now, watch
carefully and see what happens to men with bad hearts—aye,
and to women with bad hearts, who conspire against German
rule!"

What followed was more impressive because of the determination we had heard of to bring all Africa under the German yoke. In vain should the wretched natives in after years
escape by the hundreds northward in the hope of living under
British government. The fools—the "easy people"—the "folk
who gave without a price"—the "truth tellers"—the "men
who wish to forget"—the unwise, cocksure, cleaner-living,
unbelievably credulous, foolishly honest British officials would
be all gone. The *pikelhaube* and the lash, blackmail and co-
ercion would take the place of generosity. Africa would better
be back under the Arabs again, for the Arabs had no system to
speak of and were inefficient. Some Arabs have a heart—
some a very soft heart.

The crowd grew bright-eyed, little children straining forward between their elders in the bull-fight frenzy—that same
intoxication of the senses that held the Roman freemen spell-
bound at the sight of suffering.

One at a time, that the last might see the torture of the
first, the victims were noosed by the heel (one heel)—thrown
with a jerk—hauled heel-first to the overhanging branch—
and flogged into unconsciousness with slow blows, the lieutenant standing by to reprove the *askaris* if they struck too
fast, for that would have been merciful. Not until the victims
ceased to struggle were they lowered and thrown on the
ground, to lie bleeding, awaiting their turn to be hanged.

The last two—supposed to have been the culprits who
actually held the spear that pierced the marauding *askari's*
heart—were hauled up heel-to-heel together, and hanged presently in the same noose, the commandant laughing at their
struggles and Professor Schillingschen studying their agony
with strictly scientific interest.

When the last had ceased struggling Schillingschen permitted himself one more pleasure. He strolled over to us and blocked Fred's way, standing with hands behind him and out-thrust chin.

"You flatter yourself, don't you!" he sneered. He was just drunk enough to be boastful, while thoroughly sure of what he was saying. "You expect to tell a fine tale! I know the psychology of the English! I know it like a book! Let me tell you two things: First, your English would not believe you. They are such supremely cocksure fools that they can not be made to believe that another so-called civilized nation would act as they, in their egoism, would be ashamed to act! Civilization! That is a fine word, full of false meanings! Civilization is prudery—sham—false pride—veneer! Only the Germans are truly civilized, because they alone are not afraid to face naked animalism without its mask! The British dare not! They hide from it—shut their eyes! The fools! If you could tell them their story they would never listen!

"Second: You will never tell the story! Being English, you were such dull-witted fools that you did not even hide the cartridge cases, or the bones of the Masai you shot! Bah-ha-ha-ha-hah! You can escape hanging yet by telling your secret. Jail you can not escape! Try it if you don't believe me! Try to escape—go on!"

He turned on his heel and left us, striding heavily with the strength of an ox and about the alertness of a traction engine, turning his head every once in a while to enjoy the spectacle of our discomfort.

We judged it best to appear concerned, as if that was indeed our first realization of the extent of the case against us and the nature of the evidence. But we did not find it difficult. We were all three startled by the fear that in some way he had got wind of our plans, and that he meant to play with us cat-and-mouse fashion.

That night it stormed—not rain, but wind from east to west, blowing such clouds of dust that one could scarcely see across the narrow streets. Every element favored us. Even the *askari* at the cross-roads, supposed to be watching the Greeks, turned his back to the wind, and what with rubbing sand in and out of smarting eyes and fingering it out of his ears, heard and saw nothing. It was scarcely sunset when we saw both Greeks and the Goanese sneak out of the camping-place in Indian file with their pockets full of cotton waste. They had soaked the stuff in kerosene right under our eyes that afternoon.

There ought to have been a sliver of moon, but the wind and dust hid it. Fifteen minutes after sundown the only light was from the lamps in windows and the cooking fires glowing in the open here and there. Thirty minutes later there began to be a red glow in three directions. Less than one second after we saw the first indications of the holocaust a regular volley of shots broke out from the boma as the sentries on duty gave the general alarm. Less than five minutes after that the whole of the southern, grass-roofed section of the town was going up in flames, and every living man, black, white, gray, mulatto, brown and mixed, was running full pelt to the scene of action.

We waited ten minutes longer, rather expecting the Greeks to double back and begin denouncing us at once. In that case we intended to stretch them out with the first weapons handy. I sat feeling the weight of an ax, and wondering just how hard I could hit a Greek's head with the back of it without killing him. Fred had a long tent-peg. Will chose a wooden mallet that our porters carried to help in pitching tents.

But the Greeks did not come, and there streamed such a perfect screen of crimson dust, sparkling in the reflected blaze and more beautiful than all the fireworks ever loosed off at a coronation, that it was folly to linger. We each seized the load left for that last trip (Fred's included the hammer, pincers, and cold chisel for striking off the porters' chain) and started off quietly round the hill, not beginning to hurry until the hill lay between us and the burning town.

There was not much need for caution. The roar of flames, the shouting, the excitement would have protected us, whatever noise we made, however openly we ran. Over and above the tumult we could hear Schubert's bull-throated bellowing, and then the echo to him as the sergeants took up the shout all together, ordering "Off with the grass roofs! Off with the roofs!"

The white officials were more than interested, and had no time for anything but thought for the blaze. As we crossed the shoulder of the far side of the hill we could see them standing on the drill-ground all together, clearly defined against the crimson flare. Schillingschen was with them.

There was no sign of what had happened at the boma. The gang would have to emerge from a little-used gate at the northern end, provided they could break the lock or secure the key to it; otherwise their only chance was to climb the wall by the cook-house roof and jump twenty feet on the far side. I was for running to the little gate and bursting it in from the outside, but Fred damned me for a mutineer between his panting for breath, and Will, who was longer-winded, agreed with him.

"Have to leave their end of the plan to them! Let's do our part right!"

As it turned out, we were last at the rendezvous. We heard the chain clanking in the dark just ahead of us, and try how we might, could not catch up. Then, near the boat bow, Kazimoto suddenly recognized Fred and nearly throttled him in a fierce embrace, releasing all his pent-up rage, agony, resentment, misery, fear in one paroxysm of affection for the man who cared enough to run risks for the sake of rescuing him. Fred had to pry him off by main force.

"Into the boat with you!" Will ordered them. "Chain-gang first! Get down below, and lie down! The first head that shows shall be hit with a club! Quickly now!"

Clanking their infernal chain like all the ghosts from all the haunted granges of the Old World, they climbed overside and disappeared. There were more figures left on shore then than we expected. Brown we could make out dimly in the dark: he was chattering nervously, and admitted that but for Kazimoto he would not be there. The faithful fellow had broken down the corrugated iron partition and had dragged him out by main force. He was rather resentful than grateful.

"Hauled here by a nigger—think of it!"

We ordered Brown on board and below, pretty peremptorily. Lady Saffren Waldon stepped out of the darkness next, holding a rifle and two bandoliers so full of cartridges that she could hardly raise her arms. We took the load from her, and helped her overside. Fred took the rifle and succumbed to the hunter's habit of opening the breach first thing. It was a German sporting Mauser, with a hair trigger attachment and magazine, as handy and useful a weapon as the heart of man could wish. He had scarcely snapped the breach to again when a voice we all recognized made the hair rise on my neck. Fred jumped and raised the rifle. Will swore softly—endlessly.

"Gassharrrrammminy! You men took us for damned fools, didn't you? You thought to get away and leave us! By hell, no! We go or you stay! Birds of a feather fly together! One of you is American—I am American! Two of you are English—I am English, and can prove it! My friends come with me!"

Fred leveled the rifle at him.

"About face! Off back to town with you!" he barked.

"Not on your tin-type!" Coutlass yelled. "I'm no man's popinjay! Shoot if you dare, and I'll spoil the whole game! Help! He-e-e-lp! He-e-e-e-lp!"

The other Greek and the Goanese joined in the shout, the dark man setting up such an ululating screech that the very storm dwindled into second place in comparison. It was true, the unearthly yelling was carried out over the water, and very likely not a sound of it reached twenty yards inland; but it rattled our nerves, nevertheless. The skin grew prickly all up and down my backbone, and the men on the chain-gang inside the hull began shouting to know what the matter was.

Will remembered then that he was captain for the day, and made virtue of necessity.

"In with you!" he ordered. "Quick!"

With a grin that was half-triumph, half-cunning, and

wholly glad, Coutlass helped his companions over the bow, and had the civility to stand there with hand outstretched to help us in after him. We sent him below with his friends, but he came up again and insisted on leaning his weight on the poles with which we began shoving off into deeper water. It was hard work, for with her human cargo and several hundred gallons of water that had leaked through her gaping seams, the dhow was down several inches. Her hull had just begun to feel the wind and to rise and fall freely, when a white figure ran screaming down toward the water's edge and stood there waving to us frantically.

"Leave her!" said Lady Waldon excitedly, clutching my arm. I was up on the bow, just about to lay the pole along the deck and haul on the halyards. She spoke very slowly right in my ear. "That is my maid Rebecca. The faithless slut—"

Coutlass began to shout, trying to pole the dhow back to land single-handed.

"We can't leave that woman behind there!" Fred shouted, hardly making himself heard against the wind.

"Can't we!" shouted Lady Waldon. "Give me that rifle, and I'll solve the problem for you!"

But Coutlass solved it in another way by jumping overboard, over his head in deep water, taking our hempen warp with him (I had made one end of it fast to the bitts, meaning to be able to find it in the dark).

There was quite a sea running, even as close inshore as that, and for a moment I doubted whether the Greek would make it. By that time it was all we could do to see the woman's white figure, still gesticulating, and screaming like a mad thing. Presently, however, the warp tightened, and then by the strain on it I knew that Coutlass was trying to haul us back inshore. Failing to do that, for the strength of the wind was increasing, he seized the Syrian woman by the waist and plunged into the water with her. I saw them disappear and hauled on the warp hand-over-hand with all my might, Lady Waldon leaning over to strike at my hands until I

shouted to Fred to come and hold her. Then she begged
Fred again for the rifle, promising to kill the two of
them and reduce our problem to that extent if we would
only let her.

Will and I hauled the dripping pair on board, and Coutlass
carried the maid to the stern. She had fainted, either from
fright or from being half-drowned, there was no guessing
which. Then in pitch blackness with Will's help I got the
ship beam to the wind and began to make sail.

Now danger was only just beginning! I was the only one
of them all who knew anything whatever about sails and sailing. I was too weak to get the sail up single-handed, had no
compass, knew nothing whatever of the rocks and shoals, except by rumor that there were plenty of both. There appeared
to be no way of reefing the lateen sail, which was made of no
better material than calico, and I was entirely unfamiliar with
the rigging.

Behind us, as we payed before the gaining wind, was a
brilliant blaze that showed where Muanza was. Against the
blaze stood out the lakeward boma wall. I stood due east away
from it, and discovered presently that by easing on the halyard so as to lower the long spar I could obtain something
the effect of reefing.

I set Fred and Will to making a sea-anchor of buckets and
spars in case the sail or rotten rigging should carry away,
leaving us at the mercy of the short steep waves that fresh-
water lakes and the North Sea only know. The big curved
spar, now that it was hanging low, bucked and swung and
the dhow steered like an omnibus on slippery pavement.
Luckily, I had living ballast and could trim the ship how I
chose. They all began to grow seasick, but I gave them something to think about by making them shift backward and forward and from side to side until I found which way the dhow
rode easiest.

When Fred had finished the sea-anchor he got out the
tools and began striking off the iron rings on the porters'
necks through which the chain passed. The job took him two
hours, but at the end of it we owned a good serviceable chain,

and a crew that could be drilled to take the brute hard labor off our shoulders.

Coutlass meanwhile was busy on the seat in the stern beside me making Hellenic inflammatory love to Lady Waldon's maid, whom he had wrapped in his own blanket and held shivering in his arms. Lady Waldon herself sat on the other side of me, affecting not to be aware of the existence of either of them. The other Greek and the Goanese had been driven below, where they started to smoke until I saw the glow of their pipes and shouted to Will to stop that foolishness. He snatched both pipes and threw them overboard. The thought of being seen from shore was almost incitement enough for murder. They refused to turn a hand to anything that night, but sat sulking below the sloping roof of reeds and tarpaulin that did duty for a deck, wedged alongside of seasick Wanyamwezi.

It was Kazimoto who chose the least disheartened of the gang, beat them and stung them into liveliness, and set them to bailing. There was a trough running thwartwise of the ship into which the water had to be lifted from the midship well. It took the gang of eight men, working in relays, until nearly dawn to get the water out of her; and to keep her bottom reasonably dry after that two men working constantly.

I knew vaguely that the great island of Ukerewe lay to the northwestward of us. Between that and the mainland, running roughly north, was a passage that narrowed in more than one place to less than a hundred yards. That would have been the obvious course to take had we not been afraid of pursuit, had we dared get away by daylight, and provided I had known the way. As it was I intended to add another hundred miles to the distance between us and the northern shore of the lake, by sailing well clear of and around Ukerewe, trusting to the less frequented water and the wilder islands to make escape easier.

I judged it likely that the moment we were missed, the launch would be sent off in search of us, and that the Germans would search the narrow passage first. They would expect us to take the narrow passage, as the shortest, and depend on their ability to steam a dozen miles an hour to overhaul us, even should we get a long start on the outside course.

With gaining wind, a following sea, a little ship crowded to suffocation, and a sail that might blow to shreds at any minute, it was not long before I began to pray for the lee of Ukerewe, and to stand in closer toward where I judged the end of the island ought to be than perhaps I should have done. It was lucky, though, that I did.

In making calculations I had overlooked the obvious fact that, steaming three miles to our one, the launch could very well afford to take the outside course to start with. Then they could take a good look for us in the open water next morning, and, failing to find us, steam all around Ukerewe, come back down the inside passage, and catch us between two banks.

It was Lady Saffren Waldon on my left hand, looking anywhere but at her maid and sweeping the dark waste of water with eyes as restless as the waves themselves, who gave the first alarm.

"What is that light?" she asked me.

Following the direction of her hand I saw a red glow on the water to our left, not more than a mile behind.

"Reflection from the burning town," I answered, but I had no sooner said it than I knew the answer was foolish. It was the glow that rides above hot steamer funnels in the night.

"Fred!" I shouted, for fear took hold of the very roots of my heart, "for the love of God make every one keep silence! Show no lights! Don't speak above a whisper! Keep all heads below the gunwale! That cursed German launch is after us!"

We were in double danger. I could hear surf pounding on rocks to starboard. I did not dare to come up into the wind because nobody but I knew how the spar would have to be passed around the mast, and in any case the noise and the fluttering sail might attract attention.

"Look out for breakers ahead!" I ordered. "I'm going to hold this course and hope they pass us in the dark!"

# "DAVID PREVAILED"

### (I. Sam. 17:50)

*Be glad if ye know the accursèd thing*
  *And know it accurst, for the Gift is yours*
*Of Sight where the prophets of blindness sing*
  *By the brink of death. And the Gift endures;*
*Ye shall see the last of the sharpened lies*
  *That rivet privilege's gripe.*
*Be still, then, ye with the opened eyes,*
  *Come away from the thing till the time is ripe.*

*Be glad that ye loathe the accursèd thing,*
  *It is given to you to foreknow the end.*
*But they who the unwise challenge fling*
  *Shall startle foe at the risk of friend*
*As yet unready to endure—*
  *And can ye fend Goliath's swipe?*
*The slowly grinding mills are sure,*
  *Let terror alone till the time is ripe.*

*Be glad when the shout for the spoils, and the glee,*
  *The hoofs and the wheels of the prophets of wrong,*
*Outthunder the warning of what shall be;*
  *Be still, for the tumult is not for long.*
*The Finger that wrote, from a polished wall*
  *As surely the closed account shall wipe;*
*The accursèd thing ye feared shall fall*
  *To a boy with a sling when the time is ripe.*

# CHAPTER ELEVEN

IF the dhow had been seaworthy; if the crew had understood the rigging and the long unwieldy spar; if we had had any chart, or had known anything whatever of the coast; if nobody had been afraid; and, above all, if that incessant din of surf pounding on rocks not far away to starboard had not threatened disaster even greater than the Germans in the steam launch, our problem might have been simple enough.

But every one was afraid, including me who held the tiller (and the lives of all the party) in my right hand. Lady Saffren Waldon disguised fear under an acid temper and some villainously bad advice.

"Steer toward them!" she kept shouting in my ear. "Steer toward them! Ram them! Sink them!"

Coutlass, on my other hand, made feverish haste with his love-affair, fearful lest discovery by the Germans should postpone forever the assuaging of his hungry heart's desire.

"Steer toward shore!" he urged me. "Who cares if we run on rocks? Can't we swim? Gassharamminy! Take to the land and give them a run for it!"

He seized the tiller to reinforce the argument, and wrenched at it until I hit him, and Fred threatened him with the only rifle.

"Get up forward!" Fred ordered; but Georges Coutlass would not go.

"Gassharamminy!" he snarled. "You want my girl! I will fight the whole damned crew before I let her out of the hollow of my arm!"

"All right, touch that tiller again and I'll kill you!" Fred warned him.

"Touch my girl, and you kill me or get out and swim!" Coutlass retorted.

Will was up forward with Brown, looking out for breakers through the spray that swept over us continually. I watched the glow that rode above the launch's funnel, marveling, when I found time for it, at the mystery of why the cotton sail should hold. The firm, somewhere in Connecticut, who made that export calico, should be praised by name, only that the dye they used was much less perfect than the stuff and workmanship; their trade-mark was all washed out.

Suddenly Will dodged under the bellying sail, throwing up both hands, and he and Brown screamed at me: "To your left! Go to your left! Rocks to the right!"

The Germans had passed us, but not by much, for the short steep seas were tossing their propeller out of the water half the time. Because of the course I had taken the wind was setting slightly from us toward them, and I could have sworn they heard Will's voice. Yet there was nothing for it but to put the helm over, and as I laid her nearly broadside to the wind a great wave swept us. At that the Greek, the Goanese, and all the natives in the hold set up a yell together that ought to have announced our presence to the Seven Sleepers.

I held the helm up, and let her reel and wallow in the trough. Now I could see the fangs of rock myself and the white waves raging around them. See? I could have spat on them! There was a current there that set strongly toward the rocks, for a backwash of some sort helped the helm and we won clear, about a third full of water, with the crew too panicky to bail.

"Hold her so!" yelled Fred in my ear. "Don't ease up yet! If we get too close and they see us, I've the rifle! They haven't seen us yet!"

"Rocks ahead again!" yelled Will. "To the left again!"

We were in the gaping jaws of a sort of pocket, and it was too late to steer clear.

"Throw the anchor over!" I roared, "and let go everything!"

Will attended to the anchor. Fred was too anxious for the safety of the only rifle to trust it out of hand, and he hesitated. Georges Coutlass saved the day by letting go the shivering Syrian maid and slashing at the halyard with his knife. Down came the great spar with a crash, and as the dhow swung round in answer to anchor and helm, Fred, Will and Brown, between them, contrived to save the sail, Brown complaining that we were the first sailors he ever heard of who did not have rum served them for working overtime in dirty weather.

So we lay, then, wallowing in the jaws of a crescent granite reef, and watched the red glow above the German launch move farther and farther away from us. We waited there, wet and hungry, until dawn dimmed the flame from the burning roofs of Muanza, Lady Isobel Saffren Waldon loudly accusing us all at intervals of being rank incompetents unfit to be trusted with the lives of fish, and Coutlass afraid of nothing but interruption. The things he said to the maid, in English —the only language that they had apparently in common— would have scandalized a Goanese harbor "guide" or a Rock Scorpion from the lower streets of Gib. He did not mention marriage to her, beyond admitting that he had half a dozen wives already, and had been too bored by convention ever to submit to the yoke again. The maid seemed enraptured— delirious in the bight of his lawless arm, forgetful of her wetting, and only afraid when he left her for a minute.

We dared not try to cook anything, even supposing that had been possible. Forward was a box full of sand to serve as hearth-stone, but the little scraps of fuel we had brought with us were drenched and unburnable, even if the risk of being seen were not too great. Lady Saffren Waldon told us we were "toe-rag contrivers." In fact, now that she was out of reach of the men she feared and hated most, she reverted to type and tried to domineer over us all by the simple old recipe—audacious arrogance. Luckily, she slept for an hour or two.

A little before dawn, when it began to be light enough to let us see the outline of the shore, we sent Kazimoto aloft to reeve our hemp rope through the hole that did duty for block, and by the time the sun had pushed the uppermost arc of his rim above the sky-line we once more had the sail set.

The wind was still blowing a gale; the seamanlike precau-

tion would have been to lie where we were at anchor until
fairer weather; but daring is forced on the fearfullest, and
there was nothing for it but to study out the method by which
the unwieldy spar should be made to pass the mast when tack-
ing, drill Fred, Will, Brown and Kazimoto, and then haul
up the anchor and sail away before people on shore could
see us.

We had to tack toward Muanza for a quarter of a mile
with fear in our arms to make them clumsy before I dared
believe we were clear of the reefs; but when I put the helm
down at last there was neither launch in sight nor any other
boat that might contain an enemy. The southern spur of
Ukerewe stuck out like a wedge into boiling water not many
miles ahead, and once around that we should be sheltered.
The only fly in the ointment then was the probability that
the launch would be waiting for us just around the spur, or
else under the lee of another smaller island in the offing to
our left, but what we could not see in that hour could not
upset us much.

Every one clamored for food. The porters, already forgetful of the chain that had galled them, and the whips that
had flayed them day and night, demanded to be set ashore
to build a fire and eat. Lady Saffren Waldon awoke to fresh
bad temper, and Coutlass, too, grew villainously impatient.
His Greek friend, from under the shelter of the leaky reed-
and-tarpaulin deck, offered him Greek advice, and was cursed
for his trouble. One curse led to another, and then they both
had to be beaten into subjection with the first thing handy, because when they fought Lady Saffren Waldon egged them on
and the maid tried to savage the other Greek with a brooch-
pin, which brought out the Goanese to the rescue. That
crowded dhow was no place for pitched battles, plunging and
rolling between the frying-pan of Muanza and the fire of
unknown things ahead.

"One more outbreak from you, and I shoot!" Fred announced, patting the rifle. But he did not mean it, and Coutlass knew he did not. The English temperament does not
turn readily on even the most rascally fellow beings in dis-

tress. Besides, it was an indubitable fact that we all much preferred Coutlass, with his daring record, and now a most outrageous love-affair on hand, to the other Greek or the Goanese, who were now disposed to bid for our friendship by abusing him. Georges Coutlass was no drawing-room darling, or worthy citizen of any land, but he had courage of a kind, and a sort of splendid fire that made men forget his turpitude.

We were a seasick, cold and sorry company that rounded the point at last and came to anchor in a calm shallow bay where fuel grew close down to the water's edge. Having no small boat, we had to wade ashore and carry the women, Coutlass attending to his own inamorata. Lady Saffren Waldon's picric acid rage exploded by being dropped between two porters waist-deep into the water. It was her fault. She insisted one was not enough, yet refused to explain how two should do the work of one. Sitting on their two shoulders, holding on by their hair, she frightened the left-hand man by losing her balance and clutching his nose and eyes. She insisted on having both men flogged for having dropped her, and Fred's refusal was the signal for new war, our rescue of her being flung at once on to the scrap heap of her memory.

She counted with cold cynicism on our unwillingness to leave her again at the mercy of the Germans, and had no more consideration of our rights or feelings than the cuckoo has for the owner of the nest in which she lays her eggs.

"Beat those fools!" she ordered. "Beat them blue and give them no breakfast!"

"Do you see that rock over there, Lady Waldon?" Fred answered. "Go and spread your clothes to dry. When we've cooked food we'll send Rebecca to you with your share."

"If you send that slut to me I will kill her!" she answered, flying into a new fury.

"Whom do you call slut?" demanded Coutlass (and he had no compunctions of any kind—particularly none about women, and calling names. He was simply feeling gallant after his own fashion, and alert for a chance to show off.) Lady Waldon backed away from him.

"Of course," she sneered, "if you loose your bully at me, I am no match at all!"

Fred promptly kicked Coutlass until he ran limping out of range, to sit and nurse his bruises with polyglot profanity. The Syrian Rebecca went over to comfort him, and eying the two of them with either malice or else calculation (it was im-possible to judge which) Lady Waldon retreated toward the rock that Fred had pointed out.

We cooked a miserable meal, neither daring to make too great inroad into our stores before making sure we could replenish them, nor caring to make more smoke than we could help. We hoped to escape being seen even by natives, but Lady Waldon upset that part of our plan by setting up such a scream when she saw three islanders crossing a ridge three hundred yards away, that they could not help hearing her, and came to investigate. She was forced to dress faster than ever in her life before, and came running to demand that we flog all three "to teach them manners." She had perfectly absorbed the German attitude toward all black men.

From the natives we learned that there was no telegraph wire along that coast, and that the only German settlements were semi-permanent camps where they were cutting wood, for fuel for their own launch and for the steamers the British were building to serve the lake ports, Muanza included.

With that good news for encouragement we made the three natives a small present in the vain hope that they might be induced not to talk about us, and put to sea again. The weather was fairer and growing intolerably hot. Even before the sun grew high the dhow was a comfortless indecent thing, more crowded than anything Noah can have had to tolerate: and we lacked Noah's faith in omniscient guidance, in addition to sailing in a hotter latitude, and having more fleas on board than the pair he is reported to have carried.

As we crept up-coast, leaning to this or that side when the gusts of wind varied, the only enviable ones were the three in the bow, posted there to keep a look-out for the launch or any other enemy. They had room enough to sit without touching one another, and air to breathe that mostly had not been tasted half a dozen times. Fred, Will and Brown took turns commanding the fore-deck look-out, keeping it awake and its units from quarreling. The rest of us found no joy in life, and not too much hope even when Fred's concertina lifted the refrain of missionary hymn-tunes that even the porters knew, and most of us sang, the porters humming wordless melancholy through their noses. (When that happened Lady Saffren Waldon's scorn was something the arch-priests of Babylon would have paid to see.)

There was never room on the tiny after-deck for more than six people sitting elbow to elbow and back to back or knee to knee. Lady Waldon simply refused to yield her corner seat on any account at any time to any one. Coutlass refused to leave his new sweetheart, for the freely-voiced reason that then Brown might make love to her; and we did not care to send both of them below for obvious reasons. That reduced open-air accommodation to a minimum, because the reed-and-tarpaulin deck was scarcely strong enough to bear the weight of two men at a time, and we did not care to throw the whole deck overboard for fear of rain.

And by-and-by the rain came—out of season, but no less violent because of that. It rained three days and nights on end—three windless days and starless nights, during which we had to linger alongshore close to the papyrus. In order to keep mosquitoes out we had to light a smudge in the sand-box below. The smudge added to the heat, and the heat drove men to the open air to gasp a few minutes in the rain for breath and go down again to make room for the next in turn.

Sleep on shore was impossible, for thereabouts were crocodile and snake swamps, fuller of insect life than dictionaries are of letters. Poling was next to impossible, because the soft mud bottom gave no purchase. And the oars we made out of poles were clumsy affairs; there was not room for more than two boys to try to use them at a time, even if the deck would have stood the strain of more feet, which it certainly would not have done.

Lady Waldon slept seated in her corner, with her head wrapped in a veil over which the mosquitoes prospected in gangs. Coutlass and his lady-love endured rain and insects in the open, too, but suffered less, because of mutual distraction. The rest of us took turns with the natives below, lying packed between them, much as sardines nestle in a can, wondering whether the famous Black Hole of Calcutta was really such a record-breaker as they say. Brown was of the opinion that the Black Hole was a nosegay compared to our lot—"Besides which, they probably had rum with 'em!" he added.

Some of the porters grew sick under the strain of heat, fear, excitement and inactivity. The native suffers as much from unaccustomed inconvenience as the white man, and more from close confinement. The third night out the man next me began coughing, shaking my frame as much as his own as he racked himself, for we were wedged together with only the thickness of his blanket and mine between us, and I was jammed tight against the ship's side. Toward morning he grew quiet—grew colder, too. When dawn came we found that he had coughed up the most of his lungs on my white English blanket.

I gave them the blanket to bury him in, and we poled the *Queen of Sheba* inshore to find a place to dig a hole, leaving the body stretched on some tree-roots while we prospected. We should have known enough by that time to leave four or five men on guard close by; as it was, when the men still on board the dhow began kicking up a babel, Fred and I came running and jumping back through the marsh just in time to see a crocodile wriggle off into the water, with the corpse in his jaws feet first. Fred fired a shotted salute, but missed, and that ended that funeral.

By day we passed villages on higher ground, where we might have procured more food if we had dared run the risk of meeting Germans. It was likely enough the villagers were so used to dhows that they would not trouble to report having seen us in the distance; but it was perfectly certain that if we paid them a visit they would pass word along from mouth to mouth with that astonishing, undiscoverable ease that is at once the blessing and bane of governments.

So Fred wasted hot hours with the only rifle, trying to hunt

meat on a shore where all the four-legged game had been run
down by the natives, or butchered by the German machine-
guns long ago (for to teach Sudanese mercenaries the art of
rapid fire in action their officers marched them out to practise
on herds of antelope. There was game in plenty away from
the lake, but none where the German officer could conveniently
practise his profession.)

We tried to shoot ducks and geese; but a rifle at long range
is not the best weapon for that sport. We shot very few, and
then only to discover the invincible repugnance natives have
to eating "dagi" as they call all birds. We kept ourselves
alive, but did not solve the problem of the ever-diminishing
supplies of rice for our men.

Somebody thought of fishing. We found hooks in a crevice
in the *Queen of Sheba's* bow, and made lines from a frayed
rope. But although the shore was lined with traps in which
the inhabitants no doubt took fish in proper season, all that we
caught was one miserable finny specimen, all head and mouth
and tail, that the natives said would poison any one who ate it.

The truth was, of course, that they preferred rice to anything, and, African native-like, would eat nothing else as long
as rice was to be had, having no earthly notions of economy.
When the rice was all gone on the fifth day out of Muanza they
raided a banana plantation before we knew what they were up
to, and came back gorged, with bunches enough to feed them
for two or three more days.

The fat was in the fire then, of course. We paid the owners
handsomely, giving them their choice of money or blankets
when they bore down on us in long canoes demanding vengeance. They voted for blankets and money, but vowed they
would far rather have the bananas, because now their own people would be on short commons to make up for the surfeit of
ours.

We left them never doubting that they would send word to
the nearest German officer. (They told us there was a wood-
cutting station within a "few hours," and we prayed he might
be only a non-commissioned man in charge of it, but knew
that prayer was too sweetly reasonable to be answered where

the German *Gott* makes war on foreigners.) Kazimoto assured us he heard them telling one another they would make complaint against us within the day.

It remained, then, only to guess where that steam launch might be. We were approaching the northern end of Ukerewe, not a day's sail, if the light wind held, from the narrow mouth of the channel between Ukerewe and the mainland. That was the likeliest place for the launch to lie in wait; it was where we would have waited had we been pursuers and they the pursued. So we decided after a council of war to put the helm over and sail almost due westward, hoping to meet with an island where we might stop for a few days, catch fish and dry them, and caulk the leaky dhow, without the risk of letting the Germans know our whereabouts. (It is a peculiar fact that whatever the native secret system of transferring messages may be, it does not work across water.)

Not all the little gods of Africa were fighting for the Germans, although it began to seem so. An hour after putting up the helm we sighted a school of hippopotami—fifty at least, and for half a day we chased them, Fred trying to shoot one until Will and I objected to further waste of ammunition. A dead hippo would have provided us with meat enough for a month for the whole ship's company. We could have towed the carcass ashore somewhere and dried the meat in slabs. But the glare on the water made shooting very nearly impossible (Fred's eyes were sore from it); and if we should meet the Germans those remaining cartridges would be our only hope. But the diversion took us out of sight of land, and that stood us in better stead presently than tons of fresh meat.

Whether the Germans heard us, or were merely quartering that part of the lake in wait, we never knew. Probably they heard the shooting in the distance and gave chase. At any rate, within ten minutes of Fred's last wasted shot Coutlass caught sight of smoke and announced the fact with his favorite oath.

"Gassharamminy! The launch!"

At first we were all in a stew because there was no land near, where we might have beached the dhow and scattered. It was an hour before our advantage of position dawned on us, and all the while the launch approached us leisurely. She had plenty of fuel; the wood was piled high above her gunwale in a stack toward the stern; but those on board her seemed to take more pleasure in contemplation of our defenselessness than in speed. She steamed twice around us slowly before closing in; and then we made out Schillingschen's hairy shape, leaning against the cord-wood with a rifle between his hands.

"Shoot him! Shoot him, by Jiminy!" urged Coutlass, but Fred was not so previous as that. We were not yet on the defensive. We counted five rifles, in addition to Schillingschen's protruding above the launch's side, and we all took cover in the hope either that they might decide we were not the dhow they waited for, or else that they might come very close out of curiosity. For Fred had a plan of his own. Rifle in hand, he crawled under the hot tarpaulin and lay flat on the reed deck, Will crawling after him to snatch the rifle in case Fred should be hit.

"Steer straight toward 'em!" Fred called to me, as soon as it was evident that the launch did not intend to pass us by. "Keep headed toward them!"

That was not easy in the light wind, until Schillingschen tired of staring at us and gave an order to the engineer. Then they laid the launch broadside on to our bow at about two hundred yards' range, and without a word of warning opened fire on us from all six rifles, Schillingschen devoting his first attention to myself at the helm.

Our lone rifle cracked in reply, but they could not see Fred and did not guess where to shoot in order to search him out. They came no nearer, but circled slowly around us, only Schillingschen's bullets appearing to come anywhere near the target, until a yell from below showed what their real plan was and I understood why the sail was not ripped and no bullets whistled overhead. They were shooting through the planking of the dhow, endeavoring to massacre the helpless crowd below, and no doubt to sink her and drown us as soon as she was full enough of holes.

A wounded Nyamwezi came scrambling on deck, spouting

blood from his neck and crazed with fear. He jumped overboard and tried to swim toward the launch, but one of the
Germans hit him in the head at the third shot and he disappeared. Then one of Schillingschen's elephant bullets slit my
sleeve, and the next one pierced my helmet.

"Put one into Schillingschen, Fred!" I shouted, but Fred
did not answer. He kept up a very steady succession of shots
that were doing no good at all that I could see.

Another German bullet found its mark below deck in the
thigh of the Goanese. He might have known enough to lie
quiet, having some alleged white blood in him, but instead he,
too, came struggling to the after-deck, bellowing like a madman. Coutlass knocked him back below with a blow on the
chin, and he there and then threw the whole crowd into a panic
by screaming and kicking. They all began to try to swarm together through the narrow opening, and those in the rear tore
at the reed deck.

Into that pandemonium went Coutlass, armed with nothing
but Hellenic fury, thoughtful of nothing but his lady-love—
surely reckless of his own skin. He beat, kicked, bit, scragged,
banged their foolish heads together, cursed, spat, gouged, and
strangled as surely no catamount ever did. Brown leaped in
to lend a hand, and into the midst of that inferno three more
bullets penetrated, each wounding a man. Lady Waldon, mad
with some idiotic strategy of her own sudden devising, seized
the tiller and tried to wrench it from my hand. The Syrian
Rebecca, imagining new treachery and fearful for her Greek
lover, tried to prevent her with teeth and nails. The Germans
raised a war-whoop of wild enjoyment. And just at the height
of all that, Fred's three-and-twentieth shot went home.

There was a loud report, followed by instant nothing except
stampede on the part of the Germans to get out of reach of
something. Then the something grew denser; invisible hot
vapor became a pall of steam that hid the launch from view,
three more shots from Fred's rifle finding the proper mark by
sheer accident, for there was another explosion; the cloud increased and the launch stopped dead.

"That gray sheet of metal wasn't her boiler at all!" Fred

shouted back to me. "The first shot pierced the boiler when I found out where to aim! I think three of them are scalded badly—hope so!—high pressure steam—superheated—did you see? Now leave 'em to find their own way home!"

"See if you can't get Schillingschen!" said I.

But Schillingschen was invisible in the white cloud, and Fred refused to waste one of the half-dozen cartridges remaining. The light wind that bore us away from the launch also spread the screen of steam between us and them. A shot or two from Schillingschen's rifle proved him to be still alive, and still determined, but missed us by so much that we began to dare to sit upright. Then Fred went below to sort out wounded men, plug holes in the dhow, and stop the panic, and we all prayed for wind with a fervor they never exceeded in Nelson's fleet.

When Will had gone below to help Fred, the panic had ceased, two dead men had been thrown overboard, and six of the crew had been set to work bailing in deadly earnest to keep ahead of the new leaks, there was time to consider the position and to realize how hugely better off we were than if the launch had caught us somewhere close inshore. Now we could sail safely northward, every puff of wind carrying us nearer to British water and safety, whereas unless they could mend that high-pressure boiler, they would have to lie there for a week, or a month—die unless some one came in search of them. Had we holed their boiler near the shore they would have been able to take to the land until they found canoes. Good canoes, well manned, could have overhauled us hand over fist like terriers after a rat.

It was fifteen minutes yet before we were out of rifle range, and Schillingschen tried to make the most of them when the steam thinned, exposing his beefy carcass recklessly. But by the time it had thinned down sufficiently to let him really see us we were too far away to make sure shooting. He slit the sail, giving us half a night's work to mend it, and made three more holes in our planking, but hurt nobody.

That was the only launch the German government had on the lake in those days, an almost perfect toy with an aluminum hull and more up-to-date gadgets on her machinery than a battleship's engineer could have explained the purpose of in a watch. They had lavished a whole appropriation on one show. From the minute we were out of range of Schilling-schen's big-bore elephant gun we ran risk of starvation, and perhaps surprise, but no longer of pursuit, and we headed the *Queen of Sheba* as nearly as we could guess for British East with feelings that even Lady Waldon shared, for she grew distantly polite again, and complimented Fred on his cool nerve and accurate shooting.

We should have suspected treachery, for she made no attempt to retaliate on Rebecca for scratching her face. Unnatural inaction should have put us on our guard. She even went so far as to compliment the maid on "finding such a great, strong, brave man as Coutlass to cherish her." The Greek simply cooed at that—threw out his great chest and rearranged with his fingers the whiskers that had almost totally disguised him.

(There was not one of us but looked like a pirate by that time. The natives of that part of Africa shave every particle of hair from the bodies whenever they get the chance, and prefer their heads as shiny and naked as any other part of them. But the German prison system, devised to break the spirit of whoever came within its clutches, included prohibition of shaving, so that we had the woolliest crowd of passengers imaginable.)

We found it impossible to help being sorry for Lady Waldon, or even for the maid, who suffered in spite of Coutlass's kisses and strong arms. The obvious fact that the dhow was no place for a woman made us overlook the conduct of both of them over and over again, shutting eyes and ears to Lady Waldon's meanness and the maid's increasing impudence.

Lady Waldon actually began to set her own cap at Coutlass, encouraging him to boast to the porters, and pretending to admire the gift with which he told them tales in Kiswahili that would have made even her blush if she had understood the half of them. At intervals the maid grew jealous, and had to be kissed back to serenity by Coutlass, who was no less in love with her because of any mere addition to the number of his interests. He could have made hot love to six women, and have enjoyed it. There were times when he really flattered himself that Lady Waldon admired his looks and fine physique.

Food was now the chief concern. We trailed a fishing line behind us, but caught nothing. Brown said there were too many crocodiles for fish to be plentiful, but on the other hand, Kazimoto, who surely should have known, swore that the water was full of big fish, and that the islanders lived on little else. Whatever the truth of it, we caught nothing; and when we reached an island whose shore was lined with fish-traps made of stakes and basket-work we searched all the traps in vain. The natives we saw in the distance all ran away from us, and there were no crops that we could see of any kind, which rather bore out Kazimoto's story.

"Crocks' eggs are what those savages eat, I tell you!" Brown insisted. "They're wholesome and don't taste worse than a rotten hen's egg." We offered him his own price if he would eat one himself in the presence of us all; but hungry though we were all beginning to be, he refused, and we needed his example.

After that first island we began to sail among a regular archipelago, most of them scarcely better than granite rocks on which the crocodiles could crawl to sun themselves, but some of them a half-mile long, or longer. Nearly all of them were barren, but at last, when we judged ourselves well inside the British portion of the lake, we came on a very large one that had a mountain in the middle of it, and contained a fair-sized village hidden among trees.

It was dark, and we were all famished when we reached it, so when we had poled the dhow into a little bay between granite boulders big enough to hide her, mast and all, we went ashore, made fires, and served out the last handfuls of rice, skimping our own allowance to increase those of the porters, whose larger stomachs afforded vaster yearning power. They were pitiably meager rations—a mere jest—an insult to hungry men; but we found before we had cooked and finished them that we had witnesses who thought us fortunate.

They came so silently that even the porters did not notice them at first—gaunt black shadows flitting in the deeper shadows, and coming presently to squat outside the edge of the circle of firelight, until a tribe, men, women and little children, were all gathered around us burning up the darkness with their eyes.

They were hungrier than we! Our food, that looked so scant to us, to them was a very feast of the gods! They all had pieces of leather or plaited grass drawn tight around their middles to lessen the pangs of hunger, and the chief, who sat rather apart from the rest, gnawed at a piece of bark.

None of them wore any clothes. Those that had goat-skin aprons had them on behind, and they were as free from self-consciousness as the trees in winter. Some of them had spears, and they all had knives, yet none offered violence, or as much as begged. There were three or four hundred of them, at the lowest reckoning, yet they allowed us to finish our meal in the dark in peace.

There was nothing to say when we had finished. We knew what the matter was, and they knew we knew. We had nothing to share with them, and they knew that, for they could see the empty rice bags that the porters had shaken and beaten to get out the very dust. We did not know their language; even Kazimoto professed himself ignorant of any dozen words that could unlock their understanding.

Presently, under the eyes of all of them, Fred got out the rifle from its wrappings and proceeded to clean and oil it carefully, as every genuine hunter should before he sleeps.

Then it was evident at once that new hope for some reason had been born among that silent crowd. The chief, uninvited, drew nearer and watched every detail of Fred's husbandry with glittering eye.

"Give him the oily rag to suck!" suggested Brown, but that proved not to be the key to his interest, for he thrust the rag back into Fred's hand and motioned to him to continue cleaning.

Finally Fred examined the last handful of cartridges carefully one by one, and filled the magazine.  Then, after making
sure the sights were in order, he began to wrap the rifle again.
But at that the chief held out a lean long arm and stopped
him.  Coutlass sprang to his feet in a hurry, imagining that
was a signal to attack at last, but Fred ordered him to sit
down, and Lady Waldon, who seemed possessed for the once
by uncanny calmness, asked him to give her an arm to the
dhow, where she proposed to try to sleep.  Coutlass felt flattered, and obeyed.  The maid got up and followed them both
in a fury of jealousy, and they three were lost to view in a
moment among the shadows cast by our four flickering fires.
The other Greek got up and followed them, leaving the
Goanese already snoozing by the fire.

Then, just as the half of a brilliantly pale moon rose above
the papyrus, the chief came a pace nearer and touched Fred's
hand.  Then he beckoned.  Then he touched the hand again
and retreated backward.  Glancing around I saw the shadows
that were his tribe leaning toward us in strained attention,
with eyes for nothing but their chief and Fred.  Understanding there was something that the chief desired him to go and
do, Fred passed the rifle to Will and rose to his feet.

With patience that was simply pathetic the chief shook his
head and tried to explain something in weary-motioned pantomime.  Fred took the rifle back from Will.  The chief
nodded.  Fred started to follow him, and then the whole tribe
sighed, with a sound like the evening wind rustling through
the papyrus.

It being clear now that he was to shoot something, Fred
took the wrappings off the rifle, threw them to me, and walked
into the dark, the chief trotting ahead like a phantom and
glancing back to beckon about once a minute.  Not caring to
miss the play, we followed in Indian file, I bringing up the
rear.

The whole tribe rose at once and flitted along beside us on
our landward side.  We could not hear a footfall, or a breath.
They passed through dry grass without rustling, neither
stumbling nor crowding one another, but all so governed by

one all-absorbing thought that they acted in absolute unison. That the thought was food did not, even in their starving state, make them forget the crowning need for silence. We with our leather boots made more noise than all they together.

We passed along the lake shore for half a mile, until suddenly the chief, looking tall as a stripped tree in the pale uncertain light, threw up an arm and waved it in a circle. Instantly the whole tribe vanished. It was as if a puff of wind had blown them; or as if they had been figures thrown on a screen by a magic lantern and suddenly switched off at the performer's whim. Then the chief continued forward, we marching more carefully.

Now he turned to the half-right and followed a narrow track across a neck of land that jutted out into the lake. We approached a low rise, and as he drew near the top of that he went down on hands and knees, crawling up the last few yards so cautiously that I had to stare hard to be sure he was there at all.

As soon as Fred came near he made frantic signals to him to get down and crawl too; so we all knelt down and crawled behind Fred, striving to make no noise and filling the unhappy chief so full of fury at the noise we did make that he writhed in nervous torment.

On top of the rise Fred stopped and in imitation of the chief thrust his head forward very gradually. One by one we followed suit until, lying prone in line along the ridge within thirty paces of the water, we saw at last what we were after.

Bathed in the moonlight, head and shoulders clear of the mirror-like water, a great bull hippopotamus surveyed the scenery, drinking in contentment through his little placid eyes. Out there nothing troubled him, as for instance the mosquitoes troubled us. He had eaten his fill, for some sort of green stuff hung from his jaws; and he was beginning to feel sleepy, for he opened his enormous mouth and yawned straight toward us—three tons of meat on the hoof, less than a hundred yards away, stock-still, and unsuspicious!

The chief began whispering unintelligible warnings in a voice so low that it sounded like the drone of insects. Fred thrust the rifle forward inch by inch and, taking his time about it, settled himself comfortably for the shot. It was no easy shot in that uncertain light at a downward angle. The glare of the sun on the lake had troubled his eyes during the last few days. The shimmer of the moonlight was deceptive now. I wished he would pass the rifle to Will, or even to Brown of Lumbwa, who was digging his fingers into the earth beside me in almost uncontrollable excitement. But Fred was unperturbed, and the chief, who was nervous enough to detect the slightest sign of nervousness in Fred, did not seem to mistrust him for one second.

Three times I saw Fred breathe deeply, as if about to squeeze the trigger, but each time he was only *"makkin' sik-kar,"* and eased his lungs again. The target a hippo offers to a Mauser rifle bullet is not much more than half the size of a man's hand, including only the ear and eye and the narrow space between them. By daylight at a hundred yards that is nothing for a cool shot to complain about, but in half-moonlight, at that angle, it is none too much. I swore silently, wishing again and again that Fred would pass the rifle to Will, or to Brown—or to me! Yet if he had passed it to me I should have trembled worse than any one.

Visions began to haunt me of what would happen if Fred should miss! What would the effect be on wild folk tortured by hunger and keyed to the pitch of frenzy by suspense? Then, even while we watched, another problem added itself. Over on the water there began to come a wind, driving ripples and little waves in front of it. The moment those came near the hippo he would vanish from view, for they only care for moonlight when they can see it mirrored on a perfectly still surface.

I cursed Fred between set teeth, almost loud enough for him to hear me; for the hippo did move. His head was a foot nearer water-level; he had seen or heard something that alarmed him. He was in the act of sinking under water when Fred made sure of the sights at last and the rifle spoke, ringing out into the still night like the crack of Judgment Day, more startling because we had waited so long for it in such suspense.

Instantly the amazing happened. A yell burst out behind us that split the night apart. Where stilly blackness had been, now four or five hundred crazy shadows leaped and danced, murdering the silence with marrow-curdling noises intended to express joy.

Out on the water the stricken hippo pitched head downward and plunged like a mountain of meat gone mad, thrashing up great waves that were darkened with his life-blood. A whole herd, several hundred strong, emerged shoulder-high from the water to take one swift look at him and flee. The arriving wind overswept the little whirlpools they all made in the moonlight, as they dived to seek seclusion somewhere and no doubt to choose themselves a new bully after terrific fighting.

Our quarry plunged a last time, and stayed under. Now was new anxiety. In twenty minutes or half an hour he should rise to the surface again, but no man could guess where, and the wind and currents would very swiftly hide his great carcass somewhere amid the acres of papyrus unless sharp eyes were alert.

But the papyrus was friend as well as foe. In a space of time to be measured by seconds the yelling young men of the tribe had uncovered three canoes, hidden from marauding enemies among the more-than-man-high reeds, and the rest of the tribe—men, women and young ones—scattered along the shore to watch from between the stalks.

In less than fifteen minutes some one yelled, and even the very old men, who had stayed beside us to gape at Fred's rifle and our clothes and boots, began running like hares toward the sound. In twenty minutes after that, with the aid of grass ropes and leather thongs, they had hauled the huge carcass to the shore and rolled it out of the water, where it lay glistening in moonlight, stumpy, foolish, legs uppermost.

The butcher's work—the feast—did not begin yet. There was time-honored custom to obey, which Kazimoto knew all about even if those ignorant *wachenzie** would have fallen to without ceremony. He drove them off. A white man had slain that animal; therefore the white man's choice of meat was first, and he very leisurely and skilfully cut out the enormous tongue for us and fifty pounds of meat for our following before he would let them as much as touch the carcass with a dagger.

Then, though, the tribe fell to, naked, with little naked knives—tearing off the thick hide in foot-wide strips, and hacking the red flesh into lumps that they ate, raw and quivering, while they worked. The little bits of children, each chewing raw bloody meat, brought baskets for the overflow, dragging them to wherever they could find a space between the legs of struggling men, the women emptying the baskets almost as fast as the children filled them, and chewing until their jaws ran blood.

Nothing was wasted. The blood was caught in pools in part of the hide, spread like an apron on the earth, and lapped up by whoever could get to it. The very guts were gathered up in baskets to be cooked. And when the last little soft iron dagger had done its work, the blood had been drunk, and the last scrap of hide had been cut into strips, to be chewed when the meat and its memory were things of the past, the enormous ribs lay glistening in the moonlight like those of an abandoned wreck, picked as clean as if the kites had done it.

"Have we done a commendable thing?" laughed Fred, looking at the crowd's distended paunches. "There's a good bull hippo the less. We've saved the lives for a time of several hundred gluttons. They know neither grace nor gratitude."

But he was wrong. They did. They brought Fred a woman —their fattest, ugliest; which means she was skin and bone and uglier than Want, also she was more afraid of Fred than Satan is said to be of shriving. The chief led her by the hand, she hanging back and hiding her face under one

---

*Plural of *machenzie*, "man from 'way back," "rube," "simp."

arm (which left the rest of her nakedness unprotected).
He seized Fred's hand and put the woman's in it.

"Now you're spliced!" Brown explained. "Married to the
gal forever in presence of legal witnesses!"

Kazimoto confirmed the fearful news.

"Married in regular form an' accord with tribal custom!"
Brown continued, nodding solemnly.

"Divorce me — soon and swiftly, somebody!" Fred demanded.

We appealed to Kazimoto for information, but only threw
him into a quandary, and he proceeded to add to ours. The
usual price for a woman, it seemed, was cows—many or few
according as she was lovely or her father rich. In case of
divorce, custom decreed that the cows with their offspring
should be given back. The objection to any other property
than cows changing hands to bind or loose in wedlock was
that food, for instance, when eaten was not returnable.

"Married to the gal for good an' all!" Brown grinned,
nudging Will and me to note Fred's consternation. "You'd
better stay here an' take the chief's job when he kicks the
bucket—possibly you can speed the day by overfeedin' him!"

"Some men's luck," Will murmured, but stopped in mid-
sentence, for interruption came in the form of a weird figure,
gesticulating like a windmill, stumbling and careening
through the gloom, shouting as it came. Not until it was
thirty yards away did an intelligible sound explain at least
who the apparition was.

"Gassharamminy! Give me that gun!"

Coutlass burst in among us so out of breath that he could
not force through his teeth another rational syllable, but he
made his intentions partly clear by snatching at Fred's rifle,
persisting until Will and I pulled him off.

"The dhow's gone!" he panted at last. "Give me that rifle,
or come yourself! Hurry! There's a wind! You'll be too
late!"

"You're dreaming or drunk!" Fred answered, but Coutlass
refused to be disbelieved, and in another moment we were
all running as fast as we dared through the darkness to-

ward the camp-fires, where we had left the Goanese snoozing and the dhow snugly moored among the rocks.

The chief and his followers far outdistanced us in spite of their gorged condition—all except the woman, who jogged dutifully, although unhappily, behind Fred. When we reached the camp-fires they were standing gazing out on the lake, where we could just make out the bellying sail of the *Queen of Sheba* leaning like a phantom away from the gaining wind. The distance was not to be judged in that weak uncertain light. We all shouted together, but there came no answer and we could not tell whether the sound carried as far as the dhow or not.

"Gassharamminy!—why don't you shoot!" shouted Coutlass, dancing up and down the bank in frenzy. "Give me that rifle! I'll show you! I'll teach them!"

I believe I would have fired if the rifle had been in my hands. Brown, last to arrive and most out of breath, joined with Coutlass in angry shouts for vengeance. Will offered no argument against sending them a parting shot. Fred set the butt of the rifle down with a determined snort, walked over toward the fire, stirred the embers, threw on more fuel, and looked about him when the dry wood blazed.

"If she has left as much as one blanket among the lot of us, I don't see it anywhere!" he said, taking his seat on a rock.

"A blanket?" sneered Coutlass. "She has even your money! Worse than that—she has my woman! You were a gum-gasted galoot not to shoot at her!"

Fred patted the bulging pocket of his shooting jacket.

"Most of the money is here," he said quietly, and we all sighed with relief.

"Take canoes and chase them!" shouted Coutlass, beginning to dance up and down again.

"There's time enough," Fred answered. "We know the winds of these parts well enough by this time. This will blow until midnight. Then calm until dawn. After dawn a little more wind for an hour or two, then doldrums again until late afternoon. They'll run on a rock in all likelihood. If

they do we can catch them at our leisure, supposing we
can get these islanders to paddle. If it should blow hard,
then we can't catch them anyhow. Sit down and tell us what
happened, Coutlass!"

The Greek cursed and swore and pranced, but all in vain.
Fred was inexorable. We others grew calmer when the problem of who should paddle the canoes solved itself suddenly
with the arrival of fourteen of our own men. Discovering
themselves left behind, they had run along the bank in vain
hope of catching the dhow somehow — perchance of swimming through the crocodile-infested water, and returned now
disconsolate, to leap and laugh with new hope at sight of us
and of the red meat that Kazimoto had thrown on the ground
near the fire. They came near in a cluster. Will hacked off
a lump of meat for them, and they forthwith forgot their
troubles, as instantly as the birds forget when a sparrow-hawk
has done murder down a hedge-row and swooped away.

Not everything was gone after all. Kazimoto found the
pots we had cooked the rice in, and started to boil the hippo's
tongue for us.

"Come, Coutlass—sit down before we eat and tell us what
happened," Fred suggested.

The Greek paced up and down another time or two, and
at last calmed himself sufficiently to laugh at Fred's woman,
who had squatted down patiently in the shadow behind him.

"Easy for you!" he grinned savagely, squatting on the far
side of the fire. "You have a woman! Mine is God knows
where! She said to me — that hell-damned Lady Saffren
Waldon said to me—we sat all three together in the stern of
the dhow, I with my arm around Rebecca, and she said to
me—"

"I'll see if I can't make a dicker for the chief's canoes,"
Will interrupted. "We can hear the Greek's tale any old
time."

"Trade my woman for them!" Fred suggested cheerfully.
"Go on, Coutlass!"

The Greek gritted his teeth savagely. "She said—that hell-
damned Lady Saffren Waldon said, as we sat there in the

dhow, 'How about the kicking Fred Oakes gave you on the island, Mr. Coutlass? Where is your Greek honor?'—Do you see? She worked on my bodily bruises and my spiritual courage at the same time—the cunning hussy! 'That Fred Oakes will win this Rebecca away from you very soon!' she went on. 'I have watched him.'"

Fred smiled about as comfortably as a martyr on the grid. The presence of the dusky damsel, confirmed by her smell behind him, made him touchy on the subject of sex.

"Presently she said to me, 'I have my own affairs that will adjust themselves all the better for their absence when I get to British East. As for you, they will simply report you to the authorities for raiding those cattle of Brown's. Can you imagine that creature Brown forgiving you? He will have you thrown in jail! Why wait? But we must not leave the Goanese or the other porters, and we must hurry! You go,' she said, 'and send the Goanese and the rest of the porters on board!'

"So I did go. I kicked de Sousa awake, and he cursed me, because my toe landed once or twice on his thigh where the bullet wounded him. I drove him on board, and she put him to work with Kamarajes getting up the sail. Then I went off to get those cursed porters. I could not find them! The dogs had gone to the village, to find women I don't doubt! I tell you what I would do to them if they were mine!"

"Never mind that!" Fred cut in. We could all guess what form the punishment would take. "Get on with the tale! You couldn't find the porters. What next?"

"I decided to leave the dogs behind, and serve them right! I went back to the dhow in a great hurry. She was gone! Vanished! Disappeared as if the lake had opened up and swallowed her! I could just see the sail in the distance. I shouted! No answer! I shouted again. I heard Rebecca call to me! Then I heard laughter—Lady Isobel Saffren Waldon's laughter! Gassharamminy! I will run red-hot skewers into that woman when I catch her! Do you see how she has vengeance on Rebecca? Do you see now why she took sides between me and Kamarajes and de Sousa? Do you see how she has plotted? What will she do now? What will she do?"

He began to pace up and down again furiously, shaking both fists at the unresponsive stars.

"She will do Rebecca an injury! She will give that girl to de Sousa or to that old Kamarajes! We shall never catch them! Gassharamminy! Oh, Absalom! You should have fired when I told you! That she-dog has a trick of some kind up her sleeve yet! How shall we catch her? Why do we wait? Give me that rifle! I will take a canoe and go after them alone! You do not know what Greek spirit is! I am American sometimes — English when it suits me — always Greek when I am wronged!"

"You certainly have been put upon," Fred answered. "Tell us how your Greek spirit justified deserting us!"

"Why not?" snarled Coutlass. "Do you love me? What would you do to me if you could get me to British East in your power? You would hand me over as a cattle thief!"

"You bet I will!" admitted Brown of Lumbwa. "You dog, you've ruined me!"

"What did I tell you?" demanded Coutlass. "Why, then, should I not look out for myself?"

"I think we'd better leave you on this island," Fred told him quietly. "We can't trust you out of sight. The only way to prevent you from stealing this rifle and murdering us all would be to lie awake in turns."

"Bah!" grinned the Greek, striding back toward the fire. "How many cartridges have you left? Five, eh? After I had murdered all of you, how many would remain?"

"You'll have to think of a better argument than that," smiled Fred, and for the first time I suspected he was speaking in deadly earnest. Coutlass suspected it, too, and grew still. The sweat burst out on his face, and his eyes bulged from their sockets.

"You will leave me here?" he stammered.

Fred nodded, smiling up at him.

"You see, you're such an all-in scoundrel!" Brown assured him.

"You! You poor drunkard!" Coutlass turned his back on Brown, and faced Fred squarely. "You are a man, Mr. Oakes! I can speak to you as to my brother."

Fred smiled blandly.

"I will speak to you God's truth!"

Fred grinned.

"I will tell you where the ivory is!"

Fred threw his head back and laughed outright.

"I speak to you on my honor! That mother of misery, Lady Saffren Waldon, stole a map from Schillingschen. Before I would agree to set the town on fire I made her give me that for a hostage, lest she should prove treacherous and leave me behind after all! I have it now! It is marked with a circle to show where Schillingschen believes the stuff *must* be, because he has searched everywhere else!"

"If that map is worth anything," Fred countered, "how did Lady Saffren Waldon care to leave you behind with it?"

"The harridan forgot it!" answered Coutlass. "She was so delighted to get vengeance on Rebecca by taking her away from me that she did not care for anything else! She hates you! She hates me! She hates Rebecca! Those who hate—as I can hate!—would rather have revenge than all the riches of Africa! Do you think I would hesitate between money and revenge on her?"

"All right," Fred answered. "The map, then—what about it?"

"Take me with you and the map is yours!"

"Show it to me, then!"

"I must have a share of the ivory!"

"Show me the map first!"

Coutlass searched inside his flannel shirt—swiftly—more swiftly—angrily. His jaw dropped. Even between the firelight and the moonlight one could judge that his color changed —and changed again.

"Show me the map before we bargain!" Fred insisted. "Hurry, man! There's Mr. Yerkes with the canoe. We can't wait here all night!"

"It is gone!" admitted Coutlass. "Some one stole it!"

"I could have told you that in the first place," Fred informed him, rising to his feet. "I have the map in my pocket."

"You stole it?" Coutlass gasped.

"Certainly not. Rebecca stole it while she was supposed to be sleeping in your arms!"

"Gassharamminy! I might have known it! Those Syrians —she meant to give us all the slip and find the ivory herself!"

"Nothing of the sort!" said Fred. "She stole it from you, to give it to Lady Saffren Waldon! Kazimoto saw her do it— saw where Lady Waldon hid it—and stole it from her while she slept to give to me, believing it to be something of mine. Here it is!"

Fred let the end of a folded map protrude from his inner pocket just far enough for Coutlass to recognize it by the firelight. The Greek turned on his heel.

"All right!" he said ruefully, swinging suddenly round again. "If you were alone I would fight you, my knife against your rifle! I can not fight all four of you! Go away then, and be damned! I have nothing to offer. There is nothing I can do. Leave me, and I will look after myself!"

"Now you're talking like a man," said Fred.

"Leave me that woman of yours, and go to hell, all of you!" laughed the Greek.

Fred seemed suddenly possessed of a bright idea. He turned to the woman and beckoned her to rise. Then in unmistakable pantomime he went through the motions of presenting her to Coutlass. The woman gasped—stammered something that was positively not consent—stared with frightened eyes at Coutlass—shook her shaven head violently—and ran away into the darkness, pursued by roars of laughter that speeded her on her way.

"A clear case of desertion!" announced Fred judicially. "You men are witnesses!" Then he turned once more to Coutlass. "I don't think we'll leave you to raise Cain on this island. It depends on you whether we find you a lonelier island—turn you loose—or hand you over to the authorities in British East!"

"Good!" Coutlass shouted. "By Jingo, you are a gentleman! You are the best man in the world! I will treat you as my brother!"

"Thanks!" said Fred dryly.

"Aren't you men ever coming?" asked Will, striding out of the shadows. "I've made the dicker—found a man who'd been on the mainland and knows Swahili. The chief's agreeable to loan us two canoes in place of deeding you the woman. I took your name in vain, Fred, and consented to that while your back was turned—kick all you like—the deed is done! Four of his savages come with us as far as we want to go, we feeding 'em meat and paying 'em money. It's agreed they're to eat just as often as we do. They paddle the canoes back home when we're through with them. Are you all ready? Then all aboard! Let's hurry!"

# "MANY THAT ARE FIRST SHALL BE LAST; AND THE LAST FIRST"

*When the last of the luck has deserted and the least of the
      chances has waned,*
*When there's nowhere to run to and even the pluck in the
      smile that you carry is feigned;*
*When grimmer than yesterday's horror to-morrow dawns hun-
      gry and cold,*
*And your faith in the coming unknown is denied in regret for
      the known and the old,*
*Then you're facing, my son, what the Fathers from Abraham
      down to to-day*
*Have looked on alone, and stood up to alone, and each in his
      several way*
*O'ercame (or he shouldn't be Father). So ye shall o'ercome:
      while ye live,*
*Though ye've nothing but breath and good-will to your name
      ye must stand to it naked, and give!*

*Ye shall learn in that hour that the plunder ye won by profes-
      sion is nought—*
*And false was the aim ye aspired with—and dross was the
      glamour ye sought—*
*The codes and the creeds that ye cherished were shadows of
      clouds in the wind,*
*(And ye can not recall for their counsel lost leaders ye dallied
      behind!)*
*Ye shall stand in that hour and discover by agony's guttering
      flame*
*How the fruits of self-will, and the lees of ambition and bit-
      terness all are the same,*
*Until, stripped of desire, ye shall know that was death. Then
      the proof that ye live*
*Shall be knowledge new-born that the naked—the fools and
      the felons, can give!*

*Then the suns and the stars in their courses shall speedily swing to your aid,*
*And nothing shall hinder you further, and nothing shall make you afraid,*
*For the veriest edges of evil shall challenge your joy, and no more,*
*And room for the right shall shine clear in your vision where wrong was before.*
*Then the stones in the road shall be restful that used to be traps for your feet,*
*Then the crowd shall be kind that was cruel before, and your solitude sweet*
*That was wont to be gloomy aforetime and gray—when the proof that ye live*
*Is no longer the pain of desire, but the will—and the wit—and the vision, to give!*

## CHAPTER TWELVE

THE canoes were the usual crazy affairs, longer and rather wider than the average. The bottom portion of each was made from a tree-trunk, hollowed out by burning, and chipped very roughly into shape. The sides were laboriously hewn planks, stitched into place with thread made from papyrus.

Some of the men left behind were our personal servants. Counting them and Kazimoto, there were twenty natives remaining with us, making, with the four men lent us by the chief, an allowance of twelve to each canoe. If we had had loads as well it would have been a problem how to get the whole party away; but as Lady Saffren Waldon had left us nothing but three cooking-pots, we just contrived to crowd the last man in without passing the danger point, Fred taking charge of the first canoe with Brown of Lumbwa and Kazimoto, and leaving Coutlass with the other canoe to Will and me. We agreed it was most convenient to keep the Greek and the rifle separated by a stretch of water.

There is one inevitable, invariable way of starting on a journey by canoe in Africa. Somebody pushes off. The naked paddlers, seated at intervals down either side, strain their toes against a thwart or a rib. The leading paddler yells, and off you go with a swing and a rhythmic thunder as they all bring their paddles hard against the boat's side at the end of each stroke. Fifty—sixty—seventy—perhaps a hundred strokes they take at top speed, and the passenger settles down to enjoy himself, for there is no more captivating motion in the world. Then suddenly they stop, and all begin arguing at top of their lungs. Unless the passenger is a man of swift decision and firm purpose there is frequently a fight at that stage, likely to end in overturned canoes and an adventure among the crocodiles.

Our voyage broke no precedents. We started off in fine style, feeling like old-time emperors traveling in state; and within ten minutes we were using paddles ourselves to poke and beat our men into understanding of the laws of balance, they abusing one another while the canoes rocked and took in water through the loosely laid on planks.

The fiber stitching began to give out very soon after that, because when not in use the canoes were always hauled out somewhere and the dried-out fiber cracked and broke. We had all to sit to one side while some one restitched the planking. Later, when a wind came up and the quick short sea arose peculiar to lakes, we were very glad we had done that job so early.

It was only the first mile that as much as suggested enjoyment. Never accustomed to much paddling in any case, our own men had suffered from hunger and confinement in the reeking hot dhow. Then, hippo meat needs hours of cooking to be wholesome (our own share of it was still in the pot, waiting to be boiled more thoroughly at the next halting place). They had merely toasted their tough lumps in the camp-fire embers and gobbled it. The result was a craving for sleep, noisily seconded by the chief's four men, who had eaten the stuff without cooking at all, and in enormous quantities.

We began with a keen determination to overhaul the dhow, that dwindled as we had time to think the matter over; wondering what we should do with two such women in case we should capture them, and how we should prevent Coutlass in that case from acting like a savage.

"Why don't we leave 'em to make their own explanations?" I proposed at last. "We can claim our few belongings at any time if we see fit." But the suggestion took time to recommend itself.

That night until nearly morning we fretted at every rest the paddlers took—drove them unmercifully—ran risks of overturning on the slippery shoulders of partly submerged rocks—took long turns ourselves to relieve the weary men, Coutlass working harder than the rest of us. It would have been a bad night's work if we had overhauled the dhow and loosed him to do his will.

"Think of the baggage!" he kept shouting to the night at

large. "Lying in the arms of Georges Coutlass, kissing and be-ing kissed, simply to rob him—Coutlass—me! Think of it! Only think of it. She lay in the hook of my right arm and only thought of how to win back the favor of the other she-hellion! And I was deceived by such a cabbage! Wait though! Nobody ever turned a trick on Georges Coutlass more than once! Wait till we catch them! See what I do to them! I don't forget Kamarajes either, or that bastard de Sousa, also pretending they were friends of mine! Heiah! Hurry! Drive the paddles in, you lazy black men!"

It was more his hunger for revenge than any other one thing that tipped the scales of indecision and called us off the chase. A little before morning, at about that darkest hour, when the stars have seen the coming sun but the world is not yet aware of it, Fred called to us to turn in toward a barren-looking hill of granite that rose almost sheer out of the water but at one corner offered a shelving landing place. There we all clam-bered out to stretch cramped muscles and make a fire to cook the hippo's tongue, Coutlass cursing us for letting what he called idleness come between us and revenge.

Kazimoto had scarcely more than gathered an armful of wood, thrown it down, and gone to hunt for more; one of the other boys had struck a match, and the first little flicker of crimson fire and purple smoke was starting to curl skyward, when Fred jumped on it and stamped it out.

"Silence!" he ordered. "Keep still every one!" and repeated it twice in Kiswahili for the natives' benefit.

We could not see at first which way he was staring through the darkness. It was more than two minutes before I knew what had alarmed him, and then it was sound, not sight that gave me the first clue. There came a purring from the lake; and when I had searched for a minute for the source of it I saw the glow we had watched from the dhow in the storm the first night out—the telltale crimson stain on the dark that rides above a steamer's funnel, and at intervals a stream of sparks to prove they were burning wood and driving her at top speed.

"It can't be the German launch," said I.

"Why not?" demanded Fred irritably. He knew I knew it was the German launch as certainly as he did.

"How can they have patched her boiler?" I asked.

"How many beans make five? They've done it, and there she goes! No other launch on the lake can make that speed! I've heard the British railway people have a launch or two, but they're small enough to have traveled down the line on ordinary trucks. That's the German launch and Schilling-schen as surely as we stand here!"

We waited there until dawn, arguing at intervals, not daring to light a fire, nor caring to sleep, Coutlass sitting apart and laughing every now and then like a hyena.

"If the men weren't so dead beat I'd be for carrying on," said Fred.

"What's the use?" argued Brown. "We can't catch the bally launch, can we? Soon as it's daylight they'd see us, like as not. I hope to get drunk once more before I die! Schillingschen 'ud run us down, an' good-by us!"

"I'd say follow them if the men could make it," Will agreed. "But what's the odds? It's us they're after. They'll dare do nothing to the women on the dhow—in British waters."

"That's so," I agreed, not believing a word of it, any more than they. One had to calm one's feelings somehow; the men were too weary to drive the canoes another mile at anything like speed. Coutlass, who had heard every word of the argument, burst out into such yells of laughter that Fred threw a rock at him. "Curse you, you ghoul!"

Coutlass changed his tone from demoniacal delight to quieter, grim amusement.

"They will do nothing, eh? It is I, Georges Coutlass, who need do nothing! I have my revenge by proxy! Wait and see!"

Fred threw a second rock, and hit him squarely.

"Gassharamminy!" swore the Greek. "Do you know that rock is harder than a man's head?"

Fred let the boys light a fire when the sun had risen high enough to make the little blaze not noticeable. Most of the men were asleep, but though our eyes ached with the long vigil we could not have copied them. About three hours after daylight we breakfasted off slices of hot boiled hippo tongue and cold lake water, without salt or condiments of any kind, and with discontent increased by that unpleasing feast we aroused the boys and drove them into th canoes.

We forced the pace again, and picked up smoke on the sky-line an hour before noon, but it was not from a steamer's funnel. It was lazy, flat-flowing, spreading smoke with a look of iniquity about it that sent our he rts to our mouths. We paddled toward it with frenzi~d energy, and long before any of us could make out details Coutlass, standing balancing himself amidships, told ~ what we _new was true and flatly refused to believe.

"It's Queen of Sheba ~~ ~ing to the water-line!"

"Sit down, you fool, or you'll upset us!"

"She's gutted already—the flame is about finished! nothing now but smoke!"

"Sit down, you lying idiot, and hold your tongue!"

"I can see the smoke of the German launch now! Don't you all see it? Straight ad beyond the smoke of the dhow! They've burned the dhow and steamed away! I'll bet you a million pounds they've killed everybody—shot 'em, or burned 'em alive, or drowned 'em!"

"Did you hear me tell you to sit down? I'll tip you overboard and make you swim for shore—d'ye see those crocodiles? Ugh! Look at the brutes! In you go among the crocks if you don't sit down at once!"

Coutlass took no notice of the threat, but rocked the canoe recklessly as he stood on tiptoe.

"Think of their gall! By Bacchus, they're steaming for British East! I bet you five million pounds to a kick they think they've drowned the lot of us! They're going to steam in and report the accident!"

We got him to sit down at last by ordering the paddlers nearest him to throw him overboard, but nothing would stop his evil croaking any more than flat refusal to admit the truth of what he gloated over lessened our real conviction.

Long before we reached the dhow there was no room left

for unbelief. The stern planks were charred, but stood erect,
unburned yet, and the blue and white paint smeared on them
was surely that of the *Queen of Sheba*. When we came within
fifty yards the water was full of loathsome reptiles; our paddles actually struck them as they swarmed after the prey,
snapping at one another and at our canoes — long, slimy-
looking monsters, as able to smell carrion in the distance as
kites are to see.

There were garments on the water—blankets—and one
soaked, torn, lacy thing that certainly had been a woman's.
More than a dozen crocodiles fought around that. We tried
to go close enough to see whether there were dead bodies in
the dhow's charred hull, but as if the very ripple from our
paddles were the last straw, the wreck dipped suddenly ten
feet from us and plunged, the crocodiles following it down
into deep water with lashing tails—swifter than fish.

We paddled about for an hour in the blistering sun, searching stupidly for what we knew we could never find; crocodiles
remove traces of identity more swiftly than kites and crows.

"I'll bet you they thought we were on board!" gleed Coutlass. "I'll bet you they opened fire, and when we didn't answer came to the conclusion we had no ammunition. Then
they steamed close enough to throw kerosene on board and
light it! I bet you they steamed round and round and watched
the people jump as the flames drove them overboard! Or
d'you think they shot them all, and then threw them overboard and fired the dhow? No—then they'd have known we
weren't on the dhow; they'd have steamed back then to find
us; they thought we were in the dhow! They thought we were
hiding below deck! They're going to British East to take
their Bible oaths they saw us burn and drown! Isn't that a
joke! Isn't that a good one! Gassharamminy! But I'd
give my hope of heaven to know whether they shot the women
first or watched them jump among the crocodiles when the
heat grew fierce!"

We paddled to another rocky island—one that had trees on
it, and rested through the heat of the day when we had killed
all the snakes that had forestalled us in the shade. There,

after again eating hippo-tongue unseasoned and ungarnished, we held a council of war, and Fred produced the map that Rebecca stole from Coutlass.

"If we make for a township now—Kisumu is the nearest—about five and twenty miles away," said Fred, "we can give ourselves the pleasure of surprising Schillingschen, and of course we can get a square meal and some clothes and soap and so on—incidentally perhaps some rifles and ammunition. But we can't prove a thing against Schillingschen, and he has enough pull with British officials to make things deuced unpleasant for us, for a time at least. Consider the other side of it. Suppose we don't make for a station. Schillingschen reports us dead. Nobody looks for us—unless perhaps out on the lake for a hat or some scrap of clothing by way of corroborative evidence. Suppose we paddle out of this gulf and take to shore somewhere along the north end of the lake. We've no food, no tents, only one gun, next to no ammunition, nothing but money and a purpose. We don't know what chance we have of getting supplies, and particularly rifles, without letting any one know where we are, but we do know we've a clear field and a straight mark for Elgon, where rumor says—and Courtney said—and Schillingschen thinks—and this map says the ivory ought to be! The odds are against us—climate—starvation—wild beasts—savages—last and not least, the government, if they ever get wind of our being beyond bounds. Are we willing to take the chance, or are we not?"

We talked it over for an hour, Coutlass listening all ears to most of what we said, although we drove him to the farthest limit of the shade trees. We were in two minds whether or not it mattered if he listened, and made the usual two-minds hash of it. Finally we put it to a vote, letting Brown have a voice with the rest of us. He was in favor of anything that offered prospect of a gamble; and we remembered the letter in code we had given the missionary to mail to Monty. We had told him in that that we should make tracks for Elgon, and we all voted the same way.

"In other words," grinned Fred, "we're perfect idiots, and

ready and willing to prove it! Good! If you fellows had voted the other way I'd have gone forward to Elgon alone!"

It was then that Georges Coutlass took a hand in the game again. He came striding through the trees with something of his old swagger, and sat down among us with an air.

"Count me in!" he demanded.

"D'you mean in the lake?" suggested Fred.

"In on the trip to Mount Elgon!"

"We've had nearly enough of you!" Fred answered. "I know what's coming! If you don't come with us you'll tell tales? Blackmail, eh? Well, it won't work! We'll set you ashore on the mainland, and if you dare show yourself to Schillingschen or any British official, we'll run that risk cheerfully!"

But Coutlass was imperturbable for once. He laid a hand on Fred's knee, and changed his tone to one of gentle persuasion between friend and friend.

"Ah! Mr. Oakes, I know you now too well! You are not the man to leave me in the lurch! These others perhaps! You never! You know me, too. You have seen me under all conditions. You are able to judge my character. You know how firm a friend I can be, as well as how savage an enemy! You know I would never be false to a friend such as you—to a man whom I admire as I do you!"

Will Yerkes, who had tried to keep a straight face, now went off into peals of laughter, rolling over on his back and rocking his legs in the air—a performance that did not appear to discourage Coutlass in the least. Brown was far from amused. He advised throwing the Greek into the lake.

"Remember those cattle o' mine!" he insisted.

"Yes!" agreed Coutlass. "Remember those cattle! Consider what a man of quick decision and courage I am! How useful I can be! What a forager! What a guide! What a fighting man! What a hunter! What a liar on behalf of my friends! What a danger for my friends' enemies! What are the cattle of a drunkard like Brown—the poor unhappy sot!—compared to the momentary needs of a gentleman! Ah! By the ordeal! I am a gentleman, and that is the secret of it all! You, Mr. Oakes, as one brave gentleman, can not despise the right hand of friendship of Georges Coutlass, another gentleman! I know you can not! You haven't it in you! You were born under another star than that! I have confidence! I sit contented!"

"You good-for-nothing villain!" Fred grinned. "I'll take you at your word!" and Brown of Lumbwa gasped, the very hairs of his red beard bristling.

"I knew you would!" said Coutlass calmly. "These others are not gentlemen. They do not understand."

"If your word is good for anything," Fred continued.

"My word is my bond!" said the Greek.

"And you really want to prove yourself my friend—"

"I would go to hell for you and bring you back the devil's favorite wife!"

"I will set you on the mainland, to go and recover those cattle of Mr. Brown's from the Masai who raided them! Return them to Lumbwa, and I'll guarantee Brown shall shake hands with you!"

"Pah! Brown! That drunkard!"

"See here!" said Brown, getting up and peeling off his coat. "I've had enough of being called drunkard by you. Put up your dukes!"

But a fight between Brown and the Greek with bare fists would have been little short of murder. Brown was in no condition to thrash that wiry customer, and we in no mood to see Coutlass get the better of him.

"Don't be a fool, Brown! Sit down!" ordered Fred, and having saved his face Brown condescended readily enough.

"What you said's right," he admitted. "Let him get my cattle back afore he's fit to fight a gentleman!"

And so the matter was left for the present, with Georges Coutlass under sentence of abandonment to his own devices as soon as we could do that without entailing his starvation. We had no right to have pity for the rascal; he had no claim whatever on our generosity; yet I think even Brown would

not have consented to deserting him on any of those barren
islands, whatever the risk of his spoiling our plans as soon
as we should let him out of sight.

From then until we beached the canoes at last in a gap
in the papyrus on the lake's northern shore, we pressed forward like hunted men. For one thing, the very thought of
boiled meat without bread, salt, or vegetables grew detestable
even to the natives after the second or third meal, although
hippo tongue is good food. We tried green stuff gathered
on the islands, but it proved either bitter or else nauseating,
and although our boys gathered bark and roots that they said
were fit for food, it was noticeable that they did not eat much
of it themselves. The simplest course was to race for the
shore with as little rest and as little sleep as the men could
do with.

However, we were not noticeably better off when we first
set foot on shore. There was nothing but short grass growing on the thin soil that only partly hid the volcanic rock
and manganese iron ore. Victoria Nyanza is the crater of a
once enormous, long ago extinct volcano, and we stood on a
shelf of rock about a thousand feet below what had been
the upper rim—a chain of mountains leading away toward
the north higher and higher, until they culminated in Mount
Elgon, another extinct volcano fourteen thousand feet above
sea level.

It was not unexplored land where we stood, but it was so
little known that the existence of white men was said to be
a matter of some doubt among natives a mile or two to either
side of the old *safari* route that passed from east to west.
We could see no villages, although we marched for hours, the
loaned canoe-men tagging along behind us, hungrier than
we, until at last over the back of a long low spur we spied the
tops of growing kaffir corn.

At sight of that we broke into a run and burst on the field
of grain like a pack of the dog-baboons that swoop from the
hills and make havoc. We seized the heads of grain, rubbed
them between our hands, and had munched our fill before
we were seen by the jealous owners. A small boy herding

hump-backed cattle down in the valley watched us for a minute, and then deserted his charge to report to the village hidden behind a clump of trees. Ten minutes after that we were surrounded by naked black giants, all armed with spears and a personal smell that outstank one's notions of Gehenna.

We had nothing to offer them, except money, for which they obviously had not the slightest use. None of us knew their language. From their point of view we were thieves taken in the act, all but one of us unarmed as far as they knew, to be judged by the tribal standard that for more centuries than men remember has decreed that the thief shall die. They were most incensed at the four unhappy islanders, probably on the same principle that dogs pick on the weakest, and fight most readily with dogs of a more or less similar breed.

It was Coutlass who saved that situation. He instantly went crazy, or the next thing to it, wrinkling up his black-whiskered face into a caricature, yelling a Greek monologue in a refrain consisting of five notes repeated over and over, and dancing around in a wide ring with one leg shorter than the other and his arms executing symbols of witchcraft.

The chief was the biggest man—not an inch less than seven feet—black as ebony, from the curly hair, into which his patient wives had plaited fiber to hang in a greasy lump over his neck, all down his naked body to the soles of his enormous feet. Each time he came in front of that individual Coutlass paused and executed special finger movements, like the trills of a super-pianist, ending invariably in a punctuation point that made the savage shiver.

The fifth time round, to avoid the accusing fingers, the giant dodged behind a smaller man, who dodged behind a woman, who promptly turned and ran, swinging in the wind behind her a bustle like a horse's tail that was her only garment. Her flight was the touch that settled the decision in our favor. We all began to do a mumbo-jumbo dance around Coutlass, and in five seconds more the whole armed party was in full retreat, holding their spears behind them as some sort of protection against magic.

"After that," said Coutlass proudly, "will you still dismiss me from your party, gentlemen?"

"You've got to go and find Brown's cattle and return them to him!" Fred answered firmly. But we none of us felt like sending him packing until he was better fed and some provision could be made for his safety on the road. It was wonderful, the number of excuses that flocked through my mind for befriending the ruffian, and later on I found it was the same with Fred and Will. Brown, on the other hand, affected indignation at his being allowed to go with us another yard.

"Make a rope o' grass an' hang the swine!" he grumbled.

We decided to march on the village, retreat being obviously far too dangerous, and the only likely safe course being to follow up the chance success. Sleep another night in the open among the mosquitoes and wild beasts, besides making us wretched at the mere suggestion, was likely to bring us all down with fever. We preferred the thought of fever to the loneliness; for man is unlike all other nomads, and that is why the dog takes kindly to him; he must have a home of his own—a portable one, if you will—a tub like Diogenes—a Bedouin's tent—a cave, or a hole in the ground—something, so be he may rent it or own it or know for a fact he may sleep there when night comes. Life in the open is only good fun when there is cover to take to at will.

All the way along the winding foot-track leading in every imaginable direction except toward the village, and only turning suddenly toward it when we had grown disgusted and decided to leave it and try to find another, Brown kept pointing out trees with suitable overhanging arms to which we might hang Coutlass. The Greek, with eyes for nothing but the fat, hump-backed village cattle in the distance, seemed to think only of them, until Will commented on the fact, and Fred saw fit to drop a hint.

"Steal as much as a young calf, Coutlass, and we'll let Brown choose the tree! Try it on if you don't believe me!"

The villagers closed their gate against us by dragging great piles of thorn across the gap in the rough palisade, but, as Coutlass pointed out, they would have to open it up again to let the cattle in before dark, so we sat down and ate the remaining fragments of the hippo tongue—no ambrosia by that time; it had to be eaten, to save it from utter waste!

Then Coutlass once more did a first-class devil dance backward and forward this time before the gate, putting genius into it and fear into the hearts of the defenders. Kazimoto helped even more than he by discovering a native within the palisade who could speak a common tongue.

Their villagers held a very noisy council on their side of the thorn obstruction, under the apparent impression that it was sound- and bullet-proof. It was beginning to be pretty obvious that a man who advised volleying through the crevices with spears was winning the argument when Kazimoto detected familiar accents and raised his voice. After that the barricade was dragged aside within ten minutes and we entered, if not in honor, at least in temporary safety.

Luxury is a question of contrast. That evening in a hut assigned to us by the chief, squatting on the trodden cow-dung floor, leaning against the dried-mud sides, with a little fire of sticks in the midst to give us light and keep mosquitoes at a distance at the expense of almost unbearable heat, we ate porridge made from *mtama,* as they call their kaffir corn, and washed it down with milk—good rich cows' milk, milked by Kazimoto into our own metal pot instead of their unwashed gourds. Lucullus never dined better.

The feast was only rather spoiled by two things: we all had chiggers in our feet—the minute fleas that haunt the dust of native villages and insert themselves under toe-nails to grow great and lay their eggs. (Nearly every native in the village had more than one toe missing.) And the chief felt obliged to insert his smelly presence among us and ask innumerable idiotic questions through the medium of his interpreter and Kazimoto. He received some astonishing answers, but would not have been satisfied with anything more reasonable. We wanted him satisfied, and gave our interpreter free rein.

The main trouble was we had nothing of value to offer him. Money was something he had no knowledge of. He wanted beads of a certain size and color; for two handfuls of them he expressed himself willing to be our friend for life. We had to educate him about money, and Kazimoto assured him that the silver rupees Fred produced from a bag were so precious that governments went to war to get them away from other governments.

But the impression still prevailed that we were *wasikini* —poor men; and that is a fatal qualification in the savage mind.

"Why have you only one gun?"

In vain Kazimoto assured him that we had dozens of guns "at home"—that Fred's landed possessions were so vast that two hundred strong men walking for a month would be unable to march across them—that Fred's wives (Fred seemed to live under a cloud of sexual scandal in those days) were so many in number they had to be counted twice a day to make sure none was missing.

The chief had eighteen wives of his own to show. He could prove his matrimonial felicity. Why had Fred left his behind? How did he dare? Who looked after them? Had he left the guns behind to guard the women? Why did such a rich man travel without food for his men? The chief had seen us with his own eyes devour porridge as if we were starving.

To have told him the truth would have been worse than useless. To have mentioned such a thing as shipwreck would only have stirred the savage instinct to prey off all unfortunates. Failing evidence of wealth in our possession, the only feasible plan was to claim so much that he might believe some of it, and it was Coutlass, drawing a bow at a venture, who ordered Kazimoto to tell him that we expected a party in a few days bringing tents, provisions and more guns.

"There will be blue-and-white beads of the sort you long for among those loads," added Kazimoto on his own account; and that eased the chief's mind for the night. Fred gave him a half-rupee, and promised him to exchange it when the loads should come for as many of the beads as he could seize in his two fists. The chief went out to brag to the village, opening and closing his fists to see how huge their compass was; and later that night his wives had to be beaten for fighting. They were jealous because the fattest and the youngest new one had both been promised double shares.

There was another fight because our porters emerged from their hut and demanded that a barren cow out of the village herd be butchered. They made their meaning perfectly clear by taking the cow by the horns and tail and throwing her on her back. Fred decided that argument with a thick stick about four feet long.

The unusual spectacle of some one taking sides against his own men, whatever the rights or wrongs of it, so affected the chief that he entered our hut next morning disposed to hold us up for double promises of beads. It was evident we had to deal with a born extortioner. He would increase his demands with every fresh concession.

"Oh, what's the odds!" laughed Coutlass. "Promise him anything! The only loads likely to come along this way for a year or two are Schillingschen's!"

Fred told the chief he would think the matter over, and chased him out of the hut. Coutlass had given us all a new idea in an instant, and he was the only one who did not see its point—he, the only one who did not give a snap of the fingers for the laws of any land!

"D'you suppose—"

"Too good to hope for!"

"If he thinks we're dead—"

"And if he believes in that map—"

"He'll not need the map. He'll have memorized it. There's only a circle drawn on it to mark the Elgon district. All the old pencil marks have been rubbed out as he searched the other likely places and drew them all blank."

"He'll travel without military escort?"

"Sure! He won't want witnesses! He'll make believe it's a scientific trip. Remember, he's a professor of ethnology. That's how he puts it all over the British and goes where he pleases without as much as by-your-leave."

"Say, fellows! It's a moral cinch that when we broke away

from Muanza he made up his mind in a flash to return to British East and destroy us on the way. He thinks he made a clean job of that. I'll bet he loaded the launch down with stuff for a long *safari*, and thinks now he has a clear run and can take his time!"

"If that's how the cards lie, the game's ours!"

Coutlass saw the point at last and offered himself on the altar of forgiveness and friendship.

"Make me your partner, gentlemen, and if he travels within a hundred miles of this I will crawl into that Schillingschen's tent in the night and slit his throat! I would murder him as willingly as I eat when I am hungry!"

"Your job has been assigned you!" answered Fred. "When Mr. Brown's cattle are back in Lumbwa perhaps we'll give you something else to do!"

Nevertheless, Coutlass had outlined in a flash the limits of the plan. We would draw the line at murdering even Schillingschen, but must help ourselves to his outfit as our only chance of re-outfitting without betraying our presence in British East. But the plan was not without rat-holes in it that a fool could see.

"Schillingschen's boys will escape and run to the nearest British official with the story!"

"And the British official will be so full of the importance of Schillingschen and the need of protecting his beastly carcass—to say nothing of the everlasting disgrace of letting him be scoughed on British territory—and the official reprimand from home that's sure to follow—that he'll come hotfoot to investigate!"

"We'll have to provide against that," said Fred, and we all laughed, including Coutlass. Talk of provisions is easy when you have no means out of which to provide. It did not occur to include Coutlass in the calculations, or to dismiss him from them; but without exchanging any remarks on the subject it was clear enough to all of us that no such plan could hope to succeed with the Greek at large, at liberty to spoil it. We saw we should have to keep him in our party for the present.

"Don't forget," said Coutlass, more accustomed than we to seizing the strategic points of desperate situations, "that Schillingschen will have his own boys with him from German East."

"I didn't see any with him on the launch," I objected.

"He would never have come without them," Coutlass insisted. "He made them lie below the water-line out of reach of bullets at the only time when you might have seen them! He wouldn't trust himself to British porters. My word, no! That devil knows natives! He knows some of them might be British government spies! He'll have his own boys—if they can't carry all his loads he'll buy donkeys at Mumias; there are always donkeys to be bought at that place, brought down from Turkana by the Arab ivory traders. Do donkeys talk?"

At any rate, we talked, and made no bones at all about including Georges Coutlass in the conversation. It was his suggestion that we should send natives to look out for Schillingschen, and Fred's amendment that reduced the messengers to one, and that one Kazimoto. Any of the others might decide to desert, once out of sight, and we could scarcely have blamed them, for their path had not lain among roses in our company.

Kazimoto had a million objections to offer against going alone on that errand, as, for instance, that the chigger fleas would invade our toe-nails disastrously without his cunning fingers to hunt them out again. He also prophesied that without him to interpret there would swiftly be trouble between us and the chief; but we saw the other side of that medal and rather looked forward to an interval when the chief should not be able to talk to us at all.

At last, on the second morning after our arrival at the village, Kazimoto wrapped an enormous mound of cold *mtama* pudding in a cloth and went his way, prophesying darkly of murder and sudden death lurking behind rocks and trees, as unwishful to be alone as a terrier without a master, but much too faithful to refuse duty.

The chief saw a side of the medal that we had not guessed

existed. He came and sat beside us like an evil-smelling
shadow, satisfied that now we could not dismiss him, he being under no obligation to understand gestures. Curiosity was
the impelling motive, but he was not without suspicion. Fred
said he reminded him of a Bloomsbury landlady whose lodg-
ers had not paid their board and rooming in advance.

Will solved that problem by taking the rifle, and one cartridge that Fred doled out grudgingly, and after a long day's
stalking among mosquitoes in the papyrus at the edge of the
lake five miles away, at imminent risk of crocodiles and an
even worse horror we had not yet suspected, shooting a hippopotamus. Forthwith the whole village, chief included, went
to cut up and carry off the meat, and there followed revelry
by night, the chief's wives brewing beer from the *mtama*, and
all getting drunk as well as gorged. Coutlass and Brown got
more drunk than any one.

Will came back with flies on his coat—three large things
like horse-flies, that crossed their wings in repose, resembling
in all other respects the common tetse fly. He said the reeds
by the lake-side were full of them.

Remembering tales about sleeping sickness, and suspicion
of conveying it said to rest on a tetse fly that crossed its wings,
I went out the following day and walked many miles eastward, taking with me the only two sober villagers I could
find. They came willingly enough for five miles, thinking, I
suppose, that I intended to follow Will's example and kill
some more meat (although, as I did not take the rifle with
me, they were not guilty of much dead-weight reasoning).

At the bank of the fifth stream we came to they stopped,
and refused to go another yard. Thinking they were merely
lusting after the meat and beer in the village, I took a stick
to drive them across the stream in front of me, but they
dodged in terror and ran back home as if the devil had been
after them.

I crossed the stream and continued forward alone about
another mile toward a fairly large village visible between great
blue boulders with cactus dotted all about. There was the
usual herd of cattle grazing near at hand, but the place had

an unaccountable forlorn look, and the small boy standing on an ant-hill to watch the cattle seemed too listless to be curious, and too indifferent to run away. The big brown tetse flies, that crossed their wings when resting, were everywhere, making no noise at all, but announcing themselves every once in a while by a bite on the back of the hand that stung like a whip-lash. They seemed to have special liking for coat-sleeves, and a dozen of them were generally riding on each side of me. One could drive them off, but they came back at once, as horse-flies do when poked off with a whip.

When I drew near the village nobody came out to look at me, which was suspicious in itself. Nobody shouted. Nobody blocked the way, or dragged thorn-bushes across the gateway. There were black men and women there, sitting in the shadows of the eaves, who looked up and stared at me—men and women too intent on sitting still to care whether their skins were glossy—unoiled, unwashed, unfed, by the look of them —skeletons clothed in leather and dust, desiring death, but cruelly denied it.

One man, thin as a wisp of smoke, rushed at me from the shadow of a hut door and tried to bite my leg. The merest push sent him rolling over, and there he lay, too overcome by inertia to move another inch, his arm uplifted in the act of self-defense. Nobody else in the village stirred. There were more huts than people, more kites on the roofs than huts. Some of the littlest children played in the hut doors, but nearly all of them were listless like the grown folk. The only sign of normal activity was the big black earthen jars that witnessed that the women performed part at least of their daily round by bringing water from the lake.

I returned late that afternoon, walking, as it were, out of a belt of tetse flies. On one side of a narrow stream they were thick together; to the west of it there were scarcely any, although the wind blew from east to west.

"There's no fear of news about us reaching any government official," I announced. "There's a curtain of death between us and the government that even suspicion couldn't penetrate!"

# THE SLEEP THAT IS NO SLEEP*

*Ten were the plagues that Israel fled, and leaving left no cure,*
  *Whose progeny self-multiplied a million-fold remain,*
*The cloak of each one ignorance, idolatry its lure,*
  *And death the goal till, clarion-called, lost Israel come*
    *again.*
*Till then that loaded lash that bade the tale of bricks increase*
  *(Eye for an eye, and limb for limb!) shall fail not though*
    *ye weep;*
*The conqueror's heel for Africa!—The fear that shall not*
    *cease!—*
  *Desire, distrust, the alien law!—The sleep that is no sleep!*

---

*It is a characteristic of the so-called Sleeping Sickness that is decimating the tribes around Victoria Nyanza that the victim, although he goes into a coma, never actually sleeps from the time of taking the disease until the end, usually more than a year later. The natives, a tribe that came originally down from Egypt, themselves say that the dreaded sickness is a "visitation" by way of revenge on them for former sins, although what sins, and whose vengeance, they are at a total loss to explain.

## CHAPTER THIRTEEN

KAZIMOTO was gone five days, and then came preceded by
proof of the news he brought. He came in the evening. In
the morning, unaccountably from the northward, instead of
from the westward where Uganda lay, avoiding the regular
*safari* route and the belt of sleeping sickness villages, came a
genial, sleek, shiny Baganda, arrayed in khaki coat, red fez,
and bordered loin-cloth, gifted with tongues, and self-confi-
dent beyond belief.

He knew nothing of us at first, for we sat in our hut with
a smudge going, nervous about flies, even Coutlass, reckless
as a rule of anything he could not see, and perfectly indifferent to death for others, now fidgety and afraid to swagger
forth.

One of our Nyamwezi porters suddenly made a great shout
of *"Hodi!"** and came stooping through the low door, standing erect again inside to await our pleasure. We could hear
others outside, listening under the eaves. When we had kept
him waiting sufficiently long to prevent his getting too much
notion of his own importance, Fred nodded to him to speak.

"Is it true, *bwana*," he asked, "that the Germans will come
soon and conquer this part of Africa?"

"Certainly not!" said Fred.

"There is one out here, a Baganda, who says they will
surely come. He says the religion of Islam will be preached
from end to end of everywhere, and that the Germans are
the true priests of Islam. They will come, says he, when the
time is ripe, and call on all the converts of Islam to rise and
slay all other people, including all white folk, like the English, who do not accept that creed. If that is true, *bwana*,

---

*Hodi!* Equivalent to "May I come in?"

whither shall we go, and whither shall you go, to escape such
terrible things?"

"Does the Baganda know there are white men in this village?" Fred asked.

"Not yet, *bwana.*"

"Don't tell him, then, but bring him in here. Tell him
there are folk in here who say he is a liar."

The Nyamwezi backed out, and we heard whispering outside. There is precious little performance in Africa without
a deal of talk. At the end of about ten minutes the porter
again shouted *"Hodi!"* and this time was followed in by the
stranger, seven other of our own men, uninvited, bringing
up the rear.

*"Jambo!"** said the Baganda, with a great effort at bravado,
when his eyes had grown accustomed to the gloom and the
first severe surprise of seeing white men had worn off. He
was a very cool customer indeed.

"Whose pimp are you?" demanded Fred, without answering the salutation.

The man fell back on insolence at once. There is no native
in Africa who takes more keenly to that weapon than the
mission-schooled Baganda.

"I am employed by a gentleman of superior position," he
answered in perfectly good English.

"In what capacity?" demanded Fred.

"I am not employed to tell his secrets to the first strangers
who ask me!"

"Do you obey him implicitly?"

"I do. I am honorable person. I receive his pay and do
his bidding."

"Is his name Schillingschen?"

The Baganda hesitated.

"All right," said Fred. "I know his name is Schillingschen. You have boasted that you do what he orders you.
These men tell me you have said that the Germans are coming to conquer the country and destroy all people, including
the English, who have not accepted Islam!"

---

**Jambo!* Kiswahili equivalent of "How d'you do?"

The man hesitated again, glancing over his shoulder to discover his retreat cut off by our porters, and eying Fred with malignity that reminded one of a cornered beast of prey. He could control his face, but not his eyes.

"Oh, no, sir!" he answered after swallowing a time or two. "How could they tell such lies against me! I am a person born in Uganda, now a British protectorate and enjoying all blessings of British rule. I am educated at the mission college at Entebbe. How should I tell such a tale against my benefactors?"

"That is what you are here to explain!" Fred answered. "No! You can't escape, you hellion! Squat down and answer!"

"All this stuff is pretty familiar," Will interrupted. "In the States there are always people going the rounds among our darkies preaching some form of treason. Over there we can afford to treat it as a joke—now and then an ugly one, and on the darkies!"

"This is an ugly joke on a darkie, too!" grinned Fred.

The Baganda made a sudden dive and a determined struggle to get through the door, but our porters were too quick and strong for him.

"Confession is your one chance!" said Fred.

"Put hot irons to his feet!" advised Coutlass. (The native beer had left him villainously evil-tempered.) "Gassharamminy! Leave me alone with that fat Baganda for half an hour, and I will make him tell me what is on the far side of the moon, as well as what his mother said and did before she bore him!"

"Shall I hand you over to this Greek gentleman?" suggested Fred.

"Oh, my God, no!" the Baganda answered, trembling. "Hand me over to the *bwana* collector! He will put me in jail! I am not afraid of British jail! It will not be for long! The English do not punish as the Germans do! You dare not assault me! You dare not torture me! You must hand me over to the *bwana* collector to be tried in court of law. Nothing else is permissible! I shall receive short sentence, that is all, with reprieve after two-thirds time on account of good conduct!"

"Make him prisoner in the sleeping sickness village you told us about!" advised Coutlass, lolling at ease on his elbow to watch the man's increasing fear.

"Oh, no, no! Oh, gentlemen! That is not how white Englishmen behave! You must either let me go, or—"

He made another terrific dive for liberty, biting and kicking at his captors, and finally lying on his back to scream as if the hot irons Coutlass had recommended were being applied in earnest.

"What shall we do with the beast?" asked Fred. The hut was so full of his infernal screaming that we could talk without his hearing us.

"Tie him up," I said. "If we let him go he'll run straight to Schillingschen."

"Leave him here with Coutlass and me!" urged Brown. (He and Coutlass had grown almost friendly since getting drunk together on the native beer.)

"I recommend," said Will, "that we take the law in our own hands—"

The Baganda ceased screaming and listened. For some reason he suspected Will of being the deciding factor in our councils—perhaps because Will had said least.

"—take the law in our own hands, and thrash him soundly. Later on we can report what we have done to the British government, and ask for condonation under the circumstances or pay whatever piffling fine they care to impose for the sake of appearances. The point is, there's no court of law in these parts to hand him over to, and he needs punishing."

"I agree," said Fred. "Let's thrash him to begin with."

"Let's thrash him," went on Will, "as thoroughly as we've seen his friends the Germans do the job!"

"Both sides!" agreed Brown.

"Oh, no, no, no! You can not do that, gentlemen!"

"Lay him out!" ordered Fred. "Let's begin on him. Who shall beat him first?"

At a nod from Fred our porters stretched him face downward on the dry dung floor, and knelt on his arms and legs.
One of them stuffed a good handful of the dry dung into his
mouth to stop his yelling.

"Of course," said Will, rather slowly and distinctly, "if
he told us about Schillingschen, we'd have to let him off.
Let's hope he holds his tongue, for I never wanted to flog a
man so much in all my life!"

The most palpable absurdity at the moment was that there
was nothing in the hut to beat him with. There were dozens
of strips of the recently shot hippo hide hanging in the sun
outside to dry, with stones tied to the end of each, to keep
them taut and straight, but nobody made a move to bring
one in.

"Take off his loin-cloth!" ordered Fred. "It won't hurt
him enough with that thing on!"

The Baganda spat the cow-dung from his mouth and struggled violently.

"Oh, no, no!" he shouted. "I will tell! I will tell everything!"

"Too late now!" said Will jubilantly.

"No, gentlemen, no! Not too late! I tell all—I tell
quickly! Only listen! *Bwana* Schillingschen will shoot me
if he knows! He is very bad man—very *kali*—very fierce—
and oh, too clever! You must protect me!"

He could hardly get the words out, for the knees of our
porters pinned him down, and his chin was pressed hard on
the floor.

"I ordered that loin-cloth removed!" was all Fred commented. One of the porters attended to the task, and the Baganda hurried with his tale, drawing in breath in noisy gasps
like a man with asthma because of the weight of his captors
on him and the strained position of his neck.

"*Bwana* Schillingschen is sending me and many other men
—not all Baganda, but of many tribes—to go through all
parts and say Islam is the only good religion—all Germans
are high-priests of Islam—soon the Germans are coming with

very great armies to destroy the British and all other foolish
people who have not accepted Islam as their creed! All are
to get ready to receive the Germans."

"Where is Schillingschen now?" demanded Fred.

"Beyond Mumias."

"How far beyond Mumias?"

"Who knows? He is marching."

"In which direction? What for?"

"To Mount Elgon. I do not know what for."

"How do you know he is going to Mount Elgon?"

"He told me to go there and find him after my work is
done."

"How long were you to continue at what you call your
work?"

"A month or five weeks."

"So he expects to stay a long time up there?"

"Yes."

"Why?"

"I do not know."

"Has he many loads with him?"

"Very many—provisions for a long time."

"Guns?"

"Several. I do not know how many. He gives guns to some
of his men when he gets to where the government will not
know about it."

"How many men has he?"

"Not many. Ten, I think."

"How can they carry all those loads?"

"He brought a hundred porters from Kisumu to Mumias,
and there bought more than forty donkeys, sending the porters back again."

"Then are the men he has with him his own?"

"Yes."

"From German East?"

"Yes."

"What orders did he give you besides to tell these lies about
German conquest?"

"None."

"Pass me that whip!" ordered Fred. There was no whip, but the Baganda could not know that.

"He gave the same order to all of us," he yelled. "We are to stay out a month or five weeks unless we meet white men. If we meet white men we are to discover the white men's plans by talking with their servants, and then hurry to him and report."

"Ah! How many other spies has he out in this direction?"

"None."

"Why don't you pass me that whip when I ask for it?" demanded Fred.

"None! None! None, *bwana!* I am the only man in this direction! He has sent them north, south, east and west, but I am the only one down here."

"He has a lot more to tell yet," said Coutlass. "Let me put hot irons on his feet!"

Fred demurred. "He couldn't march with us if we did that!" he said with a perfectly straight face.

"Who cares whether or not he marches!" answered Coutlass. "To tell all he knows is his business! Wait while I heat the iron!"

The Baganda began to scream again, babbling that he knew no more. He assured us that Schillingschen had set the closest watch along the old caravan route, and toward his own rear in the direction of Kisumu, whence officials might come on chance errands.

"All right," said Fred. "Truss him up tight and keep him prisoner among our men in their hut."

"Our men are likely to get drunk to-night," warned Will.

"Let me watch him!" urged Coutlass. "Leave me with him alone!"

To the Greek's disgust we decided to trust the prisoner with our own men, and to keep very careful watch on them, threatening them with loss of all their pay if they dared get drunk and lose him—a threat they accepted at its full face value, but resented because of Brown's and the Greek's behavior the night before. They begged to get a little drunk —to get half as drunk as Brown had been—half as drunk as Coutlass had been—not drunk at all, but just to drink a little. We were adamant, and Brown added to their resentment by preaching them a sermon in their own tongue on the importance of being respectful toward white folk.

Kazimoto came in toward dark, foot-weary, but primed with news, and most of what he had to say confirmed the Baganda's story. Schillingschen, he said, was making for Mount Elgon in very leisurely stages, letting his loaded donkeys graze their way along, and spending hours of his time in questioning natives along the way on every subject under the sun.

Besides the fact of his leisurely progress, which was sufficiently important in itself, we learned from Kazimoto that Schillingschen's own ten boys were unable to speak the language of the country beyond a few of the commonest words —that they all slept in a tent together at night, usually quite a little distance apart from Schillingschen's—and that the donkeys were usually picketed between the two tents in a long line. He also told us the ten men had five Mauser rifles between them, in addition to the German's own battery of three guns, one of which he carried all day and kept beside his bed at night; the other two were carried behind him in the daytime by a gun-bearer.

That was good news on the whole. Coutlass went out on the strength of it and began to drink beer from the big earthenware crock in which the women had just brewed a fresh supply. Brown joined him within five minutes, and at the end of an hour they were swearing everlasting friendship, Coutlass promising Brown his cattle back, and Brown assuring him that Greece and the Greeks had always held his warmest possible regards.

"Thermopylæ, y'know, old boy, an' Marathon, an' all that kind o' thing! How many miles in a day could a Greek run in them days? Gosh!"

They two drank themselves to sleep among the gentle cattle in the circular enclosure in the midst of the village, and we—going out in turns at intervals to make sure our own boys were not drinking—matured our plans in peace.

We were too few to dare undertake the task in front of us
without the aid of Brown and the Greek. It was a case of
who was not against us must be for us, and the end must justify both men and means. We tried to work out ways of man-
aging without them, but when we thought of our Baganda
prisoner, and the almost certainty that both he and Coutlass
would race to give our game away to Schillingschen if let
out of sight for a minute, the necessity of making the best,
not the worst, of the Greek seemed overwhelming.

Early next morning, before the village had awakened from
its glut of beer and hippo meat, we shook Coutlass and Brown
to their feet none too gently, and, with the Baganda firmly
secured by the wrists between two of our men, started off,
Fred leading.

The village awoke as if by magic before we had dragged
away the thorns from the gate, and the chief leaped to the
realization that the beads he had promised his women were
about as concrete as his drunken dreams. He and a swarm
of his younger men followed us, begging and arguing—mile
after mile—growing angrier and more importunate. It was
by my advice that we crossed the stream into the sleeping
sickness zone and left them shuddering on their own side.
Our own men did not know so much about the ravages of
that plague, and in any case were willing to dare whatever
risks we despised. But we took a long bend back and crossed
the stream again higher up as soon as the chief and his beggars were out of sight. It was a pity not to keep exact faith
and give them the promised beads, if only for the sake of other
white men who might camp there in the future; but more
than two tons of hippo meat was not bad pay for their hospitality.

We wished we had as good price to offer at the villages
on our way, for sleep under cover we must, if we hoped to escape the ravages of fever; and the primitive savage, at least in
those parts, had the principle down fine of nothing whatever
for nothing. Yet as it turned out, the very man whose company we looked on as a nuisance proved to be a key to all gates.
We marched along the track the Baganda had taken. The

chiefs of all villages knew him again; and the men who dared take such a prophet of evil prisoner were looked upon as high government officials at least.

We accepted that description of ourselves, letting it go by silent assent, and explained our lack of tents and almost every other thing the white man generally travels with as due to haste. Heaven only knew what lies Kazimoto told those credulous folk, to the perfectly worthy end of making our lot bearable, but we were fed after a fashion, and lodged after a worse one all along our road. And who should send in reports about us—and to whom? Obviously white men with a prisoner, marching in such a hurry toward the north, were government officials. Who should report officials to their government? As for the tale about our having left our loads behind—are not all white people crazy? Who shall explain their craziness?

From being a nuisance the Baganda became a joke. When it dawned on his fat intellect that we were hurrying toward Schillingschen with only one rifle among us and no baggage at all, he jumped at once to the conclusion we must be Schillingschen's friends; and his fear that we intended to hand him over to that ruthless brute for summary punishment was more melting to his backbone than the dread of our imaginary whip, that had caused him to give Schillingschen away.

He tried to bite through the thongs that held him, but Will twisted for him handcuffs out of thick iron wire that we begged from a chief, who had intended to make ornaments with it for his own legs. We did not dare let the man escape, nor care to prevent our men from using force when he threw himself on the ground and wept like a spoiled child.

"I will tell you," he said at last, deciding he might as well be hanged for mutton as for lamb, "what *Bwana* Schillingschen is searching for! I will tell you who knows where to find it! I will tell you where to find the man who knows! Only let me run away then to my own home in Uganda, and I will never again leave it! I am afraid! I am afraid!"

But that was only one more reason for keeping him with

us, and no ground at all for delay. He would not tell unless
we loosed his hands first, so we pressed on, camping late and
starting early, until about noon of the fourth day we caught
sight of Schillingschen's tents in the distance, and gathered
our party at once into a little rocky hollow to discuss the
situation.

Behind us the land sloped gradually for thirty or forty
miles toward a sharp escarpment that overlooked the level
land beside the lake. At times between the hills and trees we
could glimpse Nyanza itself, looking like the vast rim of
forever, mysterious and calm. In front of us the rolling hills,
broken out here and there into rocky knolls, piled up on one
another toward the hump of Elgon, on which the blue sky
rested. In every direction were villages, of folk who knew
so little of white men that they paid no taxes yet and did
no work—marrying and giving in marriage—fighting and
running away — eating and drinking and watching their
women cultivate the corn and beans and sweet potatoes—
without as much as foreboding of the taxes, work for wages,
missionaries, law and commerce soon to come.

Schillingschen was more than taking his time, he was dawd-
ling, keeping his donkeys fat, and letting his men wander at
pleasure to right and left gathering reports for him of unusual
folk or things. We came very close to being seen by one of
them, who emerged from a village near us with a pair of chick-
ens he had foraged, followed by the owner of the luckless birds
in a great hurry and fury to get paid for them.

Schillingschen's tent could fairly easily be stalked from the
far side in broad daylight, and I was for making the attempt.
There was the risk that one of our porters might grow restless
and break bounds if we waited, or that the Baganda might take
to yelling. We gagged him as soon as I talked of the danger
of that.

Coutlass and Brown, however, were the only two who would
agree with me. Like me, they were weary to death of *mtama*
porridge, with or without milk, and the sight of Schillingschen's distant camp-fire with a great pot resting on stones in

the midst of it whetted appetite for white man's food. They
and I were for supping as soon as possible from the German's
provender, and sleeping under his canvas roof.

But Fred and Will insisted on caution, claiming reasonably
that surprise would be infinitely easier after dark. It was unlikely that Schillingschen would post any sentries, and not
much matter if he did. His knowledge of natives and natural
air of authority made him quite safe among any but the wild-
est, and these were a comparatively peaceful folk. In all probability he would sit and read by candle light, with his boys
all snoring a hundred yards away. There was no making Fred
and Will see the virtue of my contention that a sudden attack
while his boys were scattered all about among the villages
would be just as likely to succeed; so we settled down to wait
where we were with what patience we could summon.

It was a miserable, hungry business, under a blazing hot sky,
packed tightly together among men who objected to our smell
as strongly as we to theirs. It is the fixed opinion of all black
people that the white man smells like "bad water"; and no
word seems discoverable that will quite return the compliment. That afternoon was reminiscent of the long days on
the dhow, when nobody could move without disturbing everybody else, and we all breathed the same hot mixed stench over
and over.

We posted two sentries to lie with their eyes on the level
of the rim and guard against surprise. But there was so little
to watch, except kites wheeling overhead everlastingly, that
they went to sleep; and we were so bored, and so sure of our
hiding-place and Schillingschen's unsuspicion that we did not
notice them. I myself fell asleep toward five o'clock, and when
I awoke the sun was so low in the west that our hollow lay in
deep gloom.

Fred was lying on his elbow, sucking an unfilled, unlighted
pipe. Will lay on his side, too, with back toward both of us,
ruminating. Coutlass and Brown were both asleep, but Coutlass awoke as I rolled over and struck him with my heel.
Nearly all the porters were snoring.

It was a sharp exclamation from the Greek that caused me to sit up and face due westward. The others lay as they were. It was the gloom in our hollow—the velvety shadows in which we lay with granite boulders scattered between us, and no alertness on our part that saved that day, although Coutlass acted instantly and creditably, once awake.

Schillingschen stood there looking down on us, with his feet planted squarely on the rim of the hollow, and Mauser rifle under one arm. His great splay beard flowed sidewise in the evening wind. One hand he held over his eyes, trying to make out details in the dark, as stupid as we were. He stood with his back to the setting sun, exposing himself without any thought of the risk he ran, his huge, filled-out head refusing stubbornly to take in the truth of what had happened. Once convinced, the Prussian mind is not readily unconvinced. He had assured himself long ago that our party was at the bottom of Victoria Nyanza.

The second he did make out details he was swift to act, but that was already too late, although he did not know it at the moment. He threw up his rifle and laughed—a great deep guffaw from the stomach, that awoke every one.

"So, so!" he gloated. "So Mr. Oakes and his fellow escaped convicts are alive after all! Ha-ha-ho-ho! So you followed me all this way, only to forget that kites are curious! A fine comfortless journey you must have had, too! There were twenty kites wheeling over you. I counted, and wondered. Curiosity drove me to come and see. The first man who moves a finger, Mr. Oakes, will die that instant! Let your rifle lie where it is!"

It would be no use pretending the man had not courage, at all events of the sort that glories in the upper hand of a fight. He chuckled, and reveled in our predicament, taking in, now that his eyes had grown accustomed to the darkness of our hollow, the utter lack of comforts or provisions, and enjoying our disappointment. He certainly knew himself master of the situation.

"I suspect you have a man of mine down there with you!"

he announced presently. "Is not that my Baganda? Is he
gagged? Is he bound? Loose him, Mr. Oakes, at once! I
say at once! Otherwise you die now!"

He pointed his rifle directly at Fred, and the next second
fired it, but not intentionally. Coutlass sprang from behind
him, having crawled out through a shadow, and hit him so
hard with a stone on the back of the skull that he loosed off
the rifle and pitched head-foremost down among us. The
Greek promptly jumped on top of him with a yell like a
maniac's, failing to land with both heels on his backbone by
nothing but luck. As it was, he lost balance and sat down so
hard on Schillingschen's head that there was no need of the
energy with which we all followed suit, piling all over him to
pin him down like hounds that have rolled their quarry over.

The German was stunned—knocked into utter oblivion—
breathing like a sleeping drunkard, and bleeding freely from
the nose. Coutlass jumped off him and began to execute a
war dance up and down, yelling like a madman until Fred
threatened him with the rifle and Will gagged him from behind.

"Do you want his armed men down on us, you ass?"

"Gassharamminy!" he laughed. "I forgot about them!
Let us go and eat their supper!" He spoke as a man who
had full right now to be considered a member in good standing. We all noticed it, and exchanged glances; but that was
no time for argument about men's rights.

Brown was already over the rim of the hollow and making
in the direction of the tents. We called him back and compelled him to stay on guard over the prisoners, to his awful
disgust, for he suspected there was whisky among Schillingschen's "chop-boxes." But so did we! We left all our boys
with him except Kazimoto, threatening them with hitherto
unheard of penalties if they dared as much as show a lock of
hair above the rim of the hollow while we were gone.

Then the rest of us, with Fred leading and Kazimoto last
of all, crept out and sought the lowest level along which to
reach the camp. Will had taken Schillingschen's rifle and
went next after Fred. Coutlass followed so close on my heels

that more than once he trod on them, and once so nearly
tripped me that Fred called a halt behind some bushes and
cursed me for clumsiness.

But it turned out to be easy hunting. The ten boys had
tied the donkeys up to a rope in line and sat crooning while
their supper cooked at a long bright fire. We came up to
Schillingschen's tent from behind, crept around the side of it,
and in a moment had three more good weapons, I taking the
big-bore elephant gun that had dealt with us so savagely on the
lake, Coutlass seizing another Mauser, and Kazimoto adopting
the shot-gun.

The rest was child's play. We marched out of the tent all
abreast and called on the ten boys to surrender, making them
put up their hands until Coutlass had found their five rifles
and ammunition. They were too astonished even to ask questions. Accustomed to Schillingschen's despotic orders, they
obeyed ours silently, showing no symptoms of trying to bolt,
having nowhere to bolt to; but we took precautions.

Kazimoto ran back to bring our party, and we took a coil
of iron wire from Schillingschen's trade goods and fastened
every prisoner's hands firmly behind his back, including the
unconscious German's. That done, we ate the meat, beans and
vegetable supper that the ten had cooked.

Brown and Coutlass found Schillingschen's whisky after
that, and under its influence again swore ceaseless friendship
beneath the non-committal stars. While they feasted we took
Coutlass' rifle away as a plain precaution.

## PARCERE SUBJECTIS?

*When the devil's at bay*
*Ye may kneel down and pray*
*For a year and a day*
*To be spared the distress of dispatching him,*
*But the longer ye kneel*
*The more squeamish ye'll feel*
*'Cause the louder he'll squeal,*
*And at brotherly talk there's no matching him.*
*Discussion's his aim,*
*And as sure as you're game*
*To give heed to the same,*
*You regarding extremes with compunction,*
*You may bet he'll requite*
*Your compassion with spite,*
*Knifing you in the night*
*With much probonopublico unction.*

# CHAPTER FOURTEEN

For a while we looked like having trouble with Coutlass. We gave Brown a rifle, and distributed the other Mausers among Kazimoto and our best boys, but we did not dare trust the Greek with a weapon he might use against us, and he resented that bitterly. He had an answer to Fred's subterfuge that as a white man he would need a license before daring to carry firearms. "I dare do anything! I care nothing for law!" he argued, and Fred nodded.

That night we reveled in luxury, for after the life we had led recently it took time to reaccustom any of us to the common comforts. Schillingschen traveled with every provision for his carcass and his belly; and we plundered him.

We put the prisoners and our own porters in a hut in the nearest native village (less than half a mile away) under the watchful eye of Kazimoto and the shot-gun, dividing Schillingschen's two large tents between ourselves. The others offered me the camp-bed as a recent invalid, but I refused, and Will won it by matching coins. We divided the blankets in the same way, and all the spare underwear. Brown and Coutlass had to be satisfied with cotton blankets from a bale of trade goods; but when they had rifled enough to build up good thick mattresses as well as coverings, there were still two apiece for our boys and all the porters.

The chop-boxes were a revelation. The man had with him food enough for at least a year's traveling, including all the canned delicacies that hungry men dream about in the wilderness. Before we slept we ate so enormously of so very many things that it was a wonder that we were able to sleep at all.

We all hoped Schillingschen would die, for it was a hard problem what to do with him. He had no papers in his possession, beyond a diary written in German *schrift* that even Will could not make head or tail of, for all his knowledge of the language; and a very vague map bearing the imprint of

359

the British government, filled in by himself with the names of the villages he had passed on his way. There was no proof that we could find that would have condemned him of nefarious practises in a British court of law.

"And believe me," argued Will, sprawling on the plundered bed, blowing the smoke of a Melachrino through his nose, "your local British judges would take the word of Professor Schillingschen against all of ours, backed up by simply overwhelming native evidence! They're so in awe of Schillingschen's professorial degree, and of his passports, and his letters of introduction from this and that mogul that they wouldn't believe him guilty of arson if they caught him in the act!"

"Something's got to be done with him pretty soon, though," answered Fred from the floor, lying at ease on a pillow and a folded Jaeger blanket, smoking a fat cigar.

Coutlass and Brown were singing songs outside the tent and I sat in a genuine armchair with my feet on a box full of canned plum pudding. (Nobody knows, who has not hungered on the high or low veld—who has not eaten meat without vegetables for days on end, and then porridge without salt or sugar—how good that common, export, canned plum pudding is! To sit with my feet on the case that contained it was the arrogance of affluence!)

"We have his stores and his papers," said I. "We have his Baganda; and as time goes on, and his other spies begin to come in, we shall have them, too, if we're half careful. Why don't we let him go, to tell his own tale wherever he likes?"

"Maybe he'll die yet!" said the optimist on the camp-bed, blowing more cigarette smoke.

"Suppose he doesn't. We've done our best to keep him alive. He's quit bleeding. Suppose we let him go, and he lays a charge against us. Suppose they send after us and bring us in. We've his diary and his men—evidence enough," said I.

"You bally ass!" Fred murmured.

"Cuckoo!" laughed Will.

"I don't believe he'd dare approach a British official with his story," said I.

"Incredible imbecile!" Fred answered. "He has the gall of a brass monkey."

"And magnetism—loads of it," Will added. "He'd make the Pope play three-card monte."

"To say nothing," continued Fred, "of the necessity of not letting the government know we're here! Rather than turn him loose, I'd march him into Kisumu and hand him over. But, as Will says wisely, our proconsuls would believe him, and put us under bonds for outraging a distinguished foreigner."

"Well, then," said I, "what the devil shall we do with him? Offer something constructive, you two solons!"

"Have the four men we borrowed from the island bolted home yet?" wondered Will.

"They hadn't this evening," I answered. "I don't believe they'll venture home until we stop feeding them. They were hungry on their island. Our shortest commons then seemed affluence. Now they're in heaven!"

"Their canoes must be where they left them in the papyrus."

"Sure. Who'd steal a canoe?"

"Whoever could find them," Fred answered. "But they're skilfully hidden. Why don't we put Schillingschen and his ten pet blacks into those canoes, with a little food and no rifles —and show them the way to German East?"

"Because," said I, "they wouldn't go. They'd turn around and paddle for Kisumu, to file complaint against us."

"Don't you suppose," suggested Will, "that Schillingschen's own men 'ud insist on going home? Out on the water, ten to one, without guns or too much food, they wouldn't have the same fear of him they had formerly."

"That chance is too broad and long and deep," said Fred. "Altogether too bulky to be taken. Let's sleep on it. This cigar's done, and I'm drowsy. Are you quite sure Schillingschen's hands are fast behind him? Then good night, all!"

The problem looked no easier next morning, with Schillingschen recovered sufficiently to be hungry and sit up. There was a look in his eye of smoldering courage and assurance that did not bode well for us, and when we untwisted the iron wire from his wrists to let him wash himself and eat he looked about him with a sort of quick-fire cunning that belied his story of headache.

He was much too astute a customer to be judged superficially. I whispered to Fred not to shackle him again too soon, and sat near and watched him, close enough for real safety, yet not so close that he might not venture to try tricks. He said nothing whatever, but I noticed that his eye, after roving around the tent, kept returning again and again to a chop-box that stood near the foot of the bed.

Now I had unpacked that chop-box and repacked it the previous night. I knew everything it contained—exactly how many cans of plum pudding. It was the box I had rested my feet on. I felt perfectly sure he knew as well as I what the box contained, and to suppose he would sit there planning to recover canned food, however dainty, was ridiculous.

Wherefore it was a safe conclusion he was trying to deceive me as to his real intention. I put my foot on the box again, and he frowned, as much as to say I had forestalled his only hope. Pretending to watch the box and him, I examined every detail of the tent, particularly that side of it opposite the box, away from where it seemed he wanted me to look.

The human eye is a highly imperfect piece of mechanism and the human brain is mostly grayish slush. It was minutes before I detected the edge of his diary, sticking out from the pocket of Fred's shooting coat that itself protruded from under the folded blanket on which Fred had slept. It was nearer to Schillingschen than to me. After watching him for about fifteen minutes, during which he made a great fuss about his headache, I was quite sure it was the diary that interested him.

I stooped and extracted it from the coat pocket. The grimace he made was certainly not due to headache.

"Fred!" I called out, and he and Will came striding in together.

"That diary's the key," I said. "It's important. It holds his secrets!"

Will was swift to put that to the test.

"What will you offer?" he asked Schillingschen. "We want you to go back direct to German East. Will you go, if we give you back your diary?"

Schillingschen blundered into the trap like a buffalo in strange surroundings.

"*Ja wohl!*" he answered. "Give me that, and you shall never see me again!"

At that Fred threw himself full length on his blanket and took one of Schillingschen's cigars.

"Of course," he said, "you would give anything for leave to take those words back! You needn't try to hide the wince —we fully appreciate the situation! What do you say, you fellows? How about last night's idea? Who mooted it? Shall we send him back by canoe to German East, with a guarantee that if he doesn't go we'll hand over diary and him to our government?"

"Better send the book to the commissioner at Nairobi, or Mombasa, or wherever he is," suggested Will. "Then if the 'prof' here doesn't get a swift move on he's liable to be overtaken by the cops, I should say."

"Let's make no promises," said I. "I vote we simply give him time to get away."

At that the German saw the weak side of our case in a flash.

"If you dared give that diary to your government," he growled, "you would do so without bargaining with me! Why do you propose to let me go? Out of love for me? No! But because you dare not appeal to your government! Give me that diary, and I will go át once to German East, not otherwise! It is only a diary," he added. "Nothing important— merely my private jottings and memoranda."

Fred turned toward me so that Schillingschen could not see his face.

"Are you willing to start for Kisumu at once with that book?" he asked, and I nodded. He winked at me so violently that I could not trust myself to answer aloud and keep a straight face.

"Very well," he said. "Suppose you start with it to-morrow

morning. At the end of a week we'll turn the professor loose
to follow his own nose!"

Schillingschen shrugged his shoulders and refused to be
drawn into further argument. We gave him a good meal from
his own provisions, and then once more made his hands fast
with wire behind him and left him to sleep off his rage if he
cared to in a corner of the tent.

Later that morning we sent for the Baganda—gave him a
view of Schillingschen trussed and helpless—and questioned
him about the man he boasted he knew, who could tell us what
Schillingschen was after. He was so full of fear by that time
that he held back nothing.

He assured us the German was after buried ivory. There
was a man, who had promised to meet Schillingschen, who
knew where to find the ivory and would lead the way to it. He
did not know names or places—knew only that the man would
be found waiting at a certain place, and was not white.

"How did you get that information?" Fred demanded.

"By listening."

"When? Where?"

"At night, months ago, in Nairobi, outside the professor's
tent. I lay under the fly among the loads and listened. The
man came in the dark, and went in the dark. I did not see
him. I did not hear him called by name. He must have been
an old man. Speaking Kiswahili, he admitted he knew where
the ivory is. He said he saw it buried, and that he alone sur-
vives of all men who buried it. He promised to lead the professor to the place on condition that the Germans shall release
his brother, and his brother's wife, and two sons whom they
keep in prison on a life-sentence. The professor agreed, but
said, 'Wait! There are first those people who also think they
know the secret. Perhaps they do! Wait until after I have
dealt with them. Then you shall take me to the place! After
that your criminal relations shall be pardoned! Here is
money. Go and wait for me at the place we spoke of when we
talked before.'"

We each cross-examined him in turn, but could not make
him change his story in any essential. He merely exaggerated

the parts that he guessed might please us, and begged to be allowed to run before Schillingschen could break loose and get after him.

By noontime, when we gave him his second meal, Schillingschen had made up his own mind that his case was desperate and called for heroic remedy.

"All right," he growled. "I need that diary. Hand it to me and I'll tell you how to find what you're after!"

"You mean about the man who's to meet you?" suggested Fred blandly.

Schillingschen started as if shot.

"One of your men is an eavesdropper," Fred assured him with a cheerful nod. "That plug has been pulled already, Professor!"

"Let's play the cards face up!" Will interrupted impatiently. "Listen, Schillingschen. You're an all-in scoundrel. You're a spy. You're a bloody murderer of women and defenseless natives. If we could prove that we wouldn't argue with you. We know you burned that dhow with the women in it, but we've got no evidence, that's all. We know the German government wants that ivory, and we know why. We also want it. Our only reason for secrecy is that we hope for better terms from the British government. We've nothing to fear, except possible financial loss. If you prefer to come with us to Kisumu and have the whole matter out in court, all you need do is just say so. On the other hand, if you want to get out of this country before your diary can reach the hands of the British High Commissioner—you'd just better slide, that's all!"

"You've only until dawn to think it over," remarked Fred.

"You poor boob!" continued Will. "You imagine we're criminals because you're one yourself! The difference between your offer and ours is that you're bluffing and we know it, whereas we're not bluffing by as much as a hair, and the quicker you see that the better for you!"

"Oh, rats! Let's take him in with us to Kisumu!" said I, and at that Professor Schillingschen capitulated.

"Very well," he said. *"Kurtz und gut.* I will leave the

country. Permit me to take only food enough, and my porters, and one gun !"

"No guns !" said Fred promptly.

Schillingschen sighed resignedly, and we went out of the tent to talk over ways and means. In spite of our recent experience of Germany's colonial government we were still so ignorant of the workings of the *mens germanica* that we took his surrender at face value.

The problem of getting him down to the lake shore safely was none too simple. I was soft hearted and headed enough to propose that we should loose his hands, now that he had surrendered, and permit him reasonable liberty. Will—least inclined of all of us to cruelty—was disposed to agree with me. We might have overborne Fred's objections if Coutlass and Brown, returning from walking off their overnight debauch together, had not shouted and beckoned us in a mysterious sort of way, as if some new discovery puzzled them.

We walked about a hundred and fifty yards to where they stood by a row of low ant-hills. Neither of them was in a sociable frame of mind. It was obvious from the moment we could see their faces clearly that they had not called us to enjoy a joke. They stood like two dumb bird-dogs, pointing, and we had to come about abreast of them before we knew why we were summoned.

There lay five clean-picked skeletons, one on each ant-hill. One was a big bird's; one looked like a dog's; the third was a snake's; the fourth a young antelope's; and the fifth was certainly that of a yellow village cur, for some of the hairs from the tip of its tail were remaining, not yet borne off by the ants.

The skeletons lay as if the creatures had died writhing. There were pegs driven into the earth that had evidently held them in position by the sinews. Most peculiar circumstance of all, there was a camp-chair standing very near by, with its feet deep in the red earth, as if a very heavy man had sat in it.

I went back to the camp and told Kazimoto to bring one of the professor's men. Kazimoto had to do the talking, for we did not know the man's language, nor he ours.

Yes, the professor always did that to animals. He liked to

sit and watch them and keep the kites away. He said it was
white man's knowledge (science?). Yes, the animals were
pegged out alive on the ant-hills, and the professor would sit
with his watch in his hand, counting the minutes until they
ceased from writhing. It was part of the duty of the ten to
catch animals and bring them alive to him in camp for that
purpose. No, they did not know why he did it, except that it
was white man's knowledge. No, natives did not do that way,
except now and then to their enemies. The professor always
made threats he would do so to them if they ran away from
him, or disobeyed, or misbehaved. Certainly they believed
him! Why should they not believe him? Did not Germans
always keep their word when they talked of punishment?

We decided after that to let Schillingschen lie bound,
whether or not the iron wire cut his wrists. We did not trouble to go back to inquire whether he needed drink, but let him
wait for that until supper-time. The remainder of that afternoon we spent discussing who should have the disagreeable
and not too easy task of taking the professor to the lake and
sending him on his way. We sat with our backs against a
rock, with the firearms beside us and a good view of all the
countryside, very much puzzled as to whether to leave Coutlass
behind in camp (with Brown and the whisky) or send him
(with or without Brown) and one or two of us on the errand.
He was a dangerous ally in either case.

Evening fell, and the good smell of supper came along
the wind to find us still undecided. We returned to the tent
thinking that perhaps something Schillingschen himself
might say would help us to decide one way or the other.

"Better see if the brute wants a drink," said Fred, and
I went in ahead to offer him water.

He was gone! Clean gone, without a trace, or a hint as
to how he managed it! I called the others, and we hunted.
The sides of the tent were pegged down tight all around. The
front, it is true, was wide open, but we had sat in full view
of it and not so much as a rat could have crept out without
our seeing. There were no signs of burrowing. He was not
under the bed, or behind the boxes, or between the sides of

the tent and the fly. The only cover for more than a hundred yards was the shallow depression along which we had come to the capture of the camp, and that was the way he must have taken. But that, too, had been practically in full view of us all the time.

We counted heads and called the roll. Coutlass was close by. It did not look as if he had played traitor this time. Brown was sleeping off his headache in the shade. Kazimoto and all the boys were accounted for. The prisoners were safe. No donkeys were missing—no firearms—and no loads. The earth had simply opened up and swallowed Schillingschen, and that was all about it!

He had not made off with his pocket diary. Fred had that. There and then we packed it in an empty biscuit tin and buried it under a rock, Will and I keeping watch while Fred did the digging and covering up. It was too likely that Schillingschen would come back in the night and try to steal it for any of us to care about keeping it on his person.

It was too late to look far and wide for him that evening. A hunter such as he could have lain unseen in the dark with us almost stepping on him. Gone was all appetite for supper! We nibbled, and swore, and smoked—locked up the whisky—defied either Brown or Coutlass to try to break the boxes open—and arranged to take turns on sentry-go all that night, Will, Fred, and I—declining very pointedly offers by the other two to have their part in keeping watch. In spite of lack of evidence we suspected Coutlass; and we knew no particular reason for having confidence in Brown.

## THE SONG OF THE DARK-LORDS

*Turn in! Turn in! The jungle lords come forth*
 *Cat-footed, blazing-eyed—the owners of the dark,*
*What though ye steal the day! We know the worth*
 *Of vain tubes spitting at a phantom mark*
*With only human eyes to guide the fire!*
 *Tremble, ye hairless ones, who only see by day,*
*The night is ours! Who challenges our ire?*
 *Urrumph! Urrarrgh! Turn in there! Way!*

*Ye come with iron lines and dare to camp*
 *Where we were lords when Daniel stood a test!*
*Where once the tired safaris used to tramp*
 *On noisy wheels ye loll along at rest!*
*Tremble, ye long-range lovers of the day,*
 *'Twas we who shook the circus walls of ancient Rome!*
*The dark is ours! Take cover! Way there! Way!*
 *Urrumph! Urrarrgh! Take cover! Home!*

# CHAPTER FIFTEEN

THE man who tries to explain away coincidences to men who were the victims of them is likely to need more sympathy than he will get. The dictionary defines them clumsily as *instances of coinciding, apparently accidental, but which suggest a casual connection.*

Lions paid us a visit that first night after Schillingschen's escape—the first lions we had seen or heard since landing on the north shore of the lake. We prayed they might get Schillingschen, yet they and he persisted until morning—they roaring and circling never near enough for the man on guard to get a shot—he also circling the camp, calling to his ten men, whom we had transferred from the native village to the second tent under guard of Kazimoto and our own men as a precaution.

Our boys slept as if drugged, but not his. He called to them in a language that even Kazimoto did not understand, and they kept answering at intervals. Once, when I was listening to locate Schillingschen if I could, the lions came sniffing and snuffing to the back side of the tent. I tried to stalk them—a rash, reprehensible, tenderfoot trick. Luck was with me; they slunk away in the shadows, and I lived to summon Fred and Will. We tried to save the donkeys, but the lions took three of them at their leisure, and scared the rest so that they broke out of the thorn-bush boma we had made the boys build (as a precaution against leopards, not lions). Next morning out of forty we recovered twenty-five, and wondered how many of them Schillingschen got.

Remembering how we ourselves had managed, without ammunition or supplies, we did not fool ourselves with the belief that Schillingschen, with his brutal personal magnetism and profound knowledge of natives, would not do better. The probability was he would stir up the countryside against us.

He had been doing missionary work; it might be the natives
of that part were already sufficiently schooled to do murder at
his bidding.

We decided to leave at once for a district where he had not
yet done any of his infernal preaching.

"You should set a trap and shoot the swine!" Coutlass insisted. Will was inclined to agree with him, but Fred and
I demurred. The British writ had never really run as far as
the slopes of Elgon, and we could see them ahead of us not
very many marches away. If Schillingschen intended to dog
us and watch chances we preferred to have him do that in a
remote wilderness, where our prospect of influencing natives
would likely be as good as his, that was all.

Part of our strategy was to make an early start and march
swiftly, taking advantage of his physical weariness after a
night in the open on the prowl; but after a few days in camp
it is the most difficult thing imaginable to get a crowd of porters started on the march. It was more particularly difficult
on that occasion because none of our men were familiar with
Schillingschen's loads, and the captured ten, even when we
loosed their hands and treated them friendly, showed no disposition to be useful. We gave them a load apiece to carry,
but to every one we had to assign two of our own as guards, so
that, what with having lost the fifteen donkeys, we had not a
man to spare.

It was after midday when we got off at last. We had not
left the camp more than half a mile behind when I looked back
and saw Schillingschen where his great tent had stood, cavort-
ing on hands and feet like an enormous dog-baboon, searching
every inch of the ground for anything we might have left. We
three stood and watched him for half an hour, sweating with
fear lest he chance on the place where his diary lay buried in
the tin box. We began to wish we had brought it with us. I
said we had done foolishly to leave it, although I had approved
of Fred's burying it at the time.

"Suppose," I argued, "he sets the natives of that village
to searching! What's to prevent him? You know the kind of

job they'd make of it—blade by blade of grass—pebble by pebble. Where they found a trace of loosened dirt they'd dig."

"Did you bury something, then?" inquired a voice we knew too well. "By the ace of stinks, those natives can smell out anything a white man ever touched!"

We turned and faced Coutlass, whom we had imagined on ahead with the *safari*. If he noticed our sour looks, he saw fit to ignore them; but he took an upperhanded, new, insolent way with us, no doubt due to our refusal to shoot Schilling-schen. He ascribed that to a yellow streak.

"I was right. Gassharamminy! I could have sworn I saw two of you on watch while the third man dug among the stones! What did you bury? I came back to talk about Brown. The poor drunkard wants to head more to the east. I say straight on. What do you say?"

We told him to go forward. Then we looked in one another's eyes, and said nothing. Whether or not the original decision had been wise, there was no question now what was the proper course.

Instead of tiring out Schillingschen we made an early camp by a watercourse, and built a very big protection for the donkeys against lions—a high thorn enclosure, and an outer one not so high, with a space between them wide enough for the two tents and half a dozen big fires. Before dark we had enough fuel stacked up to keep the fires blazing well all night long.

Neither Coutlass nor Brown had had a drink of whisky that day, so it was all the more remarkable that Coutlass lay down early in a corner of the tent and fell into a sound sleep almost at once. We were thoroughly glad of it. Our plan was for two of us to creep out of camp when it was dark enough, and recover the contents of that tin box before Schillingschen or the blacks could forestall us.

The lions began roaring again at about sundown, but they love donkey-meat more than almost any except giraffe, and it was not likely they would trouble us. We were so sure the task was not particularly risky that Fred, who would have in-

ground where the camp had been. There was no sign of Coutlass. None of Schillingschen. A lioness and two enormous
lions stood facing one another in a triangle, almost exactly on
the spot where the larger tent had stood, not fifty yards
from us.

"Gee!" whispered Will excitedly. "We nearly stumbled
on 'em!"

"Shoot!" I whispered. My own position on the branch was
so insecure that I could not have brought my rifle into use
without making a prodigious noise. Will shook his head.

"I can see Coutlass now! Look at that rock—he's hiding
behind it—see, he's climbing! And look, there's Schillingschen!"

Neither man was aware of the other's presence, or of ours.
They were out of sight of each other, Coutlass on the very rocks
against which we had leaned to watch the tent the afternoon
before, and neither man really out of reach of anything with
claws that cared to go after them in earnest.

The arrival of the dim moon seemed to give the lions their
cue for action. The lioness turned half away, as if weary of
waiting, and then lay down full-length to watch as one lion
sprang at the other with a roar like the wrath of warring
worlds. They met in mid-air, claw to claw, and went down
together—a, roaring, snarling, eight-legged, two-tailed catastrophe—never apart—not still an instant—tearing, beating—
rolling over and over—emitting bellows of mingled rage and
agony whenever the teeth of one or other brute went home.

Even as shadows fighting in the shadows they were terrible
to watch. They shook the very earth and air, as if they owned
all the primeval bestial force of all the animals. And the she-
lion lay watching them, her eyes like burning yellow coals,
not moving a muscle that we could see.

Iron could not have withstood the blows; the thunder of
them reached us in the tree! Steel ropes could not have endured the strain as claws went home, and the brutes wrenched,
ripped, and yelled in titanic agony. Their fury increased.
Wounds did not seem to enfeeble them. Nothing checked the
speed of the fighting an instant, until suddenly the lioness

stood erect, gave a long loud call like a cat's, and turned and vanished.

She had seen. She knew. Like a spring loosed from its containing box one of the lions freed himself in mid-air and hurtled clear, landing on all-fours and hurrying away after the lioness with a bad limp. The other lion fell on his side and lay groaning, then roared half-heartedly and dragged himself away.

The second lion had hardly gone when Coutlass descended gingerly from the rock, peering about him, and listening. He evidently had no suspicion of our presence, for he never once looked in our direction. It was Schillingschen, not lions, he feared; and Schillingschen, clambering over the top of another rock, watched him as a night-beast eyes its prey. Another one-act drama was staged, and it was not time for us to come down from the tree yet.

Satisfied he was not followed and that Schillingschen was elsewhere, Coutlass crept from rock to rock toward the little cluster of small ones where, by his own confession, he had seen Fred bury the box. Schillingschen stalked him through the shadows as actively as a great ape, making no sound, as clearly visible to us as he was invisible to Coutlass.

There was not a trace of mist—nothing to obscure the dim pale light, and as the moon swung higher into space we could see both men's every movement, like the play of marionettes.

Down on his knees at last among the small loose rocks, Coutlass began digging with his fingers—grew weary of that very soon, and drew out the long knife from his boot—dug with that like a frenzied man until from our tree we heard the hard point strike on metal. Then Schillingschen began to close in, and it was time for us to drop down from the tree.

We made an abominable lot of noise about it, for the tree creaked, and our clothing tore on the thorny projections of limbs that seemed to have grown there since we climbed. To make matters worse, I stepped off the lowest branch, imagining there was another branch beneath it, and fell headlong, rifle and all, with a clatter and thump that should have alarmed the village half a mile away. And Will, not knowing what I had done but alarmed by the noise I made, jumped down on top of me.

We picked ourselves up and listened. We could hear the short quick stabs of the knife as Coutlass loosed and scooped the earth out. Among the myriad noises of the African night our own, that seemed appalling to us, had passed unnoticed; or perhaps Schillingschen heard, and thought it was the injured lion dragging himself away. (Nobody needed worry about the chance of attack from that particular lion for many a night to come; he would ask nothing better than to be left to eat mice and carrion until his awful wounds were healed.)

Reassured by the sound of digging we crept forward, knowing pretty well the best path to take from having seen Schillingschen stalking. But it was more by dint of their obsession than by any skill of ours that we crept up near without giving them alarm. Coutlass was still on his knees, throwing out the last few handfuls of loose dirt. Schillingschen stood almost over him, so close that the thrown dirt struck against his legs.

We took up positions in the shadow, one to either side, almost afraid to breathe, I cursing because the rifle quivered in my two hands like the proverbial aspen leaf. The prospect of shooting a white man—even such a thorough-paced blackguard white as Schillingschen—made me as nervous as a school-girl at a grown-up party.

At last Coutlass groped down shoulder-deep and drew the box out.

"Give that to me!" Schillingschen shouted like a thunderclap, making me jump as if I were the one intended.

The moonlight gleamed on the tin box. Coutlass did not drop it but turned his head to look behind him. Schillingschen swung for his face with a clenched fist and the whole weight and strength of his ungainly body. He would have broken the jaw he aimed at had the blow landed; but the Greek's wit was too swift.

He kicked like a mule, hard and suddenly, ducking his head, and then diving backward between the German's legs that were outspread to give him balance and leverage for the fist-blow. Schillingschen pitched over him head-forward,

## PARCERE SUBJECTIS?

*When the devil's at bay*
*Ye may kneel down and pray*
*For a year and a day*
*To be spared the distress of dispatching him,*
*But the longer ye kneel*
*The more squeamish ye'll feel*
*'Cause the louder he'll squeal,*
*And at brotherly talk there's no matching him.*
*Discussion's his aim,*
*And as sure as you're game*
*To give heed to the same,*
*You regarding extremes with compunction,*
*You may bet he'll requite*
*Your compassion with spite,*
*Knifing you in the night*
*With much probonopublico unction.*

stab rolled him over, freed himself and stood with upraised
hand to give the finishing blow. Then suddenly he saw us,
and his jaw dropped, the beastly mess that had been his well-
kept beard dropping an inch and showing where the Greek's
fist had broken the front teeth. But that was only for a second—a second that gave Coutlass time to rise to his knees, and
dodge the descending blow.

I made up my mind then it was time to shoot the German,
whatever the crimes of the Greek might be; but Coutlass had
not grown slower of wit from loss of blood. As he dodged he
rolled sidewise and seized my rifle, jerking it from my hand.
He jerked too quickly. The German saw the move and kicked
it, sending it spinning several yards away. We all made a
sudden scramble for it, Schillingschen leading, when the German turned as suddenly as one of the great apes he so resem-
bled, tripped Will by the heel, wrenched the rifle from his right
hand, pounced on the empty tin box, and was gone!

Too late, I remembered my own rifle and fired after him,
emptying the magazine at shadows.

Will's rage and self-contempt were more distressing than
the Greek's spouting knife-wounds.

"By blood and knuckle-bones! Give me that gun of yours,
will you! I go after the swine! I cut his liver out! Where
is my knife? Ah, there it is! Stoop and give it me, for my
ribs hurt! So! Now I go after him!"

We held Coutlass back, making him be still while we tore
his shirt in strips, and then our own, and tried to staunch the
blood, Will almost blubbering with rage while his fingers
worked, and the Greek cursing us both for wasting time.

"He has the box!" he screamed. "He has the rifle!"

"He has no ammunition but what's in the magazine," said
I; and that started Will off swearing at himself all over again
from the beginning.

"You damned yegg!" he complained as he knotted two strips
of shirt. "This would never have happened if you hadn't
sneaked out to steal the contents of the box!"

Suddenly Coutlass screamed again, like a mad stallion smelling battle.

for you, me and Fred Oakes! I'll stay and trick him some
more. I'll think up a new plan. I don't care if he gets me.
I'd hate to face Fred without my rifle, and have to tell him the
enemy is laying for him with it through my carelessness."

It was my first experience of Will with hysteria, for it
amounted to that. I remembered that to cure a bevy of school-
girls of it one should rap out something sharply, with a cane
if need be. Yet Will was not like a school-girl, and his hysteria took the pseudo-manly form of refusal to retreat. I
yearned for Fred's camp-fires, and Fred's laugh, hot supper,
or breakfast, or whatever the meal would be, and blankets.
Will, with a ruthless murderer stalking him in the dark,
yearned only for self-contentment. All at once I saw the thing
to do, and thrust my rifle in his hands.

"Take it," I said. "Hunt Schillingschen all night if you
want to. I'm going back to tell Fred I've lost my rifle, and
was afraid to face you for fear you'd laugh at me. Go on—
take it! No, you've got to take it!"

I let the rifle fall at his feet, and he was forced to pick it
up. By that time I was on my way, and he had to hurry if he
hoped to catch me. I kept him hurrying—cursing, and calling
out to wait. And so, hours later, we arrived in sight of Fred's
fires and answered his cheery challenge:

"Halt there, or I'll shoot your bally head off!"

Lions had kept him busy making the boys pile thornwood
on the fires. He had shot two—one inside the enclosure,
where the brute had jumped in a vain effort to reach the frantic donkeys. We stumbled over the carcass of the other as we
made our way toward the gate-gap, and dragged it in ignominiously by the tail (not such an easy task as the uninitiated
might imagine).

Once within the enclosure I left Will to tell Fred his story
as best suited him, Fred roaring with laughter as he watched
Will's rueful face, yet turning suddenly on Brown to curse
him like a criminal for laughing, too!

"Go and fetch that Mauser of yours, Brown, and give it to
Mr. Yerkes in place of what he's lost! Hurry, please!"

It was touch and go whether Brown would obey. But he

happened to be sober, and realized that he had committed the
unpermissible offense. Fred might laugh at Will all he chose;
so might I; either of us might laugh Fred out of countenance;
or they might howl derisively at me. But Brown, camp-fellow
though he was, and not bad fellow though he was, was not of
our inner-guard. He might laugh *with*, never *at*, especially
when catastrophe brought inner feelings to the surface.

"Take the shot-gun if you care to," Fred told him, as he
passed Will the rifle. "I'll unlock the chop-box presently, and
let you have some whisky!"

This last was the cruellest cut, but it did Brown good.
When Fred kept his promise and produced a whole bottle from
the locked-up store Brown refused to touch it, instead insult-
ing him like a good man, cursing him—whisky, whiskers,
whims and all, using language that Fred good-naturedly assured him was very unladylike.

Before dawn the boys, peering through the gaps between
the camp-fires, to distinguish lions if they could and give the
alarm before another could jump in and do damage, swore
they saw Schillingschen, rifle in hand, stalking among the
shadows. Nothing could convince them they had not seen
him. They said he stooped like a man in a dream—that his
beard was matted, and his shirt torn—that he strode out of
darkness into darkness like a man whose mind was gone. We
purposely laughed at their story, to see if we could shake them
in it. But they laughed at our incredulity.

"My eyes are good eyes," answered Kazimoto. "What I see
I see! Why should I invent lies?"

It was not pleasant to imagine Schillingschen, mind gone
or not, with or without three cartridges and a rifle, prowling
about our camp awaiting opportunity to do murder.

"Come to think of it," said Fred, "we've no proof he hasn't
a lot more than three cartridges. It's hardly likely, but he
might have cached some in reserve near where we found his
camp pitched. More unlikely things have happened. But the
bally man must go to sleep some time. He seems to have been
awake ever since he escaped. We'll be off at dawn, and either
tire him out or leave him!"

"I'll bet he's got one or more of those donkeys," I answered. "He'll not be so easy to tire."

"Suppose you and Will go and sleep," suggested Fred. "Otherwise we'll all go crazy, and all get left behind!"

There did not remain much time for sleeping. The porters, being used to the tents and their loads now, got away to a good start, heading straight toward the frowning pile of Elgon that hove its great hump against a blue sky and domineered over the world to the northward.

There were plenty of villages, well filled with timid spearmen and hard-working naked wives. Now that we had trade goods in plenty there was no difficulty at all about making friends with them. They had two obsessing fears: that it might not rain in proper season, and "the people" as they called themselves would "have too much hunger"; and that the men from the mountain might come and take their babies.

"Which men, from what mountain?"

"Bad men, from very high up on that mountain!" They pointed toward Elgon, shuddered, and looked away.

"Why should they take your babies?"

"They eat them!"

"What makes you think that?"

"We know it! They come! Once in so often they come and fight with us, and take away, and kill and eat our fat babies!"

All the inhabitants of all the villages agreed. None of them had ever ventured on the mountain; but all agreed that very bad black men came raiding from the upper slopes at uncertain intervals. There was no variation of the tale.

One thing puzzled us much more than the cannibal story. We heard shooting a long way off behind us to our right—two shots, followed by the unmistakable ringing echo among growing trees. Had Schillingschen decided to desert us? And if so, how did he dare squander two of his three cartridges at once—supposing he were not now mad, as our boys, and his, all vowed he was? His own ten men began to beg to be protected from him, and the captured Baganda recommended in best missionary English that we seek the services of the first witch doctor we could find.

# THE SONG OF THE ELEPHANTS

*Who is as heavy as we, or as strong?*
  *Ho! but we trample the shambas down!*
*Saw ye a swath where the trash lay long*
  *And tall trees flat like a harvest mown?*
*That was the path we shore in haste,*
  *(Judge, is it easy to find, and wide!)*
*Ripping the branch and bough to waste*
  *Like rocks shot loose from a mountain side!*
*Therefore hear us:*

   **(All together, stamping steadily in time.)**

     *'Twas we who lonely echoes woke*
     *To copy the crash of the trees we broke!*
     *Goad, nor whip, nor wheel, nor yoke*
     *Shall humble the will of the Ivory Folk!*

*Once we were monarchs from sky to sky,*
  *Many were we and the men were few;*
*Then we would go to the Place to die—*
  *Elephant tombs\* that the oldest knew,—*
*Old as the trees when the prime is past,*
  *Lords unchallenged of vale and plain,*
*Grazing aloof and alone at last*
  *To lie where the oldest had always lain.*
*So we sing of it:*

------

\*The legendary place that every ivory hunter hopes some day
to stumble on, where elephants are said to have gone away to die
of old age, and where there should therefore be almost unimaginable wealth of ivory. The legend, itself as old as African
speech, is probably due to the rarity of remains of elephants that
have died a natural death.

(All together, swinging from side to side in time,
and tossing trunks.)

> 'Twas we who lonely echoes woke
> To copy the crash of the trees we broke!
> Goad, nor whip, nor wheel, nor yoke
> Shall govern the strength of the Ivory Folk!

Still we are monarchs! Our strength and weight
  Can flatten the huts of the frightened men!
But the glory of smashing is lost of late,
  We raid less eagerly now than then,
For pits are staked, and the traps are blind,
  The guns be many, the men be more;
We fidget with pickets before and behind,
  Who snoozed in the noonday heat of yore.
Yet, hear us sing:

(All together, ears up and trunks extended.)

> 'Twas we who lonely echoes woke
> To copy the crash of the trees we broke!
> Goad, nor whip, nor wheel, nor yoke
> Have lessened the rage of the Ivory Folk!

Still we are monarchs of field and stream!
  None is as strong or as heavy as we!
We scent—we swerve—we come—we scream—
  And the men are as mud 'neath tusk and knee!
But we go no more to the Place to die,
  For the blacks head off and the guns pursue;
Bleaching our scattered rib-bones lie,
  And men be many, and we be few.
Nevertheless:

(All together, trunks up-thrown, ears extended, and stamping in
slow time with the fore-feet.)

> 'Twas we who lonely echoes woke
> To copy the crash of the trees we broke!
> Goad, nor whip, nor wheel, nor yoke
> Shall humble the pride of the Ivory Folk!

# CHAPTER SIXTEEN

WE HAD laughed at Fred's suggestion that Schillingschen might have ammunition cached away. Fred had sneered at my guess that the German might ride donkey-back and not be so easily left behind. Now the probability of both suggestions seemed to stiffen into reality.

Day followed day, and Schillingschen, squandering cartridges not far away behind us, always had more of them. He seemed, too, to lose interest in keeping so extremely close to us, as we raced to get away from him toward the mountain.

If he was really crazy, as his trembling boys maintained, then for a crazy man blazing at everything or nothing he was shooting remarkably little. On the contrary, if he was sane, and shooting for the pot, he must have acquired a big following in some mysterious manner, or else have lost his marksmanship when Coutlass bruised his eyes. He fired each day, judging by the echo of the shots, about as many cartridges as we did, who had to feed a fairly long column of men, and make presents of meat, in addition, to the chiefs of villages. It began to be a mystery how he carried so much ammunition, unless he had donkeys or porters.

Soon we began to pass through a country where elephants had been. There was ruin a hundred yards wide, where a herd of more than a thousand of them must have swept in panic for fifteen miles. There were villages with roofs not yet rethatched, whose inhabitants came and begged us to take vengeance on the monsters, showing us their trampled enclosures, torn-down huts, and ruined plantations. They offered to do whatever we told them in the way of taking part, and several times we marshaled the men of two or three villages together in an effort to get a line to windward and drive the herd our way.

But each time, as the plan approached development, ringing shots from behind us put the brutes to flight. It became

uncanny—as if Schillingschen in his new mad mood was able
to divine exactly when his noise would work most harm. Our
fool boys told the local natives that a madman was on our
heels, and after that all offers of help ceased, even from those
who had suffered most from the elephants. We began to be
regarded as mad ourselves. Efforts to get natives to go scouting to watch Schillingschen, and report to us, were met with
point-blank refusal. Rumor began to precede us, and from
one village that had suffered more than usually badly from
passing elephants the inhabitants all fled at the first sign of
Brown, leading our long single column.

We followed the herd. Its track was wide, and easier than
the winding native foot-paths; and we were willing enough
to jettison loads of trade-goods if only we could replace them
with tusks. The chase led up toward Elgon, over the shoulder of an outlying spur, and upward toward the mountain's
eastern slopes.

As long as we kept in the wake of the herd the going pre-
sented no difficulties. We knew by the state of the tracks and
the dung that the herd was never far ahead. Frequently we
heard them crashing through trees in front of us. Yet whenever we came so close as to hope for a view, and a shot at a
tusker, invariably a regular fusillade from the eastward to
our rear would start the herd stampeding with a din like all
the avalanches.

Streams by the dozen flowed down from the mountain's
sides, their banks crushed into bog where the elephants had
crossed. Our donkeys grew used to being tied by the head in
line and hauled across (for in common with all herds of donkeys, there were a few of them that swam readily, and many
that either could not or refused). The flies in the wake of the
elephants were worse than the tetse that haunted the shore of
Nyanza.

We had no trouble now from our boys. We could even let
the Baganda's hands loose. They feared the cannibals of the
higher slopes, but were much more afraid of the madman to
our right rear. Our difficulty lay in compelling them to keep
a course sufficiently to eastward, and in calling a halt each

day before men and animals were too utterly tired out. Yet, for all their hurry, we did not gain on the man who made them so afraid.

Elephants, once thoroughly scared, will run away forever. Our boys openly praised the herd in front for its speed and stamina, hoping it would continue on its course and oblige us to keep the madman with the rifle at a safe distance to our rear. But it seemed he had an easier line than we, or else his frenzy gave him seven-league boots, for he even began to gain on us, keeping along our right flank at a distance of several miles, and driving us nearly mad in the frantic effort to keep our column from turning and running away to the westward. If we had relaxed our vigilance for a moment they would have broken line and fled.

It was old volcanic country we were marching through, densely wooded, virgin forest for the most part, with earth so warm at times that it was not easy to believe the crater of Elgon quite extinct. Even at that low level we came on blow-holes nearly filled in with dirt and trash, serving as fine caves for beasts of prey. We went into one for about three hundred paces before it narrowed into nothing, and would have camped in it but for the stink. It smelt like a place where the egg of original sin had turned rotten. Fred said that was sulphur, with the air of a man who would like it believed that he knew.

At last the enemy must have made a night march, for he passed us, and the following dawn we heard him shooting to our right in front. That morning it was simply impossible to make the boys break camp. They swore that the ghost of Schillingschen had gone in league with the elephants to destroy us, and they preferred to be shot by us rather than murdered by witchcraft.

Beyond doubt they would have bolted and left us had that camp not been an almost perfect one, on rising ground with two great wings of rock almost enclosing it, and a singing brook galloping through the midst. There was only one gap by which elephant or man could enter (unless they should fall from the sky), and they closed that by rolling rocks and dragging up trunks of trees.

After a useless argument, during which we all lost our tempers and they were reduced to the verge of panic, we decided to leave them there in charge of Brown and those porters, except Kazimoto, who had rifles. The armed men promised faithfully to die beside Brown in the only place of exit rather than permit a man to pass out; and the rest all agreed it would be right to shoot them if they attempted to desert; but we left the camp together—Fred, Will, I, and Kazimoto, with Will's personal servant and mine bringing up the rear—wondering whether we should ever see any member or part of the outfit again. It felt like going to a funeral—or rather from it—more than likely Brown's.

Kazimoto and the other two should have been carrying spare rifles; but Brown had refused to remain behind unless we left him all but the one apiece we absolutely needed. We took the boys more from habit than for any use they were likely to be; and my boy and Will's bolted back to the camp almost before we were out of sight of it, Kazimoto begging us to shoot them in the back for cowards.

"Huh!" he grunted. "They are afraid of death. Teach them what death is!"

We heard Brown challenge them as they approached the camp, and hoped he thrashed them soundly. But it turned out he did not. He himself had grown afraid; for the fear of a crowd is contagious, and spreads nearly as readily from black to white as from white to black. He broke open a chop-box and consoled himself with whisky.

Forcing our way through vegetation that crowded around a spur of volcanic rock, it soon became evident that the whole of the huge herd was breakfasting not far in front of us, tearing off limbs of trees, and crashing about as if noise were the only object. We climbed and attempted to look down on them, only to discover that the part of the forest where we were consisted of a narrow belt, with a mile-wide open space beyond it between us and the elephants. The wind was from them toward us, but that did not wholly account for the amount of noise that reached us. It was the fact that the herd was twice as big as we imagined. There were elephants in every direction. We could see and hear branches breaking with reports like cannon-fire.

Kazimoto was as steady as an old soldier, a great grin spreading across his ugly honest face, and his eyes alight with enthusiasm. This was the profession he had followed when he was Courtney's gun-bearer, and he kept close to Fred with a handful of cartridges ready to pass to him, whispering wise counsel.

"Get close to them, *bwana!* Go close! Go close! Wind coming our way—smell coming our way—noise coming our way—elephant very busy eating—no hurry! No long shooting! Go right up close!"

It was easier said than done. The elephants had spread broadcast through the forest, and there was no longer one well-defined swath to follow, but a very great number of twisting narrow alleys through elastic undergrowth between great unyielding trees. We had to separate, to gain any advantage from our number, so that we emerged into the open more than a hundred yards apart, with Fred at the far left and Will in the center. Fred, with Kazimoto close at his heels, was more than fifty yards in front of either of us.

And crossing that mile of open land was no simple business. It was a mass of rocks and tree-roots, burned over in some swift-running forest fire and not yet reseeded, nor yet rotted down. There were winding ways all across it by the dozen that the elephants, with their greater height and better woodcraft, could follow on the run, but great stumps and rocks higher than a man's head (that from a distance had looked like level land) blocked all vision and made progress mostly guesswork.

However, the latter half-mile was more like level going. I emerged from between two boulders, wondering whether I could ever find my way back again, and envied Fred, who had found a better track and had the lead of me now by several hundred yards. Will was as far behind him as I, but had gone over more to the left, leaving me—feeling remarkably lonely—away in the rear to the right.

Kazimoto followed Fred so closely, stooping low behind

him, that the two looked like some strange four-legged beast. They were headed for the forest in front of them at a great pace, increasing their lead from Will, who, like me, was more or less winded. I stooped at a pool to scoop up water and splash my face and neck. When I looked up a moment later I could see none of them.

At that instant, when I could actually smell the great brutes crashing in the forest, unseen within a hundred yards of me, and would have given all I had or hoped for just to have a friend within speaking distance, a shot rang out in the forest ahead, and rattled from tree to tree like the echo of a skirmish. It was not from Fred's gun, or Will's. It was the phantom rifleman at work again. Schillingschen—Schillingschen's ghost—or whoever he was, he could not have timed his fusillade better for our undoing. The first shot was followed by six more in swift succession. And then chaos broke loose.

Toward where I stood, from every angle to my front, the whole herd stampeded. No human being could have guessed their number. The forest awoke with a battle-din of falling trees and crashing undergrowth, split apart by the trumpeting of angry bulls and the screams of cows summoning their young ones. The earth shook under the weight of their tremendous rout. I heard Fred's rifle ring out three times far to my left—then Will's a trifle nearer to me; and at that the herd swung toward its own left, and the whole lot of them came full-pelt, blind, screaming, frantic, straight for me.

There was no turning them now. None but the very farthest on the flank could have turned, given sense enough left to do it. It was a flood of maddened monsters, crazed with fear, pent by their own numbers, forced forward by the crowd behind, that invited me to dam them if I could! As they burst into the open, more shots rang out in the forest to lend their fury wings!

I glanced behind, to right and left, but there was no escape. I had come too far into the open to retreat! There were big rocks to the rear to have scrambled on, but there was no time. There was one big rock in front of me that divided their

course about in halves; to pass it they must open up, although
they would almost surely close again. I took my stand in
line with that, as a man on trial for life takes refuge behind
an unestablishable alibi.

They talk glibly about men's whole lives passing in review
before them in the instant of a crisis. That may be. That
was a crisis, and I saw elephants—elephants! I remembered
some of what Courtney had told us—some of the mad yarns
Coutlass spun when liquor and the camp-fire made him boastful. All the advice I ever heard; all my previous imaginings
of what I should do when such a time came, seemed to be
condensed into one concrete demand—shoot, shoot, shoot, and
keep on shooting! Yet my finger, bent around the trigger,
absolutely would not act!

The oncoming gray wave of brutes split apart at the rock,
as it must do, some of them screaming as they crashed into it
breast on and were crushed by the crowd behind. In the van
of the right-hand wing, brushing the rock with his shoulder,
charged an enormous bull with tusks so large that the heavier had weighed down his head to a permanent rakish angle.
He caught sight of me—trumpeted like a siren in the Channel
fog—and came at me with raised ears and trunk outstretched.
I heard shooting to the left, and more shots from the forest,
where the very active ghost or madman was keeping up a
battle of his own. I felt the fear, that turns a man's very
heart to ice, grip hold of me—felt as if nothing mattered—
imagined the whole universe a sea of charging elephants—
accepted the inevitable—and suddenly received my manhood
back again! My forefinger acted! I fired point-blank down
the throat of the charging bull. And it seemed to have no
more effect on him than a pea-shooter has on a railroad train!

I had left Schillingschen's heavy-bored elephant gun behind with Brown, considering it too cumbersome, and was
using a Mauser with flat-nosed bullets. I fired four shots as
fast as I could pump them from the magazine straight down
the monster's hot red throat; and he continued to come on as
if I had not touched him, hard-pressed on either flank by bulls
nearly as big as he.

## CHAPTER SEVENTEEN

NOBODY in camp slept that night. When the tusks had been chopped out, and our camp carried across and pitched beside Monty's — ivory weighed — lion-proof boma built — and elephant-heart portioned out to the men, who gorged themselves on it in order that their own hearts might grow great and strong; when all the myriad matters had been seen to that make camping in the tropics such a business, then there were tales to be told. We demanded Monty's first; he ours; and because his was likely to be much the shortest we won that argument.

"Wait one minute, though," he insisted. "Before I begin, have you any notion who a man with a beard could be— bruised face — broken front teeth — Mauser rifle — big dark beard cut shovel-shape—enormously powerful by the look of his shoulders and arms? I came on him three, no, four days' march back."

"Schillingschen!" we exclaimed with one voice.

"Show me Schillingschen!" echoed Brown, who was very drunk by that time, nearly ready to be put to bed. "Show me Schillingschen, an' I'll show you a corpse!"

"He's right," nodded Monty. "The man's dead. Blew his brains out with his last cartridge. Looked to me to have lost himself. Slept in trees, I should say. Clothing all torn. Hadn't been dead long when some of my boys came on him and drove away the jackals. Had he been in a fight, do you know?"

But we would not tell him that tale until we had his own.

"Mine's short and simple," he began. "Some ruffians boarded my ship at Suez, who made such eyes at me, and so obviously intended to do me damage at the first opportunity, that I talked it over with the captain (giving him a hint or two of the possible reason) and he agreed to slip me off secretly at Ismailia. It was easy—middle of the night, you know.

Perhaps the reason why my past history did not flash in review was that my time was not yet come! I continued to see elephant—nothing but elephant!—little bloodshot eyes aflame with frenzy—great tusks upthrown—a trunk upraised to brain me—huge flat feet that raged to tread me down and knead me into purple mud! I kept the last shot with a coolness I believe was really numbness—then felt his hot breath like a blast on my face, and let him have it, straight down the throat again!

He screamed—stopped—quivered right over me—toppled from the knees—and fell like a landslide, pushed forward as he tumbled by the weight behind, and held from rolling sidewise by the living tide on either flank. I tried to spring back, but his falling trunk struck me to earth. On either side of me a huge tusk drove into the ground, and I lay still between them, as safe as if in bed, while the herd crashed past to right and left for so many minutes that it seemed all the universe was elephants—bulls, cows and calves all trumpeting in mad desire to get away—away—anywhere at all so be it was not where they then were.

Blood poured on me from the dead brute's throat—warm, slippery, sticky stuff; but I lay still. I did not move when the crashing had all gone by, but lay looking up at the monster that had willed his worst and, seeking to slay, had saved me. Those are the moments when young men summon all their calf-philosophy. I wondered what the difference was between that brute and me, that I should be justified in slaying; that I should be congratulated; that I should have been pitied, had the touch-and-go reversed itself and he killed me. I knew there was a difference that had nothing to do with shape, or weight, or size, but I could not give it a name or lay my finger on it.

My reverie, or reaction, or whatever it was, was broken by Fred's voice, flustered and out of breath, coming nearer at a great pace.

"I tell you the poor chap's dead as a door-nail! He's under that great bull, I tell you! He's simply been charged and flattened out! What a dog I was—what a green-horn—what

a careless, fat-headed tomfool to leave him alone like that!
He was the least experienced of all of us, and we let him
take the full brunt of a charging herd! We ought to be hung,
drawn and quartered! I shall never forgive myself! As for
you, Will, it wasn't half as much your fault as mine! You
were following me. You expected me to give the orders, and
I ought to have called a halt away back there until we were
all three in touch! I'll never forgive myself—never!"

I crawled out then from between the tusks, and shook myself, much more dazed than I expected, and full of an unaccountable desire to vomit.

"Damn your soul!" Fred fairly yelled at me. "What the
hell d'you mean by startling me in that way! Why aren't
you dead? Look out! What's the matter with the man? The
poor chap's hurt—I knew he was!"

But that inexplicable desire to empty all I had inside me
out on to the trampled ground could no longer be resisted,
that was all. The aftermath of deadly fear is fear's corollary.
Each bears fruit after its kind.

To my one tusker Will and Fred had brought down five
and six respectively. That made twenty-three tusks, for one
was an enormous "singleton." We sent Kazimoto back alone
to try to persuade some of our porters to come and chop out
the ivory with axes, bidding him promise them all the hearts,
and as many tail-hairs as they chose to pull out to keep witches
away with. Then, since my sickness passed presently and
left me steady on my legs, Fred made a proposal that we
jumped at.

"Let's go and lay Schillingschen's ghost! If that *was* Schillingschen shooting in the forest, we've a little account with
him! If it wasn't I want to know it! Come along!"

We advanced into the forest and toiled up-hill along the
tracks the stampeding elephants had made, amid flies inde-
scribable, and almost intolerable heat. The blood on my clothing made me a veritable feeding-place of flies, until I threw
most of it off, and then began to suffer in addition from bites
I could not feel before, and from the sharp points of beckon-
ing undergrowth. My bare legs began to bleed from scratches,

and the flies swooped anew on those, and clung as if they grew there.

Will climbed a huge tree, at imminent risk of pythons and rotten branches, and descried open country on our right front. We made for it, I walking last to take advantage of the others' wake, and after more than an hour of most prodigious effort we emerged on rolling rocky country under a ledge that overhung a thousand feet sheer above us on the side of Elgon. To our right was all green grass, sloping away from us.

There was a camp half a mile away pitched on the edge of the forest—a white man's tent—a mule—meat hanging to dry in the wind under a branch—two tents for natives—and a pile of bags and boxes orderly arranged. We could see a man sitting under a big tent awning. He was reading, or writing, or something of that kind. He was certainly not Schillingschen. We hurried. Fred presently broke into a run; then, half-ashamed, checked himself and waited for me, who was beyond running.

When we came quite close we saw that the man was playing chess all by himself with a folding board open on his knees. He did not look up, although by that time he surely should have heard us. Fred began to walk quietly, signaling to the camp hangers-on to say nothing. We followed him silently in Indian file. As he came near the awning Fred tiptoed, and I felt like giggling, or yelling—like doing anything ridiculous.

He who played chess yawned suddenly, and closed the chessboard with a snap. He got up lazily, smiled, stretched himself like a great good-looking cat, faced Fred, and laughed outright.

"Glad to see you all! Did you get many elephants?" he asked.

"Monty, you old pirate— I knew it was you!" said Fred, holding a hand out.

Monty took it, and forced him into the chair he had just vacated.

"You damned old liar!" he said, nodding approvingly.

## THEY TOIL NOT, NEITHER DO THEY SPIN

*Now for opulence and place*
  *And the increment unearned*
    *We will thieve and stab and cover it with perjury,*
*Contemptuous of grace*
  *And the lesson never learned*
    *That the Rules are not amenable to surgery.*
*We will steal a neighbor's tools*
  *In the quest for easy cash,*
    *Aye, jump his claim and burrow to the heart of it,*
*But the innocents and fools*
  *Get all the goods, and we the trash,*
    *And that's the most exasperating part of it!*

—had the doctor isolate the ruffians on the starboard side while the ship anchored—some cooked-up excuse about quarantine—and kept 'em out of sight of what was happening until the ship went on again. Very simple."

"Go on, Didums—we'll be all night talking—what did you do with the King of Belgium?" Fred demanded.

"Nothing. Didn't go near the King of Belgium. I was quarantined at Ismailia on wholly imaginary grounds for fourteen days; and who should come smiling into the same lazaretto on the last day but Frederick Courtney—a very old friend of mine!"

"He was to go to Somaliland," I said.

"So he told me. He's on his way there now. Decided for reasons of his own to enter the country by way of Abyssinia. Told me of the advice he'd given you fellows, and assured me he'd seen King Leopold himself on the very matter scarcely a year before. Of course, he said, I might succeed where he failed, using influence and all that sort of thing, but he assured me Leopold was hard to deal with, and difficult to tie down. His advice was, go back to Elgon, and hunt for the stuff there."

"That's what he kept advising us," said Will. "But why should he give away his information free? And if it's good, where did he get it?"

"Courtney's no dog in the manger," Monty answered. "He told me of this man Schillingschen. Said he had sent in a report about him to the Home Government, but couldn't for the life of him get documentary evidence with which to back up his charges."

Will whistled, and drew out the diary he had rescued from the tin box. Fred nodded. Will threw it to Monty, who caught it.

"He told me this Schillingschen had searched the whole country over for the stuff—had it straight from Schillingschen's boys—I dare say you know how Courtney can make a native tell him all he knows. Schillingschen, he said, had eliminated pretty nearly all the likely places until Mount Elgon was about all there is left. Courtney said, too, that

there were always so many thousands of elephants near Elgon
that Tippoo Tib probably gathered a harvest there. We dis-
cussed probabilities, and agreed it wasn't likely he would
carry the stuff far in order to hide it. It seemed likely to both
of us, too, that if the quantity the old man hid was anything
like what rumor says, then there were probably half a dozen
hiding-places, not one. Most of the stuff may be in the Congo
Free State, and we'll do well to leave that to Leopold of Belgium and his pet concessionaires. Some of it may be near
here. I stayed in the lazaretto an extra day with Courtney,
talking it over. One other thing he remembered to tell me was
that Schillingschen had hunted high and low for Tippoo Tib's
old servants, and had finally managed to have the relatives of
that man Hassan—I remember, Fred, you called him Johnson in Zanzibar—thrown in jail in German East for some
alleged offense or other."

Monty stopped to scrape out a faithful pipe, fill it, press
down tobacco with a practised thumb, and reach toward the
camp-fire for a burning brand. Then he smoked for two minutes reflectively.

"I offered Courtney a share should we find the stuff. Knew
you fellows would agree." Pause. "Courtney wouldn't hear
of it." Pause. "Said good-by to him, and took a coastwise
trading steamer back to Mombasa. Delightful trip—put in
everywhere—saw everything. Saw a lot of the Galla—fine
tribe, the Galla."

"Suppose you cut the travelogue stuff until later on!" suggested Will.

"Landed at Mombasa, and learned the first day that you
fellows had managed to make more enemies than friends.
Put in a number of days on heavy social labor—lingered at
the club—drank too much of their infernal gin-and-black-
pepper appetizer—but made you fellows right, I think."

"We're not interested in the slumming. Go on and tell us
what you did!" urged Fred.

"That is what I did—and undid. I made friends. Soon
I had all the other junior officials in a state of mind to help
me if they could. Then I began to inquire for Hassan. They

drew the dragnet tight, and discovered him at Nairobi. A' young assistant district superintendent of police, who will rise in the service, I hope, before long, discovered a woman —who was jealous of a man—who was just then making love to the dusky damsel particularly favored by Hassan; and in that roundabout way we discovered that Hassan intended to take a trip very soon toward Mount Elgon, where, if you please, he was to take part in Professor Schillingschen's ethnological studies. On condition that he held his tongue until I gave him leave to talk, I promised that young policeman to put him *en rapport* with Schillingschen's doings as swiftly as may be. Then I returned to Mombasa, and got your code letter saying you would head this way. It all fitted in like a game of chess."

"How in the world did you get that letter so soon?" demanded Fred. "The missionary chap was to mail it in Ujiji, via Salisbury, Rhodesia."

"I suppose he simply didn't do that, that's all," Monty answered. "The bank manager told me he received it in the mission mail bag—from Ujiji, yes, but by way of Muanza, Tabora, and Dar es Salaam. It reached me in the nick of time. I must have been marching nearly parallel with you chaps for about a week!"

"If coincidence of evidence means anything," said Will, "we're all on a red-hot scent! That Baganda we have in our outfit is our prisoner. One of Schillingschen's pet pimps. He swears Hassan—or rather some old native whose name he doesn't know—was to meet Schillingschen in these parts and lead him to where he actually helped bury the ivory years ago!"

"We may have difficulty finding him," said I. "Mount Elgon's big!"

"What about Brown?" asked Monty. "I hope you haven't made him partner? I agree, of course, if you have, but I hope not!"

"Nothing doing!"

"No. Why should we?"

"Brown's all right, but a present ought to satisfy him."

We began to tell Monty about Brown's cattle that Coutlass stole, and the Masai looted from Coutlass and us.

"Were they branded?" asked Monty.

"Branded *and* hoof- *and* ear-marked," said I.

"Then they ought to be traceable, even among the huge herds the Masai have. I think I've influence enough by this time with this government to have those cattle traced and returned to Brown."

"They're his only love!" said I. "Do that for him, and he'll never wait to receive a present!"

Dawn found us still recounting our adventures and Monty alternately laughing and frowning.

"I regret Coutlass," he said, shaking the ashes from his pipe at last when Kazimoto brought our breakfast. "I regretted having to throw him out of the hotel in Zanzibar. I wish he could have escaped with his life—a picturesque scoundrel if ever there was one! I'd rather be robbed by him than flattered by ten Schillingschens or Lady Saffren Waldons. I suppose if I'd been with you I'd have killed him. It's well I wasn't. I might have regretted it all my days!"

We buried our newly won ivory under a tree, locating the spot exactly with the aid of Monty's compass, and broke camp, starting sleepless up the mountain. As Monty said:

"No use meandering around the mountain. Hassan might be higher up or lower down. If he *is* there you may depend on it he's tired of waiting. He's looking for a *safari*. Let's climb where we can be seen from miles away."

So climb we did, thousand after thousand feet, until the night air grew so cold that the porters' teeth chattered and they threatened to desert us. They grew afraid, too, remembering the tales the villagers had told them down below.

"Wow! You are not fat babies!" Kazimoto told them. "Who would eat such stringy meat as you?"

We came to caves that none of the men dared enter—vast, gloomy tunnels into the mountain through which the chill wind whistled like a dirge. Yet the caverns were warmer than the wind, and not bad camping-places if we could have persuaded the boys to take advantage of them.

The earth, too, all over the mountain and the range to eastward of it was warm in spite of the wind. In places there were warm springs bubbling from the rock, and at night and early morning a blanket of white mist that was remarkably like steam covered everything. It was a land of thunderless lightning—lightning from a clear sky, flashing here and there without warning or excuse. On the high slopes there was little or no game, and no signs whatever of inhabitants, until late one afternoon the porters shouted, and we saw an old man racing toward us along the top of a ridge.

He held his hands out, and shouted as he ran—a round-faced, big-bellied man, although not nearly so fat as when we saw him last; unclean, unkempt, in tattered shirt and crushed-in fez—a man with one desire expressed all over him—to see, and touch, and talk with other men. He ran and threw himself at Monty's feet, clasped his legs, and blubbered.

"*Bwana!* Oh, *bwana!* Oh, *bwana!*"

"Get up, Johnson!" Fred took him by the arm and raised him. "Tell us what's the matter."

"Men who eat men! Men who eat men! I had three porters to carry my tent and food. Now I have none. They have eaten them! Now they hunt me!"

"Well, you're safe," said Monty. "Calm yourself."

"But you are not *Bwana* Schillingschen! I am here to wait for him. Have you seen him? Where is he?"

Fred answered him. "Dead!"

Hassan threw himself on the ground again at Monty's feet.

"Oh, what shall I do?" he blubbered. "I am an old man. Who shall take my people out of jail? Who shall go to Dar es Salaam and make Germans give them up?"

"If you're willing to show us what you intended to show Schillingschen," said Monty, "I'll do what I can for your relations."

"What can you do? Oh, what can you do? No man but a German can make these Germans cease from punishing!"

Monty beckoned to the Baganda who had once done Schillingschen's dirty work.

"D'you see this man? This is a German spy. The Ger-

mans will be willing to hand over your relations in exchange
for a promise not to make a fuss about this man. Wait a minute, though! Are your relations criminals?"

"No, *bwana!* No, *bwana!* My relations honorable folk!
Formerly living in Zanzibar—going to Bagamoyo to serve in
German family by invitation of person attached to German
Consulate—no sooner landed than thrown in jail on charges
they know nothing whatever about. Then Schillingschen he
finding me, and say to me, 'You show where is that Tippoo
Tib's ivory, and your relations shall go free!' And Tippoo
Tib, he say to me, 'You take first step to show any man where
is that ivory, and you shall be fed to white ants by my faithful people!' And Schillingschen he catch two of them faithful
people, and feed 'em to white ants when nobody looking that
way! Schillingschen terrible! Tippoo Tib terrible! What
shall do? Tippoo Tib, he one time making me go long trip
with *Bwana* Coutlass, very bad Greek. *Bwana* Coutlass wanting ivory—me pretending showing him—leading him wrong
way. Coutlass very bad man, beating me *ngumu sana*.* All
the same, me more afraid of Tippoo Tib and *Bwana* Schillingschen. Not long ago Tippoo Tib sending me with *Bwana*
Coutlass second time, making bad threats against me if I
not lead him wrong. Then Schillingschen he send for me and
making worse threats! Oh, what shall do! Oh, what shall
do!"

"You shall show us where that ivory is!" Monty answered
him. "Stop blubbering! Get up! Look here! See this! (Get
me that diary, Will.) If the Germans won't release your relations from jail on account of this Baganda, this is a written
book that will make them do it! In this book are the names
of men who have broken treaties and the law of nations. When
the Germans know the British Government in London has this
book under lock and key, they will think it a little thing to release your relations for the sake of avoiding trouble!"

"Promise me, *bwana!* You promise me!"

"I promise I will do my best for you."

"Word of an Englishman—promise!"

* *Ngumu sana*, very severely.

"Word of an Englishman—I promise to do my best!"

That was a proud enough moment on the shoulder of a mountain, with wilderness in every direction farther than the highest eagle in the air above could see, to have that helpless, hopeless ex-slave, part Arab, part *machenzie*, put his whole stock-in-trade—his secret—all he had on earth to bargain with for those he loved—in the balance on the promise of an Englishman. It was a tribute to a race that has had its share, no doubt, of bad men, but has won dominion over half the earth and pretty much all the sea by keeping faith with men who could not by any means compel good faith.

"Then I tell!" said Hassan. "Then I show!"

But now a new fear seized him, and he clung to Monty, trembling and jabbering.

"The men who eat men! The men who eat men!"

"Pah! Cannibals!" sneered Fred. "They're always cowards!"

"Tippoo Tib, he afraid of nothing—nobody! He is hiding the ivory where men who eat men can guard it and none dare come!"

"Lead on, McDuff!" Fred grinned, shouldering his rifle.

All of us except Monty had beards by that time that fluttered in the wind, and looked desperate enough for any venture. Considering the rifles and our uncouth appearance, Hassan took heart of grace. He insisted on an armed guard to walk on either side of him, and nearly drove Kazimoto frantic by ducking behind rocks at intervals, imagining he saw an enemy; but he did not refuse any longer to show the way.

It seemed that in expectation of Schillingschen's early arrival he had camped within a mile of the place where the stuff was hidden, taking unreasoning courage from the bare fact of having the redoubtable Schillingschen for friend. But the cannibals (who must have been a hungry folk, for there were no plantations, and almost no animals on all those upper slopes) had pounced on his three lean porters, missing himself by a hair's breadth.

In hiding, he had watched his three men killed, toasted before a fire in a cavern-mouth, and eaten. Then he had run for his life, following the shoulder of the mountain in the hope of meeting Schillingschen, munching uncooked corn he had in a little bag, hiding and running at intervals for a day, and a night until he chanced on us. For an old man almost sick with fear he was astonishingly little affected by the adventure.

We took longer over the course than he had done, because he wanted to find cannibals, and teach them, maybe, a needed lesson. Fred's theory was that we should surprise them and pen them into a cavern, discovering some means of talking with them when hunger brought them out to surrender and cringe.

So we threw out a line of scouts, and pounced on cavemouths suddenly, entering great tunnels and following the course of them in ages-old lava until sometimes we thought ourselves lost in the gloom and spent hours finding the way out again.

Time and again we found bones—bones of wild animals, and of birds, and of fish; now and then bones that perhaps had been monkeys, but that looked too suspiciously like those of the fat babies mothers mourned for in the villages below for the benefit of the doubt to be conceded without something more or less resembling proof. But never a human being did we see until we rounded the northeastern hump of the mountain in a bitter wind, and spied half a hundred naked men and women, thinner than wraiths, who scampered off at sight of us and volleyed ridiculous arrows from a cave-mouth. The arrows fell about midway between us and them, but threw Hassan into a paroxysm of fear, out of which it was difficult to shake him.

"Those are the people who ate my men! That is the cavern where Tippoo Tib hid the ivory! That is where my men's bones are! See—they have torn my tent for clothing for their naked women!"

We put Hassan under double guard for fear lest he bolt again and leave us. And all that day, and all the next we hunted for cannibals through mazy caverns that seemed to ex-

tend into the mountain's very womb. There were times when
the stench was so horrible we nearly fainted. We stumbled
on men's bones. We collided with sharp projections in the
gloom—fell down holes that might have been bottomless for
aught we knew in advance—and scrambled over ledges that in
places were smooth with the wear of feet for ages. Everlastingly to right, or left of us, or up above, or down below we
could hear the inhabitants scampering away. Now and then
an arrow would flitter between us; but their supply of ammunition seemed very scanty.

At night we camped in the cavern mouth to cut off all escape, and resumed the hunt at dawn. But the caverns were
hot—hotter by contrast with the biting winds outside; and
when in the afternoon of the second day we all came out to
breathe and cool off the running sweat, we saw the whole tribe
—scarcely more than fifty of them—emerge from an opening
above, whose existence we had not guessed, and go scampering
away along a ledge like monkeys. Some of them stopped to
throw stones at us—impotent, aimless stones that fell half-
way; and Fred sent three bullets after them, chipping bits
from the ledge, after which they showed us a turn of speed
that was simply incredible, and vanished.

"Now for the great disillusionment!" laughed Will. "Hassan! Go forward, and show us where that hoard of ivory ought
to be!"

We all expected disillusionment. Brown, who was under
no delusion as to his share in the venture, scoffed openly at the
idea of finding anything buried, in a land where every living
"crittur," as he put it, was a thief from birth. But Hassan
led on in, fearless now that the cannibals were gone, and positive as if he led into his own house and would show his household treasures.

He stopped before a black-mouthed chasm, two or three
hundred yards along the smallest subdivision of the cavern,
and called for lights and a rope. We lit lanterns, and he
showed us men's bones lying everywhere in grisly confusion.

"Tippoo Tib his men!" he remarked. "They throwing

ivory in here, then byumby men who eat men kill and eat
them. I alone living to tell! Plenty men who eat men in
those days—all mountains full of them!"

He tied a lantern to a rope and lowered it down what looked
like an old vent-hole in the lava. But the little light was lost
in the enormous blackness, and we could see nothing.

"Send a man down!" he counseled.

We leaned over the edge and sniffed. There was a faint
smell of what might be sulphur, but not enough to hurt.

"Who'll go?" asked Monty, and I thought he was going to
volunteer himself.

"I go down!" announced Kazimoto cheerfully, and promptly
proceeded to divest himself of every stitch of clothing.

We made our stoutest line fast under his arm-pits, gave him
a lantern and lowered him over the edge. For fifty or sixty
feet he descended steadily, swinging the lantern and walking
downward, held almost horizontal by the slowly paid-out rope.
Then he stopped, and we heard him whistling.

"What do you see?" we called down.

"*Pembe!*" (Ivory.)

Much of it?"

"*Teli!*" (Too much!) "Oh, *teli, teli! Teli, teli, teli,
TELI!*"

His voice ended with the very high-pitched note that natives use when they want to multiply superlatives. Then he
whistled again. Next he called very excitedly.

"Very bad smell here, *bwana!* Pull me out quickly!"

# L'ENVOI

*The dry death-rattle of the streets*
*Asserts a joyless goal—*
*Re-echoed clang where traffic meets,*
*And drab monotony repeats*
*The hour-encumbered rôle.*
*Tinsel and glare, twin tawdry shams*
*Outshine the evening star*
*Where puppet-show and printed lie,*
*Victim and trapper and trap, deny*
*Old truths that always are.*
*So fare ye, fare ye well, old roofs!*
*The syren warns the shore,*
*The flowing tide sings overside*
*Of far-off beaches where abide*
*The joys ye know no more!*
*The salt sea spray shall kiss our lips—*
*Kiss clean from the fumes that were,*
*And gulls shall herald waking days*
*With news of far-seen water-ways*
*All warm, and passing fair.*
*They've cast the shore-lines loose at last*
*And coiled the wet hemp down—*
*Cut picket-ropes of Kedar's tents,*
*Of time-clock task and square-foot rents!*
*Good luck to you, old town!*
*Oh, Africa is calling back*
*Alluringly and low*
*And few they be who hear the voice,*
*But they obey—Lot's wife's the choice,*
*And we must surely go!*
*So fare ye, fare ye well, old roofs!*
*The stars and clouds and trees*
*In place of you! The heaped thorn fire—*
*Delight for the town's two-edged desire—*
*For thrice-breathed breath the breeze!*
*For rumble of wheels the lion's roar,*
*Glad green for trodden brown,*
*For potted plant and measured lawn*
*The view of the velvet veld at dawn!*
*Good-by to you, old town!*

how jealously and wakefully the Protectorate Government guarded those lonely trails. And there are folk who saw the hundred-man *safaris* that came down from that way every week or so, carrying old ivory, said to be acquired in the way of trade. But that is really all government business, and looks impertinent in print.

We did not make enough money to establish Monty in the homes of his ancestors at Montdidier Towers and Kirkud-brightshire Castle; for that would have been an unbelievable amount; it takes more than mere affluence to keep up an earl-dom in the proper style. But we all got rich.

Brown received his cattle back after a long wait, as well as a present of money that set him up handsomely for life. And certain dissatisfied Masai were fined so many cows and sheep for raiding across the border that they talked of migrating out of spite to German East—but did not do it.

A youthful red-headed, assistant district superintendent of police was unaccountably alert enough to round up and bring into court more than a dozen natives who had preached sedi-tion. And, being lucky enough to secure convictions in every case, he was promoted. The last I heard of him he was fight-ing in the very heart of German East in command of a whole brigade. So it is advantageous sometimes to do favors for stray noblemen, provided you are clever enough, and man enough to make good when the favors are repaid.

And while on the subject of favors, the four homesick islanders who had lent us their canoes and came with us all that journey, were sent back to their island followed by a launch towing two barges full of corn—free, gratis, and for nothing—*"burre tu,"* as the natives say, meaning that the English are certainly crazy and giving away food without a pull-back to it simply and solely because "the people" have too much *nja. Nja* is the nastiest word in all those languages. It means the one thing everybody dreads—the thing that only the English seem to know charms against—want—emptiness —HUNGER.

At our expense, but by the favor of the government, there went to that island food enough in boxes and strong sacks—

and seeds, treated against insects—and tools with which the wives could chop the soil up (for you can't expect the owner of a wife to work) to keep that island and its friendly folk from hunger for many a day.

THE END